UNBOUND

Praise for the Unwind Dystology

◆

Unwind

★ "Gripping, brilliantly imagined futuristic thriller. . . . The issues raised could not be more provocative—the sanctity of life, the meaning of being human—while the delivery could hardly be more engrossing or better aimed to teens."   —*Publishers Weekly*, starred review

UnWholly

"Shusterman elegantly balances the strikingly different perspectives of the three main protagonists effectively, and these dissimilar approaches to life highlight the ways in which the larger world grapples with unwinding."
—*Horn Book*

UnSouled

"Suspenseful . . . the overall premise is as hauntingly plausible as ever . . . electrifying."   —*Booklist*

UnDivided

"An action-packed, heart-wrenching conclusion guaranteed to chill readers to the bone."   —*Kirkus Reviews*

UnBound

"For fans of the series, this one will be hard to put down. A necessity where the Unwind dystology is popular, these stories are every bit as engaging and will leave readers satisfied but still hoping for more."
—*School Library Journal*

Also by Neal Shusterman

Novels
Bruiser
Challenger Deep
Chasing Forgiveness
The Dark Side of Nowhere
Dissidents
Downsiders
The Eyes of Kid Midas
Full Tilt
The Shadow Club
Speeding Bullet
Dry (with Jarrod Shusterman)

The Arc of a Scythe Trilogy
Scythe
Thunderhead
The Toll

The Accelerati Trilogy
(with Eric Elfman)
Tesla's Attic
Edison's Alley
Hawkings Hallway

The Antsy Bonano Series
The Schwa Was Here
Antsy Does Time
Ship Out of Luck

The Unwind Dystology
Unwind
UnWholly
UnSouled
UnDivided
UnBound

The Skinjacker Trilogy
Everlost
Everwild
Everfound

The Star Shards Chronicles
Scorpion Shards
Thief of Souls
Shattered Sky

The Dark Fusion Series
Dreadlocks
Red Rider's Hood
Duckling Ugly

Story Collections
Darkness Creeping
MindQuakes
MindStorms
MindTwisters
MindBenders

Visit the author at storyman.com and
Facebook.com/NealShusterman

NEAL SHUSTERMAN

UNBOUND

STORIES FROM
THE UNWIND WORLD

SIMON & SCHUSTER BFYR

New York   London   Toronto   Sydney   New Delhi

An imprint of Simon & Schuster Children's Publishing Division
1230 Avenue of the Americas, New York, New York 10020

SIMON & SCHUSTER BOOKS FOR YOUNG READERS
and related marks are trademarks of Simon & Schuster, Inc.
For information about special discounts for bulk purchases, please contact Simon &
Schuster Special Sales at 1-866-506-1949 or business@simonandschuster.com.
The Simon & Schuster Speakers Bureau can bring authors to your live event.
For more information or to book an event, contact the Simon & Schuster Speakers Bureau
at 1-866-248-3049 or visit our website at www.simonspeakers.com.
Also available in a SIMON & SCHUSTER BFYR hardcover edition
Interior design by Al Cetta
The text for this book was set in Fairfield.
Manufactured in the United States of America
This SIMON & SCHUSTER BFYR paperback edition December 2016
8   10   9
The Library of Congress has cataloged the hardcover edition as follows:
Names: Shusterman, Neal, author.
Title: UnBound: stories from the Unwind world / Neal Shusterman.
Other titles: Unwind dystology
Description: 1st edition. | New York : Simon & Schuster Books for Young Readers, 2015. |
Summary: A collection of stories about Connor, Risa, and Lev after they have destroyed the
Proactive Citizenry and are, apparently, free to live in a peaceful future.
Identifiers: LCCN 2015021458| ISBN 9781481457231 (hc) |
ISBN 9781481457255 (eBook)
Subjects: LCSH: Science fiction. | CYAC: Science fiction. | Short stories. | BISAC:
JUVENILE FICTION / Action & Adventure / General. | JUVENILE FICTION / Science
Fiction. JUVENILE FICTION / Social Issues / Death & Dying.
Classification: LCC PZ7.S55987 wUnb 2015 | DDC [Fic]—dc23
LC record available at http://lccn.loc.gov/2015021458
ISBN 978-1-4814-5724-8 (pbk)

For Steve Bocian,
who was there when I first began telling stories,
and left us too soon

ACKNOWLEDGMENTS

There are so many people to thank for the creation of *UnBound*, it's hard to know where to begin! Actually that's not true, because it all begins with my editor, David Gale, and assistant editor, Liz Kossnar. As always, their guidance through the writing and rewriting process is invaluable. Everyone at Simon & Schuster has been, and continues to be amazingly supportive: Justin Chanda, Jon Anderson, Anne Zafian, Katy Hershberger, Michelle Leo, Candace Greene, Chrissy Noh, Krista Vossen, and Katrina Groover, to name just a few.

A heartfelt thanks to my collaborators—about half the stories in *UnBound* were collaborations, and it has been a joy working with all you! Michelle Knowlden, who co-wrote *UnStrung*, *Unfinished Symphony*, and *UnTithed*; Terry Black, who conceived of, and co-wrote *UnClean*. My son Brendan Shusterman, who conceived of, and co-wrote *Unnatural Selection* with me; and my son Jarrod Shusterman, who basically did all the heavy-lifting in *UnDevoured*.

Thanks to Barb Sobel and Jennifer Widmer, my assistants, who keep life flowing around me rather than drowning me when I need time to write (which is always!) And Matt Lurie, who has been tireless in updating my website, putting together my newsletter, and keeping my social media presence alive.

Thanks to my book agent, Andrea Brown; my foreign rights agent, Taryn Fagerness, my entertainment industry agents, Steve Fisher and Debbie Deuble-Hill at APA; my manager, Trevor Engelson; and my contract attorneys, Shep Rosenman, Lee Rosenbaum, and Gia Paladino.

At the writing of this, *Unwind* is moving toward being

made as a feature film, and I'd like to thank everyone involved, including Roger and Gala Avary, Julian Stone, Catherine Kimmel, Charlotte Stout, Marc Benardout, and Faber Dewar, as well as Robert Kulzer, Martin Moszkowicz, and everyone at Constantin Films.

And of course this ten-year journey through the Unwind world never would have happened had it not been for the passion and support of the fans! This book is my gift to all of you!

UNBOUND

Contents

UnSchooled

The schoolboy bursts through the door, the first one out of the building when the bell rings. He is expected to be at home fifteen minutes after school lets out. He's not going home.

As he races through the streets, signs of the Heartland War are all around him. Burned-out cars. Rubble from blasted clinics. Crosses in the ground marking spots where soldiers and civilians on either side died fighting for their cause. This is nothing new. It's the world he knows, the world in which he grew up. He and his friends played in the burned-out cars when they were little. They played Lifers and Choicers with plastic guns and toy grenades, never caring which side of the game they were on, as long as they were on the same side as their best friends.

But those childhood days are gone. Things are much more serious for him now.

He turns down a side street that's infested with pigeons by day and rats by night, crossing an invisible line that everyone knows even without being able to see it. It's the line that marks the border beyond which law and reason cease to exist. It's called the wild zone, and every city and town has one. No one who values their property or their lives will venture there. Police have more important things to deal with, and not even the warring militias will go there anymore. The Choice Army blames all the wild zones on the Life Brigade, and vice versa. Easier to point fingers than actually do something about them.

But for the schoolboy this place and the people holed up there have a certain allure that he cannot explain. Certainly not to his parents. Whenever he's late from school, he always has an excuse they'll believe. If they knew where he really goes on those days, he can't even imagine what they'd do to him.

The buildings around him are mostly condemned. Angry spray-painted politics shout out from the bullet-marred bricks, and the windows are boarded over or just left broken.

In a narrow alley he pushes open a side door that has only one hinge to keep it upright and steps inside. Immediately he's grabbed by two teens waiting there. They push him hard against the wall—hard enough to bruise, but that's okay. He knows the drill. He knows why they have to do this. They can't be seen as weak. Even by him. Because there are other feral gangs that would use that weakness against them.

"Why you always comin' here, Schoolie?" one of his assailants asks. "Don't you got better things to do?"

"I'm here because I wanna be."

"Yeah," says the other one. "And that's all you are. A wannabe." Then, gripping his arms, they lead him deeper into the building. It used to be a theater, but the rusted seats are all stacked in the corner. The old carpet is ripped up and gathered into piles that the theater's new residents use as beds. The place is scattered with knickknacks and bits of scavenged civilization, the way a bird might feather its nest with scraps of paper woven into the twigs. The theater is the living space for about forty feral teens. They lounge on scavenged furniture; they laugh; they fight. They live. It's a very different kind of living than the "schoolie," as they call him, is used to. His life has no excitement. No passion. No adrenaline. His life is dull and in ordered control.

They bring him to Alph. The others don't know the kid's real name. He's just Alph, as in Alpha. He's the leader of this band of ferals. The schoolie, however, knows his real name, back from the days when they would play in the war-torn streets.

The kid is a year older, but he always protected the younger ones. Now that he's feral, he does the same, on a different scale. Alph is a key member of what the media likes to call the Terror Generation. He's got a scar on his face from a feral flash riot that gives him character and makes his smile impressively twisted. He's everything the schoolboy is not.

Right now, however, Alph isn't being much of a terror. He's being fawned over by a pretty, if somewhat filthy, feral girl. He doesn't seem happy to be interrupted.

"Schoolie, how many times do I gotta tell you not to come here? One of these days the Juvies'll follow you, we'll all be screwed, and it'll be your fault."

"Nah, the Juvies don't care—they're too busy chasing down ferals outside of the wild zone to care about the ones in it. And anyway, I'm stealth. I'm too smart to be followed."

"So what are you wasting my time with today?" Alph asks, getting right to the point.

The schoolie takes off his backpack and pulls out a brown paper lunch bag, but there's no lunch in it. In fact, it jangles. He hands it to Alph, who looks at him dubiously, then dumps out the contents on a dusty table beside him. Other kids ooh and aah at the glittering pile of jewelry, but Alph stays silent.

"It's my mom's," the schoolie tells him. "She doesn't think I know the combination to the safe, but I do. I took just enough so that she won't notice it's gone for a while. You can fence it long before then."

One of the others laughs—a buff kid named Raf, who could have been military if he hadn't gone feral. "He's got guts, that's for sure."

But Alph isn't impressed. "It doesn't take guts to steal from your own mother." Then he looks the schoolie in the eye. "Actually, it's pretty pathetic."

The schoolie feels heat coming to his face. He doesn't

3

know why he should care what some feral kid says to him, but he does.

"You're not gonna take it?" he asks.

Alph shrugs. "Of course I'm gonna take it. But it doesn't make you any less pathetic, Schoolie."

"I have a name."

"Yeah, I know," Alph says. "It's a sad little name. Wish I could forget it."

"I was named after my grandfather. He was a war hero." Although for the life of him, he can't remember which war.

Alph smiles. "Somehow I find it hard to imagine a war hero named Jasper."

At the mention of his name, other kids snicker.

"My friends call me Jazz. But you don't remember that, do you?"

Alph shifts his shoulders uncomfortably. Clearly he does remember, whether or not he wants to admit it. "What is it you want from me, Nelson? A pat on the back? A kiss on the forehead? What?"

They all look at him now. Isn't it obvious to them what he wants? Why does he have to say it? Just because he's not feral doesn't mean that he's not part of the Terror Generation, too. Of course, no one calls Jasper a terror but his grandmother, and she always says it with a smile.

"I want to be in your gang," he tells them.

The mention of the word brings a wave of irritation that Jasper can feel like static electricity.

Raf steps forward, speaking for Alph, who just glowers. "We are not a gang," Raf says. "We are an association."

"A limited partnership," says someone else. And that makes a few others snicker.

"Very limited," Alph finally says. "And we don't have room for schoolies. Got that?"

Jasper knows this is all a show. He knows that Alph likes him. But Jasper has to prove himself, that's all. He's got to show his value. So he goes out on a limb. He knows it might get him beaten up or worse, but it will definitely get Alph's attention.

He turns to the cavernous space of the old theater and says as loudly as he can, "How many of you can read?"

That brings absolute silence. He knew it would. Mentioning one of the three *R*s can be a call to battle. There are some things you don't say to ferals.

Nobody answers him. Even if some of them can read, he knew they wouldn't answer. Answering gives him power, and none of them want to do that. Not without permission from Alph. Jasper turns to Alph. "You need me. I can tell you what's going on out there—the stuff you don't see on TV."

"Why the hell should 'out there' matter to me?" Alph says, his voice more threatening than Jasper has ever heard it.

"Because there's this new thing I read about. It's called unwiring, or something. They say it's going to end the Heartland War, and it's also going to solve the problem of ferals."

Alph crosses his arms in defiance. "This war ain't never gonna end. And we are not a problem. Ferals are the future. Got that?"

Jasper holds his gaze. Alph's hard exterior shows no signs of cracking. No indication that he's going to give Jasper the slightest break. Jasper sighs. "Yeah, I got it, Kevin."

The fury that comes to Alph's face makes it clear that Jasper has made a critical error.

"Don't you ever call me that."

Jasper looks down. "Sorry. I didn't mean to. . . ."

Then Alph picks up something that's on the table next to the tangle of jewelry. A snow globe—one of the many weird knickknacks salvaged from the world that existed before the

Heartland War. This one shows a little gingerbread cottage magnified and distorted, submerged in water, and surrounded by swirls of fake snow.

"Tell you what, Nelson," Alph says. "I'll give you until the count of ten. You make it to the door by ten, I won't smash your skull with this thing."

"Alph, I—"

"One."

"Just hear me out!"

"Two."

Raf gets between them. "Better start running, dude."

"Three."

And so with no choice, Jasper turns to run.

"Four."

The others laugh. One kid tries to trip him, but Jasper jumps over his extended foot.

"Five."

He's almost to the door. The door guards don't try to stop him. They part to let him go, but then Alph does something unexpected.

"Six-seven-eight-nine-ten!"

With the countdown sped up, Jasper doesn't stand a chance. Just before he reaches the door he feels the snow globe connect with his back, striking a middle vertebra. He goes down. The snow globe smashes on the concrete floor.

"Man, what an arm!" one of the guards says. "Alph oughta play baseball or something."

Still in pain, Jasper gets to his feet. He's going to have a major bruise on his back—but he'll tell no one. "He could have killed me," Jasper realizes out loud. "He could have hit me in the head and killed me."

One of the door guards scoffs. "If Alph wanted to hit you in the head, he would have." Then he pushes Jasper out the door.

"You're late again," his mother says, the casualness in her tone forced, the suspicion in her voice poorly veiled. She used to manage a restaurant until either the Lifers or the Choicers inadvertently blew it up. Now all she does is micromanage Jasper.

He drops his book bag on the couch and answers just as casually. His tone isn't forced, however. He's a much better actor than his mother. "There was a meeting about school clubs. I wanted to check some out."

"What club are you interested in?"

"Fencing," he answers without the slightest hesitation.

"So violent."

He passes her on the way to the fridge. "You don't *really* stab people, Mom."

"Before you commit to anything, you should run it past your father, Jasper."

He stiffens, feeling the chill from the open refrigerator on his arm hairs. "I told you to call me Jazz."

"That's not a name," his mother says. "Take what you want and close the door. You'll let all the cold out."

He spends the rest of the afternoon doing his homework at the dining room table. It must be done, or at least deeply carved into, by the time his father gets home from work, unless he wants the next iteration of the Lecture. The lecture is always the same: all about how lucky he is to be in a corporate school at all, and how if his grades don't improve, they'll pink-slip him. "And then what?" his father would rant. "Without a corporate school, you'll have no future. You won't be any better than a feral!"

All the disgust in the world is packed into the word "feral" whenever his father says it—as if the feral kids are the source of all the world's problems. Jasper can't remember a time

7

before there were ferals. The public schools failed even before the war started, leaving millions of kids with nothing to do but cause trouble for the system that put them out on the street. Nowadays only rich kids and corporation babies get an official education. Jasper is the latter: His father works for a huge shipping conglomerate, which guarantees Jasper's place in the company's educational program.

Unless, of course, Jasper gets pink-slipped.

He's both terrified and enticed by the idea of expulsion. Maybe then Alph would see him as more than just a schoolie.

As he slaves over his homework, he begins to wonder what it was like in the old days, when education was a right, not just a privilege. He wonders if school sucked as much then as it does now.

He's still working feverishly on algebra when his father gets home. He thinks that his diligence will spare him his father's disapproval, but it doesn't. "Why do you work in the dark like this? You'll ruin your eyes, and then what?"

Jasper wants to point out that it isn't dark in the dining room; it's just that outside it's still light, and his father's eyes haven't adjusted to being indoors, but Mr. Nelson is not a man who suffers contradiction easily—especially when he's tired, and he looks exceptionally tired today. So Jasper just turns on more lights, wondering if he'll get a lecture later that night about wasting electricity. *You'll bankrupt us with utility bills, and then what?*

His father loves to lecture, and the angrier he is, the longer the lecture goes. Only once did he become physically violent with Jasper. Jasper had gotten suspended for cursing at a math teacher who deserved it, and that night his father blew like a volcano, throwing Jasper hard enough to crack the drywall. Then his father cried and begged forgiveness. Jasper knew this type of thing is rarely a one-time occurrence. In most cases it becomes a pattern—as it is for several of his friends, whose high-stress parents see their kids as the only available pressure valve. But it won't become a pattern if Jasper never gives his father a reason to hit him again. Or at least not until he's escaped to a place of safety. Where kids protect each other.

At dinner his father will often complain about the state of the world or the morons in his office. He still goes off on diatribes about the teen "terror march" on Washington, long after it ended. Maybe because Jasper once commented that he would have liked to have seen it. But tonight his father doesn't voice any opinions at dinner. He doesn't complain about work or about traffic or about anything. Jasper noticed he seemed tired, but it's more than that. He's quiet, distracted, and noticeably pale.

His mother doesn't say anything. Instead she leaves his father's medication on the counter, just in case he might forget to take it. Jasper can't stand a dinner table where the only sounds are the scraping of silverware on china. Even a lecture would be better than that. If no one will say anything, he has to.

"Is it your heart, Dad?" he asks. There are times he wishes his father would just keel over and die, but when that actually seems like a possibility, Jasper hates himself for thinking that and gets terrified that it might actually happen.

"I'm fine," his father says, as Jasper knew he would—but now the door's been opened for discussion, and his mom takes over.

"Maybe you should get in to see the doctor."

"It's indigestion," his father says, a bit louder. "I'm not an idiot; I can tell the difference."

Jasper scrapes himself a forkful of peas and speaks without looking up at him. "Indigestion doesn't make your lips turn blue."

His father puts down his silverware with a clatter. "What is this, the Inquisition?"

No one says anything for a few moments. Jasper counts peas on his plate. He ponders how to dissect his steak to get the most meat off the bone. He waits to see which direction his father's mind will go. His father does get cyanotic from time to time. Low blood oxygen. He's already had two heart attacks. He's slimmed down and exercises more but refuses to change his eating habits. The doctors say he'll need a new heart eventually. Which, to his father, is like saying he'll eventually have to clean the garage.

"Fine," he finally says. "I'll go in tomorrow and get checked out if that will make you both happy."

Jasper silently sighs with relief. He knows before the end of the week he'll be hoping his father drops dead again—but not until he comes home with a clean bill of health.

They change the dosage of his father's meds, tell him he has to stop eating red meat, and put him on some nebulous transplant waiting list. His lips aren't cyanotic anymore, and for the Nelson family, out of sight is out of mind, so Jasper's attention returns to Alph and his band of ferals.

The trick to impressing Alph is magnitude and audacity. He didn't lay claim to an old theater for nothing; Alph likes drama and spectacle. Jasper can give him that. All he has to do is keep his eyes open for an opportunity to present itself, which it does a week later. It is the confluence of three random events that sets Jasper's stage. One: His parents have a Friday night dinner party—the kind that will keep them out at least until midnight. Two: Jasper's being paid to feed the cats at the neighbors' house while they're on vacation. Three: That particular neighbor has a new sports car parked on the driveway. Candy-apple red. It's what his father calls a midlife-crisis coupe, all muscle and curves. The kind of car that sleazy salesmen call "sexy" and charge more for than it's actually worth.

But for a car like that, its parts are more valuable than the car is whole.

And so while his parents are off at their party, Jasper feeds the cats and hot-wires the car. He doesn't have his license yet, but he has a learner's permit and can drive as well as any other kid his age. The trick will be crossing into the wild zone and getting to Alph's hangout without getting jacked by other ferals on the way. He keeps a crowbar on the passenger seat in case he's forced to defend himself.

There's plenty of activity tonight. Bonfires and jam sessions and drunken brawls. Life bleeds like a wound everywhere in the wild zone. Ever since the teen march on Washington, ferals have been celebrating like it was a victory—and perhaps it was. Sure, they were subdued with tear gas and tranqs and batons, but they still proved what a formidable force they can be.

Jasper drives down the darker streets, where there's less activity and fewer chances of getting surrounded by covetous ferals. The ones he passes eye him, though. They stare at the red beast he drives. One kid steps in front of him, trying to make him stop—even smiling to put Jasper's worries at ease, but Jasper doesn't fall for it. He keeps on driving, and the kid has to leap out of the way to avoid being roadkill. If he hadn't jumped, would Jasper have hit him? He's not sure. Probably. Because if he didn't, he might be dead himself. That's the way of things in the wild zone.

When he finally arrives at the old theater, a few of Alph's street lookouts spot him and are flabbergasted.

"Is that the schoolie?"

"Nah, it can't be the schoolie."

"Yeah, it is the schoolie!"

Jasper hops out, strutting proudly. "Go get Alph," Jasper tells them, feeling like he's earned the right to give them an order.

One of them disappears inside and comes back a minute later with Alph.

"It was my neighbor's, but now it's all yours," Jasper tells him, grinning wider than the crescent moon. "A gift from me to you. I don't need anything in return." Which isn't entirely true. What he needs in return can't be quantified in dollar signs. What Jasper wants is the key to Alph's kingdom. Or if not the key, then at least an open door. A luxury car for the right to join. Jasper thinks that's more than fair. And once he disappears into the wild zone, he can say good-bye to his corporate high school and his parents' expectations and his dull, lackluster life forever. Like Alph said, ferals are the future, and Jasper's ready to be a part of that future, wherever it takes him.

"You steal this?"

"Easiest thing I ever did," Jasper says proudly.

Alph keeps a poker face. He inspects the car. Jasper impatiently waits for his pat on the back, but it never comes.

"A car like this, every part's got a molecular signature. If I try to chop it, it'll point to me from every freaking direction." Then, to Jasper's horror, he tells another kid to take it and drive it into the river. The kid seems excited by the prospect and peels out in the stolen car.

"Alph, I'm sorry," Jasper says, trying to salvage something out of this. "I just thought you'd want . . . I mean, I just wanted to show you . . . I mean, I can do better. I swear I can! Just tell me how. Tell me what you need me to do!"

Alph appraises him, then says calmly, "Come inside."

Once they're in, Alph, with a couple of the others, leads Jasper to an area separate from the rest of the theater. A broken display case. Rusted popcorn maker. It was once the theater's concession stand.

"You want to be one of us?" Alph asks.

Jasper nods.

"You think it's fun to scrounge for food and fight just to stay alive?" Then Alph lifts his shirt, showing half a dozen healed scars even worse than the one on his face. "Do you know how many knife fights I've been in? How many flash riots? Do you think I was in them for fun? Do you, for one minute, think I wouldn't change places with your lousy stinking schoolie ass?"

"You're free, Alph!" Jasper shouts. "You get to do what you want when you want."

Then Alph pushes him so hard, he hits the wall behind him. "Can't you see? I don't get to do ANYTHING I want! Because I'm too busy just trying to stay alive. And you come here with your fancy school uniform and your mother's jewelry and your neighbor's freaking car, and you think you can buy your way in? What kind of idiot buys his way into the bottom?"

Now Jasper finds himself stammering. "But—but it's not like that. I wanna—I wanna help. I wanna help all of you. I can be important to you!"

"What you need, Nelson, is to see what you have for what it is. You won life's lottery, and you want to throw it away? Why would I ever want to associate with anyone that stupid?"

The others back away, sensing what's about to happen. Jasper has no idea what to do now, what to say, other than "Kevin, I'm sorry!"

"And I told you to NEVER call me that!"

Then Alph takes a deep breath, calming himself down. Jasper thinks it's over, until Alph rolls up his sleeves.

"Clearly your skull is so dense, there's only one way to get through to you."

And then he begins pounding on Jasper. Not fighting him, but hitting him, kicking him, beating him to a bloody pulp. And what makes it all the worse is that Alph does it with such emotional detachment. He's not angry. He hasn't lost control. He's simply doing his job.

When it's over, and Jasper lies on the ground sobbing, Alph has Raf haul him to his feet. Then Alph gets in his face, speaking gently, but with a threat beneath his words as deadly as an undertow.

"You'll tell your parents you were beaten up on the other side of town. You'll say it wasn't ferals. You'll make them believe it. And then you'll go back to your lucky little life that the rest of us wish we could have, and you will make something of yourself. Outta respect for the rest of us who can't. And if you ever think about spitting out that silver spoon again, remember what happened here today. Because the next time you show up here, I'll kill you."

And then they hurl Jasper out into the street.

Jasper's parents come back early from their dinner party. Their car is in the driveway when he gets home. He knows he'll be in trouble, but his battered face will buy him clemency if he plays it right. He stumbles in the front door, wishing he could just slip into bed and pretend he'd been there all night, but he knows it's not possible.

His mother gasps then bursts into tears when she sees him. His father's anger at him being AWOL for the evening quickly fades when Jasper tells them the horrible, terrible thing that happened to him. That while he was feeding the neighbor's pets, two men broke in and kidnapped him. They stole the neighbor's car, beat Jasper real good, and were going to hold him for ransom, but Jasper slipped out of his bonds and jumped out of the moving car, and the kidnappers were so freaked, they took off. He ran all the way home.

He's taken to the hospital and treated for his wounds. He makes an official statement for the police. He looks at mug shots but can't identify either of his kidnappers. His parents idly talk about moving to an electrified-gated community—but all those communities are run by either Lifers or Choicers, and since his parents are notoriously nonpolitical, they don't want to associate with either side of the war. The incident fades. Jasper goes back to school. Life goes on. It's forgotten.

But not by Jasper.

"Unwinding," not "unwiring." It should be all over the news, but it isn't. People whisper about it, though. Jasper hears kids talk about it in school. He hears adults mumbling about it in the street.

And then there's the war. There are rumors that the war isn't coming to an end, but that it's already over. Yet an official statement is never made by either side. Usually the end of a war is a big deal. Parades, and strangers kissing in the street. But this war was different. This time both sides just slipped shamefully into the shadows when no one was looking. It's as if part of the armistice was to not talk about it. The armies just stopped fighting. The rhetoric stopped flying. Out of nowhere sanity now appears to prevail.

And bad kids are disappearing.

On a warm afternoon, less than a month after the Unwind Accord is signed, Jasper T. Nelson, looking sharp in his school uniform, shows up at a house just a few blocks away from his own. He knows who lives there. Kids always remember the homes of their childhood friends.

The woman who opens the door looks slightly hunched, as if the weight of her life is simply too much for her. She couldn't be any older than Jasper's mother, and yet she seems much worse for the wear.

"Can I help you?" she asks. "If you're selling something, I'm not buying. Sorry."

"No, I'm not selling anything," Jasper says. "It's about your son. It's about Kevin. Can I come in?"

At the mention of her son's name, the very skin on her face seems to sag. She takes a moment. Jasper can see her weighing in her mind whether to invite him in or slam the door in his face. The latter is not a possibility, however, because Jasper has surreptitiously slipped his foot over the corner of the threshold, so she couldn't slam the door on him if she tried. And if she does try, he'll scream so that all the neighbors will hear how the nasty neighbor woman just slammed a poor schoolboy's foot in her door.

But instead she chooses wisely and lets him in.

He sits in the living room. She sits across from him.

"Is he dead?" the woman asks. "Is that why you're here? To tell me he's dead?"

"No," Jasper tells her. "He's not dead."

She seems both relieved and disappointed—and miserable about both of those feelings. "He went feral almost two years ago," the woman tells him. "He's only been back once. Didn't even say why. He had something to eat, left without saying good-bye, and never came back again." Then she looks Jasper over. "You don't look like the kind of boy Kevin would hang out with."

Jasper smiles. "I'm not, but even so, I do want to help him."

She looks at him, guarded. "How?"

Then he spreads out a document in front of her, all written in legalese. In triplicate. White, yellow, and pink. "There's this new program to help ferals," Jasper explains. "It allows them to contribute to society in a meaningful way. I joined a club at my school, and we're going around talking to the parents of feral kids because we can't help those kids without permission."

"Permission," she repeats. She takes the document and starts to look it over. "What is this thing 'unwinding'? I hear people talking about it, but I don't know what it is."

Now Jasper gets to the point. "I understand the courts found you and your husband liable for the things that Kevin stole."

She leans back in her chair, suddenly seeing Jasper through a much darker lens. "How do you know that?"

"It's all public record—I looked it up on my phone. I could show you the app." He holds up his phone to her, but she doesn't take it. "Isn't there also a family that's suing you for another kid's medical expenses, because Alph—uh, I mean Kevin—broke the kid's jaw? You'll probably be paying damages for years."

Now she doesn't say anything. Good. Stunned into silence. Now to go in for the kill. Jasper smiles. "I'm sorry; I don't mean to upset you or anything. In fact, I'm here with good news. You can make all that go away! Paragraph Nine-B of the unwind order states that the liability for any offenses made by your son from seven days postconception until now falls upon the state. You won't owe anyone anything!"

She looks at the order again. Jasper can see her eyes darting over it, but he knows she's not reading. She's thinking. Weighing. Pitting her conscience against what's practical. So Jasper adds another weight on the scale.

"The court will even remove the lien they've placed on your house."

Now she stares at him as if she hasn't heard him right. "What lien?"

"You mean your husband didn't tell you? That kid with the broken jaw's got sharks for lawyers. They're trying to take away your house."

She holds eye contact with him for a moment longer. Of all the things he's said, this is the only one that isn't true, but a white lie can be justified if it leads to the proper end. The woman looks over the unwind order again, this time actually reading it. Then she looks up at Jasper with those eyes so old before their time.

"You got a pen?"

The raid happens two days later. Jasper's in a Juvey-cop car, on a ride-along. It's a perk of being part of his school's SDS club: Students for a Divisional Solution. So far Jasper is the only member, but he expects his club's popularity will grow.

Juvies descend on the old theater like a SWAT team. Kids scatter like rats. Some get away, but more are captured. Once Jasper hears the squad captain give the all clear over the police radio, he gets out of the cruiser and slips inside. He was told to wait in the car, and said that he would, but of course he was lying.

Inside, the Juvies have about a dozen kids cuffed and seated. About a dozen others are being laid out in a neat row as if they're dead, but Jasper knows they're just tranq'd.

The captain spots Jasper and frowns. "What the hell are you doing in here? Didn't I tell you to wait in the car?"

"It was my lead that made this happen, Officer," Jasper says respectfully. "The least you could do is let me see how it went down."

"It's still not safe, kid."

"Looks safe to me. Where's the leader?"

The cop glares at him a bit more, then gives up, shaking his head. "Over there."

Jasper turns to see Alph sitting alone, separated from the others, with his hands cuffed behind his head. Jasper approaches, waiting for the moment Alph looks up and sees him. The astonished look on Alph's face is perfect. At that moment Jasper decides there is no feeling in life better than revenge.

"Hi, Kevin," Jasper says with a condescending wave.

Alph's astonishment resolves into his cool poker face. "You did this?"

Jasper shrugs. "I helped," he says. "School project.

Extracurricular actually, but it'll look good on college applications."

Behind Jasper, the Juvey-cops take care of business.

"Are they all going to the North Detention Center?" he hears one of the officers ask the squad captain.

"No, North Detention is full up. They're going to East."

Hearing this, Alph looks up at Jasper and smiles. "Oh well," he says, mocking. "Guess I have detention."

"Not you," says the squad captain. "You're going to a different facility."

The smile leaves Alph's face even more quickly than it had arrived. "What kind of facility?"

"For unwinding!" Jasper says brightly. "Haven't you read about it? Oh, right, you can't read!"

Alph squirms like a fish with a hook firmly lodged deep down its throat.

"I decided to take your advice, Kevin," Jasper says. "I'm learning to appreciate all the things I have and working hard to become a productive member of society. Out of respect for those of you who can't. Oh, and here's the best part! In return for exposing a nest of ferals, *and* for getting your mom to sign the unwind order, they've moved my dad to the top of the list for a heart transplant. Isn't that great?" Then he leans in a little closer. "Hey, wouldn't it be funny if he got yours?"

"Nelson!" grunts the squad captain. "Leave the kid alone and get back out to the car. This is a ride-along, not a squawk-along."

That's when Alph makes his move. He rises in a single smooth motion and bolts toward the nearest exit. Jasper acts quickly. He grabs the tranq pistol from the captain's holster even before the officer can, aims at Alph's back, and fires. He meant to hit Alph in the same spot that Alph had hit Jasper with the snow globe, but instead the tranq hits him high on the shoulder. Good enough—it does the job. Alph goes down and is out cold in seconds.

"What the hell is wrong with you?" The captain rips the gun away, understandably furious, but Jasper is unfazed.

"Sorry—he was trying to escape—grabbing the gun was, like, I don't know, instinct or something."

The captain turns to one of the other officers. "Get him out of here!"

The officer grabs Jasper firmly by the upper arm and briskly escorts him out. They pass Kevin O'Donnell, aka Alph, aka nobody anymore, unconscious on the ground, his forehead bruised from where he hit the concrete. *That's what you get for beating the hell out of me,* Jasper thinks. *That's what you get for humiliating me. You think being feral was tough? Let's see how this works out for you.*

Outside, the officer puts Jasper in the back of the squad car, but before closing the door, he looks at Jasper, shaking his head. "You shouldn't have done that, kid."

"What's the big deal? It was only a tranq gun—it wasn't like it was gonna kill him."

"Kid, you *never* take the weapon of a police officer."

"Sorry," Jasper says again, still not feeling any sorrier about it. "I'll try to remember that."

The officer locks him into the squad car, but that's all right. His work here is done, and he can now be content with his thoughts. Today, Jasper T. Nelson can't help but feel the call of destiny. And after holding that weapon in his hands, he knows, beyond the shadow of any doubt, that tranq guns will play heavily in his future.

Unfinished Symphony

Co-authored with Michelle Knowlden

Brooklyn Ward moves through the concrete playground like water streaming through a gutter, nearly invisible, carrying flotsam and secrets in her wake. She sees four boeufs from her squad in a pickup game, shouting, the ball hurtling across the court. She melts into the shadow cast by the five-story Ohio State Home 23 and turns the corner to a side yard. She is on a mission. She cannot be seen.

After making sure no one is there to spot her, she tests the door to the south stairwell. Unlocked. Like Thor said.

Now to find out what Thor wants her to do before she goes through that door. Taking a breath, she pulls the hood of her jacket over her face and moves across the side yard to the ten-foot wall that stands between the school and the outside world. Her heart is pounding. This is the only part of the side yard that cannot be seen by security cameras, but any teachers or any state ward glancing out of the small windows might see her. She has few friends in the home and fewer privileges after Tuesday's brawl. With Thor's help, she hopes that will change.

She finds a spot in the side yard where she has a good angle on the hallway windows, all the way up to the fifth floor. Someone moves past the window on the fourth floor, but doesn't look out. If they did, they might recognize her, because that's Brooklyn's floor, a long institutional hallway lined with identical dorm rooms. There are nine other girls in Brooklyn's room: most are still fifteen, but a few have just turned sixteen like her. Most everyone will be in their rooms or the small rec lounge today, since Sunday is the only day they're allowed real downtime. The girly-girls will be all about boys and gossip and classes and clothes. The boeuf girls will be all about boys and gossip and classes and guns. Even though the girls in her room are the closest thing she knows to a family, she's in no hurry to get back to the petty squabbles and mind-numbing conversations.

No one on the fourth floor so much as glances out of the hallway window—but one level up, on floor five, Thor appears. They are partners in this mission, but he sent her down here alone, as he always does—this time, however, he didn't tell her exactly what the mission was. Today he refused to tell her until she was in position—which means it's probably something Brooklyn would balk at if she knew in advance. She wonders if Thor realizes how much more excited that makes Brooklyn at the prospect.

In the fifth-floor window, Thor flashes the sign for "all clear" and then "ground floor." The next sign she misses. When she signals him to repeat, she reads impatience in his response. He moves his hands a little more slowly, exaggerating the gestures as if to an idiot.

Headmaster.

She swallows. Really? He wants her to snoop through the headmaster's office? She spreads her hands. *For what?* And he better have a good reason. If she gets caught, it's over for her.

She sees his answer—*New state reports*—then she thinks he signs *Rumor.* Not specific and not helpful. She cuts off another string of signs that are hard to read from five floors below with an abrupt *Okay.* Satisfied, Thor leaves the window to return to his room, and Brooklyn crosses the side yard to the unlocked stairwell door.

She moves through the ground-floor hallway, taking the

long way to the headmaster's office. In the distance she hears the cries of a younger child. The echo is hollow and ghostly. No way of telling exactly where the child is. No one will calm those cries anyway. Not enough staff. *Toughen up, kid,* thinks Brooklyn, *or you'll get eaten alive.*

From outside comes the atonal sound of bouncing balls on the concrete playground. Then, from farther down the hall, she hears something different.

The musical tones of a piano.

A teacher playing? Perhaps, but Brooklyn suspects otherwise. She tracks the sound to one of the music classrooms. As it's a Sunday, no classes are being taught. No one should be in here today—it's against the rules. She quietly cracks the door just enough to peer inside.

Risa.

She should have known. Risa is Brooklyn's age, but you wouldn't know it. She seems to exist in a different place from most StaHo girls. And while other kids are terrified of breaking the rules for fear of getting unwound, Risa does whatever she pleases. A lot like Brooklyn—but unlike Brooklyn, Risa never seems to get caught. It's infuriating.

And what makes it even more irritating, is that she's good.

Brooklyn watches her dainty fingers dancing across the keyboard, playing a piece that seems too complex for two hands. Even though the practice piano is out of tune, Brooklyn finds herself soothed by Risa's playing, and while part of her wishes that a guard would stomp down the corridor and haul Risa away for discipline, another part of her wishes Risa would just play and play and play.

Piano—or any other instrument—was out of the question for Brooklyn. She didn't have the ear or know-how to infuse her playing with passion. In fifth grade Mr. Durkin actually grabbed her recorder and snapped the plastic instrument in half. *I felt an overwhelming need to put the poor thing out of its misery,* he said, and the other kids laughed.

But Durkin loved Risa. Risa was chosen for musical enrichment, while Brooklyn was hurled into the mob of kids relegated to "physical refinement." In other words, they discounted her brain and set out to build her brawn, putting her on track to become a military boeuf. Not that Brooklyn minds the physical focus of her life. She likes sports and strength training, she scores high points in marksmanship—but to know that Risa was seen as somehow better than her still makes Brooklyn stew.

If it had been anyone else but Risa, Brooklyn might be able to stomach it, but they have a history. A history that goes back nearly sixteen years to their cradle days and exploded seven years later. Perhaps everyone else has forgotten it—perhaps even Risa has—but Brooklyn is not one to let wounds go, no matter how old they are.

Still, she enjoys Risa's playing in spite of herself. So she lets the door of the music room stay open a crack and sits beside it, just for a minute or so, listening as Risa performs, taking guilty pleasure each time she stumbles and misses a note in her performance. It's good to know that little Miss Perfect isn't so perfect after all.

Risa ends the piece and begins monotonous scales, and so with Brooklyn's musical interlude over, she takes the stairwell to the staff offices. Sunday means that the headmaster isn't in his office, and it's a good time to snoop. Information is everything. Brooklyn learned that in her intermediate electronic warfare class. But she isn't using electronics to gather intel now. She will go old-school. Flipping through files, searching the desk, finding information she can use.

Hearing raised voices, she stalls in the stairwell. Luckily, she hasn't opened the stairwell door—which creaks badly and is directly across from the headmaster's office. In small increments she cracks it open, just as she had inched open the music room door to hear Risa play. This time she won't be hearing a sonata.

"No more delays, Marshall," she hears Headmaster Thomas say. "Give me your preliminary metrics now. You have till four thirty for your interim assessments—and I expect a final report one hour after testing tomorrow."

Brooklyn holds her breath. A meeting with teachers on Sunday? Even surprise government inspections happen during the week. She shivers, and not just because the stairwell is drafty. StaHo runs on rigid schedules. Departures from normal behavior scream red alert.

"Before dinner, I want the children in your charge ranked. Reports from floors four and five only. Any questions?"

Brooklyn does not wait for the questions. Any teachers leaving early will take the stairwell and see her. She eases the door closed, cutting off the voices.

Quaking, she heads upstairs and into the room of a thirteen-year-old. Even though she throws herself onto his bed, he doesn't react. Thor leans over his keyboard, his nose almost touching the screen. His room isn't much larger than a mop closet, but he gets his own room. The luck of being in a protected class.

Waiting till he realizes that she's there, she stares at the bookshelf stacked with overdue library books, the laundry bag overflowing with soiled clothes, and a half-eaten sandwich on the nightstand. The only wall decoration is a rusty mallet nicked from the handyman's tool kit. Thor's Hammer. She has no idea who started naming all the protected-class kids after gods—but Thor always rolled with it. And besides, when you're alone in a room in a StaHo, a hammer can ward off the worst kinds of intrusions.

Her attention drifts back to Thor. He still doesn't seem to have sensed her presence, and she tires of waiting.

Stretching till her foot reaches the back of his chair, she gives it a good kick.

He jerks forward, and then swivels his chair. His fingers fly. *I knew you were there, B.*

When he signs the letter *B*, his fingertips curl like a claw, his name for her. She grins. No other kid would dare give her a nickname, but she likes him making a weapon of hers.

How? she signs, and laughs when he indicates the mirror near his computer, facing the door. She laughs again when he mocks her by thumping his clawed *B* hand across his forearm. So he'd also felt her enter the room. Thor always knows. She would be suspicious of anyone else so observant—but there's no one she trusts more than Thor.

You're gonna freak when I tell you what I discovered, Brooklyn signs.

He sighs, spinning his chair closer to the bed. *You can't be in here, B. And I can't keep wiping the demerits from your records. I told you to talk to me at dinner.*

He signs with an American Sign Language abbreviated by the home dialect all the StaHo deaf kids use. They've been friends since she stood up for him on the playground nearly ten years ago, so Brooklyn can extrapolate what she sees into her hearing-world's English.

She signs slower than he does, but her fingers jab the air insistently. *We need to talk NOW. Teachers met in the headmaster's office. He wants kids ranked this afternoon. On a Sunday.*

His eyebrows raise. *Probably the state wants more data to feed their paperwork monster.*

She knows he doesn't believe that. After all, he's the one who suspected something was going on. *For just the top two floors?* she signs.

He sucks in a breath and nods. He understands as she does. Only kids thirteen and older live on the top floors.

Another harvesting so soon? . . . His fingers trail off, and his gaze meets hers.

Budget cuts? Brooklyn suggests. *So StaHo sends another batch of kids to the harvest camps?* It's something they've never done before. Keeping the size of the home's population consistent has always been at issue—around ten kids go every six months or so—but culling kids because of budget cuts? She looks to Thor, hoping he'll laugh at the very idea or just shake his head at how preposterous it is. But there's a seriousness to him now that makes her frown.

They meet eyes, and Brooklyn stops signing. Now she mouths the words for him, slowly. Solemnly. *You know something I don't?*

The teachers make Thor speak in class, or at least they try to. Everywhere else he only signs. Brooklyn never makes him read her lips unless she needs to read him. See his eyes.

Peace, Brooks, he signs back. *I know nothing, but I watch the news. You think you're at risk?*

She returns to signing. Thor's always telling her that her signing conveys only words, that she doesn't have the knack of showing emotion through her fingers. Like what Durkin said about the way she played music. That it sounded like a death rattle.

Boeufs push the limits. The headmaster can't complain that I make a good monster. She fingers in her usual boring way, hoping that Thor will miss the bitter twist in her lips and the fear in her eyes.

And you're worried that you've lost points because of that fight last week?

She looks from his fingers to his face and feels her mouth drop. How did he know?

He grins. *Don't underestimate the deaf network, B.*

She shoots back a sign not invented by the deaf. He laughs,

27

but then his face turns more serious. *Even boeufs know to kiss up to their lieutenants, B. It's the one survival skill you lack.* Thor taps her arm to make sure she gets the point. *I like you, B, because you're not political. You say what you mean. You mean what you say. But that won't win you any friends.*

She mouths at him, *The list is about rank, and how you score against the other kids. It is not a popularity contest.* Then she signs, *Will you find out where I am on the list?*

He leans back in his chair, the metal complaining loudly. She manages a smile, knowing he wouldn't care even if he heard it. He studies her somberly. *Why are you anxious, B? Your grades are fine.*

Maybe she *is* a little worried about Tuesday's fight, but he doesn't need to know that. She shrugs. *Yeah, all is good. I just gotta know.*

She feels her forehead crease with uneasiness, and Thor sees it. Now he looks worried too.

When Brooklyn changes for dinner, Abigail, one of her dorm mates, admires her Parana River shirt. Another dorm mate, Naomi, asks where she got it.

Brooklyn shrugs. "Charity closet. Some church sent a big delivery yesterday."

A ripple of excitement moves through the room, like the vapor of lemon-scented soap and mint ChapStick that always hangs there.

Abigail asks suspiciously why their DormGuardian hadn't made an announcement about the delivery, and another dorm mate asks how Brooklyn nabbed the shirt when the closet is closed on Sundays.

"I got it yesterday."

"But you said it came in yesterday," Abigail says. "It takes twenty-four hours to clean and sort them."

Brooklyn winks. "So it pays to know someone in laundry, don't it?"

Some of the girls laugh, and others stare enviously at the shirt. It's nice to be the center of attention. The focus of jealousy. She adds generously, "Next time a good haul comes in, I'll let you know."

"You should have told us this time," Naomi says, disgruntled. "You're supposed to watch out for your ward sisters."

Brooklyn musters a smile, thinking, *Yeah, right*. In a StaHo, you watch out for yourself and maybe for those in your squad. But mostly yourself, because no one else will.

"Next time," she repeats.

The StaHo dining hall holds about three hundred wards, meaning they eat in shifts in the large room painted institutional green with puke-yellow accents. She and her fellow sixteen-year-olds sit their shifts at long tables lit by high windows and low bay fluorescents. Too much light in Brooklyn's opinion. StaHo food doesn't bear close inspection.

At dinner Logan, one of her squad mates, slides onto the bench next to her. Logan is strong but bumble footed in relays and useless with nav tools. She drills him, and he gives her the latest news on food and clothing deliveries. For some reason he thinks she's getting the better deal and should be grateful for it.

"That shirt looks good on you," he says. He's sitting too close, and one of the dining room monitors frowns at Brooklyn, like it's her fault.

She hip checks him and jerks her head at the monitor still giving her the evil eye. Logan huffs and moves four inches away.

"Heard tell of ice cream deliveries later tonight. Want to meet in the kitchen stairwell after lights-out?"

Brooklyn shakes her head. "What are you, nuts? DormGuardians are on high alert after last week's brawl. And there are no deliveries on Sunday."

Foiled in his attempt to get her alone, Logan squirms a bit. He skates by on his looks and any athletic ability that depends on strength. He'll make a good boeuf because he follows orders and is quick to display muscle. Anything requiring thinking or elegance isn't in his bivouac. Through years of inactivity, his brain is about the size of the ice-cream-shaped mashed potato lump on her plate.

She likes that about him, though. Being around him is no strain. Since their squads were resorted last year and they ended up on the same one, it has become easier for her. Everyone likes Logan, and since he likes her, the rest of the boeufs accept her. She likes that about him too.

". . . and on top of that, you know how heavily new rankings get weighted."

Brooklyn chokes on her meat loaf and mash. "Huh? What new rankings?"

Logan sighs. "The ones I've been talking about. Weren't you listening?"

Hardly ever. "Sorry. I got distracted thinking about how well you did rope climbing last Friday."

He brightens. "Yeah, major points on that, right? Kip thinks—"

She couldn't care less about what Kip thinks. "Tell me about the new rankings."

He scratches his head. "Right. Sarge says the whole school's getting tested tomorrow. A real marathon. It'll be weighted against our old metrics, so all our rankings could shift."

This has to be what she'd overheard in the headmaster's office. Old rankings sent in today. Another round of testing to see what shakes out.

"Do you know why?" she asks. She swallows and tries to act unconcerned, but it's too late. She really has to work on her poker-face skills.

"Calm down—the government is crazy about reports. We're always getting tested, B."

She stiffens and then forces herself to relax. She's told Logan not to call her B. Told him about fifty times. She doesn't know why it's okay for Thor to call her B but not Logan. *Pick your battles,* she reminds herself. And she does need the lug.

"Yeah, you're right." She slides her tapioca pudding to him. He smiles happily and dives in.

"All the squads are being tested?" she asks casually.

"Our grade and higher." Logan speaks around a mouthful-glut of pudding. "Littler boeufs aren't rated till thirteen and are pretty useless till fifteen." He sounds proud of the fact that he's reached a useful age, but too thick to remember it also means he's ripe for unwinding.

This unexpected testing has to be for a harvest camp list. Feeling sick, she looks around the dining hall. She needs to know where she's ranked. She zeroes in where the deaf kids eat, napkin wads flying, fingers and elbows dancing, faces transforming with the silent stories they tell.

Thor isn't there.

After dinner she can't shed Logan. It's past time when teachers, administrators, and DormGuardians would have submitted their assessments. Thor knows the weighting algorithm StaHo uses for ranking the wards. All legal and absent of subjective malice. Right. Every staff member knows how to massage the data. And every staff member does.

If she has to wait one more minute to find Thor, she'll scream. But Logan drags her to the playground. A basketball game has already started, and his best bud Kip shouts for him to join.

"Come on, Brooklyn." Logan tries to pull her onto the court. She notes the DormGuardians watching the game. If they hadn't already turned in their numbers, she would have been tempted to impress them with her excellent sportsmanship behavior and passing skills. But unless they witness her killing someone, anything they report now is moot. Whatever nuggets of misery were in the DormGuardian's reports, it all gets hurled into the computer along with tomorrow's test results.

She rotates her wrist and fakes a wince. "Sprained it yesterday. I'd best let it heal up for the testing tomorrow." She prods him toward the court. "I'll cheer you on from the bench."

She waits about five minutes. She shouts steady encouragement and advice for Logan and one loud hoot for Kip making a basket. Racing up and down the court, Logan forgets she exists. She eases off the yard and gallops up the back staircase to Thor's room.

He's not there. She heads for the audio labs where the deaf kids hang out. Thor says it's ironic, but she doesn't get it. She taps Hera's shoulder and asks where Thor is.

Hera looks half-annoyed at the interruption, but in the same way Brooklyn's relationship with Logan gains her acceptance with the squad, her friendship with Thor earns tolerance for her with the deaf. Maybe they make fun of her "English" (she resorts to spelling out words she should know) and for "signing like a boy" and her monotone fingering—but knowing their language makes her a member of their tribe—even if just an honorary one.

Hera signs, *He skipped tonight. Said he had to finish a project in the computer lab.*

Brooklyn should have thought of that herself. Breaking through some firewalls Thor can do safely from his own computer—but hacking through the trickier ones, he'd use a computer not traceable to him. Her fingers flashing her thanks, Brooklyn heads down the east staircase and to the computer lab.

On a Sunday evening the computer lab is nearly empty except for a couple of younger kids brushing up on factory apps and Thor sitting at a back station, keeping an eye on the computer room attendant, who seems fairly disinterested and unobservant. When she slips in, he waves her over.

You were right, he signs her. *Twenty-one kids will be unwound, seven each from the academic, physical, and arts divisions.*

She tries to keep her hands from shaking as she signs back: *Twenty-one is supposed to be a lucky number.*

Thor shakes his head. *This is a very unlucky blackjack.*

His fingers fly with explanations on how he retrieved the data off the server, built matrices of the inputs, and applied his algorithm, but she doesn't care. She waves her hand to stop him, then fixes her gaze on his dark eyes and signs, *What's my ranking?*

Revealing nothing in his eyes, he swivels the screen to her. A few names jump out at Brooklyn right away. Logan is safe. So is Risa, both a decent distance above the bloodred line of the cut, and Brooklyn finds herself aggravated that she saw Risa's name before her own. Finally she finds herself. Brooklyn Ward SH23-49285. She's safe! Three spots closer to the cut than Logan—but two farther than Risa. Brooklyn has escaped the Blackjack of Doom. She'd really have to screw up tomorrow's testing to be put on the harvest camp bus!

Brooklyn feels featherlight and laughs out loud. She beat out Piano Girl by two. It's the first time since that life-altering ruckus with Risa when they were seven that she's had the upper hand. She can't remember ever feeling this powerful, this fierce, this good.

• • •

Testing day dawns damp and cool. The latter seems a good omen. Heat saps you. Brooklyn makes her best times when the temps are low. Out on the field her sarge looks them over, sneering at some, his gaze passing over others indifferently. He growls at Logan to "Move left" for no reason. Maybe Logan was a fraction of an inch too close to her again. She misses his warmth as he shifts away.

Then she realizes that the sarge is nervous, and so is the lieutenant. Do they know about the StaHo unwinding cuts? They must. She scans the bleachers for the scorekeepers and freezes when she sees adult boeufs in the stands. She sees a major in khakis, his oak clusters glinting off his shoulders in the weak sunlight. Why are they here?

"What's with the brass?" she asks Logan, her voice low, her lips barely moving.

Logan's eyes flick to the clutch of uniforms. "Don't know, don't care. Ready to put on a show?"

Brooklyn debates telling him about the headmaster's list, then figures it's kinder to keep quiet.

"Yeah." Her whisper is predatory, and she squints her eyes dangerously. "I'm ready."

Some of the squads are sent to the shooting range, but her squad is up for the fitness test first. The 2/2/2: two minutes of push-ups, two minutes of sit-ups, then a two-mile run on the track. She wishes she could be shooting first, having qualified for a marksmanship badge last year. It would give her an early lead in the rankings, and a nice psychological bump is always a good thing.

When it comes to running, Brooklyn is not the fastest on the squad, nor is she the slowest. She is a distance runner, because she knows how to pace herself for the long haul. It's the way she lives her life. The way she survives. "Slow and steady wins the race," the old adage goes. But Brooklyn is never expected to win, just to show. For her it's "slow and steady takes third place." That's always been good enough to keep her whole. At least until now. Right now she's made the cut on the headmaster's list—but she's still too close for comfort.

She pushes hard through the push-ups, but with sixty-three, only takes fourth place. Even though she about splits her gut, her fifty-nine sit-ups only get her a fifth place. Then, while glaring at the scoreboard, she catches sight of Risa in the stands with her usual pack of friends

What is Piano Girl doing here? Why isn't she practicing for her own testing this afternoon?

Risa laughs at something her friends say, and hot shame courses through Brooklyn. Is she talking about her? Making fun of her? Did she see that Brooklyn only made fourth and fifth rankings?

As if Risa could feel Brooklyn staring at her across the field, she meets her angry look. But then, that far away, she wouldn't be able to see the expression on Brooklyn's face. Brooklyn tries to put Piano Girl out of her mind, but now she's wedged in like a song you can't stop playing in your head. A distraction that Brooklyn definitely doesn't need.

As they line up on the track for the two-mile run, she sees the major staring at her from the stands as well. She meets his gaze for a moment, before leaning in to the starting stance. Nervously she checks the light on the transponder clipped to her belt. Still showing green, still streaming biometrics. At the sarge's whistle, she leaps forward.

On the first lap she's last in the pack. She fights her desire to glance into the stands, where the major—and Risa—will be watching. Beginning in last doesn't matter; all that matters is where you finish.

On the second lap, halfway through the two-mile run, a

good portion of her squad is flagging. She passes one, then two of her teammates.

She finishes the third lap in the middle of the runners. Then, in the last lap, she kicks into high gear. She catches up to Logan, who's not doing well. Beet red and sucking air like a beached walrus, he weaves as he runs. Sweat pours off him. He doesn't notice when she passes him.

Then Risa intrudes on her thoughts again, and it infuriates Brooklyn—but she realizes it's a fury she can use. She will not allow Miss Perfect to see Brooklyn be an also-ran in this race.

Brooklyn powers past the next three in her squad. Now there are only two more in front of her. When she reaches Kip, he shoots her an astonished look. Then his jaw clenches. They run side by side, Kip straining as much as she is, refusing to be bested by a girl. And then a miracle. Kip goes down! Almost shaken by her good luck, she crosses the finish line just four strides behind the boy in the number one spot.

Second. She placed second in her squad! She immediately looks for Risa in the stands, but her eyes are bleary, and she can't find her. Did she leave? Did she not see her place second? Trying to catch her breath, Brooklyn manages a smile at Logan, who almost fells her with his congratulatory shoulder slug. She peers over his shoulder to look for the major, but he also seems to have disappeared.

"Fifteen minutes," Logan crows. "You did it in fifteen minutes!"

"And four seconds." She tries to act casual, but she can't help smiling big. It's her new personal best, and she's sorry that she's missing Thor's reaction to the streamed data back at the StaHo complex.

That's when she sees Kip and the sarge huddled on the grass in the center of the track. Sarge looks unhappy, and Kip's clutching his ankle. So what? Toughen up, dude. Competition sharpens a soldier. Pain makes you stronger.

The shooting range is a long trek, at the very edge of the StaHo grounds, nearly half a mile away. She heads toward it with the rest of her squad. Thirsty, she inhales a third of her canteen and then pours a third over her head. It feels good dribbling down her neck.

She doesn't notice the clot of boeufs in front of her slowing down or the ones behind her speeding up till someone shoves her into the muscle-bound guy ahead of her. His name is Dex, but everyone calls him Pecs for obvious reasons. She bounces off him and lands on her butt. He turns, reaches down, grabs her shirt, and jerks her to her feet so fast, her head is spinning.

"What gives?" he snarls.

She pries his fingers off her shirt. "Nothing, man. Someone pushed me." She turns around, but no one is there. She looks for Logan—maybe he saw who had pushed her—but he's nowhere to be found. Half a dozen boeufs are now looking at her—mostly guys. Not a friendly face in the crowd.

She spreads her hands. "Forget it. Let's get to the firing range."

"Someone pushed you?" Pecs says. "You mean like this?"

He plants a big hand on her chest and shoves her. She lands on her ass again. Remembering Tuesday's fight and the note in her file about it, she can't take another black mark. Especially now.

Staying on the pavement, she tries an ingratiating smile. "Yep, exactly like that. You all go on ahead. I'll wait here for Logan."

She hopes mentioning Logan's name will appease them, but it doesn't. Two boeufs haul her to her feet. She balls her hands into fists and then grabs her canteen, strangling it instead of Pecs. They won't make her angry. They won't. . . .

Pecs sneers. "You think you can trip Kip and get away with it?"

That catches her off guard. "I didn't trip him. He just fell."

Pecs steps closer till she smells his stinking breath. "Kip says you did. You saying he lied?"

She feels rage from the others crash over her. She freezes. Then Pecs slowly unscrews his canteen and takes a mouthful. She doesn't expect what he does next.

He spits at her. Right in her face. In shock, she stands in front of him, the water dribbling down her face and shirt. It doesn't feel good. It reminds her of when . . .

She wipes the spray from her face with the sleeve of her T-shirt, her fury rising. She can't control herself. Her canteen is still in her hand, and so she whacks Pecs in the nose with it. He roars and reaches for her, but years of dirty fighting have honed her skills. She ducks under his hands and knees him in the groin.

"What's going on?" Sarge yells.

The lieutenant and Sarge are now standing next to her. Pecs is paddling weakly on the ground, moaning. Most of the squad melts away from the scene.

The horror of getting caught creeps over her. First she swipes at her face; the grossness of Pec's spit almost seems worse.

"He spat on me," Brooklyn says. The two men look down at Pecs. His nose is bleeding from where her canteen hit it, and his hands cup his groin.

"Get a medic," the sarge growls. Someone races back to the track.

The lieutenant studies her expressionlessly. "You're the one that started the fight last week?"

She could argue that it's never her who starts it, but she knows what the headmaster wrote in the report.

"Yes," she says. "But I didn't start *this*."

The lieutenant nods at Sarge. "I don't want her with the others. Walk her to the firing range. Now."

Sarge grabs her arm and frog-marches her all the way to the shooting range behind the others, blistering her ears with commentary for the full time it takes to get there.

He releases her near the cart. Her weapons locker is the only one left on the cart's bed. One of the plebes—a younger member of the squad—is charged with monitoring the weapons cart. Seeing the scowl on both Brooklyn's and the Sarge's faces, he steps back and lets her open her weapon locker.

Jabbing a finger at her and stopping inches away from her eyes, Sarge says, "You go last. The squad's probably gunning for you, and I won't be explaining why you got shot. Hear me?"

She nods. She's lucky they haven't already sent her back to the StaHo. She's actually surprised they're letting her finish the tests.

When they call her name, she uses every technique she's learned about relaxing and how to breathe while shooting.

In the first firing position she lines up her rifle on a barricade. She makes eight of nine good shots, but then the gun jams. Like she's been taught, she slaps, pulls, observes, releases, taps, and then shoots again. Distracted, she misses the shot.

In the second firing position she stands without the rifle supported. It malfunctions again on the second and sixth shots. She clears it each time, but now she's rattled. She misses all but four shots.

In the third position she kneels in a make-believe foxhole, but now it feels like she really *is* in a foxhole, fighting for her life. It's nearly noon and the sun is high, beating down. The rifle jams on the first shot, and she's tempted to throw it as far as she can and then stomp on it. Though the only thing she can see are the single and pop-up targets downrange, she knows her squad is watching every shot.

Five minutes later she still can't clear the malfunction. She admits defeat.

As she surrenders her weapon, she sees her score. Twelve. Miserable. Lowest score in her squad.

Logan is waiting by the gate, but before he can say anything to her, the lieutenant orders him away. The sarge takes her back to the main StaHo building alone on the army cart. He drives, and she sits on the seat next to him, the lockers and ammo boxes jouncing in the back.

Not once does he speak on the entire return trip.

Back at the StaHo she expects Sarge to escort her straight to the headmaster's office. Instead he marches her to a classroom where the rest of the squad is waiting for their written test. She slips into a seat next to Logan. Every eye is on her. Logan is frowning, puzzled and worried at the same time.

The proctor watches the clock so they can start the test on the hour. Five agonizing minutes to listen to a fly buzzing at the window.

On her other side Kip's bandaged ankle is propped on the chair in front of him. Pecs is conspicuously absent.

Then, too low for Logan to hear, Kip says, "Guess who's in the infirmary because of you?"

She refuses to look at him, keeping her eyes on the proctor.

He sings softly, "Someone's in trouble."

As the proctor sets the tests facedown on their desks, Brooklyn takes one last look at the other members of her squad. Maybe some of the girls and younger guys are looking at her with admiration for having stood up for herself. Maybe one of the older ones gives her a small nod of approval. Most are disgusted with her, though.

Her skin crawls. This is Risa's fault. If she hadn't been in the stands, Brooklyn wouldn't have pushed herself so hard. She would have realized the diplomatic benefit of taking third place in the race and not challenging Kip's asinine pride. At the thought, someone in a practice room upstairs starts playing arpeggios. Brooklyn hopes Risa's fingers malfunction during her recital. And that the whole audience spits at her.

After the written test Brooklyn only wants to scour the sweat, gunpowder, and spit off her skin. But even before she can strip down in her dorm, someone raps at the door. She thinks it might be one of the DormGuardians to hurry her along, since she's the last one out. It would mean she'd have to go to lunch reeking and take her shower later.

But no—it's just another ward. The absolute last one Brooklyn cares to see.

"Can I come in?" Risa asks.

"What, are you lost?" Brooklyn says. "Isn't your room in the south wing?"

"North," Risa says.

"Good, I'm glad you're not lost," Brooklyn tells her. "Now *get* lost."

Instead, Risa steps in, moving closer to Brooklyn. "I know it was you yesterday."

Brooklyn won't look at her. She grabs her soap and a towel for the shower. "I don't know what you're talking about."

"I saw your reflection in the dance mirror. I thought you might turn me in for being there on a Sunday."

"Who says I still won't?" She tries to push past Risa, but unlike most of the other girls, Risa's more of an obstacle than a turnstile. When Risa's shoulder doesn't give, Brooklyn stumbles, dropping the soap. "What the hell's wrong with you?" She's about to order Risa to pick it up, but Risa does so of her own volition, holding it out to Brooklyn.

Brooklyn takes it reluctantly. "What is it you want from me?"

"Just to thank you for listening," Risa says. "None of the other kids care enough to listen. Half the time the teachers don't care enough."

Brooklyn shrugs. "You're good at something," she admits. "And maybe I got some culture. Maybe I'm not the bonehead boeuf you think I am."

"I don't think that," Risa says, then grins. "Well, maybe a little."

Brooklyn finds herself fighting her own grin. "And maybe you're just a little bit of a stuck-up bitch who thinks she's better than the rest of us." It feels good to say that to Risa's face after all these years.

Then Risa nods and says, "Maybe sometimes I do act that way."

Brooklyn isn't sure how to take Risa's acceptance of her rebuke. It was always so satisfying to hate her. This is new territory. Uneasy territory.

"I've seen the way you sign with that deaf boy," Risa says.

Brooklyn tenses up, sensing an insult, or at least a dig. "That's none of your business."

"I know—I just think it's cool that you learned how to do it. It's a talent."

"A useless one!" Brooklyn growls. "There are barely any deaf people out there to use it with. Auditory tracts are cheap."

"But you still learned it for the kids in here. Maybe just for that one boy."

The fact that she's right—the fact that she can read Brooklyn so easily—makes her uncomfortable. When people know you, that knowledge can easily be turned against you. Brooklyn starts wondering if there's something she knows—or could find out—about Risa that she could use against her. Not that she would, but like old-world nukes, a balance of power could save their little world from nuclear winter.

And then Risa says, "In a way, it's not all that different from playing the piano. I mean—you use your hands to create meaning, just like I do."

Brooklyn just stares at her. What is her angle? What does she want?

"Are we done here? Because I really do have to take a shower."

"Yeah, we're done," Risa tells her. "I just wanted to thank you for liking my music. And to congratulate you on taking second place today."

"Why were you even there? Shouldn't you have been practicing for *your* test?"

"The practice rooms were all taken," Risa said with a shrug. "Besides—you stopped to listen to me. I thought I'd return the favor."

Risa turns to go, and, not wanting to let her have the last word, Brooklyn says, "You made three mistakes."

Risa turns back to her. "Excuse me?"

"When you were playing, I heard three mistakes. But if you fix those three, it'll be amazing."

Risa's smile is genuine. Almost dazzling.

Brooklyn finds Thor waiting for her just outside the cafeteria.

You scared me, Thor signs.

Why? Did you think I got unwound before lunch?

Anything's possible.

With Risa's interruption and her shower, Brooklyn hoped she'd be late enough to entirely miss her squad, but the lunch line is moving slowly today, and she can see they're all still there. Two guys from her squad, having apparently inhaled their food, are the first to leave. They pass her in the hallway as they exit the dining hall, looking like they want to shove her, or worse. Thor glares at them coldly, and they move along, as if intimidated by him. Funny how a skinny deaf kid has more power than hulking boeufs.

Another fight? Thor looks resigned as he signs.

Ignoring the question, she signs back, *How bad is it?*

This is preliminary. It's just your ranking with the boeufs and academics. It doesn't include arts kids yet—they test after lunch.

With her written test already computer scored, there's nothing more she can do. Her performance is her performance, both in the field and the classroom.

How bad is it? she signs again.

He looks around them. Through the swinging doors the dining hall is crowded and filled with watchful eyes, but the hallway is empty. There's no one listening, no one watching— and even if there were, no one could decipher their hand gestures.

Get your lunch, Thor signs. *We'll sit down and we'll talk after.*

But she grabs him before he can walk away and signs impatiently, *Tell me now!*

Then she sees the tiny tic at the corner of Thor's mouth and the dread in his eyes. He hesitates a moment more, then finally he levels the news at her. *Blackjack,* he signs. *As of now, you're number twenty-one.*

She flattens herself against the wall and slides down till her butt hits the floor. She missed the cutoff by one. She's on the harvest list. She will be unwound.

She ignores Thor kneeling next to her and his flying fingers. Everything that happened that morning crashes over her.

Thor gets in her face, shouting with his hands. *We can fix this!*

Poor kid, she thinks. *He's delusional. Nothing can fix this.*

Not after another fight. Not after that low marksmanship score.

Still, she manages one sign. *How?*

An arts kid might bump you off the harvest list, once they test, he signs. *And if not, we can bump someone else on it.*

She frowns. *How?* she signs again.

Leave that to me.

The cafeteria is only half-full for lunch. Having eaten earlier, the arts kids are now beginning their marathon of tests. The hall has a different vibe without them. The sounds are more bass, with sudden silences intermixed with gravel-rattling voices and squeaking benches. The deaf kids are there, sitting at the far end of the room, comfortable in their forest of signs—but Thor has left for the computer lab in his attempt to save Brooklyn's hide. He might be smart, but Brooklyn doubts he can influence the list at all.

As she exits the lunch line with her tray, another random lull descends. The slower eaters in her squad sit at the table under the clock. The most offensive members have already left. There are allies—or at least those who remain neutral—at the table, but still she stalls, not wanting to hear them rehash the tests, or worse, her fight with Pecs. At least he's not there. She looks around for a safe harbor away from her squad. She can't sit with one of the other squads, and she can't sit with the deaf kids without Thor there. In the end, she starts for an empty table. Ironically, if Risa were here, Brooklyn might consider joining her. As much as Brooklyn has despised her, she can't deny the fragile connection they made in her dorm room. And all that old baggage—the things that made Brooklyn feel thorny with resentment and shame—suddenly pales with the rawness of this morning's many failures.

But before she even puts her tray down, she hears, "Yo, Brooks. Over here."

From her squad's table Logan waves at her. His back had been to the doorway, and someone must have told him that she was there. Reluctantly she walks to the table. Before she gets there, several of the others leave, averting their eyes— both guys and girls. But even the ones who remain don't seem too hot on sitting with the Pariah of the Day. And of course there's Kip, complete with a bandaged ankle that he wears like a war wound. He sits at the end of the table with a trio of scrawny plebes. They'll fawn all over any older boeuf who gives them attention, and Kip always does. He gets off on being worshipped. If humans licked their wounds, she's sure Kip would make the plebes lick his.

Writhing inside, but unable to escape, she sits next to Logan.

"Bombed the written test," Logan announces cheerfully.

She's grateful that he's taken the sting out of her own failures by starting the conversation with his own. She can't help wondering whether he has really failed the written, or is he just saying that to make her feel better. Could he be on the preliminary harvest camp list too? Thor didn't tell her anyone else's standings.

"You probably did better than you think," she says generously.

"Don't see how." He seems to meditate briefly on it, and then shrugs. "Can't do anything about it now."

Not without a Thor to change his standing, she thinks, and takes a hefty bite of her burger.

"At least he didn't break a fellow soldier's nose," Kip says. The burger suddenly tastes like a turd in her mouth. One of the plebes giggles nervously.

Logan frowns at his best friend. "Man, that's not cool."

"Yeah? Well what she did was worse." Without looking at her, Kip grabs his tray and leaves. In his dramatic departure, he forgets to limp. The plebes slink after him, one girl shooting

Brooklyn a dirty look after reaching a safe distance.

Logan bumps his shoulder against Brooklyn's. "Don't worry about him. He's just sore you beat him in the two mile. And so what if you tripped him—Kip needed his ego taken down a few notches anyway."

Brooklyn bristles. "I told you—I didn't trip him."

"You know what? It's over. It doesn't matter."

But it does matter. Because Logan is taking Kip's word over hers. He thinks he's being magnanimous by forgiving her—but he's forgiving her for something she didn't do.

Logan goes on talking, not even noticing Brooklyn's slow boil. "And Pecs—I wouldn't worry about him, either. He's leaving the home soon anyways. Turns eighteen in three months." Then he looks at Brooklyn's burger. "You gonna eat that?"

She finds what little appetite she had is completely gone. She puts the half-eaten burger on his plate. "All yours."

Grinning, he wolfs it down and talks with his mouth full. It barely sounds like human speech.

"Didn't understand a word you said."

He wipes grease and mayonnaise off his mouth with his hands. "I said . . ." He speaks with exaggerated clarity. "Weird about your rifle malfunctioning."

"Yeah. Weird." She doesn't want to talk about it. Even thinking about it makes her sweat.

"No one else's did. Well, Shanda's weapon jammed a couple of times, but hers always does. You used your own rifle, right?"

"Yeah, I did." Then she thinks about it. She was the last one in line, still shaking from the encounter with Pecs and the long walk alone with the sarge. A plebe had unlocked her weapons locker before she arrived. Had he switched it with someone else's—or worse, had someone tampered with her rifle somehow?

Thoughts swirl in her head like furious hornets.

After lunch Logan slopes off to watch one of his nonboeuf friends in a jazz recital. A kid who tutors him in math.

"You should come," he says. "Get yourself a little culture."

She's about to say she likes classical better than jazz but decides against it. "Sorry, music isn't my thing." Then one of the other kids mimes the breaking of her recorder—which is apparently legendary—and it gives her all the excuse she needs to slip away and find Thor. But once she's alone, her natural paranoia rises. Had the plebe at the weapons cart given her a bad rifle? Before she knows it, she's turning for the stairwell that leads to the basement weapons cage. She keys in the digital lock, which she always knows, no matter how often they change it, and takes the stairs three at a time.

A different code opens the door at the bottom of the stairs, and through long practice, she ducks her head to avoid the camera. The basement is a warren of storage areas. An atmosphere of old paper, decaying rubber, and petroleum permeates the place. It's colder than upstairs, but not by much.

The armory is in the back. She passes the freight elevator and the long row of file rooms behind more locked doors. She's used information in those files in trade for goods and favors. She could probably find something in there that would save her now, but there's not enough time. Too bad she hadn't found a hideous scandal that could keep her safe until she turns eighteen. If she survives this harvesting, that will be her new priority.

The weapons are stored in rows behind a rigid cage of steel bars and chicken wire. She stalls on the north side of the armory, hearing a rattling inside. Between the third and fourth rows she sees someone standing at a workbench; an overhead lamp lights him and the bench. His back is to her, but he looks like the plebe who was responsible for the weapons lockers at the rifle range, a wiry kid with nasty knuckles and large ears. He was also part of Kip's entourage at lunch. Two lockers are open on the bench. The plebe is disassembling a rifle.

She's too far away to identify either of the lockers as hers. She clutches the cage bars, straining to see. In its concrete foot, the steel squeaks against her weight, and she reflexively backs away into the shadows.

"Who's there?" the plebe calls. His voice squeaks like the cage bar.

Soundlessly she flees down the long corridor, then ducks down a side hall when she hears the ponderous opening of the cage door. She finds a second stairwell, not daring to return to the main one. She fumbles the exit code and is sure the camera caught her profile leaning closer to the keypad. Can they identify her from a dim silhouette? Just one more thing she wishes she didn't have to think about.

She heads for Thor's small bedroom and is grateful he isn't there. He might have talked her out of her rampant paranoia, and she wants to let it range free.

Her thoughts buzz angry and bewildered. Did the plebe sabotage her gun and is now hiding the evidence of his tampering? And if it was sabotage, who ordered it? A plebe that age wouldn't act alone. This would have to have been planned long ahead of time, so it couldn't be Kip. Or could it? He'd never liked her, even before his catastrophic fall on the track. Maybe it was the sarge. The man always seemed to have it in for her. He treats her as if she's not a true boeuf, no matter how well she scores on tests and performs on the field. And it can't be just because of her fighting.

The lieutenant couldn't be involved in the conspiracy, could he? Maybe the sarge, but not the lieutenant. She wants to think at least one person besides Thor is on her side. Logan doesn't count. His protective power expired the moment he chose to believe Kip instead of her. Maybe she'll talk to the lieutenant about the rifle. Maybe he'll treat her fairly—and maybe Thor *can* keep her off the harvest list this time. But what about next time? She'll need to scrape deep for information that's so awful it'll keep her safe for the next two years. From now on she must protect herself. No matter who gets unwound because of it.

The recitals are finished. The art galleries closed. The committees are tallying the arts kids' final scores.

As Brooklyn heads for the staff offices, she has to step around a group of arts kids huddled in the stairwell. Two are crying. She thinks she hears Risa whispering, an edge of despair in her voice, but Brooklyn is on a mission and hurries past them.

Since she has time before Thor can run the results, she decides to see her lieutenant. No harm in currying favor in this final hour.

His office is near the headmaster's. Brooklyn uses covert measures to slip past the headmaster's office. Although she hasn't been called in to answer for the fight with Pecs, she doesn't want the headmaster to conduct an impromptu reprimand on a chance meeting.

"Sir?" She taps lightly on the lieutenant's open door.

His expression darkens seeing her. "Yes?" No welcome, no warmth in his voice.

"A moment, sir?" Maybe this isn't a good idea.

"A moment." His nod at the chair before his desk is as crisp as his shirt.

Best to get it over with. "Sir, I believe someone tampered with my rifle on the range this morning."

His jaw juts. "And do you have proof?"

"No proof, sir. But suspicions that can be—"

He waves her to silence. His eyes glint coldly. "Are you making an unfounded accusation against a member of your squad?"

"Sir . . ."

"Because soldiers don't do that. No matter what, the squad is your family, and its members are your brothers and sisters. Do you have any inkling of what that means?"

"Yes, sir." She can barely hear herself, so she clears her throat and repeats loudly, "Yes, sir!"

He leans slightly forward, his words still frosty. "I can lower your score further. Is that what you want?"

"No, sir."

"You understand what it means to be a team player?"

"Yes, sir!"

He nods and spins his chair back to his computer. "Then remember that before you waste my time again. Dismissed."

In the computer lab Brooklyn's left leg jitters. She and Thor are alone. It's late afternoon, but after a marathon of testing, no one's working on anything mundane like homework. She hears muffled shouts from the playground below—the littler kids are oblivious, but everyone else is shell-shocked.

If Thor looked morose before, he looks positively miserable now. *Remember,* he signs. *We can fix this.*

He slides to the left so she can get a better look at the screen. Her mouth goes dry and her leg stills. She's still twenty-one.

And Logan is just above the cutoff, at twenty-two.

I can switch your names, Thor signs, like it's nothing.

Then she sees the name right before Logan's. Number twenty-three. Risa. Did she flub her piano recital so badly that she's come within two spots of being unwound? Even in the shock of finding her name there, Brooklyn can't help but take a little bit of pleasure in it too. Did little Miss Perfect have stage fright? Or maybe she got sabotaged too.

Then she thinks about how Risa stopped by her dorm before lunch. How she had acted like they could be friends. Of course they never would—but now they were no longer enemies.

Her thoughts racing, she signs, *Can we substitute any name for mine?*

Thor shakes his head. *Got to be someone very close to you on the list, or it will be a huge red flag. They'll know the list was compromised, and they'll figure out who did it.*

The last thing Brooklyn wants is to get Thor in trouble. Sure, he can't be unwound, but there are other punishments. It would be simplest to bump out Logan—but can she do that to him? It wouldn't exactly be looking out for her squad brother, would it?

She points to Risa's name. *Could we use her?*

Thor considers it. He knows Brooklyn's history with Risa but doesn't bring it up. Instead, he slowly signs, *We could.* Then he waits, leaving the decision entirely up to Brooklyn.

When do I have to decide? Brooklyn asks.

I need access to the mainframe, to make the switch, and I can't get near it until the Eagle takes off.

Brooklyn glances at the hook-nosed computer-room attendant. This one is much more attentive than the weekend attendant. The Eagle eyes them with even more suspicion than he does the other kids. Apparently signing is even more suspect than whispering.

He goes off duty at five thirty, Thor tells her. *That gives you an hour to decide—but don't be late. The results become final at six—and if you miss that window, you're as good as unwound.*

It feels heady yet horrible to hold the power of life and death or—if you believe the Juvenile Authority's propaganda—living whole or living divided. But either way, it's an end. She shivers. Better someone else's end than hers.

I'll meet you back here in an hour, she tells him.

The stairwells are full of kids seeking out friends on other floors. Everyone needs someone to listen as they wail about poor performances or exult over triumphs. No one understands the true stakes. No ward except she and Thor knows of the extra harvesting this year. But every ward knows that a bad ranking could eventually lead to unwinding.

Feeling claustrophobic, Brooklyn heads for the playground to think, but DormGuardians are setting up tables there. Too bad, because in a rare moment, it's actually quiet. No basketball on the courts, no kids playing hopscotch, no one on the rusted swing set. She puts two and two together and remembers the ice cream Logan had told her about. They'll all be getting a surprise treat tonight—and everyone will know something is up when they announce it. They only give ice cream on a weekday when something truly bad happens. The last time was the day before another batch of kids was put on a bus to be unwound.

Sitting on a sun-warmed bench, she figures that even with the DormGuardians chattering about where to put the napkin dispensers, she isn't going to find a quieter spot at the StaHo. She closes her eyes against visual distractions and leans into the dappled sunlight beneath a spreading maple tree. She lets the rustling leaves envelop her.

In a few years making life-and-death decisions will be commonplace for her. On the battlefield she'll kill enemies to protect friends. As she advances, she will eventually have to choose which friends will die to protect their platoon. Her orders will end the lives of innocents caught in a cross fire or buried in a bombing raid.

The decision she makes in the next hour will prepare her for those times just as fitness and marksmanship training prepare her physically. She's making herself a better soldier, she tells herself. A better leader.

Leaving herself on the harvest list is not an option. Having a friend who knows how to alter the ranking algorithm gives her this advantage, this weapon. If you are attacked, then you defend yourself.

This is her defending herself.

Having had time to let her thoughts settle, the choice of who will take her place on the list is obvious.

Risa is smart and talented. She shouldn't be punished for having a bad day. On the other hand, Logan might be a good friend, but he's not too bright, and he's only an average boeuf. It's only a matter of time before they unwind him anyway.

She considers carefully what the lieutenant said to her. *No matter what, the squad is your family.* He meant that even if it costs the lives of others worthier than her fellow soldiers, her comrades come first.

Someday that may be true for her. To save her comrades she may one day need to level a museum, aim her rifle at a poet, or gun down an entire orchestra.

But not today. Today she will choose to save the life of a piano player instead of a boeuf.

A 5:00 factory whistle sounds in the distance, and she chuckles. In the end she made her decision in less than thirty minutes. She has time to change into the Parana River shirt Logan gave her. It seems a nice thing to do for him before he's unwound.

Her Parana River shirt is missing.

She'd worn it yesterday but not for long. She'd folded it

and put it in her nightstand drawer. It isn't there now. Did someone take it?

Feverishly she goes through her laundry hamper. The stink of dirty clothes sticks to her hands and fills her nose. She reaches the bottom of the hamper. Not there. Someone *has* taken it.

She immediately remembers that other time when she accused Risa of stealing her shirt, and the humiliation that followed, but tries to brush the thought away.

Naomi and two of her friends enter. Brooklyn's anger boils over. Naomi was jealous of that shirt yesterday. Of course she pilfered it!

Brooklyn launches herself at Naomi, shoving her against the wall, her forearm compressing Naomi's throat. Another girl shrieks, but Brooklyn's menacing growl overrides her loud protests.

"Where's my shirt?"

Naomi is unable to breathe, her eyes are wild, and her fingernails score bloody lines in Brooklyn's skin. Bucking frantically under Brooklyn's forearm, Naomi manages to overset them both, and they crash sideways onto the laundry hamper.

"Are you crazy?" Naomi vaults away from Brooklyn. "You could've killed me."

Brooklyn pushes the hamper away and starts after Naomi again, but one of the other girls, a hefty boeuf from Squad C, inserts herself between them. She's almost as big as Pecs. The memory of that fight sobers Brooklyn, but her anger still simmers.

"Give me back my Parana River shirt," Brooklyn snarls. "I know you took it."

"I didn't touch your shirt, jerk." Naomi looks in the mirror, her fingers tenderly probing her reddening neck. "Wait till I tell 'em what you did to me. Geez, I'm gonna have bruises."

"Is that your missing top?" the other girl says, pointing to a shirt wadded up on the floor behind the upended hamper.

Shocked, Brooklyn stares. Hands shaking, she picks it up. She sees the familiar insignia against the gray-green background. *PR*. Parana River.

Naomi glares at Brooklyn. "I heard about your fight with that boy this morning. Then you attack me? Man, when they're done with you, you're gonna be blood and bones on the floor."

"Let it go, Naomi."

In equal astonishment, Brooklyn and Naomi stare at the boeuf from Squad C.

The larger girl shrugs. "DormGuardians and the headmaster are in a foul mood today. They won't care whose fault it is. If you don't end this now, they'll punish you both."

Naomi glowers, then exhales explosively and kicks Brooklyn. She's an arts kid, so it doesn't hurt much. Grabbing her shower kit, Naomi and her friends slam out of the room.

Still holding her Parana River shirt, Brooklyn studies the boeuf uncertainly. "Thanks. I don't know why you did that, but thanks."

"Soldiers gotta stick together," she says. "And besides, Pecs deserved to have his nose broken."

The girl heads off toward the showers, and, thoughtfully, Brooklyn smoothes out the shirt. The Squad C boeuf made her feel kind of bad for bumping Logan, a fellow soldier, to the harvest list. Not bad enough to change her mind—just enough to make her feel miserable about it. Even so, her reasoning on who lives whole or divided still stands.

Her hand pauses from trying to dewrinkle the shirt. She accused Risa of stealing her shirt when they were seven. Was she mistaken then, too? Brooklyn's skin prickles considering how every memory of the event and everything she felt about Piano Girl since could be wrong.

She shakes away the thought. What Risa did afterward, in front of a crowd of other wards, was worse. But when she stopped by to talk to Brooklyn today, it showed that Risa was big enough to forget about childhood squabbles. Brooklyn deciding not to bump Risa onto the harvest list shows she's matured too.

She knows she can't get to the computer room too early, or the attendant will be suspicious. Best to wait until after he's gone. Brooklyn decides she'll catch Thor in his room and tell him her decision rather than waiting—but as she passes the showers, she overhears Naomi blabbing about their stupid little fight.

It infuriates Brooklyn, but, for once, she controls her temper. Brooklyn was admittedly wrong, and although it's never been in her nature to apologize, perhaps doing so will finally bring some good karma her way. Besides, a quick *I'm sorry, Naomi,* might stem off further retribution and any disciplinary action that might follow. So she'll swallow her pride and apologize. Then she'll hurry off to find Thor.

She moves toward the line of girls in the tiled bathing area, waiting their turn. Steam rolls from the showers like a hot fog, leaving the tiles slick. Brooklyn approaches Naomi, already having formed and practiced an apology in her mind—but she never gets there. Instead, she encounters someone else in line.

"Oh hey."

Brooklyn looks up. It's Risa.

"Hi," Brooklyn says. And though she already knows, she asks, "How'd your recital go?"

Risa grimaces. "Awful. I'm hoping they award points for doing a difficult piece."

They didn't, Brooklyn could say. She almost feels affection for Piano Girl, as a lifeguard might feel about someone she's saved from drowning. "Maybe they will," she says instead.

Risa moves to the sink next to Naomi and opens her toiletry

kit. Catching sight of Naomi's sore neck, she asks, "What happened to you?"

Naomi pulls on the neck of her T-shirt and mutters, "Nothing." Now that Brooklyn is there, she's not so quick to talk about it, and Brooklyn wishes Risa would just let it go—but she doesn't.

"No, really." Risa gently tugs Naomi's collar aside. "That looks nasty. You should see the nurse." Then Risa says in a low voice, "Was it one of the boys? You should report it."

Naomi jerks away and finally glares at Brooklyn. "*She* just about strangled me for no reason—that's what happened—but the nurse would have to report it, and I don't want to get into trouble."

Risa looks at Brooklyn in astonishment. Brooklyn is aware that the room has grown quiet except for the sound of the showers. Everyone is staring at her.

"Why?" Risa asks.

"It doesn't matter," Brooklyn mumbles. She looks toward the entrance, hoping to make an escape, but there are too many girls blocking the way. All she needs is to push past them and send someone sprawling on the slippery tiles. They'd say she did it on purpose.

"She accused me of stealing her shirt," Naomi says, "but it was behind the laundry hamper the whole time."

Risa looks between Naomi and Brooklyn and then bursts out laughing. "Not again!"

Feeling heat rush into her face, Brooklyn says quickly, "Let's just drop it—it was a mistake, okay?"

Then a girl behind Brooklyn asks Risa, "What do you mean 'again'?"

Brooklyn's heart is hammering. She can't bear to hear the story and her shame spoken aloud.

"When we were little, Brooklyn thought I'd taken a shirt

of hers too," Risa says with a gentle smile that might also be a little bit calculated. "She shoved me. I shoved her back. No biggie."

Don't tell them. Brooklyn feels like she's on fire, and she realizes she's signing. A lot of good that will do. She balls her hands into fists, forcing them down to her side.

And then another girl says what Risa doesn't.

"Didn't you spit on her?" the girl asks.

It's like ants beneath Brooklyn's skin.

"Yeah, I remember," the girl says. "You pinned her on the ground, and you spit in her face. It was classic."

Risa cocks her head. "Yeah. I guess I did. What can I say? Kids do dumb things."

And the other girls laugh. The brainless, heartless twitter of birds. But it's not their laughter that gets to Brooklyn. It's the slow smile that creases Risa's face. A mocking smile. A smile that says, *I was better than you then, I'm better than you now, and I will always be one rung above you, ready to step on your face. Or spit on it.*

"It was a long time ago, Brooks," Risa says.

"Yeah, right, whatever."

Brooklyn turns to leave, this time not caring who she topples to get out. No one falls, because the curtain of girls parts for her.

Minutes later she opens the computer lab door. Thor sits alone at the mainframe, no attendant in sight. The clock on the wall above him reads 5:41.

He simply signs, *Who?*

Brooklyn spells it out so there can be no confusion.

R. I. S. A.

That evening, in the crowded playground, Brooklyn Ward eats ice cream standing near Logan. He snickers at something Kip says. While the ice cream is still being served, a messenger from the headmaster's office emerges from the building and passes out notes to twenty-one wards.

Brooklyn thinks, *If I ran things here, I'd at least wait till they've finished their ice cream.* But compassion doesn't live in a StaHo.

One of the kids who gets a note is standing near them. Samson. Brooklyn remembers that he's number two on the harvest list. Supposedly he's a genius in math but is also a notorious underachiever. Genius serves no one if it never makes it out of your head.

"What you got there?" Kip asks.

"Headmaster wants to see me." Samson stuffs the note into his pocket and starts working on his ice cream again.

"What about?" Logan asks. He puts his arm around Brooklyn, and she allows it.

Samson shrugs. "Maybe someone wants to adopt me."

They all laugh. Kip jokes that maybe Samson won the lottery, and then everyone offers ideas on how Samson should spend his winnings.

Samson only grins, the loser that he is, enjoying his rare moment in the spotlight. Brooklyn says nothing, her gaze roaming through the crowd of kids.

Near the swing set, Risa stands encircled by some other arts kids. She stares at the note in one hand, with her ice-cream cone forgotten, dripping on her other hand.

The smile from before is now gone from her face. Robbed from her. Soon she will be gone, and no one will tell the story of what happened when they were seven. Because no one talks about harvested kids.

Brooklyn's gaze passes over Risa to where the deaf kids sit beneath the playground's one tree. She catches Thor's eye. His leg shields his left hand from the other deaf kids, and he signs, *Okay?*

Instead of signing back, she just gives him a small nod.

Leaning against Logan's brawny arm, Brooklyn lets her gaze sift through the crowd. After the twenty-one are taken, her rank will leave her deep in the red for harvesting. Not a problem—she has six months to improve her rating. That should be easy. Once she's taken care of that plebe who switched her rifle. Once she digs up some nice blackmail dirt she can use against someone who can secure her safety.

As for Risa Ward, she will disappear, as if she had never been born. And no great loss. It's not like she would have changed the world.

As Brooklyn looks over the kids in the yard, she wonders who will be on the next list. Or who she might put there in order to save herself. In a world where kids like her have no power, it's nice to know there are still some things she can control.

Who will she switch next time?

UnDevoured

Co-authored with Jarrod Shusterman

1 · Seventeen

When Roland Taggart steps on the wrestling mat, he feels like an animal. It's something about the way his adrenaline pumps through his veins, the bitter sting of cleaning chemicals that fills his nostrils, the way cold sweat sticks to his skin after a match—it's stimulating. It makes him feel alive.

Roland stares into his opponent's eyes for any sign of fear but finds none, only a deep hue of red with flecks of purple— pigment injections are a common fad for students these days at Continental High School. As if bleeding your school colors wasn't enough. Roland has always scoffed at the fanatic face-painting type. Today the gym bleachers are packed full of them, cheering, waving pom-poms, their screams echoing in the shells of his ear guards. And he knows his mother's voice isn't one of them, not that he cares. Lately it seems like the only extracurricular she's interested in is fighting with Roland's stepfather.

People told Roland he was in over his head, challenging a state-qualifying wrestler. Sure, beating superstar Zane Durbin means taking his spot on the team, but to Roland it means much more. It means respect. It means power.

The whistle is blown, and Zane extends his hand for the prematch handshake. He notices the shark tattoo on Roland's right forearm and smirks.

"Nice fish," he snorts.

Roland keeps his cool, offers a cordial smile, and grips Zane's hand, commencing the match. Roland moves first and grapples, eventually positioning himself for his signature move—the body lock. He uses his raw strength to squeeze Zane's torso, compressing his spine, forcing him to fold backward and collapse to the mat. Roland pounces and pins him down. But despite Roland's muscle, his opponent surges forward, tearing free from Roland's grasp and avoiding what felt like a sure win.

Roland curses himself—not just for having let Zane escape, but because he lost control. He shakes it off, gets back into his stance, and begins circling methodically. Roland steps left, forcing Zane to shift his weight right. Roland moves in a rhythm so calculated it's almost hypnotizing, and he can feel himself gaining control of the match. Roland very suddenly lowers his center of gravity all in one motion, exploding into Zane—but his opponent slips off with ease, and Roland stumbles to the ground. It seems as if every ounce of energy that Roland exerts, Zane gains in power—and now Zane is dancing around, taunting him.

He can see the amusement in Zane's gaze, and it reminds Roland of the way his stepfather would look into his eyes after a big fight with his mother. She'd be crying on the cold kitchen floor, then Roland and his stepfather would find themselves face-to-face in the doorway, his stepfather looking down at him with that same sick glint of pleasure in his eyes that screams *I own you, and there's nothing you can do about it.*

By now Roland's ears are ringing. The crowd roars from the bleachers, or maybe it's just the sound of blood rushing though his head, because within seconds he feels an uncontrollable wave of emotion surging through him. It's the same indescribable force that curls his hands into fists. That makes him hold eye contact a second too long. That lures him into confrontation—a feeling he knows all too well.

Roland bull-rushes forward, more aggressive than ever. But Zane stays calm and in one graceful motion ducks right, hooking his arms underneath Roland's. Zane thrusts backward, using Roland's own momentum against him. As soon as Roland feels his feet lifted from the mat, he knows exactly what's coming next, and he's helpless to stop it. Even before he's slammed down onto the mat, he knows this match is over.

. . . And he flashes to a time when he was a child, standing at the edge of a pier—that emotionally precarious moment just before jumping. A memory of looking down, helpless and hopeless. Not because of how far the fall was, but because he knew exactly what would happen the moment he hit the water.

2 · Eight

Today is the day that Roland is going to "grow a pair"—or at least that's what his stepfather told him as he gazed out to the horizon. Sure, a lot of kids his age jump off the pier, but heights aren't exactly Roland's forte at eight years old. Roland's grandmother moved to Southern California after retiring, which made for a good excuse to escape the land-locked summer swelter of Indianapolis for a kinder, gentler swelter—and a beach day was the only way for Roland and his younger sister to escape their parents, and their drinking. Too bad for Roland his stepfather always seemed to come up with the most creative "character-building" activities when pissed drunk, and now Roland finds himself at the supposed precipice of his manhood—namely, the San Clemente pier. Roland's stepfather has always been a throw-you-in-the-deep-end kind of guy; however, this brings a whole new meaning to the phrase.

He lifts Roland over the railing, setting him down on the thin ledge on the other side. "See. Everyone else is doing it," he slurs, failing to see that such values run contrary to that of every parent in the history of parenthood.

His stepfather is known to have a short temper, and Roland smells more than just beer on his breath. "If you jump, I'll jump too. How about that?" his stepfather says as he grabs the back of Roland's neck, making Roland tense up even more. "I promise."

Still Roland clings tight to the splintery railing, terrified.

"Do it," he commands, and digs his nails tighter into Roland's arm—and it starts to hurt. So Roland begins to cry. His tears catch in the breeze, and Roland wishes his fear could be windswept along with them—perhaps taken to another place entirely—but his stepfather's grip keeps him stuck in reality. Others take notice of the scene, which only fuels his stepfather's rage, so he tries to pry Roland's fingers from the railing, and Roland's cries quickly turn into screams.

He breathes into Roland's ear, "I'm your father. You have to *trust* me." But Roland doesn't trust him, and he knows this man isn't really his father, so Roland wraps both of his arms around the railing, clinging for all he's worth—but his stepfather is much stronger. He pulls Roland free, lifts him up, and hurls him down into the water below.

The terrifying fall. A brief sting. An abiding belief that he's going to keep sinking and drown. But then Roland surfaces, gasping for air. He reminds himself that he can swim. He confirms that, yes, he's still alive. He treads the chilly water the best he can and waits for the splash that will herald his stepfather's arrival in the water. *I'll jump too.* That's what he promised. But the telltale splash doesn't come. And only when Roland looks up does he realize why—his stepfather is frozen at the edge of the railing, clearly still trying to work up the courage to jump. He's leaning forward as if to dare himself but appears to be gripped by fear that he can't overcome. He didn't jump in after Roland like he promised. He didn't, and he never would.

3 · Seventeen

Last year Roland's guidance counselor suggested that he channel his energy into something that *builds* personality rather than punching everyone else's into submission. So now he gets to slam the mousey know-it-all from third period, and if he does it with enough conviction, it might just earn him an A. Nearly two weeks have passed since varsity challenges, long enough for everyone to forget Roland's loss to Zane—everyone, that is, except Roland. Even though practicing with junior varsity every day is a constant reminder of his failure, Roland doesn't let it get to him. Deep down he knows that he's just biding his time, waiting for the right moment to make his next move.

Roland is popular at school, not because he's particularly well liked, but because no one else has the guts to tell him otherwise. He and his group of friends, about ten in all, hang out at what they like to call the Hill, a not-so-clever name for the large elevated patch of grass located in the center of campus. The guys he hangs with are the troublemaking type, their eyes reddened by pigment injections and bodies inked like an urban interchange—as if appearing less human might prevent them from being unwound. People joke that when the Juvey-cops needed to make a quota, they'd come to the Hill and take their pick. Jokes like these don't really bother Roland, because even if they were true, he knows he would be the last to go. Roland doesn't really get in fights anymore—why should he when he has people ready and willing to do his dirty work for him? As far as anyone is concerned, Roland is the alpha of the pack. He's respected because he's fair, and above all, he's dangerously intelligent—and everyone knows it.

He spots Zane from across the quad, sporting his varsity letterman jacket, lined to the seams with patches that boast his every earthly accomplishment. The all-American jock, honor student, captain of the debate team, and perhaps the most popular kid at school. He even won homecoming king this year, not that Roland really cares about that sort of thing.

Sure, Roland has had his sights set on Zane ever since the day of the match, but today is different. Today Zane seems on edge. Vulnerable. It's not until Roland gets closer that he realizes that it's because Zane's been arguing with his girlfriend, Valerie Mills—a girl Roland dated a couple years back. He watches as Zane paces, pointing an accusing finger at her. Valerie eventually storms off, eyes black and runny with mascara.

To the rest of the school this little altercation might turn into fifth-period gossip, but to Roland it means much more. It means opportunity—not for revenge, but to take what's rightfully his. Roland watches from the top of his hill, eyes beaming, because now he knows exactly what he needs to do.

4 · Eleven

A human being is supposed to be the sum of their genes and their environment—however, Roland feels a slave to his home environment and is estranged from at least half of his biology, having never met his real father. To Roland, his life equation feels far from balanced—even though his family may appear relatively functional to the rest of the world.

As much as Roland hates it when people make the honest mistake of thinking that he is biologically related to his stepfather, there's a part of him that likes to pretend that he is—and yet another part curses the part that pretends.

It's summertime, the Taggart family is in California again, and things have gotten worse. This summer their stepfather makes both Roland and his sister keep their shirts on at the beach. A couple of puffy welts could always be written off, but at this point not even Roland could lie away the scars.

Now more than ever Roland and his sister are finding themselves out of the house. And today something brings Roland back to the pier. Roland realizes he hasn't been back here since the day his stepfather threw him in three summers ago. He still remembers the exact spot where it happened. The funny thing is that he can hardly get himself to look over the edge—he's been even more terrified of heights ever since. Roland and his stepfather never talked about that day again. In fact, he never told anyone about it—but it haunts him. Enough that he's lured back here once more. This time with his sister.

Roland turns to her. "I dare you to jump."

She shakes her head and backs up, moving away from him.

"C'mon, all the other kids do it."

"It's too far. And I don't swim good."

"I'll follow you in." Roland looks deep into her eyes. "I promise."

Roland's sister tries to back away, but Roland is a couple years older than her and much stronger. She screams when he grabs her, but no one is close enough to stop it. "It won't be so bad—you'll see." Then he picks her up and in one smooth motion throws her off the edge.

Then even before he hears her hit the water, Roland closes his eyes, musters every morsel of courage he has, and jumps, just as promised.

He surfaces just beside her, and she grabs him around the neck, holding him for dear life.

"See? It didn't even hurt, did it?"

Roland helps his sister to shore. And even though his mother, who saw the scene, goes ballistic, and even though his stepfather gives him a double helping of the belt for throwing her off that same ledge, it's all okay—because Roland needed to know who he was, but more importantly, who he wasn't. He jumped. He kept his promise. And for the first time each lash stings a little less than the one before.

5 · Seventeen

It isn't hard for Roland to find Valerie's car later that evening, stamped fresh with those bleeding-heart-hippie bumper stickers—PROACTIVE CITIZENS AGAINST UNWINDING, THE WHOLENESS COALITION, and the like. Roland watches through rows of cars in the school parking lot as Valerie bids her friends farewell after cheer practice. Roland makes his way closer, keeping out of view behind SUVs and jacked-up pickups. Valerie slips into her car and pulls the door shut, but just before it closes, Roland stops it. He sees her glance at his arm that holds open the door. She sees his tiger shark tattoo even before seeing him. She knows exactly who it is.

Roland opens the car door gently and looks down at her. "Hey, Valerie. Heard you had a rough day."

She's caught off guard. Stumbles over her words a bit. Good. It gives him the advantage. "What are you doing here?"

Rather than immediately answering the question, Roland advances forward, getting down on one knee and leveling with her. "I saw you crying today, and I just wanted to make sure everything was all right." He takes her hand and smiles, showing his teeth. Valerie pulls away, uncomfortable—Roland can feel himself already in control. So he makes his next calculated move. "I don't know . . . I felt kind of . . . protective. I don't know what that means."

Roland dated Valerie long enough to know that it would take more than sweet talk to win this game, and as expected, she keeps her cool. "It means nothing. You broke up with me. Or did you forget that?"

Her comment might evoke some feelings if Roland let it, but he doesn't. He lets it slide off. He moves close to her ear, making his voice breathy. He knows she can feel the warmth in her ear when he speaks. Feel the charge in his voice. "There's so much I miss," he tells her. "I miss kissing you. I miss the feel of it."

She shifts her shoulders, uncomfortable, but doesn't stop him. So he gently touches her cheek. "Is it crazy of me to want that again?"

He has Valerie right where he wants her—caught in his trance, mesmerized by his pretense at vulnerability. He moves his hand down her neck and grabs the back of her hair in a most primal way.

That's when she snaps out of it and pushes his hand away. He lets her. For now. "Roland, I'm sorry. I'm with Zane now, and that's not changing, no matter what you think." She grips the door handle to pull it shut, but Roland rips it open.

"And how many boyfriends is it going to take to replace all the pieces of the one you let get unwound?"

It's a dirty blow, but necessary. No one speaks of it, at least not to Valerie, but everyone knows. It was the luckless loser she chose between Roland and Zane. What was his name? Roland can't remember. That's the way it is with Unwinds.

As much as Valerie must hate him right now, Roland knows she won't look him in the eyes. Because deep down he knows Valerie will never know the answer to that question, or whether she truly played a part in that boy's parents' decision to sign an unwind order. This is the exact button Roland has been waiting to push, to detonate the entire situation. And Valerie explodes. She fights with all of her being to close the door, but Roland won't let her.

"Go to hell!" she screams—but Roland isn't finished. He puts his hand behind her head, pulling her lips to his, and forces a kiss. She struggles, but he's much stronger than she is. Valerie claws, throwing punches out of desperation, but it's no use—and as their mouths are pressed together, she sinks her teeth into Roland's lower lip, biting down. He tries to pull her off, but she doesn't let go. Not until it really stings. Not until she's drawn just enough blood.

Finally Roland pushes her off and grunts. He wipes the blood from his mouth and savors the moment, flashing her a bloody red smile. "You know what? It wasn't as good as I remember."

Valerie slams the door shut, fires up the engine, and peels out.

Roland exhales, invigorated, his bottom lip beginning to swell. He looks around, noticing that a few of Valerie's teammates saw the whole thing—three to be exact—and Roland smiles to himself, because as far as he's concerned that's just the right number of witnesses.

6 · Thirteen

The size of an ocean wave is calculated not by its face but from the trough behind it, giving it the illusion of being much larger than it actually is. But right now, for Roland, the wave that swells before him can't be measured in feet or inches, only in increments of fear.

He's no longer afraid of heights, no longer fears the jump

from the pier. He's conquered that. Now he's moved on to greater challenges.

Pulling his boogie board into his chest, Roland makes a split-second decision and dives underwater, bracing himself for impact. He goes under and a moment later emerges. It wasn't as bad as he thought. Not as bad as it could have been. He's relieved. Roland sizes up the next wave—it's intimidating, but he'll survive this one too. The crashing wall of water is beautiful even in its monstrous nature—the way the setting sun glows through its face; the way sparkles dance along its foamy crest.

Roland should have known a storm was coming in. The signs were clear, but then again Roland is far too bullheaded to back off once he's made a decision. Today was the day he was going to boogie-board the big waves. And since there was yet another screaming match occurring between his mother and stepfather, Roland knew there was only one place he could go to take out his own aggression: the sea.

"Here comes another one!" his sister shouts from the top of the pier, like his own personal lifeguard, although her jumping in is out of the question. She only did that once. And she didn't exactly jump.

Roland focuses on the next wave. It's bigger than the others. *Maybe a ten footer,* he thinks. He braces himself and takes it head-on, the ocean tide sucking him under and thrashing him around like a rag doll. The boogie board flies, and he feels it tug on the rubber cord around his wrist. By the time he reaches the surface, his ears are ringing, a shrill that crescendos into what sounds like distant screams, and it's not until Roland looks up that he realize they're coming from his sister. She's frantic, pointing to the water. Roland feels a surge of adrenaline. He pulls the boogie board back to him and focuses his attention on the water, but the sun temporarily blinds him, refracting through the surface like a prism. He panics, trying to assess his surroundings, interpret his sister's hysteria, but it only hits him when he feels something large brush past his leg. . . .

7 · Seventeen

Wrestling is always the first period of the day, and Roland knows that Zane will be there. He also knows that gossip travels at an exponential rate. So Roland makes a point to show up to practice ten minutes late, after all the wrestlers have already arrived—a controlled environment where everyone's watching.

Roland opens the gym door and surveys the room. Rows of wrestlers are stretching on the mats, per usual. He walks by carefully, scanning the faces of each of his teammates; however, Zane's isn't one of them, and only then does he realize that the coaches aren't there either.

Without warning, someone explodes into Roland's side, sending him sliding across the mat. Roland doesn't need to look up to know who it was.

Zane towers over him, his red eyes more fierce than ever before. "Keep your paws away from Valerie," he growls.

Roland reflexively jumps to his feet, getting in Zane's face. He clenches his fists, pumped full of rage, but it feels all too familiar—and it reminds him of the last time their eyes locked. The time when Roland let his emotions consume him. The time he was lifted off the ground and hurled down on his back. So this time he decides to remain in control. Rather than swinging, he forces his fists open, and responds calmly, "I don't know what you're talking about."

Apparently it wasn't the reaction Zane was looking for, because he pushes Roland even harder and snarls, "Don't lie to me."

Roland steps forward again, refusing to back down. Roland knows that fighting is exactly what Zane wants him to do; it's exactly what he expects Roland to do. And before long their teammates have started gathering around, encircling them, forcing the situation into a pressure cooker. Roland adapts to it and plays the crowd.

He shakes his head convincingly. "What the hell are you talking about?"

Already pushed to the edge, Zane doesn't buy his show. He swings a right hook, connecting with Roland's jaw, and before Roland can even react, his teammates are rushing in to break it up.

Zane fights them off, never taking his eyes off Roland. "Go get unwound," he growls.

Wrestlers go to hold Roland back, but he remains calm, he doesn't resist. Instead he smiles, letting the words roll off, and touches his fingers to his mouth, examining the blood, almost intrigued.

Coach Pratt bursts through the gym doors and makes his way to the center of the mat. "What's going on here?" he demands.

Zane fumbles his words, still too heated to formulate a coherent sentence. So Roland decides to speak for him. "We were wrestling," he says calmly.

Zane is completely taken aback.

Roland continues. "We were wrestling and things got out of control."

The coach looks at Roland's fat lip and back to Zane, who's still clenching a fist. "I oughta bench you till the next tournament."

But Roland takes up Zane's defense. "Nah, you don't have to do that. Everything's cool. It was a misunderstanding."

Coach Pratt turns back to Zane. "Is this all true?"

Zane nods. He doesn't really have a choice. And even
though Pratt doesn't fully buy the story, the explanation is
enough for him to overlook the fight. It's not uncommon for
scuffles like this to take place on the mat.

As if nothing happened, Roland strolls quietly to the center of the mat and begins his stretching routines, because even
though things didn't quite go as planned, he knows that this is
only round one. Sure, most people like to root for an underdog,
but it's human nature to side with a victim. So he grins, revealing a blood-painted smile, because this is Roland's game, and
now he's in complete control.

8 · Thirteen

Roland searches the water in terror. To him, every dark shadow
is instantly a predator; every splash sounds like a beast of prey.
He tries to convince himself that it was a fish, or maybe even
a seal. On the other hand his sister wouldn't have screamed if
that's all it was. Roland paddles violently, his body tight to his
boogie board, fighting against a riptide. He's been dragged out
too far. Dark clouds swell overhead, and the pier grows hazy in
the distance. He decides his best chance for survival is to shift
direction and paddle with the current, toward the adjacent
ocean bluffs. But Roland is already running out of strength.
His arms grow heavier with each stroke. And even though he's
moving with the current, the more he paddles the farther he
feels from land.

Whatever was there is gone. It has to be. The sea is the
only predator now.

Roland feels the shadow of a wave beginning to curl overhead. He snaps his eyes shut and clings tight to his board,
letting the sea gobble him. He thrashes about in the ocean's

underbelly until he's regurgitated to the surface once again.

Roland braces himself for the next wave, but it never comes—instead only the ringing pitch of silence. His body shakes, still on the comedown from a nasty adrenaline rush. And when Roland finally opens his eyes, everything is still. He takes a moment to catch his breath and take in his surroundings. He's alone. It's nearly dark. The pier is no longer in sight. Everywhere he looks is hazy and blue, as if trapped in the infinitude where both the ocean and sky collide.

Roland screams, but he's been dragged out too far for anyone to hear. He tries to paddle, but his arms grow weak, and the water begins to feel like gelatin. So he cries, only to have his tears swallowed by the ungrateful sea.

And then suddenly something bumps the bottom of his board.

Roland's heart quickens. He begins to hyperventilate. He feels a pulse in the water beneath him. Undulations that grow in intensity. The pressure swells until a powerful force explodes upward, launching Roland into the air, ripping him from his board.

9 · Seventeen

Roland keeps a close eye on Zane throughout practice, and it's not until the last water break that he makes his next move. Roland notices that Valerie sits on the bleachers with a few friends, waiting for Zane to finish practice. Now is the perfect time to close in. He spots Zane across the room, off the mat on the hard wood floor, navigates through a sea of wrestlers, and settles over him.

Zane looks up from his water bottle. "What do you want?" he sneers.

"I want to settle this." Roland is confident and collected.

"You want a black eye now?" Zane scoffs.

"No, I want to settle this like men. On the mat . . ." Roland decides to cut to the chase. "I want a rematch."

Zane beams arrogance. "I already beat you." And he turns his back, letting it sting.

"If you win, I'll leave her alone."

This catches Zane's attention. He stops, growling over his shoulder, "You'll stay away from her no matter what."

Roland knows all eyes are on them, so he takes another calculated risk. "And what happens if I don't?"

Zane's eyes spark red with anger, and he spins back around.

Roland grins. "Now we're talking."

Roland knows that Zane wants to make a statement, especially with Valerie there in the bleachers. However, Zane takes in his surroundings and realizes that he's cornered, unable to start another fight in front of everyone. He shakes his head, incredulous. "I don't get you, Taggart. What hell do you get out of all of this?"

"If I win, I take your spot on the team," Roland says.

Zane laughs it off with feigned bravado, but Roland knows at the end of the day he can't back down from a challenge, especially with Valerie watching. So Zane takes the bait and clicks his headgear on. "You ready to be humiliated again?"

Roland flashes his teeth, showing off a bloodstained smile. And he begins circling in his wrestling stance, ready to strike at any moment, closing in on his prey.

10 · Thirteen

The shark missed him in the first attack, but only because it caught the edge of his boogie board instead, taking out a chunk. Now it circles, its steely fin splitting water in the distance. Roland is getting closer and closer to the cliffs. He clings to what's left of his board and kicks, his leg bleeding, having been grazed by the beast. He thinks about his sister, wondering if she's found help; about his stepfather, who's probably beaten his mother's head in by now; about his screams, swept up and devoured by the wind.

When Roland finally reaches the shale cliffs, his chest is throbbing. He searches frantically along the stone wall for divots that might help him climb, but the cliff is steep and slimy, offering little to grab hold of. Roland manages to stand on his board and pull himself up, but a wave washes him off the rock's slippery surface, and he's back in the water.

The beast is coming for him. He can feel it—and his stomach knots.

The dark mass ripples stealthily through the water, terrifying in its silence.

Roland claws the wall of shale, his fingers raw and bleeding.

The predator strikes and rips away the rest of Roland's boogie board, tearing it to pieces.

Roland clamps his eyes shut, wishing that he could snap them open and wake up, safe and warm in his bed—that this would all be just a dream—but reality hits him fast.

The shark comes around again, brushing past his side.

Roland tries the rocks once more, digging his raw fingers into the shale. And this time he pulls himself up, almost out of the water.

The shark approaches one last time, even faster than before. Roland grips the next protruding stone and pulls harder. The shale stone cracks loose, sending Roland falling, rock in hand.

Roland's heart sinks to the farthest depths of his stomach, so low he feels as if he'll be dragged to the ocean floor. Maybe that would be a better way to go. The thought of it makes him wish he were dead. And he finds himself filled with hate. He hates the ocean for plotting his demise. He hates the wall of shale that mocks him. He hates the beast. But most of all he hates himself for not being stronger.

Then something begins to grow within him, an indescribable force—a powerful surge of energy like he's never felt before. And it makes Roland's fingers curl into a fist, clenching the shard of rock in his hand.

And in a split-second decision, just a moment after he hits the water, Roland kicks off from the wall, gripping the stone shard so tightly it digs into his skin. But the pain doesn't matter, because at this moment Roland is in control. Eat or be eaten. And now Roland is the beast of prey. Within seconds he's staring into the eyes of the monster—blacker than infinity itself.

It all happens so fast.

. . . Suddenly a stabbing pain grips his ankle—pulling him deeper into the abyss . . .

. . . Roland begins to feel himself drowning in his own vertigo . . .

. . . Thrashing, kicking, stabbing with all his might . . .

. . . Thrusting his spike into a soulless eye . . .

. . . Digging deeper and deeper . . .

. . . Until eventually . . .

. . . It lets go . . .

11 · Seventeen

Zane bull-rushes forward. Roland swims past him with ease. Zane shoots a double-leg takedown, and Roland dives, clamping Zane's head into a headlock. Zane tries to squirm out of Roland's vise grip, but Roland doesn't let go. Instead he flexes tighter, squeezing every breath of air out of Zane. Zane's face is turning red, and his veins begin to protrude as blood collects in his head. He gasps for air, but Roland spares him none. . . . And just before Zane loses consciousness, Roland releases.

And now Zane is bloodthirsty. He tries to stand, but he's sluggish, his motor system failing him. He swings, hitting Roland in the face. He swings again, and Roland endures them, because he knows with every swing, Zane is running out of steam. And by now they've caught the attention of the entire room. Roland lowers his hips, shoots his own double-leg takedown, more powerful than Zane's, then lifts Zane over his shoulder, driving him forward, off the mat. And in one crippling move, Roland slams him down—harder than he's ever slammed anyone before. He can hear the crunch of bone the moment Zane hits the hardwood floor.

Zane screams in pain, a shrill so earsplitting, it echoes in Roland's eardrums. Zane arches his back, convulsing in agony. It's only when Zane rolls over that Roland notices his arm snapped backward, hyperextended at such an obscene angle that it bends in the complete opposite direction.

Roland stands up, invigorated, still rushing with adrenaline as Zane kicks and screams. Within seconds everyone's there. Coaches, teammates, spectators.

Coach Pratt looks to Roland, but Roland speaks first. "He hit me again. You saw it—he kept on hitting me. It was self-defense." And, as calculated, his teammates back him up.

The assistant coach hurries over, and attempts whatever first aid he can. Zane grits his teeth, and his eyes well up. Coach Pratt starts pacing, and as it all hits him, he buries his face in his hand and shakes his head—his star wrestler is down. "A new arm could take months to transplant. . . ."

Valerie rushes to Zane and holds him, hysterical. She looks up at Roland, screaming, "What the hell did you do?"

Roland doesn't flinch; instead he looks down, wiping blood from his forearm, revealing his tiger shark tattoo. He then meets her gaze, grinning. "I won."

And like that Roland turns his back, smiling to himself. Because now he knows he's the ultimate predator. He knows he's the shark.

UnClean

Co-authored with Terry Black

1 · Jobe

Jobe Marin isn't surprised by the unwind order.

He feels no anger, just resignation. His dad's litany still reverberates: *This isn't a free ride, son. A man has to earn his seat.* Dad sees the world in Darwinian terms—you have to fight to get what's yours—and Jobe's on the side of the dinosaurs. It doesn't help that his brother and sister are wildly successful, with Greg on his way to a basketball scholarship and Brittany on the dean's list at Wellesley College.

By contrast, Jobe has dismal grades, no awards or trophies or even friends to speak of. He's exactly the sort of son Dad *didn't* want, a nonachiever with no hobbies or interests or extramural activities. He should have seen this coming.

When Jobe gets the order and the Juvey-cops show up at his doorstep, he doesn't even try to resist them. All he feels is tired and hopeless and all used up.

"Verbally confirm that you are Jobe Andrew Marin," says one of the Juvies. The one with the eyebrow twitch.

Jobe nods.

"I said verbally."

"Yeah, I'm him."

Eyebrow Twitch pulls out a card and reads from it. "Jobe Andrew Marin, by the signing of this order, your parents and/ or legal guardians have retroactively terminated your tenure, backdated to six days postconception, leaving you . . ." He drones on, reading the standard litany, but Jobe isn't listening. He looks at his parents standing awkwardly in the foyer of their modest home, his dad self-righteous and his mom uncertain. With his sister off at college and his brother at a basketball tournament, it's just his parents here to witness this. He's glad his brother and sister aren't here to have to see this sorry spectacle.

At last, Eyebrow Twitch comes to the end. ". . . all rights as a citizen thereof are now officially and permanently revoked."

An awkward silence falls. Jobe's mom starts forward as if to embrace him, but Dad grips her elbow, shaking his head. The Juvey's eyebrow twitches.

"Well, if there's nothing further, we'll be going. Thanks for your cooperation."

"Yeah," says his dad.

Jobe is bundled into a van, which takes him to a bus loaded with dozens of other kids like himself, all numb and listless, hardly knowing how they got here. They're driven to the Woodland Bounty Harvest Camp in northeast Pennsylvania, outside Wilkes-Barre—a sprawling estate smelling of rose and juniper, surrounded by cyclone fencing. Topiary hedges show an assortment of woodland animals. They're taken to a holding area and seated alphabetically at long tables, like it's some sort of standardized test.

"Jobe Marin," someone calls after a short while. He's escorted down a carpeted hallway and ushered through a door marked EXAMINING ROOM.

"Good morning, Jobe," says a man in a lab coat, smiling, but not offering his hand to shake. His name tag reads DR. FRIENDL. Jobe imagines penciling in a Y to make his name Dr. Friendly.

Jobe is seated on an examining table covered with sterile white paper that crinkles when he sits. It's like going to the doctor, if the doctor was planning to extract your internal organs and give them out like lollipops to the kiddies.

"This won't hurt," says Dr. Friendly, wrapping a rubber strip around Jobe's bicep and extracting a blood sample. He sticks the vial in his pocket, says "Wait here," and is gone for an annoyingly long time.

Jobe looks around nervously. A window shows the camp's exercise yard, where teens are playing softball, lifting weights, doing forced calisthenics. Upbeat music blasts from pole-mounted speakers, audible even through the double-paned window. Jobe wonders how he'll ever measure up, because he doesn't feel well enough for exercise.

Finally, Dr. Friendly returns with a burly orderly and a nurse carrying a tray of medical instruments. Most notably two syringes—one small and one unpleasantly large. "Standard biopsy," he says. "Just to confirm the results of the blood work." He prepares the first needle. "Anesthetic," he says. "This will only sting a little."

It stings more than a little—but that's not what troubles Jobe. What troubles him is that Dr. Friendly doesn't say anything when he approaches with the larger needle. Perhaps because this one *will* hurt. A lot.

The orderly holds him firmly to keep him from flinching. "It'll be quick," he says.

The needle goes in. Jobe grimaces, refusing to scream, although the pain is excruciating. He wonders how much more it would have hurt without the anesthetic.

At least the orderly was telling the truth. The needle is extracted. The pain begins to subside. They let him go. "You're a trouper," says the orderly. The doctor excuses himself and departs, carrying a sample jar labeled MARIN, J. His team follows him out, leaving Jobe alone.

When Dr. Friendly returns, twenty minutes later, he's smiling, but it seems forced.

"I'm afraid you can't be unwound," he says with genuine regret. "A certain number of applicants simply don't qualify. Please don't consider this a reflection on your worth."

"Why?" Jobe asks. "What did you find?"

Dr. Friendly offers an apologetic grin. "It's not my place to say. Someone will be along to collect you shortly."

The door closes, and Jobe is left alone again in the examining room. He stares out the window, watching the others prepare for a procedure he won't receive—because he's not even worth the trouble of dismantling.

2 · Heath

"We've got another one, Heath."

Heath Calderon sighs. He's sitting in an office in the Centralia fire station—what *used* to be the fire station—with a sweeping view of the town below. But now Centralia's a ghost town. It was abandoned when a fire erupted in the coal-bearing caves under the city, spewing toxic gas from dozens of boreholes. It was deemed unsafe to live here. The entire town was condemned by the Commonwealth of Pennsylvania, uprooting whole families, leaving a landscape blighted with rubble and ruin.

The perfect place for AWOLs to hide, because no one gives a crap what happens here.

"Who's the new guy?" Heath asks.

His assistant—an overachiever named Sebastian—checks a hand-scribbled notebook. "Jobe something, age fourteen. He's sick. Bad. They kicked him off the unwind list because his parts weren't worth harvesting. We found him at Wilkes-Barre General Hospital."

"How'd you get him past the guard?"

"There wasn't one. Why would they guard the worthless?"

Heath nods. "Good job, Sebastian. I think we can use him."

Sebastian beams. *That boy takes pride in his work,* Heath thinks. Even if the work involves tracking down unwinds near the end of their natural lives and bringing them here to this backwoods hideaway. Heath has a plan for how to use them, something he hesitates to talk about, except with his most trusted allies. Not even Anissa knows his plan.

The cost of leadership, he thinks sourly. He likes Anissa a lot and wishes he could share what he's doing with her. She's the smartest AWOL he knows. Pretty, too. But Heath's plan is secret, on a strictly need-to-know basis. Anissa—like everyone else—will find out soon enough . . .

. . . because he's about to strike back at the Juvenile Authority—in a way they'll never see coming.

3 · Anissa

"You won't have to lose the leg, after all," Anissa says, examining Brent Lynch's below-the-knee wound with a practiced eye. "The swelling's gone down, so has the fever, and the skin tone looks a lot better. The antibiotics are doing their job."

"Thanks, Anissa," says Brent, flipping his long hair out of his eyes. He's been confined to bed rest in this Centralia farmhouse for three days now, in a not-too-drafty bedroom, on a mattress that's mildewy but does the job. Anissa made sure he had clean sheets, fresh water, and the right black market medication—because he needed them after being infected with a tainted tranq dart.

Stupid to contaminate the organs they want to harvest, Anissa thinks, adding that to the catalog of things she hates about the Juvies.

She smiles, rebandaging the wound. "You may not ever be a track star, Brent, but you should be able to make the choice between 'walk' and 'don't walk.'" Then she adds, with a note of strong caution, "If you don't try to do too much too soon. Give your body time to heal. You're no good to anyone otherwise."

Brent nods, swiping at his hair. "Understood. I'm just glad you were here to help me. Were you, like, a med student, before . . . ?"

"Picked it up from my dad," she says.

"Was he a doctor?"

"No." Anissa smiles at the memory. "He was a firefighter."

4 · Jobe

Jobe sleeps with a little more peace than before, now that he's been rescued by this group of AWOLs. He's glad for the haven Centralia provides but not sure how to repay them, if he ever can. Each passing day saps his strength a little further, like a junker car with the gas gauge heading toward E. He knows he's dying, knows he's got only weeks to live, if he's lucky—something he'd rather not think about. He can't fathom why he's been shanghaied from Wilkes-Barre General Hospital to this remote, befouled wasteland.

They expect nothing from him. Just like at the hospital, he's given regular meals—whatever the others have managed to steal or barter from outlying neighborhoods—and otherwise left alone. His room is small and barren, with cracked plaster and a boarded-up window, but the vibe here is different from at the hospital. There, his care was obligatory. He was unwanted—but here he's clearly valued, for reasons he can't guess . . .

. . . until Heath Calderon, the leader of the group, pays him a visit.

He's charismatic, and Jobe could tell from the moment they met that Heath was in charge. It's how he holds himself. There's confidence in his body language even before he speaks.

"How you feeling?" Heath asks.

"Like the sun at sundown," Jobe mutters.

Heath pulls a chair around to face him. "I know you're not well. Hell, I know you're *dying.*" He shakes his head. "Your parents may not have known that—or didn't *want* to know it. Some people have a willful blindness about things they can't deal with. It was easier to sign the unwind order than to deal with a nasty, incurable disease."

"My dad said I was weak," Jobe says.

"He's wrong. Your issue is a medical problem. In fact, you're in a special class—what the Juvies call unclean. We've been looking for people like you."

"Why?"

Heath smiles. "How would you like to be a part of something really important?"

5 · Anissa

Anissa Pruitt feels oddly at home in this dried-up town. She helped Heath choose Centralia as the location of their camp since it was long-forgotten and seldom visited. The place reeks of despair, but it's their best hope of survival—a haven that seems to reflect their angry struggle. She keeps thinking of the mine fire still raging under their feet, the pulsing heart of Centralia, a fire that can't be extinguished and will probably burn for a hundred years.

My dad would hate that, she thinks for the thousandth time.

She's meeting Heath at the graveyard, a place others would

find gloomy, but which, like most of Centralia, is starkly appeal-
ing to Anissa—a reminder that she's still among the living. Every
bronze plaque, each weathered headstone tells a tale that's forever lost. She wonders whether Centralia's ghosts can feel the
heat of the earth below, warming up their resting places, like a
sneak preview of the netherworld they'd rather avoid.

"Enjoying the scenery?" asks Heath, coming to join her.

"I usually do. You're late."

"I had business," he says cryptically.

She shrugs. Their walks together have become a daily ritual, even though he's often late and won't explain why. It's not
romantic, not exactly, but she likes his company, even if he
doesn't talk much and hardly ever reveals anything. Heath has
secrets, a trait that's both frustrating and oddly attractive.

They set off down Locust Avenue, the main street of Centralia,
where most of the AWOLs have made their home. Weeds sprout
from cracks in the asphalt, engulfing old, rusted-out cars. The
houses have fallen into disrepair, many uninhabitable, some
stripped to the bare foundation. The air smells of sulphur—
like rotten eggs—because of gas from the burning mine. Not
many would find this beautiful, but Anissa does. It was a family
trait, after all, to find hope in the heart of disaster and plunge
into it head-on.

"You're thinking about your father again, aren't you?"

Anissa smiles. From the beginning Heath could always
read her. "This all reminds me of him, Heath."

"Because he was a firefighter?"

"Because he was a *good* one. He never gave up on anything, no matter how terrible it seemed. He'd walk right into
a burning building, like he was strolling through the park. He
said a fire wasn't made that he couldn't beat."

"Even this one?"

She grins. "Dad once said he'd like to go to the mouth of

the Centralia mine, take a deep breath, and just blow it out, like a birthday candle. He was like the Paul Bunyan of firefighters; you'd almost believe he could."

"But in the end, the fire beat him."

Anissa looks away. She appreciates Heath's frankness, most of the time, but doesn't like to be reminded of the day her father died. It was years ago, almost a decade, but the memory still troubles her.

Martin Pruitt died on the job, battling a four-alarm blaze in a seedy Harrisburg warehouse. He went in wearing a heatsuit, a computer-controlled outfit designed to make any fire survivable. The suit could keep its wearer cool and comfortable, even if the outside temperature rose past broiling. But its greatest benefit—inspired by unwind technology—was that it could *amputate injured limbs*, if necessary.

He was trapped in a burning basement, and his heatsuit recommended severing his limbs, one at a time, to conserve lifesaving oxygen. It would buy him precious minutes, time enough to be rescued—and as a firefighter, he'd be in a prime position to receive replacement body parts. But he refused, knowing the parts might come from a troubled teen who'd been forcibly taken and unwound.

"My dad could have survived," Anissa says bitterly. "But he didn't want unwound limbs. He wanted to save lives, not use others to save his own."

There's an awkward pause. A raven perches on the wall of a burned-out building, craning its neck at them. Anissa wonders what's going through Heath's mind, until he surprises her with an expression of honest sympathy.

"You must have loved him very much, Anissa."

She nods. "He loved me, too. I'm sure he never imagined I'd end up with foster parents who'd sign an unwind order."

"Selfish idiots," said Heath. "That's the problem with

unwinding—it's not about problem kids, it's about problem *adults*." He spits on the ground. "Your father was better than that."

"And it cost him."

Heath looks at her with keen calculation, as if deciding how much he trusts her. He seems to be weighing the pros and cons on some imaginary scale. Finally he lowers his voice, though there's no one remotely close enough to overhear, and says, "We may be able to change all that."

"What are you talking about?"

"I'll show you."

6 · Heath

Heath knows it's dangerous to let Anissa in on his plan, but he can't keep it from her anymore. He needs her to know. He takes Anissa into the fire station, upstairs to the barracks, which Heath has converted into a fully functioning medical research lab. It's easily the most modern part of this reclaimed town, with a portable generator, a centrifuge, an autoclave for sterilizing, and a high-powered microscope to examine samples—all lifted from a medical-supply firm in Lancaster during a midnight raid by Sebastian and some volunteers. The lab is littered with slides and beakers and pipettes, under a mountain of scribbled-in notebooks.

"This is where it happens," Heath says, perching on a lab stool.

"Where what happens?"

"Change. *Real* change." He waves her onto another stool. "It's not easy to pull off. The clappers want to do it by blowing up things. They've accomplished nothing. Brute force doesn't work; we have to beat these people at their own game."

"How?"

They're interrupted by someone coming up the stairs— it's Jobe. He's fish pale and wheezing, out of breath from the climb. To Heath he seems like an old man crammed into a kid's body.

"This is Jobe," says Heath. "He's been helping us."

"Still am," says Jobe wearily.

"And we're grateful. What you're doing here helps more people than you can imagine." Heath pulls a long syringe from a cabinet, and has Jobe get onto an examining table. He knows Anissa won't want to see this, but she needs to, so she can understand. "Jobe, I need you to lie on your side, so I can take a fresh sample."

The scrawny kid gets into position while Heath eases the extra-long needle into his lower back. Jobe grimaces but makes no sound. Heath withdraws some fluid, then pulls out the needle, squirting the viscous sample into a petri dish, forming a yellowish puddle. Liquid gold, as far as he's concerned.

"Take a look," he says, sliding the sample under a microscope, then moves aside to let Anissa squint into the eyepiece.

"What am I seeing?"

"It's what you're *not* seeing," says Heath, glad for the chance to share his secrets. This may be a mistake, he knows, jeopardizing their mission for the sake of impressing a girl he's grown fond of. But he's sure he can win her over, once she understands the full scope of his design.

"Jobe has cancer," he says bluntly. "In his kidneys, lungs, spleen, and pancreas. It's metastasized throughout his body. You should be seeing tumor markers, like fetoprotein and microglobulins, all over that sample. But you don't."

"Why not?"

"Because we've developed a cellular camouflage, a blood-borne enzyme that mimics normal body chemistry. The standard method of detecting cancer won't work. Which means

Jobe and countless others can submit to unwinding—*and be accepted* by doctors with no idea they're extracting deadly, cancerous organs."

Anissa recoils. "How does that help us?"

"Anyone who receives one will be getting a death sentence. It'll sink the program, don't you see? No one will want an unwound organ if they can't be guaranteed safe!"

"But you'd be killing people."

Heath knows that's true, but it doesn't change his conviction.

"We're killing a few . . . to save many many more."

7 · Anissa

The sense of betrayal is as great as the moment she was told she was to be unwound. But this isn't just a personal betrayal—it's treason against everything that makes them better than the unwinders. Everything that makes them human.

"Have you lost your mind?" she yells, but clearly, if his mind was lost, it happened long before she met him. This isn't just a spur-of-the-moment plan. It was premeditated, calculated, perhaps for months. This has been simmering inside Heath, like the hellish fire in the mines beneath their feet.

Only then does Anissa look to a series of shelves beside her. Dozens of petri dishes, growing God knows what. Heath has turned the lab into a seething cauldron of biological weapons.

"We have bacterial infections, cancers, viruses—and we've hidden all the biological markers," he tells her, proud of his accomplishment. "We're going to release plague after plague on those who would receive unwound parts—and the world will finally see unwinding as the horror it is!"

Her fury explodes. Before she can stop herself, she sweeps

her hand over one of the shelves, knocking off the dishes, spilling their tainted specimens. They shatter on the floor—but not before one of them cuts her hand, right between two fingers—a deep, painful slice.

Her blood drips onto Heath's research notes, smearing the paper like a red Rorschach.

"Anissa, *wait!*"

He tries to stop her, but she evades his grasp and stalks out of the lab, glass crunching under her heels.

It was Anissa who chose the firehouse as the center of their operations. All the more horrifying now that she knows what Heath is using it for.

It was once a symbol of survival for the town. Despite the evacuation, a few die-hard residents dug in and refused to leave, staying in their homes, resolute, as the town evaporated around them. Law enforcement ceased; roads went unrepaired. The Postal Service stopped delivering mail and—as a final insult—revoked their zip code.

The firehouse was the last to close.

Anissa isn't sure when they finally shut it down, sealing that big roll-up door for the last time. But before that happened, some enterprising civil servant had begged, borrowed, or maybe stolen a fully functional heatsuit, like the one her father had died in. The one that might have saved his life if he'd been less stubborn and more self-serving.

The heatsuit is kept in a little alcove off the main garage. It hangs from a hook on the wall, seeming to hover above the ground. A sign reads USE WITH EXTREME CAUTION in old, faded lettering.

This is where Anissa goes when she needs to be alone—and now she needs that more than ever.

It's become a shrine to her, that big yellow suit with the

glazed faceplate and heavy, reinforced boots. The joints are knobby and wide, each equipped with anesthetic feeds and razor-sharp scalpels, ready to sever damaged, noncrucial limbs with frightening efficiency. Anissa doesn't like to think about that, because it's not how firefighting is supposed to work. *You don't just lop off body parts; it's about standing tall and saving lives. Clearly that's not an ethos that Heath shares. His plan is all about crawling.*

She calms herself by looking up at the suit. She can picture her dad in there, wise and brave and bigger than life, close at hand like a guardian angel. She wishes she could be as brave as he was. Or that she knew what to do, like he always did, no matter what was thrown at him. She could use some of Dad's wisdom now.

She sighs, massaging her hand. She's wrapped a handkerchief around it, but it's still oozing and angry, tender to the touch.

"You probably don't want to talk to me," Heath says, coming up from behind.

"Go away, Heath." She doesn't turn around. "We have nothing to talk about."

"Oh, but we do." He steps right in front of her. "The plan is moving forward, Anissa. We need to do this."

"We need not to."

He starts to argue, pleading his case, but seems to sense the futility of it. Instead he softens a bit, tries a different approach. "Do you know why this matters to me?"

"I don't care," she says, but it's not entirely true. Anissa knows little about him, despite all the time they've spent together, their headlong flight from the Juvenile Authority, and their joint decision to make camp here. She's often wondered about Heath's history, what drives his campaign to end unwinding ("unliving," as he calls it), and how far he'll go in pursuit of the cause. She senses a window opening, a chance to learn what he seldom reveals. "Okay, tell me. Why does it matter?"

"Because of who I am. *What* I am."

"Which is what?"

"I'm not an unwind. I'm the opposite of an unwind."

She frowns, trying to understand. "Go on."

"I was born with a defective liver. The doctors said I was living on borrowed time. When I was fifteen, it failed completely. I wound up in the hospital, not expected to live more than a week, and my parents couldn't afford a replacement."

Anissa tenses, not knowing what's coming next, but knowing that it's bad.

"They couldn't afford it—but they had an alternative," Heath continues. "My brother Bryan was a stork, unexpected and unwanted, but raised with the same love they had for me. Or so I thought." Heath takes a deep breath, as if steeling himself for the next part of the story. "They sold him to black market unwinders, in exchange for a new liver and the operation to implant it. They said it was the only way to save my life. I said if that was the only way, I'd rather not be saved. I begged them not to sacrifice Bryan, but I couldn't stop them." He chokes up at this next part. "They refused to tell me whether or not my new liver was actually his. Anyway, as soon as I had healed, I ran away from home. I knew I had to help the AWOLs, but I was never one of them."

He stops talking. Anissa hesitates, unsure how to respond. She doesn't doubt that his story's authentic, and it explains his consuming obsession with unwinds. But it doesn't change anything.

"I understand now," she says, not without sympathy. "But I'll never agree to your poisoned-organ plan."

"Here's what I know: The people getting those organs don't

deserve them. They're parasites, living off the flesh of others. If they get diseased organs, they brought it on themselves."

"You think it's that simple?" she snaps. "A few people die and this all goes away? That's not how it works. They'll figure it out, find better ways of testing the organ supply, and they'll trace the contamination right back here. You'll change nothing, except to get a lot of people caught—people who trusted you, *people they'll unwind because of you.*"

Then suddenly she's grabbed from behind. She turns to find two big bruisers, ex-military boeufs, two of the dumbest but most obedient of Heath's AWOLs. She struggles, but their grip is unbreakable.

"I brought them along," Heath says, "in case there was a problem."

He nods, and she's taken away to a utility room in the firehouse, dank and smelling of old boots, where she's locked away while the plan proceeds. She's gone from being Heath's friend to Heath's prisoner.

And her hand is getting worse.

Days pass. She's allowed meals but no visitors. Heath's keeping her in isolation, probably because he doesn't want his precious plan revealed until it's been set in motion and can't be stopped. That won't be long now, she reasons, because the level of activity in the firehouse has markedly increased, judging from the background noise and shouted orders and muffled conversations.

"This can't work, you know," she tells Sebastian when he cracks open the door to slide in a plate of not-very-warm macaroni. "He's going to get you all killed."

"Don't know what you're talking about," says Sebastian, though plainly he does.

"Tell Heath I'm hurt. I need medical supplies. I cut my hand."

"My heart's breaking."

The door slams shut. Anissa's hand really is getting worse, the wound purpling, with reddish veins radiating from the point of incision—a scary, dangerous infection. She's sure it must have been contaminated with something from the petri dishes in Heath's laboratory. *Like I don't have enough to worry about,* she thinks, painfully flexing her fingers. She has to reach Heath, talk to him before it's too late.

But it already is.

8 · Sebastian

Sebastian is waiting when the empty bus pulls up outside the firehouse, and he signals a line of AWOLs, all dressed in white, to climb inside. Jobe is at the head of the line.

"Break a leg," Sebastian says.

All the teens boarding the bus are terminal patients, too far along in their particular diseases to be saved by healthy organs. Some have been given incentives to cooperate—money for their families, perhaps, or promises of a more personal nature. Others have volunteered, choosing a meaningful death rather than merely a miserable one. They've been inoculated with Heath's chemical camouflage, and they're being sent to various harvest camps for unwinding.

The pretext is that they're tithes, volunteering themselves for the good of society or whatever, and Sebastian has created a data trail that seems to confirm that: birth records, family histories, personal details. But it's all a fabrication. The truth is that they're about to unleash a biological nightmare on anyone who receives their organs.

"Sixteen, seventeen, eighteen," Sebastian says, nodding, consulting his checklist. "All present and accounted for." The door closes, and he thumps it with his palm, wishing them Godspeed.

"Excuse me . . . ," asks a timid voice. "Can you help me?"

He turns to find a pigtailed girl in a ragged dress, wearing a frayed backpack, approaching the firehouse. She looks hungry, dirty, and tired. Sebastian wonders how far she's traveled to reach them. He also wonders how she managed to get past the perimeter and enter their secret compound without being noticed or confronted. *I'll have to look into that. . . .*

"Please," she says. "I'm an unwind, or I was supposed to be. I've been hiding out, and I heard you help unwinds. Please, can you help me?"

"Of course we can," he says, smiling. "You're welcome here."

"Thanks so much."

Sebastian waves as the bus pulls out, then turns back to the pigtailed girl. "What's your name?"

But he never finds out—because she spreads her hands and powerfully claps them together, changing Centralia's geography.

9 · Blast

The clapper's blast is far more powerful than even the architects of the explosion expected. It splits the ground and strikes a pool of stagnant methane gas that has quietly accumulated over a period of decades beneath the poisoned town. The resulting detonation hollows out the fire station in a blowtorch-hot column of Old Testament flame.

Sebastian is barbecued in the first instant of the explosion. The bus flies off the roadbed like a toy tossed by a child, its frame buckling, tires and windows exploding from the heat. Buildings crumple; abandoned houses are blown off their foundations. Blazing shrapnel flies in all directions, casting a debris field the size of a stadium. Droplets of molten glass fall like rain. A road sign reading WELCOME TO CENTRALIA is flung skyward, falling to earth four miles from the post it was nailed to. The green growth overwhelming the streets is burned back, like the scene of a battle.

Those who can, flee for their lives as the inferno blossoms and rages, engulfing the town.

10 · Jobe

Jobe is sitting near the back of the bus when the clapper detonates. The bus heaves and lurches, flipping on its side, with everyone screaming and the glass windows melting (is he really seeing that?) and the whole world turned red as paint, just for a moment, like a modern version of Dante's *Inferno*.

He's thrown headlong into the rear emergency door, which snaps open under his weight. Jobe is catapulted onto the pavement, landing too hard, feeling bones break. The street burns to the touch, like a griddle, but he can't get up and run because he's broken his leg, maybe both legs. Maybe his spine. He can only crawl, trying to reach the grass, though that's burning too; he's trapped in a waking nightmare.

But even in the middle of this disaster, a part of him marvels that surprise is still possible, even for the dying, because his path to oblivion has taken a startling turn.

Heath said that Jobe would be helping more people than he could imagine. Instead, he's helping no one. He feels the bitterness of disappointment, almost worse than his injuries. His death will not count. He's become the failure his father always said he was.

Until he hears a faint voice yelling, "Help!"

11 · Anissa

Anissa is sitting in her makeshift cell when the wall splits open, like the shell of a melon. Miraculously, she's shielded from the blast wave by a bank of lockers, which crumples like tinfoil but saves her life. She staggers into the burning garage and is nearly crushed when the heatsuit topples on her. Then, before she can squirm out from under it, a beam comes down, pinning her beneath it.

I'm trapped here, she realizes, *by a machine designed to protect people from fire.* It seems the cruelest of ironies. Worse, the building is heating up around her, as the garage is consumed by flame.

She yells, "Help!" again and again, not really expecting an answer, because if Dad's death taught her anything, it's that prayers rarely get answered, miracles seldom happen, and no one's coming to save her. She can only be brave like he was and wait for the end, probably a bad one. It's already searingly hot in here and getting harder to breathe.

Then something moves.

Someone's coming toward her through the collapsed wall of the garage, crawling with painful slowness. She squints and recognizes him: Jobe, the multiple-cancer victim, the very last person she'd expect to be mounting a rescue mission. "Hang on," he says, and Anissa wonders if he's taking to her or himself.

"You're hurt," she says.

"You're trapped," he says back.

He manages to reach her and tries to dislodge the beam, without the use of his legs, but he can't—it's too heavy. Anissa rocks back and forth, and Jobe pushes, working together to free her. "Why are you helping me?" she asks, then looks into his face and doesn't need an answer; she already knows. It's too late for Jobe to save himself . . . but not too late to save someone else.

Finally the beam slides off the heatsuit, clattering to the floor, and Anissa wriggles out from under the suit.

Jobe, now lying on the ground, lets out a shuddering breath. He looks up at her, his eyes glazing, life draining from him. Yet he smiles.

"Did it," he says. "Made it count . . ." Then he releases a final rattle and is gone.

Anissa touches his face in a moment of silent commu-nion, closing his eyes. It's too late to thank him, too late to say good-bye—but even if she could, there isn't time, because she has to move, to seize the chance he's given her.

With flames licking closer, she wriggles into the heatsuit, sealing it like her father showed her, just as the ground beneath her gives way, and Anissa falls into an ocean of fire.

It's a long fall—much longer than Anissa expected. Finally she strikes the ground hard, sprawling forward. Within the suit her infected hand erupts in pain. She's lying prone on a rough, uneven surface, rock walls looming close, loose mortar tum-bling through the hole she's dropped through.

Awkwardly she climbs to her feet.

The suit adjusts automatically to Anissa's height and body size, as if it was custom fitted. The headlamp snaps on, but she can't see much—just a fiery wall of burning gas. *This isn't the basement,* she realizes. She's fallen into the blazing depths of the Centralia mine, the longest-running fire in history. Before her the burning mine snakes off into the distance. But despite the blistering heat, the suit's interior is almost comfortable, thanks to its built-in climate controls.

She tries to walk, takes her first tottering baby steps. Her infected hand feels like a knife has gone through it.

The heatsuit's faceplate display winks on, and Anissa

squints, trying to focus. The display provides an interactive readout, showing everything she needs to survive: the outside temperature, her current location, the oxygen reserves, and remaining battery power—still over 80 percent, after years of disuse. With luck, it's enough to get her to safety.

But it won't be easy.

The temperature in the mine is a searing 647 degrees Fahrenheit—enough to flash-boil her sweat away if it escaped the heatsuit's recycling system. The temperature in a mine fire can reach one thousand degrees, so she counts herself lucky. She still can't see anything, just flames curling and dancing, filling the cavern. She can only follow the moving map projected on her faceplate.

Just like Dad used to, she thinks, though it's not comforting, because he was doing that when he died.

She stumbles, jamming her hand against a spur of rock, and cries out in pain. She can't see her fingers under the bright yellow glove, but they feel swollen and tender. She wonders if the suit's biomedical scanners will detect it.

They do. On the faceplate readout, a picture of her hand appears. SEPSIS DETECTED, it says. RECOMMEND AMPUTATION. Standard procedure, she knows, is to anesthetize the injured limb and then sever it—something the suit can do automatically. But for Anissa, that's not an option.

"Amputation refused," she says.

She keeps walking, trying to figure out what happened aboveground. The Centralia camp has been attacked, maybe destroyed, by forces unknown—someone who knew where they were hiding out and decided to squash them. She wonders if they knew, somehow, about Heath's poison-unwind program, if Sebastian and his scouts were too conspicuous in hunting down candidates and attracted the wrong attention from someone who decided to destroy them. Or perhaps there was a mole, someone Heath trusted but shouldn't have. All she knows is there was a massive explosion, like a clapper's detonation, although she can't imagine why clappers would be involved. Blowing up a secret AWOL camp doesn't seem like the high-profile kind of terror they go in for.

Not that it matters. *My friends are gone,* she thinks despairingly. *Heath's gone. I warned him, but they found us too soon.*

There's a lump in her throat, an aching sadness for everyone consumed by the inferno. The ones who survived will probably be captured and taken to the nearest harvest camp. But she can't worry about that now—her priority is survival.

She checks the readout. The temperature's rising, and she's headed down, not up. The map display says SURFACE ACCESS 6.3 MILES. Worse, the suit's cooling system is starting to stutter, overloaded by the unrelenting heat. But that's not her worst problem.

She's being followed.

It's there on the map: The red blip of a second heatsuit behind her, drawing steadily closer. Anissa tries to pick up the pace, the sweat beading on her brow, her hand throbbing incessantly. She keeps glancing backward as if to spot her pursuer, but of course he's not *visible*—the rippling flames conceal him from view. Only the instruments on her heatsuit can detect him.

Until he speaks.

"Come back, Anissa," says a voice in her earpiece. She remembers Dad telling her the suits could communicate over short distances using subsonic transceivers. But the real surprise is who's talking.

"I can protect you," says Heath Calderon.

"Leave me alone," Anissa says through the heatsuit's subsonics.

"I can't let you kill yourself. This is suicide; it solves nothing. Come back with me. They won't hurt you."

"They just blew up half the town, moron! Why wouldn't they hurt me?"

"Because I cut a deal. They take me, you go free."

"Just like that."

"*Not* just like that. I gave them everything—my notes, records, whatever survived the explosion. Enough so they'll never be fooled again. Whatever threat I posed has been neutralized."

Anissa hesitates. "And in return, I go free?"

"I had nothing else to bargain for. They won't let *me* go. They only let me come down here because it's near suicide. They don't care if we burn up down here—but if I can bring you back, at least you'll have a future."

"Not much of one." Anissa flinches. "My hand's infected; it's getting worse."

"Cut it off," he says. "They'll replace it for you."

Anissa stands stock-still, processing what she's heard. She remembers Heath's brother, who was sold to organ harvesters to save him, an act so revolting that it defined his life forever. What would make him betray everything he believes in, just to save a fleeing AWOL who he doesn't even seem to like much?

"You're afraid of me," she says. "Afraid of what I may know."

"You know nothing."

"But you can't be sure of that—*because you're not Heath*."

Anissa shuts off the transceiver, pushing herself harder than before, determined to escape despite her failing health. Her pursuer—the man impersonating Heath—seems to be getting closer, though it's hard to be sure. The only thing she knows for certain is that he's got a more advanced heatsuit that can, among other things, mimic voices.

Heath has been captured or more likely killed; she knows that. They must have swooped into the wreckage of Centralia and started capturing AWOLs, rounding up survivors like ducks in a pond. Until they realized that the mine had blown open, the heatsuit was missing, and someone *had* escaped, right out from under them, into the burning maze under Centralia. And they sent someone in after her—with orders to make sure that no one escapes.

The words "sepsis detected" seem to pulse with a life of their own, like an attention-grabbing headline. The outside temperature has dropped to a balmy 619.

She wants to break into a run, but the heatsuit isn't built for that—she can only keep walking, at maximum speed, through this surreal landscape. If she slows or stops, he'll catch her. If she succumbs to the spreading infection, making her dizzy and weak and sick, he may not even *have* to catch her. She can feel her strength draining away, the pathogens in her bloodstream spreading, her world turning gray at the edges.

"You can't escape," says a soft voice.

Not Heath's voice, it's coarser and lower pitched, because the man behind her isn't pretending anymore—he's become brutally candid.

"I turned you off," Anissa says.

"I'm on an alternate frequency. We know you're Anissa Pruitt. It's time to stop running."

"Why, what's the alternative? Is there a reward for giving up?"

"A painless end," he says. "A chance to live, divided."

Gosh, thanks, Anissa thinks but says nothing. Her pursuer doesn't wait for an answer and elaborates on his proposal.

"I know you're hurt, Anissa. I know how *badly* you're hurt, because our suits automatically share information. You're in a lot of pain right now, but you don't have to be. Give yourself up, and I'll adjust your anesthetic feeds to end your pain. Then I'll get you out of here. You'll be taken to a harvest camp, and your organs will help others keep living. *You'll* keep living, through them. Isn't that better than this pointless suicide?"

"Shut off all frequencies," she says.

The voice cuts off, leaving a strained silence. He's still there, a red blip on her readout, mute but relentless.

Anissa steels herself. The mine stretches impossibly before her. Her feet are heavy, hard to lift, and the heatsuit's getting uncomfortable. She's in a race she can't win, burdened by infection, unwilling to surrender.

A part of her wants to amputate the hand and be done with it. It makes sense, because it would neutralize the infection. Amputation wouldn't *cure* her—the sepsis in her blood would have to heal gradually, over a period of time. But surgical intervention would help to kick-start her body's own recovery system.

There's just one problem: She can't bring herself to do it.

My dad wouldn't, and I won't either, she thinks, gritting her teeth. These suits were designed for firefighters ready and willing to receive unwound parts. Accepting amputation would make her complicit. This is the line she won't cross, the very thing she won't do, even if it means she'll die in this awful mine. Her one consolation is that they can't harvest her if she's dead. By the time they drag her body out of here, it'll be in no shape for organ donation.

So she keeps walking. She'll walk until she keels over from septic shock. *This is where I die, in a tunnel of fire that feels like damnation.*

Then an idea dawns.

A stupid idea, something she'd never have the nerve to try under any other circumstances. She's not sure she has the nerve to do it now. But her options are narrowing. It's either give in and let the machine amputate . . . or this.

She breaks the seal on her left-hand glove. Peels back the reinforced fabric, exposing her flesh. It's sickly red-raw, sticky and oozing, and the superheated air strikes her nerve endings, making her cry out in pain. But the worst is yet to come.

"If this doesn't work, Dad," she says, "I'm sorry."

And she jams her bare hand palm-first against the red-hot wall of the mine.

OH MY GOD OH MY GOD OH MY GOD

Don't faint, she thinks. *If you faint, you won't get up again.* But the ground is unsteady, lurching and heaving like a ship at sea, and the shock threatens to claim her because *OH MY GOD IT HURTS*, worse than anything she's ever imagined. She wants to curl up and die, wants it badly, but that merciful surrender is something Anissa can't afford and won't permit herself; she has to keep going.

The flesh of her hand is seared, but she tries not to register that. She pulls her glove back on over the ruined flesh, nearly screaming as the pain reignites, refusing to stop until the hand is covered again.

Her faceplate reads THIRD-DEGREE BURN and SEVERE TISSUE DAMAGE and, once again, AMPUTATION RECOMMENDED. But the "sepsis" message flickers and fades. *Because I burned it out of me, like putting a torch to an open wound.* She hasn't cured herself, not entirely; her blood is still tainted. But she's removed the primary source of infection and begun the process of healing. Her immune system will do the rest.

"Amputation refused," she says.

She takes a step forward. Then another. And another.

Two miles later she's still going. So is her pursuer.

With the nerve endings in her hand burned away, the pain has settled to a powerful, but manageable, throb. Her pursuer is getting closer, gaining ground. She realizes there's one last chance to lose him. Up ahead is an overhanging rock shelf, slicing across the tunnel at a place where it narrows to near impassability. Probably from a cave-in, where the support beams were burned through and couldn't carry their load. Whatever the reason, it gives Anissa the advantage. The man behind is larger and stronger, normally an asset, but here it works against him—he'll never get past this obstacle.

But can she?

She crouches, gauging the dimensions of the opening, planning her approach. The trick is not to touch the walls, because of their furnace heat—something she knows all too well. The heatsuit can survive the heat of the mine, but not if it's pressed against the near-molten stone. Anissa sidles forward awkwardly, crouching to clear the overhang. Her balance wavers and she nearly topples but manages to keep her footing. Her injured hand brushes the wall just once, with a sunburst of pain, but she bites her lip and keeps going.

She's clear. The obstruction is past. Her pursuer can't follow.

Some impossible time later, after an interval she can't clearly measure, Anissa emerges from the burning hell of the Centralia mine into a bright spring afternoon, many miles from the ruined AWOL camp. She's near a stand of gnarled-limb oak trees and rolling hills of grass and thistle and windblown dandelion. She peels off her heatsuit, like a prisoner escaping from bondage, and breathes in a lungful of air that's neither superheated nor caustic. She can almost forget the throbbing pain in her ruined hand.

They'll be looking for her; she has to keep moving. Anissa has ample time—she hopes—to find help, someone to clean and dress her wound and help her escape from the Juvenile Authority. Plenty of locals are sympathetic to AWOLs. She gives herself an even chance of getting away clean.

She turns to leave—but then hears a voice behind her.

"Help me. . . ."

A stooped figure emerges from the mine, tearing at a badly damaged heatsuit. He's a boeuf—someone Anissa's never seen, blond and buzz-cut and clearly in pain. The suit is crumpled and torn on the left-hand side, perhaps because he was too large to wriggle through that tight passage but somehow did it anyway. His left arm, Anissa notes, has been severed by the suit, just above the elbow.

He tumbles to the ground and lies still.

She checks his pulse. He's still got one. The smart move would be to forget about him, hoping he'll die, maybe even speeding the process. She admits it's tempting. Ignoring him would make her escape much easier. Getting help for him will call attention and risk her own safety. She could find a round-about way to do it—get a backwoods hunter to say he found the man, perhaps, making no mention of Anissa. But anything she tries will increase her chance of getting caught.

Should she run, or risk helping another?

Anissa smiles. She is not, nor will she ever be, like the people who want to unwind her. She is her father's daughter.

Which means her choice is obvious.

UnStrung

Co-authored with Michelle Knowlden

1 · Lev

"Do it for him," a woman says, her voice quiet but steeped in authority.

Mired in a numbing gray fog, Lev feels her cool fingers on his neck, taking his pulse. His throat hurts, his tongue feels like chewed leather, his left wrist aches, and he can't open his eyes.

"Not yet, Ma."

Like his eyes, Lev's lips won't open. Who is it who just spoke? Maybe one of his brothers. Marcus, perhaps? No, the voice is wrong. And no one in his family is so informal as to call their mother "Ma."

"All right," he hears the woman say. "You decide when he's ready. And don't forget your guitar."

The sound of footsteps recedes, and Lev slips back into darkness.

When he wakes again, his eyes open, but only a sliver. He's alone in a large bedroom with blinding-white walls. A red, woven blanket covers him. Beneath him he can feel a smooth and expensive cotton sheet, like the ones he once knew. He's on a bed that's low to the ground, and beyond its foot he sees the fur of a mountain lion on the slate floor. He shudders at the sight of it. An oak bureau faces him. It has no mirror, and for the moment he's glad.

Forcing his eyes wider, he sees unshuttered windows on the far wall, the light beyond them weakening to dusk. Or is it strengthening to dawn? There is a nightstand next to him. A stethoscope is coiled there, and for a brief, devastating moment he thinks that he's been discovered and taken to a harvest camp. Despair presses him against the cotton sheet, and he sinks into the fog that fills his head, confusing dreams with delirium and making a mockery of time. He drifts through the fog until he hears—

"When he wakes, get his name." It's a different voice. Deeper. "The council can't give him sanctuary without a name."

Cool fingers touch his wrist again. "I'll keep that in mind." He senses the woman leaning over him. He can hear her breathing. She smells of sage and smoky cottonwood. It's comforting. "Now leave us be."

He feels a prick in his upper arm, like a tranq dart, but not. The world goes hazy—but not like the fog. This is a different kind of sleep.

Suddenly he's standing in a yard, near a briefcase covered in mud that lies halfway down a hole. Outside the picket fence police are sidling toward him. No, it's not him they're interested in—it's the skinny umber kid with him. CyFi's hands overflow with gold chains and glittering stones of every color. He's pleading with the sienna-colored man and woman, who clutch each other, staring at the kid in terror.

"Please don't unwind me." CyFi's words are hoarse and choked with sobs. "Please don't unwind me. . . ."

A cool hand touches Lev's cheek, and the memory is sucked in like a mental gasp. He left CyFi days ago. He's somewhere else now.

"You're safe, child," the woman's reassuring voice says. "Open your eyes."

When he does, he sees her pleasant face smiling at

him. Square jaw, black hair tied back, and bronze skin, she's a—"SlotMonger!" he blurts, and feels his skin flush red. "I'm sorry . . . I didn't mean . . . It just came out. . . ."

She chuckles. "Old words die hard," she tells him with patient understanding. "We were called Indians long after it was obvious we weren't from India. And 'Native American' was always a bit too condescending for my taste."

"ChanceFolk," Lev says, hoping the offensiveness of his previous slur will quickly be forgotten.

"Yes," the woman says. "People of Chance. Of course the casinos are long gone, but I suppose the name was evocative enough to stick."

He sees the stethoscope around her neck—the one he had at first incorrectly thought belonged to a harvest camp surgeon. "You're a doctor?"

"A Woman of Medicine, yes—and as such I can tell you that your cuts and bruises are healing, and the swelling of your wrist is much reduced. Leave the brace on till I give you leave to shed it. You need to gain a few pounds, but once you taste my husband's cooking, that shouldn't be a problem."

Lev watches warily as she sits on the edge of his bed and studies him.

"But your spirit, child, is a vastly different matter."

He withdraws, and her lips purse ruefully.

"Healing takes time; for some more time than for others. Tell me one thing, and I'll leave you to rest."

He stiffens, reflexively on his guard. "What?"

"What is your name?"

"Lev Calder," he says, and regrets it immediately. It's been almost three weeks since he was dragged by Connor from his limo, but the powers that be are still looking for him. It was one thing to be traveling with CyFi, but to give a doctor his name—what if she turns him over to the Juvenile Authority?

He thinks of his parents and the destiny he left behind. How could he have wanted to be unwound? How could his parents have made him want it? It fills him with an unrelenting fury at everyone and everything. He's not a tithe anymore. He's an AWOL now. He'd better start thinking like one.

"Well, Lev, we're petitioning the Tribal Council to allow you to stay. You don't have to tell me all you've been through—I'm sure it was horrible." And then her eyes brighten. "But we People of Chance do believe in people of *second* chance."

2 · Wil

He stands in the doorway, watching the boy sleep. His guitar hangs down his back, warm from the sun, strings still humming.

He doesn't mind being here, though he was sorry to have to leave the forest. His time accompanying the sounds of shivering leaves, whirling dust devils, and powerful Chinook winds is always special to him. There's calming joy in transposing nature to music. Adapting the chords of yellow-shouldered blackbirds, prairie dogs, and wild pigs. Bringing their voices into each movement he plays.

Wil brought Dad's leftover blackberry crumble to the forest with him. Una brought some elk jerky and a thermos of cinnamon-spiced chocolate. She sat with him beneath a spreading oak while he played, although she left before he finished, as it was her turn to clean the workshop.

His guitar always sounds a little melancholy when Una leaves.

The AWOL boy that his mother has taken into their home has been awake for a day now, but he hasn't come down for anything, even meals. Dad offered to carry him, but Ma said he needed more time.

"Can't fret over AWOLs," his father told her. "They never stay long, and they're too desperate to be grateful." But Ma just ignores him. She's taken the boy under her protection, and that is that.

Wil wonders how the boy can sleep when the sun blasts through the windows over his head, and the roar of tribal construction in town echoes down the ravine. The boy's chest rises and falls, and then his legs churn beneath the sheets as if he's running. Wil is not surprised: AWOLs know much about running. Sometimes he thinks that's all they know.

Wil is confident the boy will be calmed. Wild animals, rattlesnakes, and feral teenagers go quiet in Wil's presence. Even when his guitar hangs silent on his back, his presence calms them—perhaps in anticipation of what he'll deliver. Although Wil's just a teenager himself, he's got old-soul style, a storyteller vibe that he got from his grandfather—

But he doesn't want to think about his grandfather now.

While he considers what music may reach this AWOL, the boy wakes. His wide pupils constrict, revealing pale blue eyes that focus on Wil standing in the doorway.

Wil takes a few steps into the room and sits on the mountain lion skin, swinging his guitar into his lap in a single, practiced movement.

"My name's Chowilawu," he tells the boy, "but everyone calls me Wil."

The boy stares at him guardedly. "I heard you talking yesterday. The medicine woman is your mom?"

He nods. The kid looks about thirteen—three years younger than Wil—but something about his eyes makes him seem like he's going on one hundred. More old-soul style, but of the world-weary kind. Life has done a number on this AWOL.

"Okay if I play my guitar here?" Wil asks, his voice as gentle as he can make it.

The boy squints suspiciously. "Why?"

Wil shrugs. "It's easier for me than talking."

The boy hesitates, chewing on his lip. "Sure, okay."

It starts that way with them. Being an AWOL breaks kids' spirits—makes them distrustful of the world. But since they can't see the trickery in listening to a guitar, or how Wil's music breaks through barriers that betrayal built, they surrender, listening to his fingers caress the strings; his music finally gives voice to their souls' sorrow.

His ma took a music-therapy seminar at Johns Hopkins, but she only knows its theories. Wil has seen how music heals since the day he picked up a guitar on his third birthday. Not all the AWOLs and not all ChanceFolk with sick spirits heal, though. Some are too far gone. Too early to tell into which camp this boy will fall.

Wil plays for two straight hours, until he smells lunch and feels the cramp in his back. The AWOL sits on the bed, having been awake and listening the whole time. His arms are wrapped around his legs; his chin rests on his knees; his eyes stare at the blanket. The chords of Wil's music fade to silence.

"Time to eat." Wil gets to his feet, his guitar swinging over his shoulder to hang down his back. "Probably soup and corn bread. You coming down?"

The boy reminds him of a rabbit, frozen, trapped between staying or fleeing. Wil waits, letting the quiet hum in widening ripples till the boy unwraps his arms from his legs and gets off the bed, standing straighter than Wil expected he would.

"My name's Lev. I was a tithe."

Wil accepts this with a nod and no judgment. Maybe this kid will be okay after all.

3 · Lev

Lev watches Wil wash the dishes after lunch, still thinking about what possessed him to tell Wil that he's a runaway tithe. Giving out too much information can only make things worse for him. Then a dish towel hits him in the face and drops to the counter.

"Hey." Lev glares at Wil, wondering if it was thrown in anger. Wil may be big as a bear, but he has a teddy-bear grin.

"You can dry the dishes. Meet me at the end of the hall when you finish."

Lev never did dishes at home: That was the servants' job. He's been sick, too. Who makes sick people dry dishes? Still, he does the job. He owes Wil for the one-man concert. He'd never heard guitar playing like that before—and Lev's folks were big on the arts, making sure their kids had violin lessons, listening to the Cincinnati Pops most Thursday nights.

But Wil's music was different. It was . . . real. For two hours, and strictly from memory, Wil played a little Bach, Schubert, and Elton, but he mostly played Spanish guitar.

Lev thought such wild, complex music would be too hard to listen to in his weakened state, but it was just the opposite. The music lulled him until it seemed to sing through his synapses: notes rising, sweetening, spinning in perfect synchronicity with his thoughts.

He hangs the towel after he finishes drying the dishes and thinks about going back to his room, but he's curious about Wil. He finds him at the end of the hall, closing his bedroom door and putting on a light jacket. He looks somehow incomplete without his guitar. Evidently Wil feels the same. His hand fingers the doorknob; then, with a sigh, he opens the door again and retrieves his guitar, and a jacket for Lev, too.

"Are we going somewhere?" Lev asks.

"Here and there." Which seems a logical answer for a guy like Wil, but the answer makes Lev think about being unwound. The dispersal of every piece of him. Here and there. Lev climbed the rez wall desperate for some sort of sanctuary, but what if he put too much faith in rumors?

"Is it true that reservations are safe for AWOLs?" he asks. "Is it true that People of Chance don't unwind?"

Wil nods. "We never signed the Unwind Accord. So not only don't we unwind, we also can't use unwound parts."

Lev mulls that over, baffled how a society could work without harvesting organs. "So . . . where do you get parts?"

"Nature provides," Wil says. "Sometimes." An enigmatic look crosses Wil's face like a shadow behind his eyes. "C'mon, I'll show you around the rez."

Moments later they stand on an open balcony, staring down almost four stories to a dry creek. Across the narrow gulf is the wall of a cliff, which mirrors the one into which Wil's family's home is carved. Other homes hewn right out of the red stone face them. They appear to be of ancient design, yet somehow modern and carved with diamond precision. New-world technology serving ancestral respect.

"Not scared of heights, are you?" Wil doesn't wait for an answer but makes sure his guitar strap has his instrument secure on his back, then hops on a rope ladder. He climbs down, sometimes sliding for yards at a time.

Lev swallows nervously, but not as nervously as he might have three weeks ago. Lately he's been doing plenty of dangerous things. He waits till Wil reaches the bottom, then he grits his teeth and follows him. With his left wrist still in a brace, it's hard, and his stomach rolls every time he looks down, but Lev grins when he reaches bottom, realizing why Wil made him do this. The first thing an AWOL loses is his dignity. By allowing Lev to climb the rope alone, Wil gave his dignity back to him.

When Lev turns to Wil, he's surprised to see that they're not alone.

"Lev, this is my uncle Pivane."

Lev cautiously shakes the large man's hand, keeping an eye on the shiny tranq rifle cradled in his left arm. His deerskins are worn, and the long graying hair escaping from its rawhide knot makes him look scruffy—but there is no mistaking the designer quality of his boots or the Swiss watch on his wrist. And that fine Uruguayan rifle was probably custom made.

"How did today's hunt go?" Wil asks. It should be a casual question, but Lev catches how intently Wil looks at his uncle.

"Tranq'd a lioness, but had to let her go: She was nursing." Pivane rubs his eyes. "We're heading to Cash Out Gulch in the morning. Rumors of a male down there. You coming with us for once?"

Wil doesn't answer, and Lev wonders at the sly look Pivane gives his nephew. Lev assumed all ChanceFolk hunted, but maybe that's just a myth. Just like everything else in his life has been.

Pivane spares a glance at Lev. "You look better than when I found you. That arm okay?"

"Yeah. Better. Thanks for saving me." Lev can't remember being rescued. He can't remember much after dropping off the wall except the sharp pain in his wrist, then lying in the leaves and pine needles, certain that this was what dying felt like.

Pivane's gaze sharpens on Wil's guitar. "Are you going down to the medical warren today? Are you going to visit your grandfather?"

"Maybe not" is all Wil says.

The man's voice roughens, becoming almost an accusation. "Medicine folk and musicians don't get to choose who their hands heal. Or whose way they smooth for dying." Then he points a finger at Wil. "You do it for him, Chowilawu." A moment of uneasy eye contact between them, then Pivane takes a step back and shifts his rifle. "Tell your grandfather we'll bag a heart for him tomorrow." Then he nods a solemn good-bye to Lev and leaves, using not the ropes but an elevator that Lev did not see, and Wil did not see fit to show him.

They walk into the village. Lev, so used to bland, sienna suburbia, feels out of place among the red-cliff homes, the whitewashed adobes, and the sidewalks of rich mahogany planks. Although the place appears at first to be primitive, Lev knows upper crust when he sees it, from the luxury cars parked on the side streets to the gold plaques embedded in the adobe walls. Men and women wear business suits that are clearly ChanceFolk in style, yet finer than the best designer fashions.

"What do your people do here?"

Wil throws him an amused look. "My people as in 'SlotMongers' in general, or are you asking about my family in particular?"

Lev reddens, wondering if the medicine woman told Wil how he'd accidently called the ChanceFolk by the rude slang name. "Both, I guess."

"Didn't do your homework before scaling our wall?"

"I needed a place to hide and had no time to be choosy. A kid at a train station told me that since your people are protected, I would be protected too. And that you know the legal mumbo jumbo to make it stick."

Wil relents and offers Lev a brief history of the tribe. "When my grandfather was a kid, the rez made a bundle— not just from gaming, but from some lawsuits over land usage, a water-treatment plant, a wind farm that went haywire, and casinos we didn't want but got stuck with when another tribe rolled on us." He shrugs uncomfortably. "Luck of the draw. We've got it better than some tribes."

Lev looks down the street, where the curbs gleam with gold. "Way better, by the look of it."

"Yeah," says Wil, looking both embarrassed and proud at the same time. "Some tribes did wise investing with their casino cash; others squandered it. Then, when the virtual casinos got ritzier than the real ones and it all came crashing down, tribes like ours did very well. We're a Hi-Rez. You're lucky you didn't jump the wall of a Low-Rez. They're much more likely to sell AWOLs to parts pirates."

Lev has, of course, heard of the wealth chasm between the rich tribes and the poor ones, but as it was never a part of his world, he never gave it much thought. Maybe people this rich don't need to profit off AWOLs. Still, he tries not to let his spark of hope ignite. He has quickly learned that hope is a luxury the hunted can ill afford.

"Anyway," says Wil, "my tribe knows the law and how to use it. In fact my dad's a lawyer and has done pretty well for our family. My mom runs the pediatrics lodge in the medical warren and is well respected. We get rich tribal kids from all over North America coming here for healing."

Lev wonders at the irony in Wil's voice but feels awkward about asking him more questions. His mother always told him it was rude to talk about money, especially if you didn't know the person well. But on the other hand, after listening to Wil play the guitar for him, he feels he knows Lev better than much of his own family knows him.

Wil stops before a small storefront at the end of the street. A carved oak sign says LUTHIER. He tries the handle, but it's locked. "Huh. I wanted to introduce you to my fiancée, but I guess she's taking a break."

"Fiancée?"

"Yah," says Wil. "It's like that around here."

Lev looks up at the sign above the door, feeling increasingly ignorant. "So . . . what's a luthier?"

"Guitar maker. Una is an apprentice to the rez's best."

"You mean there's more than one?"

"It's kind of a tribal specialty." Wil looks around, clearly disappointed, and Lev realizes this was less about showing him around than it was about showing him off to his fiancée. "Ready to go back yet?"

But Lev is tired of hibernating at Wil's house. Besides, if that petition is approved, this could be his new home. The thought gives him a strange chill, excitement laced with fear of a future so new and unknown. There have never been unknown quantities in his life. Until a few weeks ago everything was carefully laid out for him, so he never needed to consider the concept of possibilities. But now there are possibilities enough to make him dizzy.

"Show me more. How about your schools? What kind of school would I go to?"

Wil shakes his head, laughing. "You really don't know anything about us, do you?"

Lev doesn't dignify that with a response—he just waits for an explanation.

"Very young kids learn what they need to know from extended family and the neighborhood elders," Wil explains. "Then, as their talents and passions are recognized, they're apprenticed to a master in the field, whatever that field is."

"Seems kind of narrow to learn only one thing."

"We learn many things, from many people," Wil says, "as opposed to your world, where you're taught all the same things, by the same people."

Lev nods, point taken. "Advantages and disadvantages to both, I guess."

Lev thinks Wil will just defend his tribe's ways, but instead he says, "Agreed." Then he adds, "I don't always like the way things are done here, but the way we learn works for us. It even prepares kids for university every bit as well as your system. We learn because we want to, not because we have to, so we learn faster. We learn deeper."

Then Lev hears a young voice behind him.

"Chowilawu?"

Lev turns around to see three kids, maybe about ten years old, staring admiringly at Wil. The kid who spoke is skinny as an arrow and strung as tightly as a bow. He has a pleading look on his face.

"Something wrong, Kele?" Wil asks.

"No . . . it's just . . . Elder Muna asks if you'll play for us."

Wil sighs but grins, as if he feels put upon and flattered at the same time. "Elder Muna knows I'm not permitted to play lightly. There must be a need."

"It's Nova," Kele says, indicating a girl beside him, her eyes downcast. "Ever since her father divorced his spirit animal, her parents have been fighting."

"It's bad," Nova blurts out. "My ma says she married an eagle, not a possum—but he was the only accountant in his office who wasn't a possum. So now they fight."

Lev wants to laugh but realizes that this is no laughing matter.

"So shouldn't I play for your parents, not you?" Wil asks her.

"They won't ask," Nova says. "But maybe some of what you give me will rub off on them."

Wil looks to Lev, offers him a shrug, and agrees to perform. "Not too long," he tells them. "Our new mahpee can't have too much excitement on his first waking day."

Lev looks at him, puzzled.

"'Mahpee' is short for 'sky-faller.' It's what we call AWOLs who climb the wall and drop into the rez as if they've fallen from the sky."

Elder Muna, a white-haired woman, meets them at the door a few streets away, clasping Wil's hands with both of hers, asking him about his parents. Lev looks around the round room with its many windows. The maps on the walls and the computer stations make the place resemble a classroom, but only slightly. A dozen children mill about in what appears to be total mayhem: Two argue over a helix on one monitor, one child traces a path on a map of Africa, four act out a play that could be *Macbeth* if Lev remembers his Shakespeare correctly, and except for the three who have shanghaied Wil, the rest are playing some complicated game on the floor with a pile of pebbles.

Elder Muna claps once, and the children instantly look her way, see Wil, and swarm him. He shoos them away, and they stampede to the center of the room, jostling for the best place on the floor. Wil settles on a stool, and all the kids start shouting their favorites at him. But Elder Muna silences them with a raised hand.

"The gift is for Nova today. She will choose."

"The Crow and Sparrow song," Nova says, trying to hide her delight with a solemn expression.

The song is markedly different from the music Wil played for Lev. This tune is bright and joyous, evoking perhaps a different kind of healing. Lev closes his eyes and imagines himself a bird flitting through summer leaves in an orchard that seems to go on forever. It captures, if only for a few moments, a sense of an innocence recently lost.

When the song is done, Lev raises his hands to clap, but Elder Muna, anticipating this, gently takes his hand before he can and shakes her head no.

The group of kids sits in silence for a good thirty seconds, filled with the aftermath of the song. Then the elder releases them, and they all go back to their games and learning.

She thanks Wil and wishes Lev luck with his new journey, and they leave.

"You really are amazing," Lev tells him once they're out on the street. "I bet you could make millions outside the rez with your music."

"It would be nice," Wil says wistfully, almost sadly. "But we both know that's not going to happen."

Lev wonders at his sadness, because if you never had to worry about unwinding, it seems to him that you could do anything. "Why no applause?" he asks. "Are people here that afraid of clappers?"

Wil laughs at that. "Believe it or not, we don't have clappers on the rez. I'd like to believe that's because people here don't get angry enough to become suicide bombers and make their blood explosive . . . but maybe it's just that we vent our anger at the world in different ways." Then he sighs and says, with more than a little bitterness, "No, we don't applaud because it's not our way. Applause is for the musician, and the musician is 'just an instrument.' Accepting applause is considered vanity." Then he looks at his guitar, stroking the strings with his fingertips, peering into its hollow, like maybe something will speak out from inside. "Every night I dream of cheering crowds and wake up feeling guilty for it."

"Don't be," Lev tells him. "Where I come from, everyone wants to be cheered for something. It's normal."

"Ready to go back?"

Lev isn't sure whether he means Wil's home or back to the world outside of the rez. Well, Lev isn't ready to do either. He points down a winding path. "What's down there?"

Wil huffs, his mood clearly darkened by Lev's talk of

adoration. "Why do you need to see everything? Maybe there are some places it's best not to go!"

Lev stares at the ground, feeling more hurt by the rebuke than he wants to admit.

When he looks up, Wil is staring with pain at the cliffs on the other side of the village, then down the winding path. "The medical warren is down there," he tells Lev. "It's where my mother works."

And then Lev recalls something. "And where your grandfather is?"

Wil nods, saying nothing for a moment . . . and then he takes off his guitar and leaves it hidden behind a boulder. "Come on. I'll take you there."

Lost in thought, Wil walks down the cobblestone road. His face looks grim, and Lev leaves him alone, wrapped in memories of his own. Clappers remind him of the last time he saw Connor and Risa, and guilt prickles him. They rescued him, and in his own uneasy ambivalence between his past and his future, he betrayed them. Connor and Risa pretended to be clappers, solemnly applauding in grand rhythmic sweeps, and it caused a panic. They escaped. He hopes. The truth is, he has no idea what befell them. They could be unwound by now. In a "divided state." The more he thinks about it, the more he despises that euphemism.

The road curves outside the village toward the wide fissure in the cliff and dips into a gulch filled with gleaming one-story buildings separated by greenbelts.

"This first building is the pediatric lodge," Wil explains tersely as they pass. Wil doesn't stop, but Lev peers through the windows and into the patios, hoping to see the medicine woman. He sees other healers and groups of children, but not Wil's ma.

Lev shoots a look at Wil and sees his eyes glued on someone

ahead: a short girl with warm almond eyes, a cascade of feathers woven into her vest, and a faint smile that reminds Lev of Risa. She is standing in front of another medical lodge, stalling at the door, when she catches sight of Wil.

Even before they speak, Lev realizes that this must be Wil's fiancée. There's a connection between them perhaps even more powerful than Wil's connection with his guitar. As Wil approaches her, Lev thinks they might kiss, but instead Wil reaches for the beaded ribbon restraining her hair and unties it, sending her shiny black locks cascading down her shoulders.

"Much better," he says with the slightest of smiles.

"Not for the workshop," she points out. "It'll wrap around a saw blade, and my head will get cut off."

"Now that's what I call unwinding!" Wil says with a smirk. She gives him a glare that's more like a visual rim shot, and he laughs.

"Una, this is Lev. Lev, Una."

"Hi."

"Nice to meet you, Lev." She snatches at Wil's hand, but as he's much taller than her, he easily holds the ribbon out of reach. "Give it to me, Wil." Then, as if she's had years of practice, she leaps and yanks it from his hand. "Ha!" Winking at Lev, she says, "Take notes, Little Brother. If you hang with this one, you'll need that move."

Lev isn't sure why she's calling him Little Brother, but he feels pleased.

Una studies Wil. "Is your uncle back?"

Something intense passes between them. Lev notices that this lodge has CARDIOLOGY carved in large wood letters above the door.

"Yeah," Wil says. "Didn't find anything. So are you here to see my grandfather?"

"Someone has to," she says. "He's been here for weeks, and how many times have you visited?"

"Stop it, Una. It's bad enough I get it from my family."

"You get it because you deserve it."

"Well, I'm visiting now, aren't I?"

"Then where's your guitar?"

Something crumples in Wil's face, and Lev looks sideways, not wanting to see the tears building in his eyes. "Una, I can't do it. He wants me to soothe him into death. I just can't do it!"

"It doesn't mean he'll actually die."

Wil's voice gets louder. "He's waiting for me when he should be waiting for a heart."

And although Lev knows none of the particulars, he touches Wil on the arm to get his attention and says, "Maybe he's waiting for both . . . but he'll accept one if he can't have the other."

Wil looks at him like he's seeing him for the first time, and Una smiles. "Well said, Little Brother," says Una. "I suspect if you were one of us, your spirit animal would be an owl."

Lev feels himself go just the tiniest bit red. "More like a deer in headlights."

Lev follows them inside and to the far end of the building, where a spacious round room is subdivided into four open alcoves. It feels less like a hospital and more like a spa. There are large windows framed in rough-hewn wood. Blooming flowers decorate the walls, and in the very center is a fountain gently drizzling water over a copper sculpture made to look like a stylized dream catcher. There is state-of-the-art medical equipment in each alcove, but placed discreetly, so as not to disturb the calming nature of the place.

Of the four beds, only two are occupied. In the one closest to the door rests a young woman who breathes irregularly, her lips tinged blue. In the farthest bed is a gaunt old man, who looks tall even lying down. Lev stalls in the hallway with Wil and Una until Wil takes a deep breath and leads the way in, mustering a smile.

His grandfather is awake. Seeing them, he chuckles delightedly, but the laugh turns into a ragged cough.

"Grandfather, this is Ma's patient Lev. Lev, this is my grandfather Tocho."

"Please sit," Tocho says. "Keep standing around me and I'll feel like I'm already dead."

Lev sits with the others but scoots his plush chair slightly back, disturbed at how pasty the old man looks, his face drawn and his breathing ragged. Lev sees the family resemblance, and it unnerves him that this frail man probably looked like Wil sixty years ago. This man is dying for lack of a heart. It reminds Lev of the heart he might have provided someone. Did a person die because Lev kept his heart for himself? There's still a part of him that wants to feel guilty for that, and it makes him angry.

Wil picks up his grandfather's hand. "Uncle Pivane says he'll bag a mountain lion tomorrow."

"Always tomorrow with that one," Tocho says. "And I suppose you'll play for me tomorrow too?"

Wil reluctantly nods. Lev notices how he won't meet the old man's gaze. "I don't have my guitar today. But yes, tomorrow for sure."

Then Tocho wags a finger at Wil. "And no more talk of changing my guide to a pig." He smiles hugely. "Not happ'nin'."

Lev looks to Wil. "Pig?"

"Nova's dad isn't the only one who divorced his spirit guide. My dad writes petitions to the council all the time asking to switch people's animal spirit guides to something more . . . helpful. It's no big deal."

Tocho's expression is mutinous. "Big deal to me. Lion

chose me." He turns weakly to Lev. "My grandson thinks I should change my spirit guide to a pig, just so I can have a new heart quick and easy. What do you think?"

Lev knows that this is a test. Tocho isn't really seeking Lev's opinion; he wants to know Lev's heart. Will he say what he believes, or will he say what those around him want to hear? And whose side will he take?

Wil throws Lev a forbidding look, but Una nods at Lev, giving him silent permission to speak. "This is all new to me," Lev says. "I don't think I would want an animal part . . . but sir, I think whatever lets you keep your dignity is the right thing to do."

Wil's frown is so severe, Lev tempers his answer just a bit. The old man is testing Lev, but Wil is too.

"But on the other hand, if the heart of a pig saves your life, you could take it for now, and then get a lion heart when they find one."

The old man grins. "Why stop there?" he says. "Add the heart of a goat, and I can juggle them." Then he begins to laugh-cough again.

Lev isn't sure whether he passed or failed anyone's test. "Uh . . . maybe I should wait outside." Lev starts to get up, ready to make his escape, but Una stops him.

"You'll do no such thing. It's refreshing to hear an outsider's view. Isn't it, Wil?"

Wil considers it. "We can learn things from the outside, just as they can learn things from us. And if an old tradition ends your life before its time, then what good is it? Not many mountain lions on the rez anymore, but there are plenty of pigs, mustangs, and sheep. It makes no sense to insist on a part from his animal spirit guide. Choosing a different animal is simple logic. Shouldn't a flush of logic beat a straight of tradition?"

"Neither," Lev says. "In games of chance nobody wins but the house."

A beat of silence, and Una throws her head back and laughs. "Definitely an owl," she says.

Tocho locks his eyes on Wil. "I will hear you play tomorrow," he says. "You will smooth the path of dying for me. You shame me by refusing. You shame yourself."

"I will play for your healing only, Grandfather," Wil says. "After you have a new heart."

The old man stares stonily at his grandson, his earlier good humor gone. He turns toward the window, shutting them out. The visit is over.

"While your people focused on the business and science of unwinding, the tribal nations' scientists worked on perfecting animal-to-human transplant technology," Wil tells Lev on the way back to Wil's cliffside home. Una left Wil with a halfhearted kiss on the cheek and returned to the luthier workshop. Wil waited until she was gone before he retrieved his guitar. "We overcame organ rejection and other problems caused by interspecies transplant. The only thing we can't use is animal brain tissue. Animals don't think the way we do, and it just doesn't take."

"How come you didn't share with our scientists?" Lev asks.

Wil looks at him as if it's a stupid question. Maybe it is.

"We did. They weren't interested," Wil tells him. "In fact, your people condemned it as unethical, immoral, and just plain sick."

Lev has to admit that a part of him—the part that was indoctrinated into a world where tithing and unwinding were accepted—agrees. Funny how morality, which always seems so black-and-white, can be influenced so completely by what you were raised to believe.

"Anyway," Wil continues, "our legal powerhouse crafted an intricate set of laws, based on traditional belief systems, for using this technology. When ChanceFolk come of age, they take a vision quest and discover their spirit guide, which can be anything from a bird to an insect to a larger animal. Of course, after the council transplant laws came down, it was amazing how many kids, coached by their parents, came up with pig guides."

Lev doesn't quite get it until Wil explains that, aside from primates, pigs are biologically closest to humans. "Mountain lion is a worst case," Wil says. "Vastly different biology from humans, and on top of it, carnivores weren't created to last as long as plant eaters, so the hearts give out quickly."

"So what's your spirit guide?" Lev asks.

Wil laughs. "I'm even more screwed if ever I need an organ. It was a crow that spoke to me." And then he becomes silent for a moment. Pensive. The way he gets when he plays. "They call my music a gift but treat it like an obligation. I am shameful if I don't use it the way they see fit." He spits, leaving a dark spot on a boulder as they pass. "I would never accept a human part, Little Brother . . . but there are many things your world has to offer that I would take."

"Like a cheering crowd?"

Wil considers it. "Like . . . being appreciated."

4 · Wil

Wil knows he's opened up too much to Lev. An AWOL is supposed to open up to *them*, to find solace in their acceptance, not the other way around. He vows to shutter his heart a little more securely.

The next day Wil's spooning out breakfast porridge for Lev

and himself when his father calls. Ma takes the call in the study, expecting bad news, but then comes out to put it on speaker because it turns out to be the kind of news everyone should hear.

"We bagged a mountain lion a half hour out in today's hunt," Wil hears his father say. "Pivane is already harvesting his heart."

Intense relief reverberates through the house. Even Lev, who met Grandfather only once, seems overjoyed.

"Wil, go now and tell your grandfather," Ma says. "And be quick about it. For once, good news will travel faster than bad."

Wil grabs his guitar and asks Lev to come along. He even takes Lev in the elevator rather than making him struggle down the ropes.

"You're a stubborn man, Grandfather, but you finally got your lion heart!" Wil says, swinging his guitar around, ready to play some healing tunes even before the transplant.

"Stubbornness is a family trait," the old man says flatly. Wil notices that his grandfather is looking at Lev, not because he's giving Lev his attention but because he's avoiding eye contact with Wil. It makes Wil uneasy.

"What's wrong, Grandfather? I thought you'd be happy."

"I would be, if the heart were mine."

"Excuse me?"

Grandfather twitches a finger at the crowd around the other patient's bed. Wil barely noticed them when he came in, so intent was he on giving Grandfather the news—but apparently the news had already reached him. The woman in the other bed is in her late twenties or early thirties. The family around her seems very happy in spite of her dire condition.

"The heart is to be hers," Grandfather says. "I've already decided."

Wil stands up so quickly that the chair crashes backward. "What are you saying?"

"I'm a poor risk, Chowilawu. Too old for it to make sense when there's someone younger with a better chance of survival. Her spirit guide is the lion too."

"It was found by your family," Wil fiercely announces, loud enough for the woman to hear. Good. He wants them to know. "It was found by your family, which means it is meant to be yours and no one else's."

His grandfather's gaze drifts again to Lev, and that makes Wil angry. "Don't look at him. He's not one of us."

"All the more reason. He'll be objective. He won't be clouded by a family's emotion."

Lev takes a step backward, clearly not wanting to be a part of this any more than Wil wants him to be.

"It's your heart" is all Lev says.

Wil is about to relax, relieved to have Lev on his side, until Grandfather says, "You see? The boy agrees with me."

"What?" both Wil and Lev say in unison.

"It's my heart," Grandfather explains. "Which means I have full legal right to decide what happens to it. And I choose to gift it to the young woman over there. I will hear no further discussion."

Fury and grief nearly overwhelm Wil. He storms out of the cardiology lodge—but there is no escaping this. Word of Grandfather's decision reaches the rest of the family quickly. Within the hour, while Wil still stews and storms outside, ignoring Lev's attempts to calm him, his family begins to arrive: his parents, then Uncle Pivane. He sees Grandfather's closest friends arrive. He sees Una. They've all been called to give the old man their good-byes. They've come for the final vigil.

"Do it for him," Ma says gently as she enters the cardiology lodge. "Please, Wil, do it."

He waits outside until everyone has gone in, even Lev. Then he takes the long walk down the hallway toward the round room at the end. The woman in the other bed is wheeled past him, followed by her family. She is already prepped for surgery.

Inside the room his family sits on chairs and on the floor. Lev has held a chair for Wil. His grandfather's weary eyes are fixed on him as he takes his spot. He begins to play. At first he plays healing songs, but the tempo is too fast. He's playing them too desperately. No one stops him. Then, in time, the songs evolve into traveling threnodies: tunes meant to ease one's passage from this world to the next.

Over the next few hours Wil melts so completely into the music that his family ignores his presence. He hardly listens as they all say their good-byes, or as his grandfather speaks about the spirit's journey from its failing temple to other realms. He ignores Lev, who appears more out of place than ever with the family. Una crouches next to Lev near the window, listening to Wil play, but he won't look at her. Wil catches a glimpse of his dad's face, etched with sorrow. His father still wears his hunting gear, as does Uncle Pivane, although his uncle is stained with the animal's blood. There is the smell of a bonfire coming from outside the lodge, the giving of thanks, the exuberant singing of the young woman's family.

As the day wears on toward twilight, Tocho almost seems to dissolve before them, giving in to the call from beyond. Then, very near the end, he reaches out to stop Wil from playing, motioning him closer.

He has one last request for Wil, and he whispers it with long spaces between the words. Wil agrees; he hasn't the strength to argue about tomorrow, because his grandfather has only today.

The promise made, Wil loses himself in the music again,

faintly aware of his ma in her hospital whites solemnly taking his grandfather's vitals and shaking her head. Wil plays as his grandfather's breathing slows. Wil plays as his uncle Pivane quietly weeps. Wil plays, the music of his guitar covering everything, until it carries his grandfather's soul to a place Wil cannot see. And when Wil finally lifts his fingers from his instrument, there is nothing but overwhelming silence.

5 · Lev

In the very center of the rez, miles from its many villages, sprawl the ChanceFolk burial grounds. Many families have adopted the Western use of caskets, more traditional ones bury their dead wrapped in a blanket, and some still invoke the most ancient ritual of all. Although levels of tradition in Wil's family are very mixed, his grandfather was as old-school as they come. His funeral is of the ancient kind.

Tocho is placed on a high platform made of cottonwood and heaped with boughs of juniper. Reed baskets, decorated with lion teeth, are filled with food for the afterlife and hung from poles. A fire is lit, and smoke leaps into the wind. Lev watches carefully, storing the memory.

"Our ancestors believed that the breath of the dead moves to the Lower World," Una explains to him.

Lev is shocked. "Lower World?"

"Not hell," Una says, understanding what he's thinking. "It's the place where spirits dwell. Down or up—neither of those directions has much meaning in the afterlife."

Lev can't help but notice Wil standing apart from everyone else, as if he's suddenly the outsider. "Why isn't Wil taking part in the ceremony?" Lev asks Una.

"Wil followed our traditions because he loved his

grandfather. Now he must decide for himself whether to follow the traditions or not. And so must you."

Lev first thinks she's joking. "Me?"

"When your residence petition is approved, you will be an adopted son of the tribe. In addition to protecting you from your unwind order, the adoption will make this your official home. Like everyone else here, you'll eventually choose on which side of the rez wall your spirit belongs."

Lev tries his best to wrap his mind around this. He hasn't thought that far ahead: finding a safe place he can truly call home.

"Wil's grandfather gave you a gift, Lev," Una tells him.

Lev can't begin to imagine what it might be. Anticipation stirs in him.

"He gave the same gift to Wil, but Wil doesn't know it yet. You see, on his deathbed Tocho asked Wil to take you on a vision quest."

Suddenly the wind changes, and their eyes tear from the smoke.

There is a communal quest in ten days' time, and Lev is added to the group to honor Tocho's dying wish. Wil joins them as well, also to honor his grandfather's final request.

The vision quest starts with a sweat lodge. It's total chaos trying to keep a bunch of ten- and eleven-year-olds occupied while sitting around hot rocks, being steamed nearly to death. They drink gallons of salted cactus tea and leave the sweltering heat of the lodge only to pee, which isn't often since they sweat out almost everything they drink.

Lev, who always felt the youngest of any group he was in, is now the oldest. As if he didn't already feel out of place.

After the sweat lodge, they hike into the mountains. No food on a quest either: just thick, noxious drinks that taste like weeds.

"The sweating and fasting prepare the body for the vision quest," Wil tells him. Pivane is in charge of the quest, with Wil as a reluctant sidekick. "Of course, my uncle and I get real food." He is almost taunting. Lev knows Wil is here only because he promised his grandfather.

On the first night one kid has a vision that he tells the others at their meager liquid breakfast the next day. A pig spirit led him to a courthouse and told him he'd be a judge.

"He's lying," announces Kele, the skinny, hyper kid who often seems to speak for the others. "How much you wanna bet his parents told him to say that?"

Wil begins to call the boy out on it, but Pivane raises his hand and lets it go.

"If the boy has a true vision," Lev overhears Pivane tell Wil, "he will choose it over the lie."

On the next day there is an archery competition. Luckily for Lev, he took a liking to archery a few years back and placed silver in a citywide competition. Unfortunately, that doesn't help him here. He takes last place.

On the third day Lev falls and tweaks his wrist again. He has forgotten what clean feels like, and he's covered with mosquito bites. He's miserable and uncomfortable, and his head is pounding.

So why then does he find this to be the happiest week of his life?

Every night they build a fire, and Wil plays his guitar. It is the highlight of the day. So are the stories that Pivane tells: traditional folktales. Some are funny and some are strange. Lev likes to watch the kids around him lean close to the storyteller, their eyes wide with wonder.

On the fourth day everyone is antsy. Lev isn't sure if it's the effects of not eating or a storm brewing in the mountains to the north. The kids are simmering in the muggy morning stillness.

When Ahote spills his weed drink on Lansa, the two boys fight with such fury it takes the combined might of Lev, Wil, and Pivane to separate them.

It doesn't help that Lev feels like he's being watched. He stares into the forest every time a bird erupts from a tree or a twig cracks. He knows it's probably nothing, but all the uneasiness from his time as an AWOL still has him paranoid. His twitchiness spreads to the younger kids, till Pivane finally sends him off for a break.

At first it's a relief to be alone in the small pup tent, but soon the deerskin walls press down on him and the smell of dirty socks drives him outside. He can hear the others washing the breakfast mugs in the clearing. Chin low, he sits in the small thicket of tents, wishing the storm would finally break and get it over with.

"Lev?"

Looking up, he sees Kele fidgeting in front of him. Kele sits down, but he won't look directly at Lev at first. When he finally does, Kele says, "I had my vision last night."

Lev doesn't know what to say. He wonders why Kele came to him rather than Pivane or Wil.

"So you saw your spirit guide?" Kele seems stuck on what to say next, so Lev prompts him. "It wasn't a pig, was it?"

"No . . ." Kele draws the word out. "It was a sparrow, like my name."

Lev is struck by this. Seems right that the spirit guide would mean something special to a kid, unless of course it's to be a source of organ replacements.

"So what happened?"

"Something bad." The boy whispers so quietly that Lev has to lean forward to hear him. He shivers.

"What was bad?" All the fears that have been haunting him this morning return.

"I don't know." Kele looks at him, nervously crushing leaves to powder. "But I saw you leaving. You won't, will you?"

Lev feels as if an arrow has hit him in the chest, and he can't breathe. He tries to remember what Wil told him. The hunger and the sweating can cause hallucinations and strange dreams. Or maybe someone suggested to Kele that mahpees always leave, and so he dreamed it.

"I'm not leaving," he says, and he's reassuring himself just as much as Kele.

"In the vision you were running," Kele tells him. "People wanted to hurt you . . . and you wanted to hurt them back."

6 · Wil

Earlier that morning Wil told Pivane he was going off to gather firewood, but in reality he just needed to get away. Find a place to think. Now he sits on a cliffside boulder that gives him a fine view of the forest and a clearer perspective on his life. He can see the camp from here, or at least part of it, and although he does intend to come back with firewood, he doesn't intend to do it for a while.

Wil can no longer deny the resentment building inside of him. It's been building since long before his grandfather's funeral. *Wil, play us a song for healing. Wil, play us a song for calming. Wil, play us a song for celebration, for soothing, for patience, for wisdom.* The tribe has used him like a music machine. No more. He doesn't have an on/off switch. Maybe it's time he played music for a different reason; one of his choosing.

And so when this vision quest is over, and he has fulfilled his promise to his grandfather, even if Lev stays, Wil will not. He resolves that it is time for him to leave the rez and blaze a fresh future for himself, and for Una, too . . . if she decides she loves him more than she loves the rez.

7 · Lev

Lev tries not to shudder at the prospect of Kele's vision. Lev has dreamed of himself running too. And he's dreamed of revenge. Not against anyone in particular, but everyone at once. The world at large. It's a feeling as dark as the storm clouds on the horizon, and it won't be easy to dispel.

"We're in the rez, surrounded by walls and laws that protect us," he tells Kele with more confidence than he feels. "There's no one to run from here," he adds, more to himself than to Kele.

Then, barely a moment after the words are out of his mouth, something cracks in the woods again—and this time he hears screaming. High-pitched shrieks of surprise. Maybe even terror.

Lev launches himself toward the clearing, with Kele on his heels. The kids are standing, staring at Pivane, who lies facedown in the dirt.

A tranq bullet whistles by Lev's ear and embeds in a log inches away from Kele's foot.

"Get down!" Lev yells, and pushes Kele to the ground, his arm shielding him. The other kids follow his lead, diving down just as a storm of tranqs flies through the camp. Frantically Lev looks around for Wil but doesn't see him anywhere.

It's all up to Lev.

He's only a couple of years older, but the rez kids are looking to him for help. He shifts to "protect mode," as he had for CyFi.

While Lev scans the surrounding trees, frantic thoughts

jostle for attention: *They've found me. They're taking me to a harvest camp. I'll be tithed after all.* And although he's scared, his anger overwhelms the fear. This is supposed to be a sanctuary. ChanceFolk are supposed to be protected. But are mahpees? Maybe someone on the rez turned him in before his petition to the council could be accepted.

Kele shifts impatiently under his arm. "Why don't we shoot back?"

But Lev has no idea where Pivane's tranq rifle is—and even if he had it, he has no idea where to shoot.

"Stay here," he orders Kele and the others. "Don't move till I tell you." Then, like a soldier, Lev uses his toes and elbows to crawl low across the clearing. One of the kids has a tranq flag in his leg and is unconscious. Another got hit in the back. The rest are okay. Where the hell is Wil?

His ear pressed to the ground, Lev feels the tramp of feet, and into the clearing stride three men in dirty battle fatigues, mismatched as if they found their clothes in a thrift store. The three are barely men. They seem no older than nineteen or twenty. They are not ChanceFolk—they're outsiders.

One of the kids—the youngest girl in the group—gets up to run.

"Pakwa, no!" Lev yells.

Too late. The lead pirate, with a quick flick of his wrist, fires his pistol, tranqing her in the back of the neck, and she goes down, unconscious.

"Well, well, well," the oldest of the three says. He's tough, missing an ear, and he handles his gun like he was born with it. *Van Gogh,* thinks Lev. *Cut his ear off for the woman he loved.* But Lev imagines that this guy's ear was cut off by someone else. Probably in a fight. The second guy is squinty-eyed, like either he's got bad eyesight or he's so used to glaring at people that his eyes stayed that way. The third guy has big teeth and a straggly beard, which, taken together, make him look like a goat. "What a lovely nest of SlotMongers we've found," says Van Gogh.

Lev, his mouth dry, gets up to face the attackers, putting himself between them and the kids on the ground.

"This kid's sienna!" says the goat, stating the obvious.

Van Gogh is amused. "One wonders what a nice sienna boy is doing running with SlotMongers." The guy sounds like he was raised in high-class boarding schools, but he looks as ragged and hungry as the others.

"Exchange program," Lev says. "I hope you know that violence against People of Chance on their own rez is punishable by death." Lev doesn't know if this is true, but if it's not, it should be. "Leave now and we'll forget this ever happened."

"Shut it!" says Squints, taking aim at Lev with his tranq pistol.

"These 'Mongers are all underage," says the goat.

"Which means their parts are worth even more on the black market." Van Gogh reaches down and tousles Kele's hair. "Isn't that right, lamb chop?"

Kele pulls away and smacks his hand. Squints raises his gun to tranq him, but Van Gogh doesn't let him.

"We've wasted enough ammo. Save it until we need it."

Lev tries to swallow his fear. If there was any doubt as to what these lowlifes were, it's gone. They are hunters of human flesh. Parts pirates.

"Take me," Lev says, hardly believing he's saying it. "I'm the one you want. I'm a tithe, which means I'm worth more on the black market than other AWOLs."

Van Gogh grins. "But not nearly as much as the right little SlotMonger."

Suddenly there's the *pfft* of a tranq shot, and Squints's eyes go uncharacteristically wide before he falls to the ground with the flag of a tranq in his back.

8 · Wil

At the first sound of a rifle crack Wil's attention snapped to the clearing. He saw Pivane fall to the ground, and Wil was instantly on his feet, running back to camp. His heart hammering, he circled the camp quietly, slipping into Pivane's tent to grab his rifle. Then, having found an unseen position from which to fire, he shot the tallest one, who dropped like a bag of bones.

Now, still wielding his uncle's rifle, Wil emerges into the clearing, his aim trained on the leader, but the leader is quick. He pulls out an old-fashioned revolver—the kind that takes only real bullets—and shoves it against Lev's temple.

"Drop it or I kill him."

They freeze in a standoff.

"Thirty-eight caliber, my friend," the gunman says. "You can tranq me, but your friend will be dead before I hit the ground. Drop the rifle now!"

Wil lowers it but doesn't drop it. He's not that stupid. The leader considers the action, then takes the pistol away from Lev's head, shoving him to the ground.

"What do you want?" Wil asks.

The leader signals his remaining conspirator—the goat-ugly one with the scraggly beard. He pulls something from his pocket and gives it to Wil. "We found this posted in Denver last week."

It's a flyer on bright red paper that reads SEEKING PEOPLE OF CHANCE PARTS. TRIPLE RECOMPENSE FOR SPECIAL GIFTS.

Light suddenly dawns. Parts pirates? These intruders are parts pirates?

"People of Chance are protected," Wil says. "We can't be unwound."

UnStrung

"Hardly the point, Hiawatha," the leader says, smoothing his oily hair over an ear that doesn't exist. "This requisition isn't strictly legal, which makes it very profitable."

"So let's cut to the chase," says the other parts pirate. "Any of these here kids got special skills?"

A moment of silence, then Lansa says, "Nova can do high math. Algebra and stuff."

"Oh yeah, Lansa?" says Nova, "Why don't you tell them how good you are with a bow and arrow?"

"Both of you shut up!" yells Lev. "Don't turn on each other. That's what these dirtbags want!"

The goat-faced one glares at Lev, then kicks him in the side.

Wil advances on Goat Face, but One Ear raises his pistol at Wil. "Let's all take a deep breath, shall we?"

Lev lies in the dirt, the grimace fading from his face. He makes eye contact with Wil to let him know that he's okay. Hurt, but okay. Wil has never felt so powerless. He thinks of his grandfather. What would he have done?

"Such lovely choices," the leader says, looking at the batch of kids. "Perhaps we'll take the lot."

"Do that," says Wil, "and our entire tribe will hunt you for the rest of your miserable lives, and I promise you those lives won't be long. . . . But that won't happen if one of us goes of our own free will."

"That's not yer choice to make!" says Goat Face. "We choose!"

"Then choose wisely!" Wil says. Near his uncle he sees his guitar where he left it at breakfast, propped against a log. Everything seems to go quiet, though dimly he's aware of the two pirates talking to each other. Plotting. Choosing.

Wil knows how he can protect the children. He knows how he can save Pivane and Lev.

He lays his uncle's rifle on the ground and walks to his guitar.

"Hey," Goat Face yells at him, and scoops up Pivane's rifle. "Where do you think yer going?"

Wil picks up his guitar and sits on the log. He knows it's the only weapon he needs.

He thinks of Una and the last thing she said to him. She had carved him a pick of rare canyon sinker wood—trees lying submerged for months in the Colorado River—and she gave it to him when he left for this vision quest. Now he pulls it from between the strings and turns it over in his fingers, thinking of her words:

I will not miss you, she said, clearly meaning that she would but refusing to say it out loud.

He kisses the pick and puts it in his pocket. He will not waste it on the likes of these monsters. He will play with his bare fingers. He will play a song of their greed. Of their malice. Of their corruption. He will entice them until they are so consumed by their own lust for money that they will see him as their shining meal ticket and forget the others.

"Tell me what this is worth," Wil says, and begins to play.

The music soars through the camp. He starts with a complicated baroque piece, then a fiery ChanceFolk traditional, and finishes with the Spanish music he loves best, but all angry. Accusing. Music that is both glorious and stirring, yet at the same time a secret indictment of the men he is playing for. Each piece makes his fingers tingle and electrifies even the trees surrounding them.

As always his audience waits in a charged silence long after the last note is played. Even the leader's gun is pointed at the ground, as if he's forgotten he's holding it. Then something happens. Something different.

Someone claps.

He looks at Lev, still sitting in the dirt, gun oil smudged on his neck, mud on his cheek. Lev's eyes are fixed only on Wil. He claps with all his might, bringing his hands together powerfully, shattering the silence with his singular applause. Then Kele joins in, then Nova, then all the kids who are still conscious. It becomes rhythmic, as the applause falls into unison.

"Stop clapping!" the goat-faced pirate screams. His face pale, he points a shaking tranq rifle at Lev. "Stop it! You're freaking me out."

The other one laughs. "You'll have to excuse my associate. You see, his brother died in a clapper attack."

Looks like they blew up the wrong one, Wil wants to say, but he realizes that the quickening pace and rising volume of their clapping says it much better than words.

Finally the chorus of applause falls off, with Lev's loud clapping the last to cease, leaving his hands red from the passion of it.

The lead parts pirate holds eye contact with Wil and nods, sealing Wil's fate. "You've got yourself a deal." Then he orders his comrade to tie the others up.

"What about Bobby?" Goat Face asks, pointing to their tranq'd accomplice.

The leader spares a single look at the unconscious pirate, aims his revolver, and puts a bullet in his head. "Problem solved."

Then the two of them duct-tape the kids' hands and feet and tie all of them together, weaving a rope through their trussed limbs. Kele almost spits at them till he catches Wil's warning look.

Goat Face ties Lev alone to the tree near where Pivane lies, leaving Lev struggling against the tight ropes.

As he winds the rope around the tree, securing Lev's legs, he watches Wil warily as if he expects to be attacked.

"Let me say my good-byes," Wil asks the leader.

The man sits on the log where Wil played his guitar, waving his tranq pistol as a warning. Apparently Wil is now too valuable to shoot with real bullets. "Make it quick."

"Wil, what are you doing?" Lev whispers. "These guys are for real. You don't come back from a Chop Shop."

"My choice, Lev. It's your job now to take care of these kids. Calm them. Reassure them. Pivane will wake up in a few hours. You'll all be fine."

Lev swallows and nods, accepting the responsibility.

Wil summons a wry smile for Lev before the parts pirates take him and his guitar away. "Thanks for the applause, Little Brother."

9 · Lev

In the village three hours later Lev leans against Pivane's dusty truck, only half listening as Pivane tells the sheriff what happened. He watches the kids rushed to their cars and taken home. Only Kele looks back and waves good-bye to Lev.

The sheriff returns to his car to relay the report and then heads back up the mountain to retrieve Bobby, the dead parts pirate—probably wishing it was one of them who took him out, and not one of his own gang.

Lev can't help but notice the cold glare that the policemen throw at him before they leave.

"Your petition to join the tribe has been denied," Wil's ma tells him, the pain in her voice partly for him and partly for her son who will never return. "I'm sorry, Lev."

Lev accepts the news with a stoic nod. He knew this would be the decision. He knew because of the looks everyone has given him since he returned from the vision quest. Those who know him see him as a walking gravestone with Wil's name etched on his sienna face. Those who don't know him see only a harbinger of the world that so cruelly took Chowilawu away. Wil's music—his spirit—cannot be replaced by any musician on the rez. The wound will be raw for a very long time. And there's no one they can blame for it. No one but Lev. Even if they allow him to stay, Lev knows the rez can no longer be his sanctuary.

Pivane volunteers to drive him to the reservation's northern entrance: immense bronze gates bookended by towers of green glass. Lev leans forward to see the bells in the towers and the rearing, life-size, bronze mustang suspended above the gate. Wil told him that fine, nearly invisible wires and a clear glass bridge support the mustang. When Chinook winds blow through the valley, children gather, hoping to see the horse escape its fetters and fly away.

"Where will I go?" Lev asks simply.

"That is for you to decide." Pivane leans across him and retrieves his wallet from the glove compartment. Then he hands Lev a huge wad of cash.

"Too much," Lev manages, but Pivane shakes his head.

"By accepting this gift, you will honor me . . . and you will honor him," Pivane says. "The children told me how you offered yourself to the pirates before Wil did. It was not your fault they chose him over you."

Lev obediently shoves the money into his pocket. He shakes Pivane's hand as he gets out of the car.

"I hope your spirit guide takes you to a place of safety. A place you can call home," Pivane says.

Lev closes the door, and in a plume of dust the truck disappears down the street. Only then does it occur to Lev that he has no spirit guide. He never completed his vision quest. There is nothing and no one to guide him through this dim, foggy future.

A security guard nods as he exits the pedestrian gate, and Lev heads for a bus stop a hundred feet away. He sees nothing else but a barren plateau, spotted with sage, which stretches to the horizon, not quite as barren as he feels inside.

He counts the money Pivane gave him, and it will carry him far indeed, but not far enough, because there is nowhere far enough away from all the things he's experienced since the day he was sent off to be tithed.

Wil healed him with music, taught him the way of his people, and saved him from the pirates by sacrificing his own life.

All he was able to give Wil was applause.

The bus schedule shows the next departure is in thirty minutes. He doesn't bother checking the destination. Lev knows that wherever it leads, his path ahead is dark. He has nothing left to lose. A burning fills his emptiness. A powerful need for revenge drives him now.

As he looks at his hands, he begins to see a purpose for his applause. It's a powerful purpose that will make his anger known . . . and tear the world to shreds.

10 · Wil

Like a crow Wil has flown over the rez wall, but not as he imagined. Deep down, he still expects his Tribal Council—or even the American Tribal Congress to somehow rescue him.

But no one comes.

The pirates drive him not to a Chop Shop but to a private hospital. In this upscale, designer clinic of glass walls, soft lights, and wall-size murals of cascading color, he sees no patients. He is treated like a rock star by an extensive staff and is provided any food he'd like, but he's not hungry. He's offered any music, the latest movies, games, books, or television, but nothing distracts him. He only watches the door.

On his third day a neurologist, a surgeon, and a severe-looking blond woman come in and graciously ask him to play his guitar. Despite heartache, Wil plays flawlessly, and they are duly impressed. He still expects that somehow his playing will open their hearts and set him free. He still expects someone from the tribe to come to his door with good news. But no one comes.

On the fourth day, at dawn, he's put in restraints. A nurse gives him a shot, and he feels woozy. They roll him into an operating room: bright lights, white walls, monitors bleeping, sterile, cold. Nothing like the surgical lodge at home.

He feels numb despair. He is being unwound. And he comes to his end alone.

Then he sees a face in the operating room he recognizes. Although her hair is hidden by surgical scrubs, she doesn't wear a mask like the others. It's as if his seeing her face is more important than the sterile environment. He's not surprised to see her again. He played his guitar for this woman. She never told him her name, although he heard the others call her Roberta.

"Do you remember me, Chowilawu?" she asks with the hint of a British accent almost Americanized. "We met yesterday." She pronounces his name flawlessly. It pleases him yet troubles him at the same time.

"Why are you doing this?" he asks. "Why me?"

"We have been searching for the right Person of Chance for a very long time. You will be part of a spectacular experiment. One that will change the future."

"Will you tell my parents what happened to me? Please?"

"I'm sorry, Wil. No one can know."

This shakes him worse than death. His parents, Pivane,

Una, the whole tribe grieving his absence, never knowing his fate.

She takes his hand in hers. "I want you to know that your talent will not be lost. These hands and the neuron bundles that hold every bit of your musical memory will be kept together. Intact. Because I, too, treasure that which means the most to you."

It's not anything close to what Wil truly wants, but he tries to cling to the knowledge that his gift of music will somehow survive his unwinding.

"My guitar," he manages through chattering teeth, ignoring the fact that he can no longer feel his toes.

"It's safe," Roberta says quickly. "I have it."

"Send it home."

She hesitates, and then nods.

Wil's unwinding proceeds at an alarming rate. All too soon a wave of darkness crashes over him. He can no longer hear Roberta. He can no longer see her.

Then, in the void, he senses someone lean close to him. Someone familiar.

"Grandfather?" he hazards to say. He cannot hear himself speak.

"Yes, Chowilawu."

"Are we are going to the Lower World?"

"We will see, Chowilawu," his grandfather says. "We will see."

11 · Una

There is never anything official.

No communication confirming Wil's unwinding, because kids taken by parts pirates simply disappear.

In the end, however, the rez does receive evidence of Wil's

demise. His guitar is delivered home with no note and no return address.

Una cradles the guitar in her arms and remembers: Wil building mountains for her in a sandbox when they were five. The quiet delight in his eyes when she asked him to marry her when they were six. His grief as Tocho died, while she and Lev sat watching. The touch of Wil's hand on her arm when he said good-bye.

In every memory is his music, and she hears it again every day, playing in the wind through the trees to tease and torment her. Or maybe to comfort her and remind her that nothing and no one is ever truly lost.

Una tries to hold on to that as she lays Wil's guitar on the workshop table. There is no body; there is only the guitar. So she gently, lovingly, unstrings it and prepares it for the funeral pyre in the morning.

And she tells no one of the strange hope she cradles in her heart, that somehow she will hear Wil's music again, loud and pure, calling forth her soul.

Unnatural Selection

Co-authored with Brendan Shusterman

1 · Colton

The deep, resonant clang of a Buddhist *ghanta* snaps Colton to attention, the heavy sound of the bell echoing through the marketplace. Before this he was just drifting, lonely, like a jellyfish at sea, through the vendors and crowds. Every so often a soldier passes him, but more often than not, he sees only tourists and locals. It doesn't matter that three days ago there had been a coup here in Thailand. It doesn't matter that Myanmar, formerly Burma, formerly Myanmar, formerly Burma, is (big surprise) Burma again, and the current regime has been threatening to drop bombs on Bangkok for harboring enemies of the state. It is, as Colton has already surmised, business as usual.

Like the Burmese, Colton isn't quite sure who he is anymore. He's halfway between one thing and another. Neither here nor there, fish nor fowl. Who he was and who he will be are connected only by the fine, nearly invisible thread of who he is now. He can't yet decide whether to be terrified or energized by the spectrum of personal possibilities before him.

The sweet smell of lychees brings Colton to a vendor who smiles wide and sells him four for what would have been pocket change back home. Colton puts his hands together before his face as if in prayer—a common thank-you in this part of the world—and the vendor returns the gesture.

There is a reason Colton is in Thailand and why he's

decided he isn't leaving. Thailand has outlawed unwinding. In fact, they were one of the first countries to speak out against it and sign the Florence Agreement—a plea that was ignored completely by the United States, as if it were written by her enemies. Colton knows the name of every country that retracted their statements and turned to unwinding—which was most of them—but Thailand held firm. Now Thailand is somewhat of a haven for AWOLs from China and Russia. But just next door is Burma. The heart of darkness.

Colton heard stories about the Burmese Dah Zey, or "Flesh Market." Everyone had. How they would keep you alive during a week-long unwinding process, taking part after part while you suffered in a cell, slowly losing more and more of yourself to buyers across Asia. The Dah Zey became the stuff of horror stories around AWOL campfires, but the scariest part was that no one knew truth from fiction. Colton does know that they are so powerful they now run Burma from the shadows, pulling the strings while they pull their parts. But that's not why he's here, and he has to keep reminding himself of that. As much as he'd like to stop the Dah Zey, he has no means to do so. *It's not David versus Goliath,* he tells himself. *It's David versus a hostile universe that was constructed in the wake of the Heartland War.*

Colton shifts his backpack and tries to make it sit right. It won't, though it only holds his clothes—nothing sharp or bulky. He packed light when he ran away.

As far as he's concerned, his parents are monsters as bad as the Dah Zey. How they could have signed his little brother's unwind order is a question he asks himself over and over each day as he sits at cafés and restaurants, in tuk-tuks and temples. He looks for an answer. He never finds it.

His brother never saw it coming, and Colton never really found out how it went down. Colton came home from school one day, and Ryan was gone. His parents told him he'd been sent to his aunt's—to get him away from the bad influences at school—although other parents would say that *Ryan* was the bad influence. Colton kept calling his aunt, wanting to talk to his brother, but she never answered or returned his call. That's when Colton began to worry.

He denied the possibility. Yes, Ryan was more defiant than Colton had ever been—but is that enough reason for a divisional solution? He finally got through to his aunt. At first she tried to sound normal, making excuses as to why Ryan couldn't come to the phone. Then she finally broke down and told him the truth.

A week later Colton pawned everything he could find of value in the house, got himself a false passport, and left for good. He never said good-bye or left any sort of explanation. *Let them wonder*, he thought. *Let them wonder why their straight-A, college-bound son disappeared. Let them cry the tears they should have cried for Ryan.*

He told no one he was leaving—not even his friends. He was there one day, and the next he was on the other side of the planet. He suspected his brother had a similar problem, only more divided.

That was a month ago. Now he wanders the streets of Bangkok, in that dizzying place between possible futures.

He peels one of the lychees and takes a bite, its sweet flavor unlike anything he could get in the West. Looking around, he takes notice of how many obvious AWOLs he sees in this part of town. Many of them are adults now. He wonders how many would still be unwound by their parents today, if they had it to do over again. One of these former AWOL kids shouts at him for blocking the road and throws a half-eaten hamburger at his head. As it bounces off him, he figures that at least one of these kids still would be unwound.

At the sound of a girl's laughter, he turns to a small

restaurant where stray cats wind through patrons' feet. A blond girl with a wide smile laughs at the cat rubbing up against her leg. She's maybe sixteen and covered in tattoos from head to toe. Angels, demons, tigers, and clowns fill out a veritable circus of ink. A nose ring pierces her septum. She'd look like a bull ready to charge if she weren't still smiling. He sits at an adjacent table, and then makes his move.

"So how long you been on the run?" he asks.

"What makes you think I'm running?" she responds in a thick Cockney accent.

Britain, Colton thinks. Just another country that reneged and made unwinding a legal and acceptable practice. In fact, they were the first ones to come up with the term "feral teens."

He smirks. "It's written all over you." Then he adds, "Like a dare."

She puts out a cigarette that he just notices; so much about her draws attention, the cigarette was the least of it. She says, "You're right. Been AWOL for two months now. How about you?"

"A month or so," he tells her. It's a half-truth. He chooses not to tell her that he isn't an AWOL—that he left of his own free will. There's a sort of triumph in taking on the role that he wishes his brother could have had.

She looks him over, reading him far too well, and narrows her already suspicious eyes. "You're lying." Then she gets up to leave.

This girl is a strange one, he thinks. *There's something off about her, more so than most AWOLs.* He finds it intriguing. Alluring. As she tries to slip away, he instinctively stands in her way, trying to think of something witty to say that might keep her there. Nothing comes out, but they make eye contact. She stops and stares into his eyes.

"Hazel eyes, yeah?"

"Yeah," he says.

"Nice."

"Listen—us AWOLs gotta stick together," he says. "I'm sure you know how dangerous it can be out on these streets. You could get arrested for vagrancy. Or worse—sold to the Dah Zey."

She smiles, showing yellow-stained teeth that Colton finds oddly alluring, and says, "You don't know a thing about danger, Hazel."

Her name is Karissa. She doesn't give her last name, even though he asks for it. She tells him that she left it in England with her bloody parents. He gets that. At first he tells her that he left because he found his own unwind order. Like the Akron AWOL. But eventually he tells her the whole story about his brother and the real reason why he left home. In turn she tells him her story, emptying her broken life out onto him like he's a shrink. It's a lot to take in.

He finds out she has a place. They talk till nearly midnight, and by then, she's ready to take him back to it. They stroll through the streets and get into a tuk-tuk, a small, three-wheeled taxi. When he looks to his left, she's gotten out on the other side. She winks at him and hurries off as the tuk-tuk takes him away without her.

"American?" asks the tuk-tuk driver in an uninterested tone.

"Yeah," he says, equally uninterested and shocked he's just been ditched by the girl.

"I'll take you home now," he says. Colton gives the driver the address, but he doesn't seem to be listening. "Yeah, yeah, take you home . . ."

Exhausted, Colton dozes, waking up every time they hit a rough patch of road—which is every few seconds. After a particularly bad bump, Colton opens his eyes to see he's in a part of town he's never seen before. It's impoverished, so unpleasant that not even brothels will open up shop here.

"Yo, man—this is not where I live," says Colton, irritated.

"Shortcut, shortcut," says the tuk-tuk driver. "Get there soon."

Colton looks around. *This idiot must have gotten lost,* he thinks.

The tuk-tuk stops in front of a large, gray building that dwarfs the rest, like a mausoleum in a sea of tombstones.

"What the hell—"

Then the tuk-tuk driver gets up and leaves. He just runs off into the darkness, abandoning Colton there.

Colton knows this is bad, but his body is slow to move. He tries to get up, but his legs feel like rubber. Has he been drugged? He labors out of the tuk-tuk. The world spins around him. The few people in the street at this time of night give him fearful looks. Or perhaps they are looks of pity. Either way, they don't gaze at him for long before shuffling off—as if looking will curse them somehow.

Colton tries to stumble away, but before he can get anywhere, he runs into a soldier who seems to appear out of thin air.

"Whoa, whoa. Where you going?" says the soldier in Thai—Colton can understand that much.

"The hell outta here," Colton answers in English. "Move!"

"No, no. You come with us," the soldier says, now in heavily accented English.

Colton tries to push past, but a second soldier comes out of the darkness, slamming a rifle butt to the back of his head. His vision spins worse than before. The hit doesn't knock him out, but it does make him stumble into the arms of the first soldier, who laughs.

Colton rubs his head and feels blood. *Gotta get outta here,* he thinks. *Gotta get out of here fast.* But now there are more of them, and he's surrounded. *These aren't soldiers,* he realizes. *They're police officers.* Two officers grab him and drag him into the dead gray building.

"Colton Ellis," the Thai man behind the desk says in perfect English. On his head is a beret. He smells of cologne and wears the smile of a used-car salesman. Behind him a grenade launcher casually leans against a file cabinet, upon which are a coffee machine and an old-school microwave.

"Look . . . ," says Colton. "What's this all about? What do you want? Money?"

Even as Colton says the words, he knows that can't be why this is happening, but he has nothing else with which to bargain.

The man seems to know this and ignores him, waiting an uncomfortably long time before speaking again. Just before Colton starts pleading, the man says, "When I was a boy, I stepped on a land mine. A land mine put there by Americans during the Vietnam War long before I was born. I lost my leg. I thought I'd lost it for good, but then came the Dah Zey."

The man takes a sip of his coffee, seeming to savor the taste as much as he savors Colton's wide-eyed reaction. Colton looks around for something he can use to hit the man and escape. There's nothing within reach. The grenade launcher is close enough only to mock him.

"My parents were poor, but the Dah Zey offered free parts to anyone who had lost a limb due to American explosives. Thousands of people who thought they would have to beg in the streets for the rest of their lives suddenly had new leases on life. But there was a catch: The Dah Zey needed us as enforcers, agents, and merchants. I like to think of myself as all three."

"Let me out of here! This is a mistake! My . . . my parents are rich! They'll pay you double what the Dah Zey will!" It's all he can think to say, and he knows it's probably true. But they think he's an AWOL Unwind. How can he convince them he's not?

"The unwind order that they signed surely says otherwise."

"But they didn't! They never signed one!"

He just ignores Colton. "Karma has already decided your fate," he says as if by rote—he's had the same conversation hundreds of times. "I bring balance to the world. Justice. In a way, you are the greatest sort of martyr. The reluctant one. In the grand scheme of things, it is an envious position." Then he picks up his phone and makes a call. "Yes, Sonthi. I have him now. Just what you were looking for. Yes, hazel eyes. I'll send him to you now." He ends the call with *"Laeo phop gan mai krap."* A standard Thai good-bye.

That's when Colton realizes . . . hazel eyes . . . it was the AWOL girl who noticed that. How could he have been so stupid?

Colton tries to plead for his life again, but the man raises his voice and cuts him off.

"They'll take you now. And you needn't worry—the Dah Zey is not what the American media makes it out to be. Well, maybe it was back when Thuang was running it, but things have become more civilized since then. You will be treated well."

"Yeah, your Juvey-cops treated me real well too. This is illegal, you know. You're finished if the Thai government finds out about this."

"That is why you must be unwound . . . ," he says, his face growing serious. "And your brain discarded."

Colton didn't think he could be any more horrified than he already was. "Shelled? I'm being shelled?"

"The Dah Zey doesn't deal in gray matter. Too unpredictable. You know too much. Who's to say all those brain bits won't exert some of your will over the recipients? The last thing the Dah Zey needs is a piece of your mind turning up in the wrong place."

"No!" shouts Colton, realizing that there is an alternative even worse than just unwinding. "My brain will stay quiet. I swear! Even divided! Just don't shell me."

The man smiles sympathetically. "Just think of yourself as the humanitarian aid America never gave us." And he gestures to the guard waiting at the door to take him.

The truck rumbles down the highway with Colton bound and gagged in the back. He knows he's headed to Burma now. If he's lucky, a military convoy might stop them and open the back of the truck—but he knows that such a thing is very unlikely. They're probably taking an unregulated road or one where the soldiers have been paid off. His head throbs, and he curses the girl who turned him over.

After what seems like days with scant rations of food and water, they pull him to his feet and drag him out like a corpse into the mud of a Dah Zey harvest camp.

2 · Kunal

"Come, Kunal! Must I wait for you? The truck is already here."

"Yes, Doctor. Coming, sir."

Kunal hates that the doctor forces him to take the long walk to the front entrance of the camp. He thinks he's doing Kunal a kindness by allowing him out of the Green Manor to witness the deliveries, but Kunal would much rather stay within the manor's gates. These long walks do nothing but make his ankles ache.

The truck stops in the muddy expanse between the infirmary and the Eastern Refinery. This place used to be an opium farm, before unwound parts became more valuable than heroin. They don't call them Unwinds here, though. The Burmese phrase for it is *a htwat* "harvest." That's all the AWOLs are to them. The cinder-block buildings that used to be opium refineries have long since been subdivided into cells for the Unwinds who move through here at a steady pace.

The doctor watches every delivery with a pair of binoculars, keeping his distance. He brings Kunal along to hold his binoculars, because apparently they're too heavy for the doctor to wear around his neck.

There are guards everywhere. A show of force for kids who are too frightened, weak, and sleep deprived to fight back, even if they tried. The Dah Zey love overkill. That's why there are three outer gates before reaching the camp. They are a box within a box within a box.

A Burmese man in military camo approaches. Sonthi. He's an imposing figure. Kunal is convinced that he was once part of one military junta or another that ran the country for its fifteen minutes of power. If this place is a factory, then Sonthi is the floor manager.

"Mixed bag today," Sonthi tells the doctor. "Many interesting eyes."

"Injected?"

"Natural," Sonthi says.

"All the better."

About a dozen kids are manhandled, stumbling in the mud as they're herded toward the infirmary. Kunal wonders how much they know about this place. How much they've been told about what will be done to them. Do they know about the shelling? Better if they don't. At least their demise will be painless—something they might not be expecting. But after all, on an old opium farm there is no shortage of morphine. Kunal worries more for the ones who don't get unwound. But that's not something he can ever say out loud.

The doctor lowers his binoculars and hands them to Kunal. "Shouldn't there be more?"

Sonthi rolls his shoulders uncomfortably. He glances at Kunal, and Kunal glances away, afraid to meet his eye or draw the man's attention in any way. "We expect another truck tomorrow," Sonthi says, and the doctor sighs.

"Go back, Kunal. I should be done here in an hour. Draw me a bath before I return—and please mind your posture."

"Yes, Doctor." Binoculars in hand, Kunal makes his way back to the Green Manor, trying to mind his posture and ignore his aching ankles.

3 · Colton

He waits alone in a small room, too terrified to even move. The only light spills through slats in the wood. There's nothing in the room but an old examination table and a chair. Finally a man comes in, dressed casually, but with the requisite stethoscope around his neck. "Hello, Colton," he says. "I am Dr. Raotdanakosin. I know this is a mouthful, yes? Laotian names are long and never used twice. You can just call me Dr. Rodín."

Colton doesn't want to call him anything. "Are you the one who's going to unwind me?"

Dr. Rodín laughs. "No, no—I see to your health. That is all. Others will do the deed when the time comes. Please say 'aah.'"

He gives Colton the standard checkup. It seems oddly normal for such a dire circumstance. Rodín's demeanor is that of any physician. Somehow that makes Colton feel even worse—to be reminded of something normal in the midst of this nightmare. There's also something else about him that Colton can't place. Rodín is a doctor, yes, but Colton senses that he's also playacting the role. Colton can tell that he's more than just the camp's doctor.

"You came far," Rodín says as he examines Colton's ears. "Only to get caught. A shame, yes?"

"How long?" Colton asks. "How soon will they . . . do it? "

"The Dah Zey works on its own schedule," Rodín says. "Who can say?"

Then, when he's done, he steps back and does an overall assessment. "Healthy. You were not on the run for long, am I right?"

Colton hesitates. Will a nod get him unwound faster? He doesn't know, so he doesn't respond at all.

"Are they really going to shell me?" he asks, knowing the answer, knowing how pathetic he sounds asking.

Rodín considers Colton, looking at him a moment too long. *No, he doesn't look at me,* Colton realizes. *He looks at my parts. He looks through me. He sees dollar signs.* "Brain disposal is official Dah Zey policy," Rodín says, "but there are alternatives to shelling." Then he turns to go, but just before he leaves, he adds, "There are alternatives to unwinding as well."

He's taken to a gray cinder-block building and thrown into a room with a dirt floor and four other Unwinds. There are three boys and a girl, who perhaps they mistook for a boy in the dark, but they didn't care enough to correct their mistake. *These kids couldn't possibly look more defeated,* Colton thinks. There's nothing in the room but five straw mats, an ancient tube TV that probably doesn't work, and some sort of prewar disc player. Obsolete technology that seems left there to mock them.

"Looks like you had a fun ride, mate," says a muscular Australian boy who looks about seventeen. The kid has a real loser vibe, like he was beating up geeks before he was on the run.

Colton tries to say something, but he's still shaking.

"Not much for words, are you?" says the kid. "I'm Jenson. Welcome to the Magic Kingdom."

The Magic Kingdom is apparently what they've been calling this place. Jenson explains that it started out as some Unwind's idea of a joke, but the name caught on among the guards. Now it's official. It's one of the seven Dah Zey harvest camps—the one closest to the Thai border, which is barely half a mile away.

Jenson points to the two Thai boys, the smaller of whom is huddled in a corner fighting back sobs. The other one, a bit heftier, sits with his legs crossed in lotus position, a relaxed expression running contrary to the other boy's tears.

"Gamon's the crying one," says Jenson. "I don't think he speaks English. The other is Kemo. Won't hear a peep outta him. Kemo was planning to join a Buddhist monastery, but his parents sold him to the Dah Zey to pay for his father's gambling debts instead. And Gamon was sold to pay for his brother's wedding." Then Jenson kicks Gamon—not hard enough to hurt, but hard enough to display dominance. "Stop your bawling!" Jenson orders. Gamon's sobs settle to whimpers. "He acts up each time someone new shows up—like he wants to prove he's the most pathetic AWOL in the world." Then Jenson takes a good look at Colton. "You're not gonna be a problem, are you? I'm tired of problem AWOLs."

"Sounds like you've been here awhile," Colton says.

Jenson gets a bit uncomfortable. "Yeah, well three weeks feels like forever when you're a guest of the Dah Zey."

As for the girl, she doesn't introduce herself, just curses at Colton when he says hello. According to Jenson, she's a Russian AWOL who claims to be a political prisoner. "She says she's a *pravda*—a Russian clapper—and that she's killed seventy Dah Zey members."

"Is true!" she insists. "I will kill you if you say is not."

Colton suspects she's delusional. After all, a clapper in this environment would have detonated long before getting hurled into this room, but he knows her delusions are what get her through the day. In a way she's not really lying, because she actually believes it—and she believes that the Russian government will pay for her release so they can extradite her for trial. "Pravda" can't be older than fourteen.

Jenson's story is the same as Colton's, without the girl. He got in the back of the wrong tuk-tuk, and it took him to the gray building. Jenson had heard stories about it from other AWOLs and started to run as soon as he saw where he was, but they tranq'd him. He admits he was being foolhardy, but no one had bothered him in the months he'd been hiding. He fell into a state of ease. When they passed the Cap-17 law in America, he thought he'd be safer. But Asia's different.

"That's crazy about the girl, eh," says Jenson, when Colton tells him about Karissa. "She'll get what's coming to her, though."

"I hope so," says Colton, smiling for the first time since he's gotten there. "I just wish I could be the one to dish it out to her."

The camp is full of groups of kids in small rooms. Every morning they're flushed out, squinting into the light as guards line them up and inspect them. Kids are pulled out of the line to be unwound. After that everyone else breathes easy. The guards count them, feed them watery protein paste of an origin Colton does not want to consider. They're checked for injuries, rashes, and new diseases. The kids with issues are sent to the infirmary, where Dr. Rodín will have a look at them. The rest are sent back to their rooms.

The old TV, to Colton's amazement, actually does work. At lineup that morning Jenson traded discs with some other kids for a pair of fresh movies. They're all old films that nobody has seen or cared about since before the Heartland War, but it's better than staring at the cinder-block walls. Or at each other.

Apparently it's Jenson's ritual to put on a movie after morning inspection. Today's features an invisible alien in a jungle not unlike the one around them. As if they now need something invisible to worry about.

"Why does the Dah Zey bother to keep us entertained?" Colton wonders out loud.

"Who knows?" says Jenson. "Maybe it makes them feel better about themselves. Their watered-down version of mercy."

At a particularly suspenseful part of the movie some new misery must occur to Gamon, because he begins sobbing again, louder than the TV's tiny distorted speaker. That's when Jenson snaps and begins whaling on Gamon, brutally beating him, swearing and cursing—probably the very type of loose-cannon behavior that got him on an Unwind list to begin with. "I TOLD! YOU! TO SHUT! THE HELL UP!"

"Jenson! Enough!" Colton struggles to pull Jenson off the poor kid, who doesn't even defend himself. Jenson looks at Colton as if coming out of a trance. "He . . . he was asking for it," Jenson says weakly. "He was ruining the movie. . . . He had it coming. . . ." But not even Jenson buys his own argument. Gamon is a bruised, bloody mess. He pulls himself into a ball, his sobs sounding no different than before the beating.

Then Kemo breaks concentration and rises in a calm, fluid motion. All eyes turn to him as his slow, steady footfalls bring him to Jenson. Even though Kemo is more than a head shorter than Jenson, his presence makes the larger boy shrink.

"You just damaged their property," Kemo says in perfect English. "You know what they do to you if you damage their property, don't you?" Colton is taken aback for a moment by Kemo's calm, by the thought of them as property, and by Kemo's unexpected command of English.

Jenson doesn't say anything but backs away, flexing his fingers and looking at his bloody knuckles. His blood? Probably not.

Kemo turns his back to him. "Yes, you know." Then he returns to where he was meditating and reassumes lotus position.

So the stories about the Dah Zey are true, then, Colton thinks, *or at least Kemo believes them.* But he has to ask. He approaches Kemo.

"What do they do?"

Kemo doesn't respond. His face is unreadable.

"What do they do, Kemo?"

It's Pravda who answers from across the room. "Many things," she says. "Maybe you vill get to see." And she smiles as if she might want to see herself.

Jenson doesn't say anything. He just goes to the back wall and sinks to the ground, putting his bloodied hands to his head, no longer interested in an alien that rips out people's spines.

The next morning, when they are lined up for inspection, Sonthi the overlord—if that's what you call such a person—looks them over. He wears camo, as if he's living in an eternal war.

Sonthi stops by Gamon, quickly noticing his bruises and swollen face. The kid shivers and whimpers.

"Who did this?" he asks, looking to the others.

No one says anything.

So he approaches Colton, grabs his hands, then turns them over to look at his knuckles. Satisfied, he moves on to Jenson and catches him, very literally, red-handed. Sonthi glares at him until Jenson looks away, then Sonthi turns to all the members of their little cell squad. "Guilt for one is guilt for all." He turns to the guards around them. "Take them to the Haunted Mansion."

Colton has a feeling this will not be a fun ride.

They're marched across the harvest camp, passing five other buildings, each larger than the one they're being housed in. Colton wonders if they're all full of Unwinds awaiting their fate. There's no way to tell from the outside, since there are no windows.

At the far side of the camp there's one building that stands alone. It looks like it was once an elaborate residence, or maybe even a temple, but now it's covered with forest growth and moss. Pravda suddenly tries to bolt, but she never gets past the guard beside her, who grabs her and pulls her back in line.

Sonthi opens a heavy door and leads them in.

The inside is spotless. Oddly so, considering the exterior. The stone walls echo with strange noises from deeper in the structure. Grunting and panting. Gibbering and licking. Colton feels the perpetual knot in his stomach seize tighter.

The narrow entry corridor leads them to a huge open-air courtyard. Around them are doors. Many, many doors. It is from behind these doors that the sounds come.

"Ah! Mr. Sonthi! You bring me visitors, yes? Welcome to the Green Manor!"

173

Dr. Rodín descends a grand staircase into the vast court-yard, his arms wide in a warm gesture of greeting, followed by a dark-skinned teen—not umber, but perhaps Pakistani or Indian. He lumbers with an odd side-to-side gate.

Rodín reaches them and claps his hands together. "So these five have been exceptionally well behaved—and you thought you'd treat them to a glimpse of creation, yes?"

Sonthi is clearly annoyed but remains respectful. "No. They've caused trouble. They are here as punishment."

Now it's Rodín's turn to be annoyed. "Yes, well, we do see things differently."

"What is this place?" Colton dares to ask.

Rodín smiles at him. "This place I call my factory of miracles."

That causes Sonthi to stifle a guffaw.

Rodín indicates the boy who came down with him. "This is Kunal, my valet."

The boy nods to them respectfully, but his eyes dart back and forth between Rodín and Sonthi with practiced caution.

"Show them, Kunal," says Rodín, and Kunal obediently goes to a huge tree with gnarled, twisted limbs in the middle of the courtyard and begins to climb—but not quite the way another person might climb it. His movements are disturbingly graceful. Like a chimpanzee. It is then that Colton realizes that Kunal doesn't have feet. He has a second pair of hands grafted in their place.

Pravda gasps, Jenson looks terrified, Kemo almost loses his composure, and Gamon just whimpers.

Kunal returns, hobbling in a perverted right-side-up hand-stand. None of the kids can look at him.

"Perhaps you should show them Marisol," says Sonthi.

"I was just about to suggest the same thing." Rodín leads

them to one of the many doors on the edge of the courtyard. Kunal produces a key from an overstuffed key chain and opens a door, and Rodín ushers them in.

There's a girl in the room. Or something that was once a girl. Now it looks more like an alien one might find in a prewar movie. She has four eyes, each a different color, with cheekbones that are way too low in order to accommodate the extra pair of eyes. And she has four arms.

"Isn't she a wonder," Rodín says, gazing at her in bemused admiration.

Colton does his best to keep from hurling what little food is inside him. Pravda loses the same battle, and Kunal hurries off to get towels to clean the mess.

"She can be off-putting, I admit," Rodín says. "Exotic creations are an acquired sight, much like exotic foods are an acquired taste."

It stands there in the corner of the small cell, almost, but not quite, cowering.

"Please . . . ," begs Jenson. "For the love of God, please take us out of here."

Rodín ignores him. "Marisol, are you happy here?"

"Yes, Dr. Rodín," she says timidly, not meeting his eyes with any of hers.

"You are pleased with what we've done for you, no?"

"Yes, Dr. Rodín." Her voice is dead. Resigned. Colton looks down to see that there is a heavy shackle on one of her legs. Just in case she's less happy than she cares to admit.

Rodín reaches into his pocket and puts a piece of candy into each of her four hands. One by one she lifts the candy to her mouth—but the fourth one connects with her cheek instead and falls to the ground.

"We're still working on eye-hand coordination on Marisol's

lower left arm." Then he tells them how he hopes, in time, to create a girl with eight arms. "A living, breathing version of Kali, the Hindu goddess," he says. "What a price that would fetch on the black market, yes, Sonthi?"

Sonthi raises his eyebrows and nods. Colton suspects he might not like this place either, but with the Dah Zey, it's all about money. It's then that Colton begins to understand the power structure here. At first he had wondered why Sonthi allows the doctor to do the things he does. But now Colton understands. This palace is Rodín's; the camp is Rodín's. Everyone here, including Sonthi, works for the doctor.

"Tell me," Rodín says. "Which of our guests has been a problem today?" He looks at Colton when he says it, smiling at him, and Colton has to look away. "Is it this one? The one with the eyes?"

"We all have eyes," Colton says under his breath.

Sonthi grabs Jenson's shoulder and pushes him forward.

"This one," Sonthi says. "He beat the crap out of the little one. We warned him before, but he doesn't listen."

Rodín looks Jenson over like he might appraise a painting. "Yes, well, I know a way to make him listen." Then he nods to the guards. It takes three of them to drag Jenson away, kicking and screaming.

Colton and the others are taken back to their room in silence. The message is clear without Sonthi saying a thing. Cause trouble, and you become Rodín's next experiment.

"What do you think they'll do to him?" Pravda asks, sounding much more frightened and innocent than she had before their visit to the mansion.

Colton doesn't want to think about it, but Kemo speaks. Since returning, he has tried unsuccessfully to pervade the air with peace. Clearly he can't find any of that peace within himself. His meditations are getting shorter, and he spends a lot of time reciting mantras under his breath while pacing. "Whatever they do," says Kemo, "I hope Jenson's transformation has meaning for him."

That just makes Colton angry. "How can you even say that? What kind of 'meaning' could it have?"

Kemo remains calm, or at least fakes it. "Everything has meaning, or nothing has meaning," he says. "Which world would you rather live in?"

Gamon has stopped crying. It seems the Haunted Mansion has gotten through to him. He still doesn't talk, but he doesn't cry. Pravda just huddles alone, picking at the skin of her elbows until they're raw and bleeding. Colton wonders if the Dah Zey will punish her for damaging their property.

Apparently the question is moot, because the following day, she's taken at inspection for unwinding. She screams and protests as they all do, cursing in half a dozen languages, but it changes nothing. In the end she's led off to one of the other windowless buildings—the one where the actual unwinding is done. He hopes for her sake that it's quick.

It's just before they are sent back inside that Colton catches sight of Rodín, lurking in the background, holding a pair of binoculars. When he takes the binoculars away, Colton can tell that he's not surveying the scene; he's staring right at him. The boy with the eyes. He smiles at Colton. Yesterday that smile made Colton look away, but this time he refuses to let Rodín intimidate him. Colton holds the doctor's gaze, without smiling back.

In their cell no one speaks of Pravda. To do so would be bad luck, and they need all the luck they can get.

"Whose fate is worse?" Kemo ponders aloud. "To be shelled and unwound, or to be an experiment?"

It's not the question that bothers Colton but the calm way in which Kemo asks it—as if it's a hypothetical and not the reality they're facing. "How can you even compare them?"

"I can't," says Kemo. "Not really. A shelled unwinding is different from a regular unwinding. Without a brain there's no question that one is dead, even if one's flesh lives. And with death come the mysteries of what lies beyond. Death I am ready for. But to become one of Rodín's . . . things?" Kemo shivers. "And yet as a thing, one lives on, presumably with one's own brain." Then Kemo looks through Colton with a question that rings with the solemnity of a ghanta bell. "Are you tempted?"

"No!" says Colton. "Absolutely not! I'd rather be shelled."

But Kemo grins because he knows that Colton isn't entirely sure.

The day after Pravda is taken they are given a new cell mate. The door to their holding tank bursts open, and the guards drag in a girl. A girl who's covered head to toe in animal tattoos.

"You can't do this, you bastards!" shouts Karissa, flinging her arms as the guards struggle to hold her still. "How can you do this to me?"

They throw her to the ground and leave. Colton is the first to approach her, taking great pleasure in her newfound misery. "Let me be the first to welcome you."

"Oh crap!" The fight seems to drop right out of her when she sees him. She rises to her feet, brushing blood from her mouth.

"Is this the girl who turned you in?" asks Kemo, stalking closer. His calm presence has suddenly become coolly menacing.

Karissa backs all the way to a spider-infested corner. "They made me do it!"

"Really." Colton moves closer to her, not sure what he plans to do, but enjoying the fact that she's frightened of his righteous rage.

"They have my sister!" Karissa blurts out, bursting into tears that are convenient, but perhaps sincere. "But if I bring them AWOLs, they won't unwind her. Fifty AWOLs in exchange for her freedom. That's what they promised."

"Let me guess," says Kemo. "You gave them forty-nine, and they made you number fifty."

Karissa appeals to Colton. "What would you have done if it were your brother?"

"Leave him out of this!" In his stupidity Colton had told her the whole story the night she destroyed his life. "You knew I wasn't an AWOL, but you turned me in anyway."

She has no defense for that other than to look down and say, "I had to save my sister."

Gamon looks back and forth between them, clearly not comprehending, but at the very least getting the emotional gist.

"Do you really think they honored their end of the bargain?" Colton says. "I'm sure she was unwound weeks ago."

But Karissa shakes her head. "No. I call every week, and they let me talk to her. I know Marisol is still alive!"

"Marisol . . . ," says Kemo, then glances to Colton. "Yes, you're right. She is still alive." But he tells her nothing more, and as furious as Colton is at Karissa, he won't tell her what her sister has become. He's not that cruel.

"You know her?" Karissa asks. "Where is she? Is she nearby?"

No one says anything.

"Tell me where she is," Karissa offers, "and I'll let you in on a little secret."

Colton is intrigued but guarded. "What kind of secret?"

179

Karissa smiles and takes her time. Colton crosses his arms, expecting a lie or a trick or both.

"I might know a way out of here," she says.

"Hmm," says Kemo. "You mean other than leaving in small refrigerated boxes?"

"There's information out there, if you know where to find it." Then Karissa launches into a history lesson—all about Burma in the old days. "A while back—before unwinding and before the Dah Zey even existed—the military junta that ran Burma secretly hired North Korean engineers to build tunnels."

"What for?" Colton asks dubiously.

Karissa shrugs. "To escape a coup? To hide weapons? No one knows for sure—but the point is, this place, after it was an opium farm and before it was a harvest camp, was a military training ground. The only building that still exists from those days is on the north end of the camp. They took an old temple and turned it into a palace for the general."

"The Haunted Mansion!" Colton says. Karissa looks at him funny. "Go on," he says.

"There are pictures in the public nimbus that show this place—or at least how it looked all those years ago. There's an old well right in the middle that leads down to the tunnel. I was trying to find where it exits, so I could sneak in and save my sister—but all I know is where those tunnels start, not where they end."

"So," says Colton, "they could lead right to another Dah Zey stronghold."

"Or," says Karissa, "they could lead to freedom. . . ."

At the next inspection, a whole host of kids are pulled out of the line and dragged off to be unwound. If there's any rhyme or reason to whom they choose, Colton can't see it. He's become used to the dread of inspection. Used to the relief of being allowed to return to the horrible little holding cell, as if returning there is some sort of triumph.

Rodín doesn't keep his distance today. He's right at the front line, checking sores, determining the quality of the product and who might need medical attention to bring up the price of their parts. But Colton knows why he's really here. He's looking for subjects. As Rodín moves down the line toward him, Colton gets an idea. It's probably a very bad idea, but it's a desperate measure in a very desperate time. He steps forward out of line and waits to be noticed.

A guard lifts his rifle butt, moving as if to strike Colton, but Colton knows he won't. Not in front of Sonthi, who is farther down the line, and definitely not in front of the doctor. Mustn't damage the merchandise.

"I want to volunteer," Colton says as soon as the doctor sees him standing here. He's horrified by his own words but also energized by the risk he's taking. "I want you to change me, Dr. Rodín. I want to be something new. Something different. Something great."

Rodín smiles like he's just unwrapped the perfect present. "A volunteer. I very rarely get volunteers. Few are so brave."

Colton knows Rodín already had him pegged. If it wasn't today, it would be tomorrow or the day after. Then he would be a prisoner. But now he's a willing subject. It could make all the difference.

"And what sort of creation would you like to be?" Rodín asks.

Colton swallows and tries to sell it. "I surrender to your imagination."

Rodín looks him over, judging him, trying to read him. "You fear the shelling."

"We all do," Colton tells him. "But it's not just that. I want something . . . more."

Rodín turns to the guard, speaking in Burmese. The guard nods. Colton has no idea what he says, but then Rodín smiles at him again. "I must complete the inspection," Rodín says. "Then we shall talk."

After Rodín is gone, Kemo turns to Colton, his calm entirely shaken. "Why?" he asks. "Why would you do such a thing?"

"To save us," Colton whispers. "If the tunnel exists, I'll find it. Give me three days, then at inspection on the third day, demand to see your sister," he tells Karissa.

"Why would they let me?"

"They will," Colton says, sure of it. Sonthi will bring her, if only to see the look on her face. "The hard part will be convincing them that Kemo and Gamon should come too, but I have faith you'll figure out a way."

Karissa gives him a twisted grin. "You're a regular Akron AWOL," she says.

Colton shakes his head. "I'm not a hero—I just want to survive."

"I'm sure that's what Connor Lassiter said when he tranq'd that Juvey-cop and took a tithe hostage."

"And what if you can't find a tunnel?" Kemo asks.

"Then we're no worse off than we are now."

"*You'll* be worse off," Kemo points out, and Colton agrees—but he can't stand the frying pan any longer. He's ready to take on the fire.

When inspection is done, and the others return to their dingy gray holding pens, Rodín, speaking Burmese, Lao, or some hybrid of the two, instructs the guards, and they roughly grab Colton. Rodín stops them right away, chastising them. They release Colton but stand close as they escort him to the moss-covered stone palace.

"You'll have a private room here in the Green Manor,"

Rodín tells him after they've closed the wrought-iron gates behind him. Colton wonders if he knows that everyone else calls it the Haunted Mansion.

"All your needs will be taken care of." He waves his hand, and Kunal comes running. Or hobbling.

"We have a volunteer."

"Yes, Dr. Rodín."

"Show him to chamber twenty-three."

"Yes, Dr. Rodín."

Rodín turns to Colton. "I've been teaching Kunal English. I intend to bring him into the West and impress the world with what we've done here."

Colton finds that very unlikely. Rodín is as delusional as Pravda is. Was.

Kunal obediently leads Colton across the courtyard, and Colton looks around, trying not to be obvious about it and trying to ignore the sounds coming from the rooms that border the courtyard. Creations he doesn't even want to imagine reside in there. He focuses his attention toward the middle of the courtyard. Karissa talked of a well in the center, but now there's only a huge, gnarled tree—the one Kunal had climbed at the doctor's request.

"So, can you say anything more than 'Yes, Dr. Rodín'?"

"My English getting better," Kunal says.

Colton looks down at the hands connected to his ankles. He wears fingerless leather gloves on them.

"Were you a volunteer?"

Kunal doesn't answer him.

"Are you happy with . . . with what he made you?"

Kunal stops and takes a good look at Colton, and while Colton tries to read his emotions, he can't. He's not sure if Kunal is friend or foe. Has the doctor really won him over?

"My brain, my body still here," Kunal says. "Better that than no."

"Agreed—but that doesn't answer my question."

"No understand you."

"I think you do."

They reach the back of the large courtyard—a place where the strange sounds fade away—and Kunal opens a warped wooden door with an old-fashioned key on his bulky, jangling key ring. The room itself, as the doctor had promised, looks far more comfortable than the crowded cell he had been in. Only the best for a volunteer.

"You here," Kunal says. "Maybe doctor come bring lunch. Maybe I come. Maybe nobody come." Colton glances out at the tree again, which rustles in the breeze.

"Have you climbed all the way to the top?" Colton asks. "Have you tried? I'll bet you could."

"I no talk no more."

Kunal locks him in and hobbles off, but an hour later Colton sees him through the small window of his room, swinging through highest branches of the huge tree.

Late in the afternoon of that first day Rodín has Colton brought to his office on the second floor, away from the sounds coming from the many rooms below. They discuss Colton's future.

"Such a spectrum of possibilities, yes?" The doctor says, brightly.

Colton can't keep his knee from bouncing. That's all right. He forces all his anxiety into that knee so that it doesn't show anywhere else.

"I have a shipment coming in next week," Rodín tells him. "The wings of a wandering albatross—three-point-five-meter wingspan—the largest in the world. They've been infused with human DNA, to overcome cross-species tissue rejection."

Colton just nods, keeping his jaws clamped tightly closed,

because if he doesn't, he might scream. The doctor takes his silence for thoughtfulness.

"You must be imagining what it would be like to fly, yes?" Then the doctor glances down at Colton's lower half. "Of course human legs are far too heavy for flight—but legs were made for walking. What need for them if you can fly?"

Colton tries to hold on to the first thing Rodín said. *Next week.* If this is to be his fate, it won't happen until next week. By then maybe he can find that tunnel and be out of here.

"But perhaps we should think about highlighting those hazel eyes of yours. Eyes are lost in one's face, do you not think? But imagine them in the palms of your hands. How much more useful they would be!"

"Are those my choices?" Colton finally asks. "Eyes in my hands or albatross wings?"

Rodín frowns. "Do you have something better? Something you dream you could be? Something the human body cannot do in its natural, inferior form?"

Colton takes a deep breath. What possible variation of awful could he propose? Something that would keep most of him intact? But more important, something that would take a long, long time to prepare.

He imagines the albatross wings, which leads him to think of a Pegasus, which leads him to think of—

"Centaur." He cannot believe he's even considering it, much less saying it out loud.

The doctor laughs. "You reach for the stars, yes? Centaurus, the brightest constellation in the southern sky. Like me, you are enamored with the mythological. This I can respect." The doctor taps his chin thoughtfully. "I've thought of it before, of course, but such an endeavor is fraught with complications. The spine must bend at a sharp angle; the central nervous system must be effectively fused—and the operation itself? Risky.

Very risky." He looks at Colton a moment more, then he slaps the table. "But if you're up for the challenge, then so am I!"

He rises, full of excitement, and Colton begins to laugh. He finds none of this funny, and yet still he laughs and doesn't know why. The doctor takes his laughter as a sign of some sort of connection.

"We shall find a horse of the proper size. Chestnut, I think—to match your hair. It will take several weeks to infuse human DNA."

Several weeks. That was the reprieve Colton was hoping for! Colton is ready to congratulate himself on his own cleverness, until Rodín says:

"But first we must give you a larger heart. I'll make that this week's priority."

"What?"

"You can't expect a mere human heart to pump all the way to your hindquarters."

"No—but . . . but won't you need time to infuse it with human DNA too?"

"Usually yes—but I happen to have the heart of a bull already prepared. I had plans to make a pair of minotaurs to stand on either side of the palace entrance—but that can wait; this is so much more exciting." Rodín claps his hands in delight. "What a wonder we will create!"

Dizzy now, Colton holds on tightly to his chair, praying he can get off this ride before its terrible conclusion.

4 · Kunal

The bed this boy has made for himself is worse than any the doctor could have devised. Kunal thinks his mind must be broken, like that poor Russian girl. Or maybe he truly does fancy himself as the makings of mythology.

The first procedure—the heart transplant—is scheduled for Friday, just three days after his arrival at the Green Manor. The boy's heart will be sold on the black market, and in its place will be a beef heart more than twice its size.

Kunal is there as the doctor has his second conversation with the boy. The preoperative discussion. "Of course we'll have to enlarge your chest a bit," Dr. Rodín casually tells him, "but that's simple enough."

Kunal watches Colton, but he shows no hint of a reaction. How could he not be terrified? Kunal was terrified when he was the focus of the doctor's attention—but then Kunal didn't volunteer. He was selected.

Perhaps that's why this American boy is treated differently from the others.

"You will lock him in his room at night, but allow him to move about the manor during the day," Rodín instructs Kunal. "But keep a close eye on him. Escort him wherever he goes."

"Why, Dr. Rodín?" Kunal dares to ask. "Why he get no chains?"

The doctor looks at him, affronted. "You question me?"

"Only to understand."

Rodín sighs. "This boy will most certainly die. If not after this procedure, then after the next. Progress cannot be made without the experiments that fail, no? But I admire this boy's bravery. The least I could do is allow him his humanity for a day or two."

Kunal does not like the idea that he is now the valet to some spoiled American kid—but knowing what he's in for softens Kunal's judgment just a bit.

The next morning Kunal gives Colton the grand tour of the Green Manor—or at least the places that Kunal is allowed to go.

The library full of mildewing books. The shrine—for before men resided in this place, the gods did. And the veranda, which looks out over an electrified fence to the jungle and Thailand in the east—its border barely a kilometer away, so tantalizingly close.

There are, of course, guards all over the grounds, and although they grip their weapons tighter when they see Colton, they know that he is not to be touched. Not until he's touched by the doctor's scalpel.

Kunal makes the mistake of bringing Colton near the north wing. And the sounds make Colton stop in his tracks. They are different from the sounds in the front sections of the manor. Those are merely sounds of the aftermath. Ruined beings scrabbling and babbling, trying to comprehend their fun-house existence. But in the north wing—these are the sounds of souls in transition. The hollow howls of purgatory.

In spite of Kunal's attempts to direct Colton away from the north wing, the boy moves toward a heavily bolted double door, beyond which they can hear muffled moans and weakened wails. Rodín's own *Gates of Hell*.

"Recovery room," Kunal reluctantly tells Colton. "Some live; some die. Some worse than die. You no want here. You be here soon enough."

Kunal grabs his arm to pull him away, but Colton shakes him off.

"Shhh."

Kunal looks around to make sure there are no guards observing them, for the doctor does not like Kunal to linger by the north wing. Then they hear within the chorus of groans a single voice begging for help. English. Australian accent.

"Your friend," Kunal says. "He survive. So far."

"What did Rodín do to him?"

"Don't know yet. Will know when he gets out."

It's as they're walking away from the recovery room that Kunal catches something in Colton's eye. Something more than an acquiescence to Rodín's experimental plans. Something rebellious. *Perhaps,* Kunal thinks, *there is more to this American boy after all.*

5 · Colton

All of Colton's hope now lies in a tunnel that may not exist. The tree in the center of the grand courtyard remains the center of Colton's attention. He circles around it again and again, trying not to look suspicious. The roots are as heavy and as gnarled as the limbs. If there was ever a well here, it has been destroyed by the tree's relentless growth.

"You want climb?" Kunal asks him. "Better to climb now. Won't be able to later. Either you dead, or you a horse. Climb now. I show you."

One thing about Kunal, he doesn't mince what few English words he knows. Colton looks up at the tree and shakes his head. "Rodín won't be too happy with you if I break my neck."

"I help," Kunal says. "Come."

It seems Kunal's only joy is his newfound ability to climb this tree, and Colton thinks how amazing it is that humans can adapt to whatever is thrown at them. If Colton survived, will he be able to adapt? He's not ready to imagine what life for him might be like if his unthinkable operation is successful.

As they approach the tree, Colton sees a small hole between two large roots, no larger than a fist. Colton kneels down to inspect it.

"Bad there," Kunal says. "Pythons."

"I thought Burmese pythons live *in* trees, not under them."

Kunal shrugs. "Rats, then. Big. Many big things in Burma."

Still, Colton kicks at the hole, and some dirt falls in, making the hole a little bit bigger. He smiles and looks up at Kunal, who has already begun to climb, and joins him in the lowest branches of the tree. Immediately a guard comes over to shout him down, because while Kunal is allowed to climb, Colton is not—but that's all right. Colton climbs down, salutes the guard, and heads back to his room, knowing all he needs to know.

Colton realizes that if he's going to escape he needs someone with access. An inside accomplice. So that night when Kunal brings dinner, Colton risks it all.

"Kunal, what if I told you that there's a way you can escape from this place?"

Kunal only laughs. "I say you crazy."

"That hole beneath the tree is more than a rat hole. It's a tunnel. I'm pretty sure it leads out into the jungle—maybe even over the border into Thailand."

That gives Kunal pause for thought.

"Do you want to leave here, Kunal? Think about it!"

Kunal's eyes begin to moisten. "What for me out there?"

"Whatever it is, it's better than what you have here. You don't have to be the doctor's trained monkey."

Kunal backs away angrily, and Colton knows that was the wrong thing to say.

"I bring you breakfast at seven. You no talk to me; I no talk to you." And he quickly leaves, his key chain jangling as he hobbles off.

6 · Kunal

The American boy is crazy. This proves it. And yet Kunal can't get Colton's voice out of his mind. *You don't have to be the doctor's trained monkey.* That's all he is, isn't he? A pet. An animal that the doctor can teach to do tricks for his amusement. Climb trees. Speak English.

That night Kunal ices his aching ankles as he always does, but later, after all but the night guards are asleep, he leaves his upstairs room. Stealthily he creeps along the balcony that circles the courtyard to the spot where the tree's heavy branches come close to the building. Then he leaps into it, shimmying down in silence until he reaches the base. To the guards on patrol the tree is a blind spot. Their attention is on the gates, the doors, the barriers that either keep people in or keep people out.

Ignoring his fear of what might be down there, Kunal scrapes at the dirt around the hole between the roots, using all four of his hands, until he creates an opening more than a foot wide. He can't see down into the darkness. He drops a stone in. It takes at least a second before he hears it strike bottom. Colton is right; this is more than just a hole. Quickly he covers it with leaves and twigs. No one must know about this. The doctor has many secrets. Now Kunal has one too.

In the morning Sonthi arrives with three AWOLs: Colton's two remaining roommates and a girl with tattoos who Kunal has not seen before.

Kunal hurries to the doctor's side, knowing it is the best place to be when something happens that's not on the schedule. Were he anywhere else, and the doctor called for him, he'd take out his wrath on Kunal, rather than just order him about.

"She wishes to see her sister," Sonthi says with a wide grin. "I thought it was time."

The doctor scowls. "Since when is it your job to think?"

Sonthi takes the rebuke in a simmering silence. Kunal knows he despises the doctor, but this is the doctor's camp, and in the Dah Zey disrespect to a superior is punishable by death.

Then the girl shouts, "You bastards broke your bargain with me! Now I'm going to be unwound, and my sister is still a prisoner. The least you can do is let me say good-bye."

The doctor ignores her. "And what about these other two?"

Sonthi shrugs. "They insisted on coming with her. I told them if they come they won't be coming back. So I guess you have two new volunteers."

7 · Colton

Colton hears the commotion at the gate, and through his small bedroom window he sees Karissa and the others with Sonthi. Right on schedule. The doctor isn't pleased, and Kunal seems anxious, shifting his weight from one hand to the other. Colton leaves his room, which Kunal unlocked earlier today, and hurries over.

"So I guess you have two new volunteers," he hears Sonthi say.

"I don't need volunteers today," the doctor says, and waves his hand dismissively. "Take them out of here. Their insolence should be rewarded with unwinding."

The guards grab all three of them, but just then Kunal spots Colton approaching and meets his gaze.

What Kunal does next changes everything.

Colton watches as Kunal reaches down and jangles his keys ever so slightly, then gives Colton a nod. That nod says, *I'm on your side. I'll be your accomplice. Your inside man.* It occurs to Colton how a single nod can alter the world.

"Wait," says Colton. "You do need them, Dr. Rodín."

All eyes turn to him. The other kids seem shocked to see him not in shackles. He steps over to Gamon. "Look at how slight this one is. You need someone small for your albatross wings, don't you? And Kemo—he sits all day with palms turned heavenward. Put eyes in those palms, and then let him tell you what he sees."

Stunned silence—even from the doctor.

"And this one . . ." Colton glares at Karissa. "The AWOL catcher. You *should* let her see her sister. Then add her inked arms—after all, she'll be a close biological match, and it will bring you one step closer to having your Kali."

Karissa looks at them in building confusion. "My arms? What are you talking about? What is he talking about?"

Then Sonthi laughs long and loud. "It looks like you finally found a kindred spirit, doctor. Too bad you must put him under the knife."

Rodín looks at Colton with something bordering on awe or at least admiration. "Very well, then."

He orders the guards to put Gamon and Kemo in a holding cell and sends Kunal to open Marisol's room. Sonthi personally escorts Karissa to visit her sister. Colton doesn't go—he remains in the courtyard with the doctor.

"You and I are of a like mind," Rodín tells him. "It gives me more incentive to make sure you survive your procedures."

Then, from Marisol's cell, Colton hears Karissa's soul-searing wails of shock and grief, along with Sonthi's endless laughter.

8 · Kunal

The unexpected hope of freedom is enticing yet terrifying. His life here is awful but tolerable. What would his life be out there, in a world that will see him as a monster? He could live alone, a recluse at the edge of civilization, bothering no one, and no one bothering him. Is that the life he wants?

These are questions he can't answer—all he knows is that freedom is desirable above all things. He cannot let his fear cloud his judgment. And so, well past midnight, he leaves his room once more, a plan fully formed in his mind. A plan he might be able to pull off.

9 · Colton

Colton paces his room in the dark. He can't sleep; he can't even sit for long. They will come for him at dawn to prep him for his operation. Soon, his chest will be expanded, and the heart of the bull will be installed in place of his own. Unless Kunal comes through.

"You wait," Kunal told him when he locked Colton in his room that night after dinner. "You wait, I come."

"And the others?"

Kunal didn't answer him. "You wait."

The moon moves halfway across the sky before Kunal shows up at his door. His keys do not jingle. The lock turns slowly, quietly. Colton's heart seem to rise so he can feel it beating in his neck. *His* heart. Kunal is here, which means he will keep his heart. If the tunnel truly is a tunnel. And if the guards don't kill him before he reaches it.

He sees Kunal silhouetted as the door opens. "Come, come," Kunal whispers. "No time." He gives Colton a handgun—and he doubts it's loaded with tranqs. Colton has never held a weapon before, but he knows he'll use it if he has to.

It's only as he steps out of his room that he sees the others. Kemo, Gamon, Karissa, and Marisol, her silhouette spiderlike in the darkness. Kunal has armed them all.

Colton would make a beeline for the tree, if it weren't for one thing. Jenson isn't with them.

"We have to get Jenson," Colton whispers.

"No," says Kunal. "You leave now. He stay. Too late for him."

But Colton knows he'll never be able to live with himself if he doesn't try. "Take them to the tunnel," he tells Kunal, then holds out his hand. "Give me the key."

Kunal hesitates but only for a moment. He finds the key on the key ring but can't take it off, so he hands the entire ring to Colton.

"You stupid. Very stupid." Then he leaves with the others.

Alone, Colton creeps in shadows to the double doors of the recovery room. Even at this time of night it's not silent in there. There are still moans and the faint, hopeless wails of the damned. He waits for a guard to pass on his rounds, then he goes to the door, unlocks it, and slips in.

The first thing that hits him is the stench. Both medicinal and septic at the same time. It's hard to keep from gagging. The lights are scarce and dim, and he's glad for it, for in each alcove is another one of Dr. Rodín's recovering experiments.

And that's exactly what they are—experiments more than creations. Colton can almost hear the hypotheses the Doctor was attempting to investigate.

Can a brain be housed somewhere other than a skull?

Can a mythological Janus exist, with two faces on the same cranium, forever facing in opposite directions?

Can a giant be created by stacking spinal columns?

And these were the ones that survived their procedures.

Colton couldn't even imagine the miscreations that didn't.

And then there's Jenson.

"Who's there?" Colton hears him say. "I know you're there—I can hear you!"

Colton moves closer to the hospital bed on which Jenson lies, ankles and wrists secured to the frame of the bed. An intravenous tube feeding into his arm.

"Don't pretend you're not there! I hear you!"

"It's me, Jenson. It's Colton."

At first it seems as if nothing's been done to him . . . but as he turns his head in the direction of Colton's voice, Colton can see that Jenson no longer has eyes. Instead he has a second set of ears where his eyes should be.

I know a way to make him listen, the doctor said. Colton shudders.

"Help me, Colton. Get me out of here."

Colton tries, but the keyholes on Jenson's shackles don't match any of the keys on Kunal's key chain.

"Please, Colton! You've got to! You've got to."

"I'm trying. . . ."

And then from outside come shouts in Burmese and gunshots. He hears a girl scream. Is that Marisol? Karissa? More gunshots, and then a barrage of machine-gun fire. Something's gone wrong! Colton takes a step away from Jenson to peer out the door.

"No, don't go!" Jenson wails. Then quieter. "If you can't free me . . . then kill me. Please, Colton. I don't want to live like this."

Colton understands. He wouldn't want to live like this either. He pulls the pistol from his waist and aims it at Jenson's scarred forehead.

But he can't pull the trigger. He can't. He just can't.

"I'm sorry, Jenson," Colton says. "I'm sorry." And he turns

and runs, knowing that if he does live through this night, he'll never be able to forgive himself for his moment of weakness. For his failure to give Jenson what he truly needed.

10 · Kunal

Kunal blames it on the moon. Had it been a moonless night, they would have been under full cover of darkness. He should have waited a few more hours, until after the moon set—but he was anxious, and it clouded his judgment. Now all could be lost.

He hears the shout of the first guard, which draws the attention of the second. He can't see them yet, but knows the direction the shouts are coming from. Marisol panics, running toward the tree—but she doesn't know where to go. She's heading toward the wrong side. Karissa goes after her. Then one of the guards fires. It hits Karissa, and she goes down in a scream of pain, but that doesn't stop her. She rolls over and begins firing the gun Kunal gave her in the direction of the guards.

Then the small Thai boy—was his name Gamon?—loses control. He has not said a word since he was brought here, but suddenly he runs out into the center of the courtyard, screaming a war cry at the top of his lungs. Kunal had taken whatever weapons he could carry when he raided the armory. He hadn't given much thought to which weapons he handed to who. Gamon has a submachine gun, which he now fires wildly at anything that moves.

And it's just the diversion that they need.

"The left side of tree," Kunal tells Kemo. "Between the roots. Go now!"

Kemo runs, grabbing Marisol, while Karissa limps behind them. The guards' attention is on Gamon, who has already taken down at least four. Lights come on upstairs—but not the big floodlights—which means there's still time, if they can just make it to the tree.

11 · Colton

Colton races into the courtyard, not quite sure what he's seeing. Bodies litter the ground. He doesn't know whose they are. Then he's grabbed. He turns, ready to use his gun this time, but it's Kunal.

"Go now!" Kunal tells him. "Now! Last chance!"

They run to the tree, taking the long way to keep under the overhang of the upstairs balcony, shielded from the moonlight.

In the courtyard, whoever's screaming and firing that machine gun is taken down by a shot to the head. Was that . . . was that Gamon?

"Down there! Go!"

They're at the roots of the tree. Something smells awful. All around them, a terrible stench. *Smells like gasoline . . .*

Kunal pushes him, and Colton plunges down the hole that's barely large enough for him to fit, birthing him from one world into another.

"Are you okay?" It's Kemo. Karissa's there and Marisol. Karissa groans. She's been shot, but she's alive.

Colton turns to the hole, expecting to see Kunal climbing down behind him—but he doesn't come.

"Kunal!" He's already failed one friend today; he can't fail another. He climbs a pile of broken bricks back up toward the hole.

"Colton!" shouts Kemo. "What are you doing?"

The gunshots have stopped. Colton pokes his head out from between the roots. Kunal is nowhere. But someone sees him and is running toward him. It's not Kunal. It's Sonthi. He raises his gun—

And suddenly the whole world is engulfed in flames.

12 · Kunal

The moment Colton slips into the hole, Kunal is grabbed from behind, pulled away from the tree, and thrown to the ground, pinned there by none other than the doctor himself.

"You evil, ungrateful little bastard! What have you done?"

There's a gun in Kunal's hand, but the doctor slams his hand against the ground until the gun falls free. He grapples, but the doctor pins both his hands to the hard earth. "I'll have Sonthi unwind you alive bit by bit until there's nothing left of you."

"You forget something, doctor," Kunal says. Then he smiles. And with a hand that used to be a foot, he plunges a knife deep into the doctor's neck. Rodín barely has time to register his surprise before he dies.

With no time to lose now, Kunal pushes the doctor's body off him and looks toward the tree. Sonthi has seen the hole and is running toward it—but he hasn't seen Kunal. The man's gun is raised, aiming at the hole. Kunal grabs his own gun and raises it too—but instead of aiming at Sonthi, he aims at the base of the tree.

Kunal fires the flare gun. It hits a large root, and the tree, which he drenched in gasoline an hour earlier, bursts into flames.

13 · Colton

He falls back down into the tunnel, his hair and eyebrows singed.

"What the hell?"

Kemo has just finished tying off the wound on Karissa's leg. The light from the flaming hole flickers around them, illuminating a tunnel that heads into absolute darkness.

"Do we know where it goes?" Kemo ponders.

"Away from here," Marisol says, wrapping all four of her arms around herself.

"I couldn't save them," Colton says, looking at the flaming hole in the tunnel roof. "Not Jenson, not Gamon, not Kunal."

"No," agrees Kemo. "But you saved *us*."

Colton nods, knowing that it will have to be enough. He turns from the flames that have now begun to spill down the walls like lava and leads them through the tunnel into a darkness full of hope.

14 · Sonthi

The floodlights come on two minutes too late. They're not needed anymore, because the tree blazes, lighting up the entire courtyard.

"In the morning I want proof that they burned down there!" Sonthi yells with a fury that could shake mountains. "I want to see their charred bodies!" The tree ignited quickly, and he suspects an accelerant. Perhaps it was some sort of plan the AWOLs had that went awry. If so they'll be consumed in their own flames. He orders men to get fire hoses to douse the flaming tree. The AWOLs no longer matter. The top priority is putting out this goddam fire before the whole place goes up in flames.

That's when that talking monkey Kunal comes up to him, tugging at his arm.

"Mr. Sonthi! Mr. Sonthi! They kill the doctor! They steal keys and kill the doctor!"

Sonthi grunts and looks over to where Kunal is pointing. There, on the ground, a dozen yards away, lies the doctor, with a knife protruding from his neck. What a mess this whole thing is. What a stinking mess. How could this have happened?

Then he studies Kunal, whose eyes are wild and panicked. "What should I do? What should I do?"

And Sonthi laughs. In the midst of this miserable night, he laughs. "Take acting lessons," he tells Kunal.

Kunal just looks at him, confused. That's all right; let him wonder. Sonthi is no idiot. He knows the AWOLs didn't kill the doctor. They had no reason to—their only goal was to escape. He wouldn't be surprised if Kunal helped them, and then used their escape as the perfect cover for killing Rodín. He could blame the AWOLs, and no one would ever know the truth. Yes, the more he thinks about it, the more he realizes that's the real play here. That's exactly how it went down.

Sonthi supposes he could turn Kunal in. Punish him for it. But why? After all, he's done Sonthi a favor. He's managed to get rid of the doctor, leaving Sonthi in charge of the camp. If anything, he should be rewarded.

"What should I do, Mr. Sonthi?" Kunal asks again.

"Draw me a bath," Sonthi says. "Draw me a bath in the doctor's private suite." Then he thinks for a moment and adds, "But first draw one for yourself."

Kunal gives him that same confused look.

"Didn't you hear me? You stink! Go take a bath in the doctor's quarters. As long as you like. That's an order."

"Yes, Mr. Sonthi."

Kunal hobbles off in that weird way he has, but there seems to be a spring in his step that wasn't there before.

And that makes Sonthi laugh and laugh and laugh.

15 · Colton

Six weeks later he sits at the same restaurant where he met Karissa, eating panang curry and reading a newspaper in Thai. He's picking up the language faster than he thought possible. He can easily read the headline. It says PARTS-PIRATE RING DISCOVERED IN POLICE FORCE.

The face of the police chief who first turned him over to the Dah Zey is right beneath the headline, looking far less smug and condescending than when he spoke to Colton.

A tuk-tuk speeds by. It was weeks before Colton could bring himself to ride in one again, but even the driver who brought him to the gray building was arrested. They'd likely never even get a trial. With the way the Thai abhor unwinding, he won't be surprised if they just disappeared.

Kemo disappeared in his own way as well, after their escape. He's in Laos now, at a monastery in Luang Prabang. Colton has no idea what happened to Karissa and her sister. After they stumbled out of the forest and rediscovered civilization, they quickly went their own way. He assumes they're together, dealing with Marisol's very particular issues. Colton finds he's not even curious. All that matters to him is that they're alive and no longer his problem.

The harvest camp is still there, just across the border. So are half a dozen other Dah Zey camps. He can't fight them directly, but he can battle their agents here in Bangkok. The Thai police force is more than happy to use him, the same way the Dah Zey used Karissa. But rather than catching AWOLs, he's begun working undercover to expose parts pirates. It's dangerous work, but he's paid well, and it's rewarding in other ways. He knows that each parts pirate he cleans off the street means dozens of AWOLs saved. Those AWOLs will never know him and never know what he's done for them, but that's all right. At least he's beginning to atone for the ones he couldn't save from the Haunted Mansion.

He stirs the rice into his curry and takes a taste. The sun is setting. Pretty soon the tourists will be out in full force to experience the Bangkok nightlife, and Colton will get to work.

For a moment—but only a moment—he pauses to think of the life he left behind. The comfort of his family. The grief and sense of betrayal when they unwound his brother. But it's as if that were another lifetime. Colton smiles. He's no longer the person he used to be. He's become something entirely different.

UnConfirmed

Hayden approaches the West Palm Beach mansion driving a rental car. He still finds that amazing. A year ago he was public enemy number four—just behind Connor, Risa, and Starkey. But now people in airports call him Mr. Upchurch and hand him the keys to Toyotas and Hyundais, with a smile, like none of that ever happened.

"I listen to your radio show all the time, Mr. Upchurch," said the gushing clerk when she rented him the car. "You're so *clever!*"

He grinned and gave her the answer he gives everyone who gushes at him. "Not clever enough to get this for free!"

The funny thing is, about one third of the times he says that, they do give it to him for free, whatever it is. A meal, a movie ticket, a pack of gum at the convenience store. All he has to do is drop his name, then they'll recognize his voice, and the magic ensues. Sometimes the cost is the ten seconds it takes to pose with someone for a picture—which is ridiculous, because it's his voice that's become famous, not his face—but who is he to argue with free lunch?

The rental car was not free, but he's not paying for it. The big bad media conglomerate that sponsors his radio show gave him a corporate credit card. He finds that even more absurd. How is this not theft? He doesn't want to think about it too deeply. If this is his fifteen minutes of fame, he intends to milk it dry. No guilt, no regrets. Maybe therapy when it's all over, but damn it, no regrets.

The woman he's come to visit is just a few years older than

him. Twenty-one, maybe twenty-two. Nouveau riche, as they say. Rags to riches in a most spectacular way. Hayden is here by her personal invitation. He's never met her, though they do have some key mutual friends.

He announces himself at a street-side intercom and a wrought-iron gate slowly swings open to a semicircular drive-way and the mansion beyond. It's an ostentatiously pink Floridian palace with the requisite palm trees, balconies, and red-tiled roof. Lots of "curb appeal," as a Realtor might say, although behind the gate you can't really see the house from the curb—which, for residents in this kind of neighborhood, is its appeal.

Hayden is greeted at the door by a butler. An actual butler.

"Miss Skinner is expecting you," he says in the mournful, lugubrious sort of voice one might expect a butler to cultivate. "This way, Mr. Upchurch."

The house is as elaborate on the inside as it is out. Lots of marble and designer furniture and expensive art. It looks like something one might see in an interior-decorating magazine—and not in a good way. It looks more like a model home than an actual one. Cold and false.

The butler leads him all the way through the house and out a pair of french doors to a backyard pool. Grace Skinner isn't lounging by the pool. Instead, she's on the far side of it, in front of a little guest house. She sits there with an easel, painting. As Hayden approaches a step behind the butler, he can see her canvas. It's a dog. Or a horse. Or a giraffe. He can't be quite sure. It's either avant-garde or just very, very bad. She is so absorbed in her work, she doesn't notice that they've approached.

The butler politely clears his throat. Twice. She finally looks up.

"Oh, lookee lookee who came right outta the radio!" She

stands up—as tall as Hayden, and he's pretty tall. She reaches out her hand to shake, but then pulls it back before he can. "Bad idea. Not unless you want your hand covered in oil paints. Stuff's a bitch to get off your skin. And don't even get me started on clothes."

"Shall I bring more lemonade?" the butler asks.

"Yeah, yeah, good idea," Grace tells him. The butler takes a platter with an empty carafe and heads to the house.

"Sit, sit, sit," she tells Hayden. He does, a bit bemused by her chummy manner. He likes her far more than he likes her house.

She points to her painting. "What do you think?" she asks, but doesn't wait for an answer. "It sucks, right?"

Hayden smiles. "Yes, but with a rare kind of passion."

"I do it because I like to, not because I'm any good. You want good art, go back in the house. The walls are full of it."

"Yes, I noticed," Hayden says. "I suspect it's not your style."

Grace shrugs. "I got some artsy-fartsy woman with high heels and some kind of accent to decorate the whole place, on account of I woulda filled it with sad clowns and stuff on velvet. Not the kind of 'aht' rich people are supposed to like."

"But it's your house—you should fill it with the things you like."

Grace waves the thought away. "I might own it, but it's not where I live." She points to the guest house. "This is where I live. The big house is too cold and scary-lonely at night. I got it because I could. And because it's supposed to be an investment."

She tells him all about how her deal with Rifkin Medical Instruments for Sonia's organ printer made her a king's ransom, and how some highly strategic investments of her own parlayed it into a true embarrassment of riches. "I got these financial advisors who tell me don't do this and don't do that—but my

investment strategies always pay off and make them look like
morons—which is why I keep them. I like makin' people who
think they know everything look like morons. So anyways, now
I got more money than God, as they say. Well, maybe not God,
but his cousin at least. If he had one. Does he? Well, if he did."

Hayden laughs out loud, and Grace looks a bit embarrassed—
which was not his intent. He just finds her attitude so refreshing.
"So what are you going to do with all of it?" Hayden asks.

Grace shrugs. "Play," she tells him. "Maybe buy an amusement park or something. And give a bunch away to folks who
deserve it." She looks to the mansion. "I've been throwing par-
ties for poor people in the house, to keep the place from being
so empty all the time—and everyone deserves a fancy night out
in a place you gotta be invited to—especially poor folks who
never get invited nowhere by anyone who isn't family. I buy 'em
gowns and tuxedos that they get to take with them when they
go, and I feed 'em the kind of meat you don't gotta put ketchup
on. I make 'em *my* family, on accounta my real one didn't work
out so well."

She looks away then, probably thinking about her brother.
Hayden never met Argent, but he knows he played a crucial
role in saving Connor from a ruthless black marketeer.

"So I imagine you invited me here because you want me to
interview you on my radio show," Hayden says.

"I don't wanna talk about that yet," she says. The butler
arrives with lemonade and chocolate chip cookies. "Eat, drink,
and be merry," she says. "Isn't that how it goes?"

"There's a second part to that expression," Hayden points
out. "But it's not nearly as much fun."

"So you were with Connor and Risa down in Sonia's basement the first time they were there, huh?" she asks with her
mouth full of cookie.

"Once upon a time."

"Wasn't no fairy tale, I'm sure."

"A different kind of 'grim.'"

"And then you was with them in the airplane graveyard. That's where you started the Radio Free Hayden thing, right?"

"You know a lot about me."

Grace shakes her head. "Just the stuff Connor told me. And the stuff you say on your show. You know, you talk about yourself an awful lot."

"I know; it's a bad habit."

"So where are they?" Grace asks, and says no more as she waits for his answer. When he isn't forthcoming, she adds, "I mean, you were closer with them than just about anybody, so you gotta know where they are now, right?"

Hayden sighs. "Not exactly."

The fact is, ever since that infamous TV interview that Connor and Risa did more than six months ago, he hasn't heard from them. No one has. He could hardly blame them. Hayden wasn't there—he just heard about it like everyone else. It was a big deal. An interview on a national prime-time talk show. How the guy got a gun into the studio audience is still a mystery—there were metal detectors and security up the wazoo, and then some. It was, after all, their first public interview after their testimony before Congress—the testimony that shamed lawmakers into making the moratorium on unwinding permanent. But there are still plenty of people who support unwinding, and they're not going to let that dark era of history go without a fight.

Connor or Risa or both of them would be dead now, had it not been for the actions of some anonymous woman in the studio audience who saw the shooter rise and pushed his arm as he fired.

There, before the world, on live TV, the beloved host of a beloved talk show was shot through the chest by the stray bullet and killed. He never had a chance. Risa and Connor were spirited off the stage by security and neither has been seen since.

"C'mon," Grace cajoles. "You know where they are—you hafta know!"

"If they want to say hidden, why would they tell a blabber-mouth with a nationally syndicated radio show?"

Grace considers that. "Good point. Damn."

There are a few theories out there, of course, as to where Risa and Connor are. Some people think they've joined Lev on the Arápache Reservation and are enjoying peaceful sanctu-ary there. Others say that Connor, Risa, and Connor's family entered the witness protection program, and all have brand-new identities. With faces that recognizable, Hayden can't imagine how they'd remain anonymous for very long. Conspiracy kooks think they're in a high-security prison or dead. Religious kooks think they've been raptured. Every tabloid claims unconfirmed sightings, and the WHERE'S CONNOR? and WHERE'S RISA? T-shirts that were so popular before they resurfaced at the Washington rally are back in vogue. Too bad for them. The more they try to hide from their legend, the more it asserts itself.

Hayden, on the other hand, has no problems with fame or infamy. He loves the vitriolic haters as much as he loves the fans who adore him. To be the cause of such passion tickles him to no end. And of course there's the free stuff.

"I got a theory," Grace says. "And I'm very good with the-ories. Theories and games and strategies. So tell me what you think."

"I'm listening."

"Connor needed something from his parents before he could forgive them for reals. He needed a sacrifice. So after that awful interview thing, he gave them a choice. Either leave their lives behind and disappear with him and Risa, or say good-bye to him forever. They would live out their lives without him, knowing that he never forgave them for signing his unwind order."

"So in your scenario, what did they do?"

"I can't be certain, but I *do* know that they sold their house. I heard that the guy who bought it is gonna turn it onto some kind of public attraction, you know, like Graceland, although I can't see it—I mean it's just a house. But then, Graceland is also just a house—I been there and I wasn't all that impressed—so I guess it's possible. Anyway, I think they accepted Connor's challenge. They took off and they're all together."

"Where?"

"Somewhere mobile," Grace says. "My first thought was the opposite, of course. That they hunkered down in Alaska or some other place where they'd stay put and have no outside contact. Nobody sees them, and they don't gotta see no one else, living off the land. But you know Connor—that's not him. His life's all about motion. He's like that shark he's got on his grafted arm—he's gotta keep moving or die. So I think they got themselves some sorta sailboat or catamaran. Nothing fancy. I mean, his family wasn't rich. Just a simple kind of boat, and maybe they're tooling around the Mediterranean, minding their own business, hanging out in smaller, less-traveled ports. Or maybe they're using their boat to save AWOLs in places where there's still unwinding. That'd be Risa's idea, and although Connor'd say he doesn't want to do that anymore, he's just saying it so that Risa can convince him. And his parents get behind it, because again, it's part of the deal: Love me; love my choices. And maybe they'll come back someday and maybe they won't. But I think they're happy. Not happily-ever-after kind of happy, because no one gets that. I mean we all get sick, and get hit by trucks, and fall out of love, and stuff—but I swear I can see Connor and Risa dangling their feet off that catamaran, saying, *Sure as hell beats Sonia's basement.*"

Hayden has to laugh again, because the way she paints it, he can see it too.

"The proof, though," Grace says, "will be the brother. Luke, or Lucas, or whatever his name is."

"What about him?"

"They'd want him to finish school. They won't leave him behind, though, so five'll get you ten that he's enrolled in some boarding school that's not too far from the Mediterranean Sea. Maybe Barcelona or Athens, or Ephesus, or Nice. Find a Luke, or a Lucas, who just started a few months ago at some boarding school out that way, where they teach in English, and you'll know I got it right."

Grace smiles, proud of herself, treating the whole thing like it was a fait accompli. Like a mathematical proof beyond reproach. Then her smile fades. She pours herself some lemonade and pours more for Hayden, even though he tells her he doesn't want any more.

Then she says, "I didn't ask you here to talk about Risa and Connor. Well, I guess maybe I did, but that's not the main reason."

"Right," says Hayden. "Your interview. How Grace Skinner became the name behind organ printing. How she became worth half a billion dollars in less than a year. A true American fairy tale."

Grace slams down her glass hard enough to make half the lemonade shoot out. "First of all, I'm only half of the name behind the printer. It's the Rifkin-Skinner Biobuilder. Rifkin made it—I just handed him Sonia's broken prototype, and he got it to work, and I still feel pretty damn guilty I didn't insist they call it the Rifkin-Rheinschild Biobuilder, after Sonia and her husband, but I figured it was too hard to spell, and after all I'd been through I wanted some credit. Second of all—like

I said—there are no fairy tales, American or otherwise. And third, I don't do interviews, because they make me sound stupid, and I'm tired of sounding stupid, because it makes me *feel* stupid, and I never want to feel stupid again. I got enough money so that no one calls me stupid to my face, but I don't want them saying it behind my back neither."

"I don't think you're stupid, Grace," Hayden says very honestly. "Yes, there are some things you lack that other people have—but you compensate. There are things you can do that put everyone else to shame. I don't think you're low-cortical. I think you're deep-cortical."

"If I do an interview with you, others won't see it that way."

"So if I'm not here to set up an interview, why am I here?"

"I want you to find my brother."

Hayden takes a deep breath.

"I want you to put out a plea to your listeners. You got a lot of them—they'll listen to you."

"Grace—Divan Umarov's plane hit a mountain. The debris field stretched for miles—there were no survivors. . . ."

"I know—but I got a feeling. . . ."

"A theory?"

"No!" she says, frustrated. "I ain't got enough to have a theory. All I got is a feeling and I can't let it go. They didn't find any part of him. And if there's no proof he's dead . . ."

"Grace, there are lots of people who are dead with no proof."

"I know that! And I know I can't let it go. You got listeners. I'll put pictures of him up online. You just gotta get your listeners to look."

"From what Connor said, half his face was gone, and the black market guy promised him a new one. Even if he survived the crash, and is alive, what good will a picture do? He won't look the same."

"Why can't you do it? Connor would want you to do it, wouldn't he? He would want it!"

"He would tell you exactly what I'm telling you now."

Grace's face gets red like a child about to throw a tantrum. "Get out of here. I don't want to talk to you no more. You're just like everyone else, sayin' Argie's dead, when I know in my heart that he's not. He's not!"

Hayden stands up. "Grace, I'm sorry."

"Just go. Take some cookies with you, or else I'll eat them and I already ate too many."

And although it goes against all his instincts, Hayden says, "Okay, I'll do it. I'll put an all-points bulletin out on Argent—but on one condition."

"What."

He's about to ask for an interview. It's what he wants. His listeners will love it. But he's not going to blackmail her. It's not his style. Besides, he can do a whole show about her without even having to have her there. And he does love to hear himself talk. So, instead of asking for an interview, he says, "On the one condition . . . that you invite me to your next party. I'll even bring my own tuxedo."

Grace smiles. "And bring a date," she says. "A girl or a boy, I don't care."

Hayden chuckles. "Maybe both," he says. "One on each arm. They can go dance while I schmooze."

He does the public plea just as he promised. Argent Skinner—oddball unexpected hero who helped save the Akron AWOL from being sold for parts on the black market. Has anyone seen him? His sister has pictures up on her website. He looked like this. Might not look like that anymore. Might look only half like this. Then Hayden opens up his show to callers. His producer always hurls him the most bizarro ones. Good for ratings. One guy talks about the black market and says he knows a guy who knows a guy who knows a girl who escaped from the Burmese Dah Zey. And that she has four arms. Go figure. Another caller says that Argent Skinner is really just an anagram of the Stark Green Inn in Stark, New Hampshire, so that must be where he's hiding. When faced with the fact that the Stark Green Inn was in existence long before Argent Skinner was born, the caller suggests some form of time travel. It's all very amusing and entertaining, but, as Hayden suspected, this train leads to various suburbs of nowhere.

It's the other things that Grace talked about that stick in Hayden's mind, however, and, in his spare time he does some hacking. He doesn't have the skills that Jeevan does, wherever he is these days, but Hayden can bludgeon his way through a firewall in a pinch. What he finds is a particular picture on a school website. The American School of Marseille, perched on a hill above the sunny Mediterranean Sea. The picture is of a lacrosse team, everyone smiling after a big win, or pretending to smile after a big loss, one can never be quite sure. In the back row is a kid tagged as Lucas Saltries. There is a familiar look about him. His smile. His eyebrows. But the proof of this particular pudding isn't in some vague family resemblance— it's in the name. Hayden sincerely doubts that Argent Skinner has anything to do with the Stark Green Inn . . . but Saltries is most definitely an anagram of Lassiter.

UnTithed

Co-authored with Michelle Knowlden

1 · Miracolina

Daytime smothers her in vibrant colors. The sun illuminates secrets she holds close. Night is better. It flows in hues of gray and black and streetlights that don't disturb the shadows. She slips through darkness like vapor.

Sometimes Miracolina is uncomfortable in her evolving relationship with her mother and father. Her parents chose her embryo self to save her brother. Then chose her to be a tithe to save dozens of people. Then they didn't sign the unwind order when she turned thirteen. She knows they did it out of love. She is learning to be grateful.

Most times she's glad to be around her folks. But if she doesn't act like an ordinary fourteen-year-old girl, her father turns moody and her mother cries. She spent her entire life preparing her body to be divided. She needs time to reboot for this unexpected future.

She once read that sometimes you have to *act* like you believe until you *can* believe. In pretending to be ordinary and pretending to be glad she has this long, unpredictable future, maybe she's learning how to live like a normal girl.

After she was brought home from her "adventure" as they call it—the adventure that brought her all the way to Tucson, Arizona, with a notorious tithe-turned-clapper-turned-rebel— nothing was the same. Her parents thought it would be uncomfortable for her at their old church, so now they go to a new one. Now they attend a larger Roman Catholic church in an older suburb of Chicago that reminds her of the formality, ceremony, and beauty of the cathedrals of Rome. And because her parents wanted to give her a fresh start, she now goes to the parochial school near the church. Whatever.

You'll make new friends, her parents told her. *And no one has to know what happened.*

But her only real friends at her old school were tithes. She doesn't know how to make regular friends.

Most days at school aren't so bad. They wear uniforms. Even though the skirt is a bright plaid of red and navy blue, the blouse is white, like the clothes she wore when she was a tithe. White is either the absence of color or the presence of all colors, depending on how you look at it. The whiteness of the blouse feels familiar, but on the other hand it tethers her too uncomfortably to her abandoned purpose—so now, when she isn't wearing the school uniform, she wears black. Like the nuns. Besides, black blends better into the night.

Miracolina still has dreams of the time she escaped the Cavenaugh mansion with Lev, only to be taken by the parts pirate. The nightmare always comes in the early morning hours. And in her waking hours, she thinks too much about Lev as well. She's not sure what that means.

She's pretty sure he's dead. He must be. When she last saw him, the Juvey-cops were rounding up the kids at the airplane graveyard for unwinding. Then she was tranq'd. Then she was in a police car, being spirited back to her new old life.

But what if he's alive? Is he still an AWOL? If she saw him again, would she slap him silly or throw her arms around him? And if he *is* alive, does he think about her as much as she thinks about him?

With a long future stretching before her, she knows she

shouldn't waste time thinking about someone who is probably dead. Better to focus on church, on saving lives, and on other matters of eternity.

"Not cheese puffs, please," says one of the guests at the soup kitchen. "If I have to eat another cheese puff, I'll barf." Even though it's warm inside the community center, he wears a long, woolen coat. "Do you have potato chips?"

The best thing about the new church is the soup kitchen and thrift store in their community center. They give bags of groceries to the needy. They serve dinner during the week and a special supper after mass on Sundays. Clothing is distributed in the evenings and on Saturday mornings with coffee and cookies. They even have beds for those who want them. There are lots of opportunities for a girl like Miracolina to help out. She works in the community center every chance she gets. It's not exactly donating a liver, but it's something.

"Coming through," a nun yells. She slips a full vat of sloppy-joe mix into the steam table in front of Miracolina. "I may have made this batch a little spicier than usual—so make sure you warn people."

Sister Barbara (named after Saint Barbara, who was beheaded by her father in the third century) runs the community center with Father Lawrence (from Saint Lawrence, roasted over coals in Panisperna). Miracolina learned about martyrs in religion class last week. The idea appeals to her.

On the other side of the counter a tiny girl with fat pigtails waves a chocolate chip cookie at Miracolina. "Thank you!" the girl says, and hurries off before Miracolina can say "You're welcome."

As she spoons coleslaw next to the sloppy joes on their plates, a boy in line catches her eye. For a moment she thinks he looks like Lev and almost drops the plate. Then she sees that it's not Lev. In fact it really doesn't look like him at all.

She puzzles over what made her think of Lev, when a thought electrifies her. The way the boy ducks his head and mumbles his "thank you" when she hands him his meal is what an AWOL does.

She glances out of the window to see Father Lawrence on the street, talking to some of the homeless in line. Father Lawrence can usually tell if one of their younger guests is running from an unwind order and does what needs to be done. Maybe the boy snuck past him. Or maybe the boy told him he was eighteen. No way is he eighteen.

"Hey, Mira," Sister Barbara says.

"It's Miracolina, Sister," she says politely. When she finishes spooning coleslaw on the next few plates, she turns to the nun—and cringes. Sister Barbara is waving a red Hawaiian blouse like a bullfighter.

"Someone dropped it in the donation barrel yesterday, and I thought of you. It'll look so much prettier than all those black outfits you wear. What do you think?"

She wouldn't wear something that gaudy even by papal decree. "I couldn't take something meant for the homeless, Sister. And it's a little bit flashy for me."

"Nonsense." Sister Barbara holds the shirt up against Miracolina. "You're young. You could use a little flash."

Which is funny, because the nuns often complain about how provocatively other kids dress. But apparently there are limits to modesty as well.

Miracolina gently pushes the Hawaiian shirt away. "I appreciate the thought, Sister Barbara, but my mom chooses my clothes." Which is mostly a lie, as her mother has been buying bright shirts and dresses for Miracolina even flashier than this one. She prefers black and wishes the adults in her life would leave her alone about it.

Miracolina seeks out the AWOL-looking boy again. He sits as alone as he can at one of the long tables in the dining room, scarfing down his food as quickly as humanly possible. He glances furtively around at the other guests. Then he pockets the orange and the bag of cheese puffs that come with dinner and gets up to leave.

2 · Bryce

Every smart AWOL knows that a soup kitchen can be like a mousetrap. Tempting eats can trigger the iron arm of the law to swing around and snag the unwary. Juvey-cops are always staking out shelters and soup kitchens. Bryce had watched this one for hours before deciding that it was safe, then had tagged along behind a family that he vaguely resembled to get past the priest who monitored the line. Priests are unpredictable when it comes to AWOLs. The Vatican has never taken an official position on unwinding, which leaves priests the rare privilege of following their conscience rather than papal policy. The man might let him in or might turn him away or might call the Juvies. Best to avoid the confrontation entirely.

It's not the priest who troubles him now, though—it's the girl who served him his meal. She keeps looking at him. *Maybe she likes me,* he thinks. *Or maybe she likes the reward she'll receive for turning me in.* Not that the Juvies would pay much for him. It's not like he's the Akron AWOL. He steals a glance at her while she's busy scooping out food. She's cute in a restrained, every-hair-in-its-place kind of way. He wonders if she's working here for community-service credit in school or because she actually wants to work here. Then he finds himself irritated by his own curiosity. "Curiosity dismembered the dog" is an expression known by all AWOLs. He's known more than one AWOL who got caught because they stuck their nose somewhere it didn't belong because they were curious. He will not make the same mistake. Whatever this girl's interest in him, he's got to treat it as if she's a threat and get out as quickly as he can and never come back. It means more scavenging trash cans for food, but there are worse things.

3 · Miracolina

When she sees the boy get up to leave, Miracolina turns to Sister Barbara and says quickly, "Would it be okay if I left early, Sister? I have a test tomorrow." Another lie for confession.

Sister looks surprised but nods. Miracolina unties the apron, slips on her sweater, and hurries through the dining room. The boy is gone.

Dusk is already settling into night as she reaches the sidewalk. She looks left, then right, and finally spots him turning a corner. The church is in a middle-class neighborhood, but the area goes bad fast as the boy heads toward the freeway. She keeps a safe distance between them. He doesn't seem to hear or sense her behind him. She's been tailing AWOLs and Juvey-cops for a few months now and has gotten good at it.

When Miracolina was a tithe, she thought AWOLs were the worst sort. Criminals guilty of stealing a body that no longer belonged to them—allowing others to die because they were cowards. But ever since her misadventure with Lev, she's much more ambivalent about it. In fact, it keeps her up at night. It's become a bit of an obsession. She talks to Juvey-cops and muscled boeufs who track down runaways. She listens to them boast about their arrests. They don't seem to care about the lives saved by the lungs and livers going to cancer patients or the hearts going to cardiac patients or the lives improved by corneas and brain sections. It's adrenaline and quotas to them. A competition. A game. Nothing more.

Some nights she sneaks out in search of AWOLs when her parents are asleep. Sometimes she finds them; sometimes she doesn't. The adrenaline-charged fear of being alone in dark corners of the city has become like a drug to her. When she does talk to AWOLs, she finds that some are the criminals she thinks them to be. They run because they have broken any number of laws and feel little to no remorse for it. Whether their hearts were this toxic before they went AWOL is anyone's guess. That's just a very small fraction of AWOLs. Most of the ones she's met aren't so bad. They're basically decent kids and certainly have something to offer the world. A lot of them care so much for their friends or for fighting against unwinding that they would sacrifice their lives.

Kids like Lev.

Miracolina slips into a covered bus stop when she sees the boy ahead skirt a freeway overpass and head for a dimly lit pedestrian bridge instead. Her curiosity rises. He's moving toward a really seedy area. Her mother would just die if she knew Miracolina spends time there.

The boy still doesn't seem aware that she's following him. Her boots clang on the metal walkway, but the wind roaring around them and the cars thundering on the highway below muffle her passage.

She loses sight of him when she reaches the end of the walkway at the spiral staircase to the ground. She doesn't see him walking the main avenue to the factory district or the road to the dump or the streets to the bars, tattoo parlors, and strip joints that fill this part of town.

Perhaps she lost him and should go home. They're expecting her soon, and after her last disappearance, they're sure to overreact. And anyway, this boy is probably another of those loser AWOLs who can't tell her more than what she already knows.

But what if he is the one? What if he knows the secret? What if he can tell her how to turn herself from a bucket of spare parts into a normal girl?

With one hand on the staircase rail and one foot pointed back to the church, she grinds her teeth. She hates this worst of all. Not knowing what decision to make. Feeling that voice in the back of her head telling her that she should be more like Lev. In spite of the fact that he was a no-good clapper with a price on his head.

Tired of waffling, she runs down the stairs as fast as she can in pursuit, fighting the urge to go home. She resolves to give up if she can't pick up the trail in a minute or so.

Out of breath once she reaches street level, she hesitates for just a second, trying to decide which street the kid would have taken, when he grabs her from the gloom beneath the stairs.

"Who are you?" he rasps. With wiry strength he pulls her close to him. He stinks of sloppy joes and filth.

The AWOL underestimates her. She twists from his grip and shoves him hard. He smacks against the staircase and slides into the trash and weeds. When he starts to scramble away, she jumps him and pins his skinny self to the ground. Sometimes a healthy diet and keeping yourself fit for parts donation comes in handy.

"Settle down," she hisses. "I'm here to save you."

4 · Bryce

This must be the ultimate humiliation—not just to be bested by a girl, but to be bested by a girl who serves slop in a soup kitchen. He tries to wriggle out from under her, but the girl's got moves and keeps him pinned.

"Stop squirming, or I will hit you so hard you'll think you've entered the divided state." Then in one smooth motion she lifts him halfway to his feet and tosses him to the other side of the staircase, where they will be hidden from view of the nearly empty boulevard. The meager streetlights have come on, but the space behind the staircase, which smells of dirt and urine, is mostly dark.

"I'll kill you before I let you turn me in," he threatens, although he's not entirely sure whether he could follow through on the threat.

The girl is not intimidated in the least. "What about 'I'm here to save you' is unclear?" she says. "You can't be low-cortical, so you must just be stupid."

He ignores the insult. "Save me how? You mean go-back-to-that-church-and-confess-my-sins kind of saving? Because that's not going to happen."

"Your immortal soul is your problem," she says. "I'm talking about saving your hide, because in spite of your unwind order, it's only semiworthless, not entirely worthless." She shifts slightly so that the streetlamp lights her. "What's your name?" she asks.

Seeing her clearly makes him feel easier, but not easy enough to answer.

"Are you a Juvey-cop?" he asks.

She hoots. "Do I look like a Juvey-cop?" She straightens importantly. "I know what you're up against—I used to run with AWOLs."

He throws her a doubtful look, and she qualifies it.

"Well, with one AWOL in particular."

"What does that have to do with me?"

"Everything. That priest—the one at the soup kitchen—

Father Lawrence, he looks for AWOLs and does what his con-science tells him to do. He gets them to safety—and I'm a key part of that safety net." Then she looks him in the eye and asks, "Do you want me to save you or not?"

Bryce doesn't need some church girl to save him; he's been saving himself since he turned thirteen and his stepmother signed his unwind order. On the other hand, he could use someone who knew a safe way out of town . . . but safe passage can be expensive.

"I don't got any money."

"I don't want money. I just want to ask a question."

He tenses, which she must have seen even in the shadows. "But the question can wait. Let's go."

He doesn't move. "Go where?"

"I know people who can take you to where you'll never have to worry about harvest camps again."

She heads for the sidewalk and waits for him. Still feeling wary, he joins her.

She sticks out her hand. "My name is Miracolina Roselli."

He gingerly shakes it. "I'm Bryce Barlow."

She squeezes his hand hard. "Pleased to meet you, Bryce."

About four blocks later she opens the door to a small store between a pawnshop and a tattoo parlor. The sign above the door says JACK AND JILL EXTERMINATORS. On the roof floats a huge roach balloon. In the window a poster states virtuously WE USE ONLY ENVIRONMENTALLY SAFE PRODUCTS TO RID YOUR HOME OF PESTS.

Bryce stalls on the sidewalk. "Exterminators? I'm not a roach—I don't want to be exterminated."

"It's a cover for an AWOL rescue operation," Miracolina says impatiently. "It's supposed to be ironic. Now get in before someone sees you."

That makes him jump inside, and she shuts the door behind them.

226

The front office looks more like a school counselor's office than an exterminator's place of business. She holds open the small swinging door at the counter and prods Bryce through it. At the back of the office she rings a bell.

Immediately a voice sounds through the intercom, too distorted by static to distinguish whether it's male or female.

"Are you here for our termite special? A free inspection and ten percent off if you decide to use our service. Good till the end of the month."

It's a pretty lame code, but the girl presses the button and speaks into the grille as serious as if she works for the CIA.

"My fire ants are back."

In a moment the door cracks open. "That you, Miracolina?"

"Yeah, Jack. I got an AWOL here name of Bryce Bower. . . ."

"Barlow." Bryce corrects her.

"Bryce Barlow. Can you take him?"

"Of course."

A man in his late twenties with thinning red hair opens the door wider. He yells over his shoulder, "Jill, we got a guest."

A woman immediately appears at his side, the top of her head barely reaching his chin. She's wearing a moose oven mitt on her right hand and a wedding ring on her left. With a radiant smile, she pulls Bryce into a hug. He hasn't been held by anyone since forever, but after about five seconds he pats her back awkwardly. When she releases him, he has to turn away because he doesn't want anyone to see how watery his eyes have gotten.

"I'm so happy you showed up, Bryce. We have about a gallon of stew left over from dinner and several pieces of my famous rhubarb pie. Hope you're hungry."

Bryce, glancing at her oven mitt, says, "I could eat a moose, ma'am."

"Sorry, not on the menu," Jill says. "And don't be calling me ma'am. It's Jill." She leads him down the long hallway.

5 · Miracolina

Miracolina starts to follow, but Jack stays her with a hand to her elbow. "Let's talk."

They return to the office, and he peeks through the blinds for a second before turning to face her.

He smiles, but it fades quickly. "You've become our biggest customer, girl. How many AWOLs have you brought us? Five? Six?"

"Eight," she says. "Bryce makes eight."

He tries another smile, but it vanishes as he looks through the blinds again.

"What's wrong?" she asks.

His forehead has more worry lines than she remembers. Suddenly he looks decades older. "We lost thirty-one kids last week. Parts pirates took a van in Milwaukee. Two days later, they clobbered the safe house in Saint Louis."

She sucks in a breath. "Were any of them mine?"

He shakes his head. "No. But I'm not sure how long we've got before one of the kids that got taken cuts a deal with the pirates and tells them where we are and what we're doing. Don't bring any more kids till we find a new place and a new cover."

She frowns. "But what if . . ." She fizzles to a stop seeing the wretched look in his eyes.

Jack nods to the back of the house. "I can't trust anyone till I find out who's selling us out. I'm keeping intel down to just family—and now you. We got twenty-seven kids upstairs. Twenty-eight with Bryce. Later tonight we'll be driving them out in three vans to different safe houses, but I don't want you coming around here again. Hear me?"

She shivers, knowing the danger they're in, and feels absolutely furious that she can do nothing to help. "I hear you,

Jack. Promise me you'll tell Father Lawrence when you've got a new place. He'll let me know." She jerks her head to the back door. "Can I tell Bryce good-bye?"

Walking through the narrow house, she wonders what she'll do if she can't save AWOLs. This is how she keeps on living whole when she still has such a hard time believing she should be. She has a mission. Which she just lost to parts pirates.

Remembering the parts pirate that kept her and Lev imprisoned, she seethes.

In the kitchen Miracolina finds Jill ladling a second helping of stew into Bryce's bowl. Even after dinner at the soup kitchen, he's eating like he's starved. The boy must have gone shy, because he's pulled his hoodie low over his face. Jill's brother, Griffin, is wiping down the stove. He's got a shaved head and a bushy beard, but like Jill, he has a smile that can melt ice.

Jill pats Miracolina's cheek. "Eat some pie, girl." Then she nudges her brother. "Come on, Griffin. We got packing to do."

They leave Miracolina alone with Bryce, and she takes the chair across from his. Although she hears rustling through the walls, floors, and ceiling around her, for a building holding so many hidden kids, it's unnaturally quiet.

She's ready to ask her question, the one she asks all the AWOLs she finds, but Bryce pushes the hood off his head and leans closer to her.

"You trust these people?" he asks.

"Of course I do!"

"Even the guy with the beard?"

Miracolina looks at Bryce closely. "Why?"

Bryce shrugs. "Just asking." Then he holds up his bowl, which is empty again. "Could you get me some more?"

Miracolina goes over to the stove and fills his bowl again.

"You should pace yourself," she says. "Eat too much, too fast and—"

But she never finishes the thought. Because when she turns back, Bryce is gone.

6 · Bryce

It might be nothing. It might be just the paranoia that infiltrates every AWOL's thoughts. But it's a protective paranoia—it's there for a reason—and more often than not, when Bryce has had a bad feeling about something, caution has saved his life.

The guy with the beard might not be the same guy.

And even if it is the same guy, it might not be what Bryce thinks. What he saw in the alley last week might have nothing to do with AWOLs. For all Bryce knows, the guy is a tobacco dealer, selling cigs on the side to earn some spare cash. Who knows, maybe the money the guy makes dealing goes right into their AWOL-saving operation.

Or maybe not.

Bryce has a pretty sweet setup. There's an alley a few blocks from the "exterminators" behind a row of bars and pawnshops. There are three Dumpsters back there. Two are still in use, but the third one is in such bad shape, the lid has rusted shut—but there's a huge hole in the back, large enough for a person to climb through. He's filled it with pillows and sofa cushions and even has a sleeping bag he scarfed from a donation bin. So far no one's found his personal safe house.

He squeezes behind the Dumpster and climbs inside, belly bursting from all he's eaten, and peers out through one of many bullet holes in the old trash bin. No activity in the alley this early at night. Later there'll be things going on, though. It can be a regular entertainment zone out there. Mostly Bryce ignores it. The scum of the world doesn't bother him in his private domain, and he has no interest in bothering them. But once in a while he does see things. Like the time he was turning into the alley, and he passed two men in some sort of clandestine deal.

A lot of guys look like that, he tells himself. *It wasn't him. And if it was, why should I care? It's not my problem.*

But it becomes his problem again ten seconds later when someone climbs through the hole in the trash bin, invading his personal domain.

7 · Miracolina

"Don't be so surprised," says Miracolina, shining her phone light in his face. "You're not exactly a stealthy AWOL."

"Be quiet!" Bryce snaps. "No one knows about this spot— and if someone out there hears you . . ."

She lowers her voice to a whisper. "Why did you run?"

"I have my reasons."

"Something scared you, didn't it?"

"Will you lower your voice?"

Miracolina takes a deep breath, returns her voice to the faintest of whispers, and lowers her phone so it's not in his face anymore. "I need to know what spooked you."

Bryce doesn't say anything for a moment. Then he finally tells her "I saw someone who looked like Griffin taking money in this alley last week."

"Money for what?"

"I don't know."

Miracolina leans back against the rough trash bin wall. Could Griffin be selling them out to parts pirates? It seems unthinkable, and yet they know there is a leak. It has to be someone on the inside. Miracolina knows what she has to do.

"They're transporting all the kids in a few hours. So if he's making deals in this alley, then he'll be back tonight." She thinks about it and nods. "I'll wait here with you." She already called her parents, telling them she's staying overnight at the church to help in the shelter. They trust the nuns to take care of her. Tonight she's just compounding lie upon lie.

In the oblique light of her sideways phone she catches Bryce giving her a faint grin. "You don't mind being in a Dumpster with an AWOL?"

Miracolina thinks back to the time she was trapped in the tiny luggage compartment of a bus traveling cross-country with Lev. They barely had room to breathe, and Lev had to pee in someone's shampoo bottle. She smiles and finds it odd that this has somehow become a pleasant memory.

"I can handle it," she tells him.

An hour later, to Miracolina's profound despair and disappointment, Griffin makes an appearance in the alley. Both she and Bryce watch through the trash bin's bullet holes as he meets with a man who appears to be missing an ear. Although they speak quietly, and they're at least twenty yards down the alley, she hears enough of the conversation to know that Griffin is the one selling them out.

The question is, will Jill believe her, or her own brother? Then she realizes she doesn't have to convince her if she has evidence. So she raises her phone to the small hole and opens her camera app.

The roach balloon bobs mockingly over Jack and Jill Exterminators, looking far more threatening than it ever did before. They waited ten terrible minutes in the Dumpster after

Griffin left, afraid they might bump into him on the way back. Neither Jack nor Jill are answering their phones. The call goes straight to voice mail. Just as well; this has to be done in person, and Miracolina knows she can't bring this to Jill—she has to tell Jack. He'll know how to break the bad news to her that her brother has betrayed them. Miracolina doesn't want to see the disbelief and dawning despair in Jill's face. She doesn't want to be the one responsible for wiping Jill's smile away, perhaps forever.

The steel security screen is already down over the window, and the door is locked. No sign that anyone's inside. It's always like that after hours. Signs of activity would be suspicious. Miracolina jabs the bell and looks up at the camera she knows is hidden above them, to the left of the entrance, and gives a thumbs-up.

The door buzzes open, and Miracolina pushes Bryce through. The door from the front office to the back hallway is ajar, which means they don't have to go through the intercom code-talk to get in. They both slip through the front office and into the hallway that leads to the kitchen. It's quiet. Too quiet. For a second she thinks that Jack moved up the transfer, and the vans have already left with the kids. Which would mean they're on their way to being captured by parts pirates. Then she chides herself for panicking. It hasn't even been a half hour since they'd seen Griffin in the alley. She hears movement ahead of them, someone shuffling through cupboards, and they hurry to the kitchen . . .

. . . where Griffin is making himself a sandwich.

"Is that the AWOL AWOL? I'm surprised you were able to drag him back."

There's no sign of Jack or Jill anywhere. Bryce turns his back, opening the fridge and lowering his head to look inside. Miracolina can't imagine he'd be hungry at a time like this, and then she realizes that if he had seen Griffin last week on the way to his Dumpster, Griffin could have seen him. That was why he kept his hood low when he was here the first time. That's why he's poking his head into the fridge now. She stands in front of him, hoping it's not obvious to Griffin what they're doing.

"Can you check if there's a bed downstairs for him?" Miracolina asks.

Griffin spreads mustard with a rather sharp steak knife—but that's not the weapon she's worried about. There's a gun in his belt. It's most likely loaded with tranqs, but that's little comfort.

"He doesn't need a bed. We're moving up the transfer. I've already got my van, and Jack and Jill are out picking up the other two now. We should be ready to go by midnight." Then he goes to the fridge and pulls Bryce away. "Dude, y' can't leave the door open like that. Everything will spoil."

He closes the door and catches sight of Bryce's face. He studies it a moment too long. Then he frowns. "Why do you look familiar, kid?"

Miracolina feels an awful sinking feeling—but Bryce grins.

"I was just here for dinner, remember?"

"No—I've seen you before that. . . ."

Still Bryce just shrugs it off, playing the part for all he's worth. "Everyone says that, sir. I got an average-looking face."

Griffin isn't buying it. Shielded by Bryce, Miracolina gropes for something on the counter. Anything to use as a weapon.

Griffin's eyes narrow. "Were you hanging around an alley last week, off of Pershing?"

Miracolina grabs a glass pot full of hot coffee at the same time Bryce issues a general denial about hanging about in alleys of any kind, but it's too late—he's already been made. Griffin raises his gun, and Miracolina hurls the coffee in his face, then throws the pot at him.

As Griffin crashes against a cabinet, the gun goes off, a tranq dart embedding in the wall behind Miracolina. Fear gives them wings as they race upstairs, and Miracolina fervently thanks God when they find the door at the top unlocked. Behind them, Griffin is cursing and wailing his fury, clambering up the stairs, just a few feet away.

She slams the door and locks it, hoping that Griffin doesn't have the key with him. But even if Griffin had one, he's not in the frame of mind to use it. He begins kicking and hurling his substantial weight against the old door, until it crashes off its hinges.

Dressed for their night journey, kids are coming from bedrooms and bathrooms into the hallway to see what the commotion is. "Parts pirates!" Bryce yells, hoping that for these AWOLS it will be like yelling "fire" in a crowded theater.

A small Asian girl with pink barrettes pats him on the arm. "No, that's just Griffin." Then she gulps as Griffin storms forward, waving the gun.

The kids start to back away.

Now Miracolina builds on what Bryce said. "He's a traitor! He's selling kids to the black market! He's selling them to the Burmese Dah Zey!"

She has no idea if that last part is true, but it gets the desired response. The kids stop backing away and begin to make a stand. The little Asian girl and three large boys move forward.

"Stop!" yells Griffin. "I'm warning you!"

He tranqs two of the boys, but five more kids replace them.

Then the girl with the pink barrettes leaps at him, delivering the nastiest flying kick Miracolina has ever seen. It pushes Griffin against the wall, knocking the gun from his hand. And in an instant they are all over him. A dozen frenzied kids, punching him, smacking him, kicking him—Miracolina's afraid they might actually tear him apart.

Griffin's angry protests degrade to desperate pleas for them to stop.

Then Miracolina picks up the tranq gun. It slides comfortably into her hand. One by one the kids see her holding the gun as she moves toward Griffin, and they peel off him till only the girl with pink barrettes is left, sitting on his chest, punching him with enthusiasm. Bryce pulls the little girl away.

Griffin is bloody and bruised. It seems the fight has left him, but Miracolina will not take anything for granted. She holds eye contact with Griffin for a moment. Making sure he sees her raise the gun.

Griffin is not the least bit repentant. "You stupid little—"

She fires before he finishes the thought, and the last word comes out as a pained grunt. The dart embeds in his sternum. One second later he goes limp, out cold.

Miracolina sighs, knowing that she'll be lining up for confession tomorrow with Father Lawrence. Not for shooting Griffin, but for enjoying it.

When Jack and Jill return with the extra vans they need for the evening's operation, they realize very quickly that the situation has changed once they see Griffin tied up and unconscious. Miracolina shows them the incriminating pictures—but even without them, Jack and Jill believe her.

Jill is furious, and heartbroken—but to Miracolina's surprise, she's also relieved.

"Now that we know where the leak is, no more of our kids will fall prey to parts pirates on our watch."

Since Griffin knew the location of the new safe houses, the plan is abandoned, and Jack spends the rest of the night on the phone, arranging a secure location. They still need to leave tonight—there's no telling how many people know the kids are here. Best to abandon this location as soon as possible.

The question still remains what to do with Griffin. They can't turn him in—because sheltering AWOLs is currently just as illegal in the eyes of the law as pirating parts. They'd all be arrested.

It's Bryce who comes up with the solution. "Leave him here," he says. "When you take the kids to the new safe house, just leave him. He'll wake up, and everyone will be gone without a trace."

"And since he's already been paid for information," Miracolina adds, "he'll be more worried about retribution from the black marketeers than tracking you down."

Half an hour later the kids are loaded into the vans. Father Lawrence shows up to drive the third one. He's never afraid to get his hands dirty when salvation is involved—even if it's just salvation from the Juvenile Authority.

Miracolina notices that Bryce lingers, not getting in either of the three vans with the other kids. She hopes it's just because he wants to spend more time with her.

"You wanted to ask me a question," he asks her. "What was it?"

Somehow it seems odd to ask after all they've been through, but it's a question she asks every AWOL she helps.

"How do you dream of a future when you're not supposed to have one? How do you keep going when the world has disowned you?"

Some kids laugh when she asks the question. Others shrug it off and don't have an answer—but Bryce, to his credit, seriously thinks about it.

"I keep reminding myself that I'm right, and the world is wrong."

"But how do you *know*?"

He smiles. "I believe," he tells her. "I don't have your kind of faith, but I got faith in myself, and right now that works for me just fine."

Jack, having triple-counted the kids, tells Bryce there's room for him in his van, and Bryce tells him what Miracolina was fearing he might.

"I'm not going."

Jack tries to persuade him, but Bryce cuts him off. "Decision's final. I've been on my own for more than a year. I'm used to it. I like it that way. I'll be okay."

"And if you're not?" Jack asks.

"Then it's my own fault," he says. "I can live with that."

"You won't live with anything if you get caught," Miracolina points out. "You'll be unwound."

"I'll take that risk."

A few minutes later the vans drive off, leaving Bryce and Miracolina alone, dawn just beginning to break through a still, silent haze.

"Walk me back to the church," Miracolina asks him—although it's more like an order than a request. He's happy to do it.

"So, Bryce Barlow," Miracolina says playfully as they walk, "what do you want to do with this life you're not supposed to have?"

"Tons of things," he tells her. "I just don't know what they are yet, but that's okay. One thing I know—one thing I can feel in my bones—I'm going to be important. I'm going to *matter*. And people are going to know my name."

"You already matter to the kids you helped save today," she tells him. "Even if they don't know your name."

"Yeah, it's funny how that works, isn't it?" he says. "I mean, look at you—I bet you've touched the lives of lots of people who don't know your name. You're like this invisible connection between hundreds."

She stares at him, his words striking something deep within herself, and suddenly she understands. Her desire to be divided is not about the annihilation of self, but of the expansion of herself in the service of others. Being divided would connect her to hundreds, but there are many fulfilling ways to connect, aren't there?

"Thank you," she says as they reach the church.

He laughs. "For what?"

"Just because," she says. "Because I'd rather say thank you than good-bye."

"Well, in that case, you're welcome."

Then he turns and disappears into the misty dawn.

In the community center of the church some of the sisters are already getting breakfast ready, while the shelter guests still sleep.

"You're here early today, Miracolina," says Sister Barbara. "Don't you ever sleep?"

Miracolina yawns. "Once in a while." It's Saturday, isn't it? She'll spend some time here, then go home and sleep the rest of the day.

"Maybe you can help Sister Vitalis with her tapestry. She can't see well enough to do the work, the poor dear."

Sister Vitalis, named after the martyr Saint Vitalis (buried alive under a pile of rocks), sits in a corner trying to repair one of the church's tapestries. She seems to work at it morning, noon, and night with endless patience.

"Let me help you with that, Sister," Miracolina says, and the nun is more than happy to share the work.

Live like Lev. Miracolina thinks. That was the battle cry of the rescued tithes back in the Cavenaugh mansion. Do not give in to the urge to extinguish oneself in the waters of the world, but instead be a light above those waters to help guide the way.

Thank you, too, Lev, she thinks. Like her brief time with Bryce, she now realizes that her tumultuous friendship with

Lev is a gift. She can only hope he is still alive, so that she can someday repay him.

Sister Vitalis puts the tapestry into Miracolina's lap, graciously allowing her to take over. Now she knows she doesn't need to surrender her eyes to be the eyes of an old nun. And she doesn't need to surrender her sense of self to connect with others.

Besides—she's only fourteen. She has her whole life to be a martyr.

Rewinds

1 · 00039

Jigsaw. Rubik. Twist twist twist.

He chews on his thoughts like a piece of gum that has long since lost its flavor. 00039 still believes he might one day make sense of those thoughts. He has no choice but to believe, because losing the hope of having hope would be unimaginable. Almost as unimaginable as his existence.

"I know you all must be angry. Confused. You have every right to be."

School of salmon. Gaggle of geese. Murder of crows.

There are many others here in this group of diced-and-sliced souls. All are like him. They are ugly. They are scarred. They pass their timeless days babbling their own particular incoherencies. And fighting. Always fighting. But with whose hands do they fight? Does anyone know?

"I'm here to ease you through this. To help you find yourselves—and you will, I promise you that."

Pretty boy. Media star. First of his kind.

Different parts of 00039 remember the young man addressing them. He was the sparkling example of what could be. He was the dream before the nightmare. Camus Comprix. Unlike the dozens of rewinds gathered here on Molokai, Camus Comprix has gentle seams instead of jagged scars. Unlike them, his many flesh tones are well designed and symmetrical, expanding out from a dynamic sunburst in the center of his forehead. Unlike them, his hair, filled with textures and tints, redefines the very concept of style. He is a work of art. Unlike them. And yet he claims to be one of them.

00039 knows he is no work of art. Even though he has never seen himself in a mirror, he knows because he can see versions of himself reflected in the rewinds around him. All of them are in their teens, with no specific age. They are a mix of many ages. All of them are caught between what they once were and what they might become.

How did this happen? How did this terrible state of existence come to be?

Jigsaw. Rubik. Twist twist twist.

If only he could think more clearly. . . .

"I've been where you are," insists Camus Comprix, the golden child. "I know how painful it is—but you *will* integrate. The pieces do come together if you keep working at it."

It's comforting to hear, but nothing 00039 has seen here proves it. The only rewind ever to fully reintegrate is the one addressing them. If only 00039 could be just a little bit of what Camus is, it will be enough. So instead of resenting him, the rewind makes a decision to admire him. Camus was rewound, just like them. Yes, with much greater care, but he was rewound from bits and pieces of others.

00039 remembers his unwinding. Or rather, he remembers echoes of dozens of unwindings. When he first awoke, and regained awareness, he thought that he was living in a divided state—that the Juvenile Authority's propaganda must be true, and this is what it felt like to be alive, but divided. Soon, however, he came to realize that this was something very different. And when he realized what he was, he felt ashamed.

"What happened to you was a crime," Camus Comprix

says. "I can't change that. What I *can* do is teach you to live with dignity."

The rewind next to 00039 turns to him with disturbingly empty, mismatched eyes. "Snake," he says pointing to Comprix. "Janus. Lucifer." Then he smiles a twisted grin. "Lincoln, Kennedy, King," he says. "Bang bang! Police have no leads."

00039 doesn't know what he means and doesn't want to. Whatever it is, it's unpleasant. He ignores the rewind beside him and turns his attention back to Camus Comprix, so sharp in his military uniform, so convincing in his eloquence. 00039 wants to believe everything he says is true.

Messiah. Communion. Hallelujah.

Yes—perhaps this first born rewind *can* save him.

2 · Cam

He leaves the ward sick to his stomach. Not from what he sees, but from what he feels. There is no level of hell deep enough for Roberta and her colleagues. Yes, Roberta was sentenced to life in prison, but it's not enough. No punishment could *ever* be enough for having created these poor creatures.

No, Cam tells himself. *Not creatures. They are human beings.* Cam has finally come to see himself as human. It was a struggle to get there—to truly believe it. How much harder will it be for these rewinds, who do not have the advantages he had? They were not made from hand-picked parts. They were not created from the best of the best—they were hashed together from a random pool of Unwinds, without regard for anything other than their ability to hold a weapon. They were to be the start of a slave army—for when you're a collection of parts, you're not a person. You're property.

At least that's how General Bodeker saw it. Well, he's in

prison along with Roberta, and now the world has been left to deal with their prototype army of rewinds.

Cam, now a hero, volunteered to tend to them, and the military was more than happy to put them in his hands. Although Cam was just a cadet, everyone agreed that there was no one more suited to oversee the rewinds on Molokai.

The military sees him as a glorified babysitter—keeping the rewinds under guard and out of public sight. They don't care if the rewinds ever find peace and purpose. But Cam does.

"That was a good speech," says the military doctor catching up with him as he exits the rewind dormitory building. "I'm not sure they understood any of it, but it was very . . . inspirational." They head for the main complex nearly half a mile away. A golf cart is available to take him, but Cam would rather walk.

"Most of them understood," Cam tells him.

The doctor dons shades to guard his eyes from the harsh Hawaiian sun. "Yes, I suppose you would know."

Dr. Pettigrew clearly resents Cam's presence here. Good. Let him resent it. The man's orders were clear—he is to answer to Cam as if Cam is his superior officer. His resentment is a nuisance but not an obstacle. Cam will do what he needs to do here.

"The females seemed more attentive," the doctor says as they take the path leading toward the mansion, which is still the center of operations.

"The girls," corrects Cam. The doctor might see them as animals, but Cam won't let that mentality take hold in the way he speaks of them. There are fewer girls among the rewinds, reflecting Proactive Citizenry's bias in the creation of this prototype army. Cam is even more sympathetic to the girls than he is to the boys. Seeing them nearly brings him to tears each time. He has to remind himself that it could have been worse. Roberta could have created them all sexless.

Cam stops walking halfway between the rewind building and the mansion. Tall cane and bamboo rise behind him, hiding the rewind building from view. Before him are taro plants, to the edge of the cliffs—even from here he can hear the pounding surf. Molokai was once a leper colony, as isolated as a place could be. The world would be happy to make this a rewind colony and never think about it again. People can't abide the thought of killing them—but they do want to make the rewinds go away. That won't happen on Cam's watch.

"Planning a picnic?" asks the doctor, impatient at Cam's moment of reflection.

"I want you to set up appointments with each of the rewinds," he tells the doctor, who stares at him as if he hasn't heard correctly.

"Appointments? You can't be serious. With all due respect, they have the cognitive capacity of chimpanzees right now."

"And if we want to change that, we will start treating them as human beings, not a mob of apes."

Still the doctor hesitates.

"Or maybe you don't want that to change," Cam suggests, reading the man more deeply than he'd want to be read. "Maybe it's easier for you to see them as less than human."

The man bristles. "Spare me the psychoanalysis."

Cam smiles. The doctor is pushing forty, and he's being given orders by someone half his age. Cam allows himself a moment—but only a moment—to gloat over his position. "Appointments with each of them," Cam repeats, before continuing on to the mansion. "Beginning at nine tomorrow morning. And you'll be there with me for each interview." And he strides off, knowing the doctor has no choice but to make it happen.

• • •

Cam lives in the wing of the mansion where he first came to consciousness. Even with all the negative memories, this is, and has always been, home.

He finds Una out back, sitting in a lawn chair in the expansive yard overlooking the sea—the same place where he once looked at stars with the Girl He Can't Remember. He's learning to come to terms with that absence of memory. It's a melancholy that is filled by the presence of Una.

He quietly comes up behind her. She's just finished tuning one of his guitars and has begun to play it. She plays well, but never plays for others—and certainly not for him. She'll only play when she thinks no one is listening. He waits a few yards behind her, listening, until she senses his presence and stops.

"The humidity here warps the wood," she tells him. "Can't get a single instrument to sound right."

"Sounded fine to me."

She huffs at that. "Then they must have gotten your ears from the bargain basement."

He gives her an obligatory chuckle and sits beside her. "We should have brought one of *your* guitars with us. To show them how it's done."

"I'm sure there are plenty of my guitars on the islands," she says proudly. "People have crossed oceans for my instruments." Finally she takes a moment to assess him. "You spoke to the rewinds today, didn't you?" she asks. "How did it go?"

"Fine, I guess," Cam tells her. "No surprises." And then he adds, "I wish you would have come."

The air is too warm for a chill, but she shifts her shoulders and back as if she's had one. "It wasn't my place to be there. I would have been just one more thing to confuse them, and you know it."

"We're here to do this together," he reminds her.

Then she looks him dead in the eye. "Then give me something to do. I'm not an accessory for you to wear on your arm."

Cam sighs. "How can I give you something to do when I don't really know how to play this myself?"

Una considers that, then gives the guitar a single decisive pat. It resounds with a gentle thud. "Tell you what. You work on your melody, and I'll find my own harmony."

"The perfect combination," Cam says, then he reaches behind her, pulling the tie from her hair and letting her hair fall free.

"Stop that!" she says. "You know I hate that!"

But he knows she doesn't. He knows she puts that tie there just for him to pull it out. He smiles and playfully says, "Tell me how much you despise me."

"More than anything in the world," she answers, clearly suppressing a grin.

"Tell me how sorry you are that you married me."

She glares at him, but it's all for show. "I didn't marry you," she points out. "I married your hands."

"I'm sure there's a hacksaw somewhere on the compound if those are the only parts of me you want."

She puts the guitar down on the grass. "Just shut up, you stupid quilt." Then she grabs him and kisses him, biting his lower lip just enough for it to hurt. She'll never kiss him without first insulting him. He's grown to enjoy that almost as much as her mildly painful kisses.

Then, as she lets him go, she says something she's never said before.

"I don't know whose lips I'm kissing, but I'm starting to like them." Then she pushes him back in his chair so hard he almost falls over backward and thrusts the guitar at him.

"Your turn," she says. "Play something." And then gentler. "It'll relax you. Maybe give your mind a break from the rewinds."

He holds the guitar, which has grown warm from the midday sun. "Should I play something of Wil's?" he asks.

She looks at the hands that had once belonged to her fiancé, Wil Tashi'ne, and says gently, "No. Play something of yours."

And so he pulls together a brand-new tune for Una from the random fabric of this multitextured day. A tune that feeds and underscores the growing bond between them, without forgetting the ominous tone of the task before them.

3 · 00039

The rewind is escorted to a room down a winding hallway that he knows isn't winding at all. It's straight. It's only his mind that sees it otherwise. He knows that now. He knows that walls that seem crooked are not, and that oddly angled windows are actually perfect rectangles. The more he tells his mind this, the more his mind begins to accept it. Even his muscles are learning to cooperate when he walks. Camus Comprix was right. Integration will come, if he makes it happen.

They lead him to a room, and in that room sits none other than Camus and the doctor, who has never talked directly to him, just around him. About him. As if he's not present. While the doctor looks at his tablet, tapping in notes, Camus rises and smiles warmly, extending his hand in a gesture of greeting. 00039 puts his hand out to shake, but realizes he's thrust forth the wrong hand.

"Red mark. Fumble. Typo," he says.

Still, Camus smiles and waits for him to switch hands,

which he does. He shakes 00039's hand. "The word you're looking for is 'mistake,'" Camus says without an ounce of judgment.

"Mistake," repeats the rewind, owning the word and taking pride in that ownership. Good word. Meaty word. He'll remember it.

"You'll make a lot of them," Camus says. "And that's okay."

00039 nods and points to his own head. "Jigsaw. Rubik. Twist twist twist."

"Ha!" says Camus Comprix. "Tell me about it! Being rewound is like a puzzle in four dimensions!" He sits and gestures for the rewind to sit as well. The doctor continues taking notes, looking up occasionally, content to be excluded from the conversation.

Still not knowing what this is all about, the rewind says the only thing he can get out. "Riddler? Riddle me this?"

Camus takes a moment to decipher it, then finally gets it. "Ah! Big question mark on his chest, right? You're asking me 'why.' Why are you here."

00039 nods, but then realizes he shook his head instead. Still Camus knows what he meant.

"You're here so that we can get to know each other. And for me to help with anything you're having trouble with."

00039 takes a deep shuddering breath. Is there anything that he *isn't* having trouble with? It's not only a matter of where to begin but how to express it. First are the Enemies. The Enemies have been troubling him since he noticed them. He holds his hands up so Camus and the doctor can see the Enemies for themselves.

"Left-right," he says, looking from one hand to the other and back again. "This"—he raises his left hand, which is pale sienna—"hates this," he says, raising his other hand, which is a deep shade of umber brown.

The doctor looks to Cam, and Cam nods in understanding.

"Okay," says Cam. "So you've got one umber hand, and one of your brain bits is racist. Well, that brain bit is just going to have to learn to deal with it."

00039 nods, not entirely sure that's possible, but willing to let Camus take him for the ride.

"Think of it this way," Camus says. "There are a hundred men inside a submarine. They come from different places, different backgrounds. Some are decent, some are creeps, but they all have to work together or that submarine goes down. You're the submarine. The crew will learn to work together—trust each other, even—because they have to."

00039 nods. The only submarine that comes to mind is yellow, but he knows that doesn't matter. It's the function Camus Comprix is talking about, not the form.

"There's one more reason you're here," Camus says. "If you ask me, I think it's the most important one." Then he leans forward, giving more weight to what he's about to say. "You're here to find your name."

The rewind can't fully comprehend the thought. The brand on his ankle says 00039. That's the only designation he knows. The concept of being anything else makes the various parts of his brain chafe and itch.

"I'll bet there are lots of names kicking around your internal community," Camus says.

It was something that 00039 never considered before, but now that it's been suggested to him, the names come dropping out of his mouth. "Sean Ethan Armando Ralphy Deavon Ahmed Joel—"

The doctor looks up, raising his eyebrows. "Remarkable!"

Camus puts two pages in front of the rewind. On those pages are lists of names. "These are the kids who were unwound to create all of you. Find a first name, a middle name, and then a last name that really speak to you. Rewind your own name from this list, and that's who you'll be."

00039 furrows his brow as he concentrates, enough to make the seams on his face ache. He knows this is important. The first important thing he's been asked to do since being rewound. A number of names on the list have been crossed out. Names that other rewinds must have already taken. But more than half of them still remain. As he looks over the list, some names leap out at him as if rising off the page. With the name Keaton comes a flash of a blue room covered in posters and draped with dirty clothes that rarely made it to a hamper. With Miguel comes the memory of Christmas. And the last name Shelton almost makes him stand up and shout, *Here!*

He points to those three names. The doctor taps them out on his tablet, and Camus crosses them off the list. No one would have those names but him.

"It's a pleasure to meet you, Keaton Miguel Shelton," says Camus. He holds out his hand, and Keaton shakes it—getting the handshake right the first time.

He returns to the dormitory feeling he's accomplished something. And later that night, he receives a present in a box labeled for Keaton M. Shelton. It's a prewar plastic toy. A Rubik's Cube courtesy of Camus Comprix.

4 · Cam

The rewinds all receive names. There are far more names on the list than there are rewinds, so no one leaves without a choice. None leave feeling slighted.

Cam works to remember each of their names and faces. At first it's hard to tell them apart; they all have shaved heads that have barely begun to grow in, and the asymmetry makes it even harder. The human mind is designed to recognize faces, not mosaics, and the hodgepodge nature of their features leaves little for the mind to grasp. It isn't until Cam starts focusing on the scars that he begins to tell them apart. Every rewind has their own individual scar pattern. Soon he knows many of them by name—but not all of them. There are those who keep their distance, lurking in shadows whenever he's around. Cam chooses to let that go. If he gives them space, and enough time, they'll come out of their shells when they're ready.

Una has found her harmony. She now wields a camera, documenting the colony's progress.

"I have to choose my images wisely," she tells Cam. "I have to show the rewinds as both triumphant and tragic. People have to see them as human, but must always remember what a bad idea it was to create them."

Cam knows what she says is true, but it still hits him in a very personal place. "Like it was a bad idea to create me?"

"Oh please," says Una with a dismissive wave. "Why must it always be about you?" But then she considers it a little more seriously. "The world is full of bad ideas that turn into wonderful things," she says, and gives him a peck on the cheek.

5 · Keaton

Spirits are high in the rewind ward after naming day. There are fewer fights, more laughter. There are hints at real communication between the rewinds. Keaton is happy to watch, enjoying the change. The sense of a future is so much more compelling than an endless present.

He watches two kids attempt a game of checkers. They get

a whole five minutes into the game before one of them flips the board in anger, and guards have to pull them apart. Five minutes! That's a great start. Tomorrow it might be ten!

Then someone raps Keaton hard on the shoulder. He turns to see the rewind with hollow, mismatched eyes.

"Dirk," he says, and raps Keaton on the arm again. "Dirk Mullen. Dirk Zachary Mullen."

He keeps hitting Keaton until Keaton says, "Dirk. Yeah. Got it."

"You—me," Dirk says. "Part—part." And he holds up his right hand. It's the exact same shade of brown as Keaton's left hand—and Keaton realizes that those hands came from the same Unwind. They're a matching pair.

Suddenly Dirk grabs Keaton's umber hand with his. It feels strange yet familiar clasping those hands together.

"Brother-self," says Dirk. "Hand of my hand."

Dirk doesn't let go. Finally Keaton repeats, "Hand of my hand," and Dirk, satisfied, releases his grip.

"You—me, take no prisoners," Dirk says, then laughs. "Police have no leads."

The guards begin herding the rewinds into the cafeteria for dinner, and Keaton slips away from Dirk Zachary Mullen, finding a crowded table to make sure that Dirk can't join him if he wanted to.

Keaton eats, but he has no appetite because all he can think about is Dirk and those eyes. Most of the rewinds' eyes are mismatched—but it's more than that when it comes to Dirk. There was something Keaton saw in Dirk's eyes, and it frightens him. Because the something he saw . . . was nothing.

6 · Cam

Cam decides to allow the rewinds outside.

Not outside the compound's fence, of course, just outside of the rewind ward. Some who express an interest are given jobs, to add to their self-respect.

"Menial labor," Dr. Pettigrew notes, "is probably all they can hope for."

Cam won't dignify that with a response. For their leisure time Cam gives a group of them basketballs, and they are allowed to play on the court by the main mansion. Unwinds, Cam recalls, were monitored in harvest camps so that prices could be put on their muscle groups. Cam makes sure there are no video cameras watching them now as they play.

Cam still runs the many paths of the Molokai compound. He encourages the rewinds to run with him, leading by example. "Sound body will bring a sound mind," he tells them. "Teach your muscles to work together, and the rest of you will follow."

Some run with him; others walk the route more slowly, unable to coax their reformed selves into the complex concert of a jog. Some don't come at all. Cam won't force them. Everyone has a different timetable.

"Is it really wise to give them this much freedom?" Dr. Pettigrew asks, clearly thinking Cam a fool for not keeping them locked up in the ward. If it were up to the good doctor, the rewinds would be turned into institutional vegetables, unable to function outside of the rewind ward.

"They'll all be free eventually," Cam tells him. "They should learn how it feels now." He knows that the doctor is sending reports back to their superiors. Cam can only hope that they'll take Pettigrew's reports with a grain of salt—and that his own progress with the rewinds will be proof of Cam's approach.

But what if they want what the doctor wants? What if they don't care about rehabilitation—what if they simply wish to brush all these rewinds under a rug and make the world forget about them?

He must believe that if he can prove their value—their humanity—his superiors will see what a mistake it is to keep them locked away.

After today's run Cam finds Una in the mansion's grand living room. It's a place of many memories. It holds the mirror where he first saw himself. The large tabletop computer interface where Roberta coaxed his reintegration through pictures and torturous mental exercises.

Today Una also has pictures open on the table face. Her photos. She scrutinizes them intently.

"Come here. I want to show you something," she tells him.

The desktop is awash with digital photos of the rewinds, but she moves her hands across the tabletop screen, swiping most of the images aside and centering three. They aren't the best of her photos; these are grainy, and pixilated—as if they were taken from a distance, then enlarged. They are all of the same subject.

"This rewind here. Do you know him?"

Cam is a bit embarrassed to admit that he doesn't. Although he's made great efforts to treat each rewind like an individual, there are those who fall through the cracks—or rather, hide in the cracks. This is one of them. He probably stays out of sight when Cam is around. Cam knows he must have had a meeting with him, but he was probably one of the silent ones who didn't meet Cam's eye.

"Take a closer look," Una says. Then she enlarges the central photo. He has one umber hand and badly mismatched eyes that just seem to be staring off into nowhere. "He disappears when he sees me, so these are the only pictures I have of him." She thrums her nails on the glass surface. "Something about him bothers me."

Cam can see why. There is a vacancy about him that is . . . unique. Looking at him is like looking into an empty bag. "It's as if . . . ," Cam begins to say, but then banishes the thought before it has time to surface. Instead he says, "Hmmm . . . It looks like he's having trouble integrating."

Una takes a deep probing look at him. Cam hates when she does that. "It's more than that, and you know it."

"All I know," Cam says, his voice rising just the slightest bit, "is that every rewind has to be given time, and the chance to become who they are."

"What if they're not becoming anybody?" Una asks. "Not every collection of parts makes a whole."

Lockdown! The thought hits Cam like it used to in the old days. When there was a thought so dangerous, he dropped a firewall of self-preservation in front of it. He doesn't let the word escape his lips, however. Instead he clamps his jaw shut until the impulse passes and says in a whisper that's almost threatening, "Careful, Una . . ."

But Una is not one to tread lightly. Not even in a minefield. "Why?" she asks. "You think one soulless rewind means you all might be?"

This time Cam lets his mind go into lockdown rather than face the question.

7 · Keaton

Keaton twists, twists, twists the Rubik's Cube, never seeming to come closer to solving it. He gets a single row of matching colors, but trying to get the next row ruins the first. He fights through his frustration and tries again.

"You know, there's a trick," a guard tells him. "I can show it to you."

He holds out his hand, but Keaton holds the cube out of reach. "No. No trick. Figure it myself."

"Fine," says the guard. "Have it your way."

Keaton tries to give all his attention to the toy but can't help but be distracted by 00047. The one named Dirk.

Dirk is making plans. Keaton knows it but can't be sure what those plans are. That rewind isn't just dark; he's opaque, like obsidian, jagged and sharp. For a while Keaton watched Dirk try to win the favor of other rewinds, but no one would have anything to do with him. He's been shunned from the pack. They all sense that something is wrong with Dirk, although none have put words to it. Now Dirk just lingers and lurks, eats and sleeps. And he watches through those eyes that don't seem to have anyone living behind them.

"Bad one, that Forty-seven," one of the rewound girls says to Keaton. Most of the others still refer to Dirk by his numeric designation. "Ten-foot pole."

"I hear that," Keaton tells her. And although Keaton wants to keep a ten-foot-pole distance, Dirk is always singling him out for conversation—perhaps because Keaton's cold shoulder isn't quite as cold as everyone else's.

"You, me, vroom-vroom!" Dirk says. "Born to be wild, hand of my hand."

"Yeah, sure, whatever."

But "whatever" isn't enough for Dirk. "You, me, Oswald, Ruby, Booth, then bail. Police have no leads." He smiles an empty grin that couldn't be more chilling on a skeleton and grabs Keaton's arm, nails digging in. "Butch and Sundance."

Keaton tugs free. For a moment he thinks he's taken Dirk's hand with him, because he can still feel those fingertips gripping his arm long after he's gone.

The ward doors are left open during the day on Camus Comprix's orders. He doesn't want them to feel like prisoners. The doctor blusters about it, but he blusters about everything. He's placated when extra guards are put on duty.

The compound is well fenced off from the rest of the island. In most places it's a double fence with a twenty-foot no-man's-land between, but not everywhere. There's one spot where a jogging path is separated from an outside road by nothing but a single fence. It's where locals will sometimes gather to get a glimpse of the rewinds they've heard about but haven't seen.

It works both ways. The rewinds want to look out as much as the locals want to look in.

On this day Keaton takes the perimeter path, telling himself that he's just going for a jog, but he knows that's an excuse.

There are a few cars on the road, parked there on the other side of the fence. A few islanders wait for a rewind to show his face. Some are actually native Hawaiians, but just as many are sienna transplants from places they chose to get away from.

Keaton rests from his run, and a Hawaiian girl, sixteen, maybe seventeen, cautiously approaches the fence.

"Hello?" she says, like it's a question, not a greeting.

"Hi," Keaton says. "Scared? Don't," he says. Then corrects himself. "Don't be scared. I mean."

"Okay . . ." She seems a little scared anyway.

"Keaton," he says.

"Keliana," she answers.

Keaton points to his face. "Ugly. Right?"

But Keliana shakes her head. "No, just . . . weird."

It makes Keaton smile. He can deal with weird. And his smile makes her smile.

And then suddenly something eclipses them both.

Out of nowhere Dirk hurls himself against the fence like an animal, gripping it with his hands. Keliana gasps and jumps back.

"PROM NIGHT!" shouts Dirk.

"PROM NIGHT—BACKSEAT!" he snarls at Keliana with the nastiest of grins. "MAKE YOU LIKE IT! MAKE YOU LIKE IT!"

"Ew!" Then Keliana looks at Keaton like Dirk is somehow his fault, and she runs away.

"No!" calls Keaton desperately. "Him not me! I'm not him!" But it's too late. Keaton turns to Dirk. "Hate!" Keaton snaps at Dirk. "Hate you!"

Dirk doesn't seem to care. He just holds up his left hand. "Hand of my hand. Me, you, same."

The first rock hits the fence with a resounding rattle. The second one gets through, hitting Keaton on the arm.

He turns to see that the other island kids have armed themselves and are throwing stones at the two of them.

"Get lost!" they yell. "Stinking monsters."

"Ground beef!" one of them says, and the others laugh and start repeating it. "Ground beef! Ground beef!" Dirk is the first to run, but Keaton stands his ground a moment longer, until a rock hits his forehead and he realizes it's no use. They'll keep throwing stones as long as he remains a target.

"Ground beef! Ground beef!"

So he turns, leaving the path, and heads into the dense brush to escape them. His only consolation is that Keliana wasn't throwing stones too.

Rewinds sleep the sleep of the dead. Maybe because they've tasted it. When Keaton dreams, they're mostly variations on memories even more disjointed than normal dreams, because the memories are from dozens of different people. But when he dreams of things he's seen after his rewinding, those images are almost as sharp as waking life. He has a dream of Keliana. Of walking with her on Molokai's finest beach, which happens to be part of the colony compound. Is it so wrong for him to be dreaming of her? The doctor keeps expecting the male rewinds to be attracted to the girls among them—as if they are their own species. In nature even the most hideous of creatures are attracted to one another. But rewinds are not a species. The girls find the boys frightening and repulsive to the core, and the boys' disgust is returned in equal measure. There will be no brides of Frankenstein among this bunch. Keaton suspects no girl in the outside world will want to be with him, but the rules of dreams are different.

How infuriating it is, then, when he is shaken out of the depths of such a fine dream.

"Shawshank! Shawshank!"

It's Dirk. He whispers into Keaton's ear so close it doesn't sound like a whisper at all.

"Go away."

But Dirk won't leave him alone. "Shawshank! Now! Now!"

"Go away! Not your friend!"

Dirk grabs his umber hand. "Hand of my hand. You, me, now!"

Finally Keaton sits up, and Dirk points to the door of the ward. "You, me, now!"

The last thing Keaton wants is to get involved with whatever trouble Dirk has in mind, but somehow he's become Dirk's keeper.

There are two guards on duty at the rewind ward. One for the girls and one for the boys. Currently the male guard is not at his post—probably on a perimeter check. Security cameras are everywhere, but few of them are on. They are leftovers from when the facility was bustling with activity. Now it's just the two wards of dispossessed souls.

At the door, which is always locked from the outside, Dirk produces from his pocket a Proactive Citizenry security pass featuring the picture of some serious-looking man.

"Finders keepers," says Dirk.

No surprise there. The rewinds are constantly finding things left over from Proactive Citizenry's reign of this place. He taps the pass to the reader, and the door unlocks.

"Sesame," Dirk says with the same flat affect with which he says everything. But Keaton's emotions are anything but flat. Half of him wants to turn around and return to the comfort of his bed, but if he does, and Dirk gets into some kind of trouble, it will be bad for all of them, so Keaton follows the soulless rewind into the cricket-filled night.

In the stark silver light of a gibbous moon, Dirk leads them to the fence where the locals threw stones at them. The fence is high and rimmed with several rows of tranq-coated barbed wire. With a single prick you're rendered unconscious and fall, landing hard enough to break bones, and maybe your neck. For a rewind still integrating, he wouldn't be surprised if they just popped apart like Legos. The thought makes him queasy.

"Pointless," Keaton says. "Can't climb out. Pointless." He grabs Dirk's arm. "Back now. Late. Sleep. Better for you than this."

But Dirk shrugs out of his grip and walks farther down the fence . . . to a spot where there's a hole in the chain link, just big enough to squeeze through. Clearly the chain link was cut by bolt cutters—and probably from the outside. He once heard guards complaining about how the locals would sneak onto the property since some of the island's best beaches are on the compound. They rarely did it in the days of Proactive Citizenry because their guards shot trespassers on sight. But Cam's guards are all armed with tranqs, which are much less intimidating if you're not an AWOL unwind. Dirk must have found this hole the other day and concealed it. Now there's no barrier between them and the outside world. Keaton feels his heart begin to pound so painfully in his chest, he's afraid it might bounce right out.

"No!" Keaton says. "Not out there. Not yet. Not ready. None of us." Although he knows that's not entirely true. Some of them might be ready. He certainly feels he is. But Dirk is not. Keaton suspects that he never will be. Maybe that's why Dirk feels the need to break out.

Dirk looks at him with cool curiosity. "You, me?" he says. "Frank and Jesse? Police have no leads?"

"No!" Keaton insists. He can't deny there are plenty of rebellious brain bits that see a hole in a fence as an opportunity, but his will is beginning to exert coherence. Submariners. They must work together for the good of all, and right now, sailing back to port is the best strategy. "Go back now. Sleep. Forget this."

Dirk shrugs. "You lose," he says, then slams a rock he's been concealing into Keaton's head, knocking him out cold.

8 · Cam

Cam's ringtone is unique. He designed it himself. The first strains of Mozart's *Eine kleine Nachtmusik*, layered over "Hey Jude," layered over a Coltrane sax riff. It all blends together perfectly. Far better than he does, but it's a constant reminder at his lowest moments that a mash-up can either shine or clash—it all depends on the care one takes with it. At 2:19 a.m., however, he despises his ringtone. There are few who know his personal number, and none of those who do would call him at this hour unless there was an emergency.

He wants to let it go for a second ring, but Una stirs, and he doesn't want this—whatever it is—to wake her up, so he answers it, hurrying to the bathroom and closing the door.

As he suspected, the news is not good. There's been a breakout in the boys' ward.

"Two male rewinds are AWOL," Dr. Pettigrew says—his voice, as always, like an accusation. The idea of there being such a thing as AWOL rewinds, like AWOL Unwinds, sticks in Cam's mind like some bad stew meat.

"Two of them? Do we know which ones?"

"Thirty-nine and Forty-seven."

"Names, please."

"I don't know off the top of my head."

"And where was the guard?"

"He's got a million excuses. Didn't I tell you we needed more guards at night?"

Cam resists the urge to lash back. Told-ya-sos don't help the situation, but as much as Cam hates to admit it, Pettigrew was right. But before he allows this to rattle his confidence, he lays out a course of action. Scour and secure the perimeter of the complex. Then work inward. The most important thing is that they don't get off the grounds. If they do, the situation could mushroom far beyond any hope of damage control.

When he steps out of the bathroom, Una is already up and dressed. "Have they checked if any vehicles are missing?" Clearly she heard his side of the conversation.

"I'll take care of this; go back to sleep."

"Spare me the chivalry—you can use all the help you can

get." She tosses him his pants, then ties her hair back with a ribbon. For once he resists the playful urge to pull it out.

9 · Keliana

The party goes late. They always do. She probably should have stayed at her friend's house and slept on the couch—but her friend's furniture always smells like wet dog. Or maybe it smells of her friend's brother, who smells like wet dog. She should have stayed, but her house is only three blocks away. A five-minute walk. And the town of Kaunakakai is notoriously safe. Usually.

There are no silent nights in Molokai. The dark hours are alive with crickets and katydids. Sometimes the chorus can be deafening. As she walks home from the party, she has the sense of being watched. But of course that's typical. Whenever she walks alone in the dark, she feels that way. It's human nature. A primal survival instinct crying wolf. The feeling is no stronger today than any other time, so she dismisses it as she always does.

It isn't until she turns the key in the lock that a shape emerges from the shadows. His hand covers her mouth before she can scream—a hand that doesn't match the rest of him.

He pushes her inside, and although she struggles, he's much stronger. She knows it's a rewind, but until he speaks, she doesn't realize that she's seen him before.

"Prom night!" he says. "Win the bet!"

It's the horrible one from the fence. She sees his eyes now. Dead. Lifeless. That void in his eyes makes it all the more awful. She breaks free and finally screams—but realizes she's alone in the house. Her father works the night shift, and her mother is at a teacher's conference on Maui. The neighbors must have heard, but will they get here fast enough to stop him from reliving whatever horrific prom night his fragmented brain remembers and whatever twisted bet that particular unwind made with his sleazy friends?

She races to the kitchen, thinking she'll escape through the back door but realizing how unlikely that is. The kitchen has weapons, though. She reaches for the knife drawer, but he tackles her to the ground from behind. With her hand firmly on the drawer handle, the entire drawer comes out, sending knives and skewers and wooden spoons flying across the room—which means he has access to as many potential weapons as she does.

Standing above her now, he starts blathering out names. "Audrey, Katrina, Camille, Hazel!"

Are these girls that some unwind in his head once victimized? It isn't until he adds Andrew to the list that she realizes that they're all hurricanes.

"Category five!" he shouts over her screams. "Surf's up!" He's calling her a storm, and he intends to tame her.

As he moves toward her, she thrusts her hands out across the floor and grabs the first thing she can, swinging it at his head. It's an iron ladle. Not what she wanted, but she swings it hard enough to open a seam on his forehead. She swings again and again, and it keeps him at bay just long enough for a neighbor to arrive at the back door, pounding, then kicking the door.

The doorjamb splinters, the man bursts in, and the unwind turns tail, pushing past him—but not before grabbing the pistol from the man's hand. The rewind—now armed—disappears into the night. Only now that he's gone does Keliana burst into sobs, allowing herself to be comforted by her neighbor.

10 · Keaton

He regains consciousness, knowing he's not in his bed but not yet realizing where he is, or why he's there. Then awareness begins to shoot back at him in staccato machine-gun bursts. Outside. Perimeter fence. Hit in the head. Dirk! It was Dirk!

What time is it? It's still night. Does anyone know they're gone? Probably. There's a gash on his temple. It's stopped bleeding. He's sure he didn't lose much blood, but he's still dizzy when he gets up. Concussion? Possibly. Not important now. What's important is finding Dirk. So Keaton squeezes his way through the hole in the fence, birthing himself into a world he might be ready for, but is certainly not ready for him.

He follows the road for more than a mile until he reaches a portside town. It's still dark, and morning seems no closer. There seems to be a lot of activity for this time of night. Lights are on in many homes. Cars are on the street. It doesn't occur to him to think why. He's too focused on searching for Dirk. He will be hiding in the shadows. Lurking. That's what Dirk does. Even in the light of day he lurks. It's only when he sees a line of people with flashlights that Keaton realizes this is a search. It seems half the town is up, and Keaton knows who they must be searching for. What the hell did Dirk do?

Keaton hurries to duck into the cover of some bushes, but one of the flashlights catches him.

"Look there! I think it's him!"

They start running in his direction, and he pushes through the bushes and into a backyard, leaps a hedge, and is out on another street. But there are people everywhere. He's spotted again, and another half dozen people take chase. At the end of the street, headlights light him up for everyone to see.

"It's him!" someone shouts. "Look, he's got one umber hand and a cut on his forehead—just like Keliana said!"

He spins, looking for an escape route, but there is none.

He's surrounded on all sides, and he knows that the crowd around him senses triumph. They move in.

"No!" he shouts. "Eraser! Fumble! Red X!" He forces the right words. "Mistake! You're making . . . a mistake!"

And a boeuf-looking teen closest to him—one of the ones throwing stones the other day—glares at him with a brutal look of hatred and says, "You're the one who made a mistake. And it's going to be your last."

11 · Cam

"This could be worse," Una tells Cam as they drive the short distance to Kaunakakai, followed by a whole military entourage.

"Really? How?"

"The girl could have been hurt, but she wasn't."

Practically the same moment the security detail found the hole in the perimeter fence, the call came in from the Kaunakakai sheriff about the attack.

"One of your damn monsters came after a girl." The sheriff had spoken with such seething vitriol in his voice it made Cam wince. "I want you to know I'm authorizing the use of deadly force."

Cam pounds the steering wheel of the jeep hard enough to bruise his hand.

"Easy," says Una, "that won't help anyone." Then she adds, "Besides, those hands were meant for better things."

He takes a deep breath and tries to dispel his frustration. This is entirely his fault. He should have given in to everyone else's paranoia. He should have treated them like prisoners. He should not have let his personal feelings get in the way. Maybe the rewinds need to prove their humanity before it can be granted to them. But he knows it's not all the rewinds, is it? There's only one that's a problem. One that's profoundly different from the others. Number 00047. Dirk Mullen. Even when he chose his name, he just pointed randomly to the page, as if he didn't care. As if he knew his existence didn't warrant a name. For so long Cam had obsessed over whether or not he himself had a soul. Now he realizes he must. Because he's seen into the eyes of one who doesn't, and that void within—whatever it is— is the very definition of hell.

"Of all the rewinds to escape, why did it have to be Forty-seven?"

"What about the other one?" Una asks.

"Keaton," Cam says. Dirk might still be a number, but Keaton is not. "I wouldn't be surprised if Forty-seven killed him."

"I hope not," Una says. "He's a good kid."

"They all are," Cam points out, then has to qualify. "All but one."

They're headed to the police station, but a commotion on what should be a quiet residential street pulls their attention. Shouts and headlights and revving engines, like some sort of street race—then the blast of a shotgun followed by silence.

"I was wrong," Una says as they turn a corner and race toward the crowd. "This *couldn't* get any worse."

12 · Keaton

Five minutes before Cam and Una hear the gunshot, the mob's emotion reaches a fever pitch. They will have justice. They will not wait for it to be meted out; they will take it themselves.

Keaton cannot speak. They have gagged him. But what would it matter if he could? They did not listen to his protests before; why should they listen to him now? They have their man. He fits the description. And what are the chances, really, that there'd be two rewinds running around town? Much less two rewinds with one umber hand and a cut on the forehead?

Keaton knows from their angry shouts what Dirk has done. Not the details but the gist of it, and it's enough. He doesn't blame the crowd for what they're doing. Were he one of them, he might do the same. Or maybe not. Because their choice of punishment is far too visceral, and Keaton feels the terror of every single Unwind within him. A hundred screams fill his head.

They have him stretched out on the ground in the middle of an intersection with ropes tied to each arm and each leg. The ends of those four ropes are tied to four vehicles, each pointed in a different direction. The ropes are slack now, but they won't be for long.

The boeuf-looking teen gets in his face—the one who probably threw the first stone the other day. He's so incensed, spittle flies from his mouth when he speaks.

"You're gonna die, you know that, don't you?"

"You tell him, Todd," goads one of his buddies.

Keaton doesn't give him the satisfaction of mumbling from behind the gag.

"This is what they used to do to people who didn't deserve to live," Todd says. "Back when punishment fit the crime. It's called quartering. We're gonna pull apart what never shoulda been put together in the first place."

Engines rev. He feels vibrations in the ropes. They pull just taut enough to make his joints ache. He can hear people in the crowd talking to one another. Some are entirely on Todd's side and wait for this horrible circus to commence. But there are other voices too. "This is going too far," he hears a woman say. "Someone should stop this."

Someone. Not her. The faint voices of protest aren't really

interested in stopping this, Keaton realizes. All they want is to assuage their own guilt, so after it happens, they can say to themselves, *Well I wanted to put an end to it, but nobody listened.* Which makes them just as complicit as the others.

Engines rev again. He closes his eyes and tenses his muscles, but he knows that he is no match for the horsepower in those four vehicles.

Then he hears a girl's voice. She's cursing. She's yelling at people to get out of her way. He opens his eyes to see her pushing through the crowd. Her eyes are red from crying. Her jaw is hardened in resolve—but as she looks at him, her expression changes. Her head tilts a bit. She suddenly looks confused. Troubled, but in a different way than she was just a moment ago. Keaton recognizes her, too. This is the girl who came up to him at the fence. The one who was kind to him. Keliana. He resolves to hold eye contact with her for as long as he can, until the cars throw their transmissions into gear, which will be any second now.

"This isn't him!" she says. Quietly at first, then again, more loudly. "This isn't him!"

Todd storms to her like he might strike her but doesn't. "What do you mean it isn't him? Of course it is!" He tries to move her away from Keaton. "You let us take care of this! He's hurt you enough."

"No!" She shakes him off and comes closer to Keaton. "You can't do this!"

Todd ignores her and raises his hand, signaling the drivers.

Then a shotgun blast rings out. It brings everyone to silence.

Another man—a police officer, maybe the sheriff—comes forward, holding the shotgun he has just fired into the air.

"She says you have the wrong rewind. You want to go to prison, Todd? Not just for murder, but for killing the wrong man?"

"It's not a man!" screeches Todd.

"That's right," says the sheriff calmly. "It's a boy. Now cut him loose."

That's when Cam and Una arrive on his other side.

"Untie him, or I swear to you, every one of you will be held accountable!" the sheriff warns. The spirit of the mob seems to melt into the ground. It's no longer a mob but a bewildered group of people, sheepish and ashamed. Now people crowd around Keaton, untying him. It's Cam who takes the gag from his mouth, and Keaton coughs, choking on his own saliva.

"It's all right, Keaton," Cam says. "It's all right."

He tries to stand, but his joints ache from the strain, as if he'd been on a medieval rack. Una helps him to his feet. He turns and finds Keliana, who is still there, but keeping her distance. He holds up his umber hand to show her. "Not me!" he says. "Left hand, not right!"

"I know," she says.

Then the sheriff calls out to the crowd. "Everyone better get yourselves home before I remember who was here tonight."

People begin to meander away, then, from the edge of the crowd, someone says, "Hey—where the hell is my Harley?"

13 · Cam

Cam's brain has begun to feel disjointed. Fragmented. It always does when stress starts to overwhelm him. He can't let it happen. Not now. *Lockdown*, he says to himself, and clamps down on his panic. The crew of his own personal submarine must not mutiny.

The first clue to Dirk's whereabouts is the missing motorcycle. While the mob was focused on lynching Keaton, Dirk must have snuck in right behind them and, masked by the mob's frenzy, taken off. Now he's loose to do whatever damage he intends to do. Cam suspects the attack on the girl will not be an isolated incident. Unless they can catch him, it's going to be a rampage, and there's no telling how bad it will be.

A part of Cam wants to run, just like Dirk trying to escape the mob's judgment. But he can't. He won't. He looks at Una, and, as always, her presence stabilizes him.

"You didn't make him," Una says, reading him better than he reads himself. "What he did—what he is—it's not your fault."

"No," Cam admits. "But the fact that he escaped—that *is* my fault. Which means I'm accountable for anything that he does."

There's nothing she can say that can soften that reality.

"I'll deal with the fallout later," Cam says. "What matters now is that we catch him."

As he looks around, he sees more and more military personnel from the compound arriving, not quite outnumbering the mob, but their presence begins to subdue the worst of the hatemongers even more than the sheriff's presence had. Some people leave, but more linger, probably anticipating a more accurate reckoning. Not mob justice, but at this point any justice will do.

With the support of troops under his jurisdiction, Cam tells the sheriff, "We'll take it from here. This is our problem."

But the sheriff isn't about to yield. "It stopped being your problem when your *thing* attacked that girl." For a moment it looks like there's going to be a standoff, until Keaton comes between them.

"Sunset!" he says. "Into the sunset!"

Keaton sputters and grimaces, trying to force coherence to his thoughts.

"What's this one babbling about?" asks the sheriff, with no patience for it.

"Shh!" says Cam, and gives Keaton time to form his thoughts.

"Ride . . . into the sunset," he says. "Dirk. Dirk doesn't know. He doesn't know!"

And Cam gets it. "Dirk doesn't know we're on an island!"

Keaton smiles. "On the nose! Dirk doesn't know!"

Cam has become pretty familiar with the roads on Molokai. For Dirk, taking off into his metaphorical "sunset," couldn't have been west, or he'd have passed right through the most populated part of town. He would have headed east, away from the populated areas. He'll be on Kamehameha V Highway, which wraps around the eastern tip of the island and doubles back along the north shore.

"How could he not know this is an island?" the sheriff asks.

"His mind hasn't integrated as well as the others," Cam explains. "He probably can't think clearly enough to figure it out. The moon has already set, so he'll have no way to gauge his direction, and it's a slow curve going around the eastern tip, so he'll think he's going straight. We just have to cross a few miles to the north shore, and we'll catch him as he loops back."

"And if you're wrong?" the sheriff asks.

"I'm not," Cam says, then looks to Keaton. "We're not." But just to be sure, Cam sends a fleet of jeeps down Kamehameha V Highway in pursuit. Then he and the bulk of his forces cross the narrow width of the island to the north shore and wait for Dirk to arrive.

14 · Dirk

Me. Wheels. Road. Squint. Face. Wind. Vroom-vroom. Ocean on the right. Ocean on the right. Smarter than them. Faster than them. Vroom-vroom. Ocean on the right. "Born to be Wild." Steppenwolf.

Lone wolf. No one catches a lone wolf. Stupid people. Killing Keaton. Stupid Keaton. Saw them do it. Saw them tie him. Rope, rope, rope, rope. Car, car, truck, van. Stretch Armstrong. Couldn't watch. Took Harley. No one saw. Stupid people.

Parts of me know how. Clutch. Accelerator. Vrooom-vrooom. Parts don't know how. Make 'em learn fast. Almost fall. Learn quick or die.

Me. Me. Me. Not like other rewinds. Know that. Hate that. Think they're better than me. Better than them. Hate them. Keaton dead. Hate all the rest. Make them pay.

Still night. Still of the night. Morning soon. Let freedom ring. Far from here. Vroom-vroom. Ocean on the right. Heading south? North? Doesn't matter. Free either way. Find something pretty. Curvy. Prom night. Make her like it. Win the bet. Make them all like it. Smarter than them. Stronger. Stupid girl. Find her someday. Kill her for hurting me. But not now. Later. Later than you think. Dawn. Horizon. Ocean on the right. And ahead? And ahead?

No!

Can't be! Jeeps and police and boeufs. Roadblock. And Camus Comprix. Can't be faster than me. How are they here? How?

And Keaton.

Dead? Not dead? Ghosts. All ghosts. Are they?

Bird at my ear.

Not a bird. A tranq.

Missed.

Nowhere to go.

Pffft. Missed again.

Ocean to the right. And a pier. Nowhere else to go. Vroom-vroom. Road, road, then wood. Wheels on rattling wood. A shack at the end of the pier. Nowhere else to go.

15 · Keaton

The sharpshooters aren't all that sharp. "It's the tranqs," they complain. "They don't behave like standard bullets. It's not our fault we missed him." No one wants to take responsibility for Dirk.

No one but Cam. Keaton can see the torment in Cam's face. He wishes he could ease it. All Cam did was try to give them some dignity. It worked for Keaton. It worked for all the others. But not for Dirk. Because Dirk is different. Dirk is missing the spark. Which means there's nothing holding him together but stitches.

There's a small burger joint at the end of the pier. This is where Dirk goes to take refuge. The motorcycle skids out from under him as he nears it. He gets up limping. The sharpshooters try to tranq him again. They take down a seagull. It would be funny if things weren't so dire. One tranq shatters a window, saving Dirk the trouble of having to do it himself. He shoots back once with his stolen pistol—a wild shot that disappears into the dawn, then he climbs in through the broken window to escape the barrage of tranqs. *Does he understand what happened?* Keaton wonders. *Has it finally occurred to his fragmented mind that they're on an island? That all things here come full circle?*

"He's cornered," Cam says.

"He's armed," Una warns.

"He could jump," suggests the sheriff. "Swim to shore and escape."

Keaton shakes his head. "Davy Jones," he says. "Sink. Drown. Rewinds can't swim. Not yet. Must learn again. Harder than motorcycle."

One of Cam's military officers suggests they take the whole building out. "A single mortar shell could do it."

"That pier is a landmark," the sheriff points out.

The officer shrugs. "Doesn't a landmark need to be on land?"

"We're not blowing anything up," Cam announces. "Can we get close enough to shoot a canister of tear gas inside? Smoke him out?"

They throw ideas back and forth. Keaton has one of his own, but he's not going to tell them. They'll just dismiss him.

Keaton begins to walk down the pier.

"What the hell is he doing?" shouts the sheriff. "Get back here!"

Keaton ignores him. Let them tackle him or tranq him. That will be the only way to stop him. He knows what he needs to do. Hand of my hand. He and Dirk are, in some twisted way, family, and family takes care of its own. Cam must understand this, because Keaton hears him say, "Let him go."

Dawn evolves into sunrise in the minute it takes to reach the shack at the end of the pier. There's blood on the motorcycle lying on the wooden slats of the pier. Blood on the windowsill Dirk climbed over. Behind him military boeufs take position on the pier, weapons drawn, but keeping their distance. Keaton glances back at them once. Then climbs through the window.

Dirk sits in a corner. His pants are ripped, and his leg is torn open from when he flew off the bike, right along one of his rewound seams.

"Dead!" Dirk shouts, waving the gun carelessly "Saw you! Dead!"

"Almost dead," Keaton says calmly. "They let me go. Knew it was you, not me."

"Stupid people."

Keaton sits beside him. Says nothing. He waits to see what Dirk will do. He wonders if Dirk will shoot him. Or maybe, realizing there's no way out, shoot himself. But then it occurs to Keaton that Dirk would never do that. It's a choice that Dirk is incapable of making. You have to be alive to kill yourself. A wave of pity suddenly washes over Keaton. What must it be like to go through the motions of life, yet not be alive? Keaton knows he himself lives, because he has compassion for this poor unfortunate creature before him. A creature that is doomed to be nothing more than a collection of parts.

Dirk suddenly grabs his hand. "Hand of my hand. Die with me? Butch and Sundance?"

As one stray memory in Keaton's internal community recalls, Butch Cassidy and the Sundance Kid died in a hopeless shootout. Keaton has no desire to re-create that scene. "No," says Keaton, and instead says, "George and Lenny."

Dirk looks at him questioningly. He doesn't get the reference. Just as well.

"Give me the gun, Dirk." It is perhaps the first complete self-motivated sentence he's said.

Dirk's dead eyes narrow. "Why?"

"Because I asked."

"Why?"

Dirk holds the gun tighter. He aims it toward Keaton, and Keaton studies his eyes for a hint of anything. But no. There is no torment, no remorse, no fear, or even resignation. He could shoot Keaton. But he doesn't. Instead he hands the gun to him.

"I shoot bad," Dirk says. "You better. Talk better, think better, shoot better."

"Probably," admits Keaton.

"You go shoot them. Shoot them all. Is what we have to do. Take no prisoners."

Keaton looks at the gun in his hand. His umber hand doesn't know how to hold it, but his sienna one does. In fact it feels almost familiar. He wonders what that's about, but then decides he'd rather not know.

"No prisoners, Dirk."

16 · Cam

This was a mistake. He knows it. Just one more in a whole series of mistakes. He should have gone in there himself. Yet he knows if he had, Dirk would have shot him dead in an instant. Keaton was the only one who stood a chance. But how do you reason with a creation that knows no reason? Not even its own reason to be?

"We can still take out the structure," suggests his mortar-happy officer. "If all else fails."

Then a single gunshot splits the morning, sending the gulls flapping from the pier like a release of doves. Cam holds his breath.

The front door of the burger shack opens, and Keaton steps out. The gun is in his hand by his side. All weapons on the pier are trained on him.

"Lower your weapons," Cam orders.

They obey. Keaton walks down the pier toward Cam and puts the gun in Cam's hand.

"Done" is all Keaton says. Then he climbs into the passenger seat of the nearest jeep and closes his eyes, waiting for whatever's coming next.

There's an old leper cemetery by a rustic white church on a western Molokai bluff. Dirk is buried with a small ceremony by a military pastor. No one else is in attendance but Cam and

Una. The pastor says his litany by rote. Words about God's mercy, everlasting life, and how Dirk's soul is now remanded to the Almighty. It makes Cam grimace, feeling himself a hypocrite to be party to the travesty. But then who is he to decide if Dirk truly was soulless? Better to err on the side of grace.

The whole incident of Dirk's escape and subsequent death is reported to Cam's superiors in Washington. Dr. Pettigrew writes a scathing indictment of how Cam handled it—but it is balanced by the account of the sheriff, who, to Cam's surprise, commends Cam for his leadership in the crisis.

In the end there is no official inquest or investigation. Not even the obligatory slap on the wrist.

"Are you disappointed?" Una asks him once things slip back into a shade of normality around the compound.

"Actually, yeah. A little." The truth is, the whole Molokai compound is an albatross around the neck of the military, and the rewinds are so unloved as to be completely ignored. Now Cam realizes that he's no different. He was once the military's shining star, now he's the reminder of their unchecked hubris. Clearly they'd rather not be reminded.

"Being ignored has its advantages," Una is quick to point out. "Dignity doesn't grow under a microscope."

Three weeks after the incident there is a day of rejoicing. A new milestone in the lives of the rewinds. Six of them—three boys, three girls—the six most well-integrated—will begin attending Molokai High School. Tenth grade—arbitrary since their internal communities range from thirteen to seventeen, but it seemed unnecessarily cruel to make them freshman. To Cam's surprise the suggestion of allowing the rewinds to attend Molokai High came from the local population—perhaps as a response to the hatemongers. Sometimes prejudice can be slapped upside the head by tolerance. Especially now that people in town have come to see Keaton Shelton as a sort of folk hero.

The night before their big day Cam and Una hold a dinner for the six school-bound rewinds in the formal dining room where Proactive Citizenry once wined, dined, and bribed the movers and shakers of the world. No longer are these rewinds wearing drab convalescent scrubs. The boys are in jeans, with comfortable shirts, and Una made a trip to Honolulu to find the latest fashions for the girls.

Dinner conversation is upbeat and only a little bit disjointed and stilted. After dessert the half dozen rewinds cajole Cam and Una to play guitar for them, an impromptu duet that ends the evening. It took the rewinds themselves to convince Una to play in front of an audience—something Cam could never do on his own.

Then the evening concludes, but as the others board golf carts that will take them back to the rewind ward, Keaton lingers. He comes up to Cam and points at his own temple.

"Someone here played guitar, but badly." Then he holds up his umber hand. "This hand played drums, I think, but no memory of it." He sighs.

"How are you feeling about tomorrow?" Cam asks him.

Keaton smiles. "Got butterflies. But they're good." Then he thinks for a moment. "Hardest part . . . is that I don't know what I don't know."

Cam gets that. Every one codes and stores memories differently. When it comes to education, a rewind's mind can be like swiss cheese. Keaton might know the history of the world but have no concept of the order of it all.

"You'll figure it out," Cam tells him. "Be patient."

Keaton accepts the advice. "Left a present for you," he says, and nods toward the living room. Then he turns and boards a golf cart with two of the rewind girls, who laugh and talk with giddy anticipation about tomorrow's reentry into the human race.

Cam can't help but smile as they ride off.

"Look at you," Una says, taking his hand. "The proud papa."

"Nah," he says. "Just an older brother."

Una goes upstairs. It'll be an early, and eventful, day for all of them tomorrow. A momentous day. Best to get a good night's sleep. But before heading upstairs for the night, Cam detours through the living room. At first he doesn't see Keaton's gift, because it's just sitting on a coffee table, masquerading as a paperweight. When he finally notices it, he laughs with pleasant surprise.

Sometimes the most meaningful gifts are the ones that come back to you. And for Camus Comprix, no gift could be more meaningful than an old Rubik's Cube, perfectly solved.

Unknown Quantity

1 · Argent

Argent Skinner could not keep the right half of his face.

He had desperately wanted to. He had watched through the UNIS machine's little window as Nelson was unwound. He found himself unmoved by the man's screams and found he had no pity whatsoever for Nelson. Argent wondered if that made him a bad person. Well, who cares. He saved Connor Lassiter, who has since been rewound and is kicking ass in Washington. That made Argent a hero even if no one ever knew—and every hero should be allowed to enjoy at least one moment of revenge.

The plane was already in the air by the time UNIS was done with Nelson—but Argent had then realized his dilemma. If Argent brought the biostasis container holding the right half of his face to Divan, Divan would know what he had done. Divan Umarov, king of the Western world's organ black market, believed Argent to be too dimwitted to even conceive of doing something so brash. It was a perception that worked in Argent's favor, allowing him to get away with many things . . . such as relabeling all of Connor's crates.

Little did Divan know that the parts his buyers paid millions for weren't Connor's parts at all. They belonged to some random AWOL whose name Argent couldn't remember.

If Divan knew what Argent had done to Nelson, Argent

would become an unknown quantity in Divan's eyes. That would be a problem. Divan had allies and enemies; anyone who fell somewhere in between could end up dead. Ever since the day that Risa escaped with most of Divan's Unwinds, the man had been ordering the death of anyone he had questions about.

So Argent denied himself his ultimate victory and sat back as all of Jasper T. Nelson was sold off piece by piece to greedy buyers. Divan never even knew that lot 4833 wasn't one of his AWOLs.

That was months ago. Now Argent bides his time, serving as Divan's valet to the best of his ability, waiting for the day the man keeps his promise to Argent and allows him to choose a new face—a whole one—to replace the scarred half of his own and the biobandage that covers his right half like a mask. Argent has no doubt that his employer will keep his promise. Divan Umarov is many things, some of them unthinkable, but Argent knows that above all else, Divan is a man of his word.

2 · Divan

Business could not be better. With the United States government caving to the conscience of its people, leading to the temporary halting of all unwinding, the call for parts worldwide has been great. Prices have tripled, and Divan finds he cannot keep up with the demand. If the ban on unwinding becomes permanent, and spreads to other nations, he and the Burmese Dah Zey will be the sole sources of quality parts. And since the Dah Zey does not deal in brain tissue, he will have a distinct advantage.

The Dah Zey knows this and wants him taken out of play more than ever before.

For this reason Divan has been forced to purge his ranks of anyone he does not trust and to keep himself at a level of paranoia that, considering the circumstances, could save his life.

Today Divan watches a news clip over and over in the vaulted "great room" of *Lady Lucrezia*, an Antonov AN-255—the largest aircraft ever built. All the comforts of home, at thirty-seven thousand feet. His valet comes in with a carafe of coffee.

"Skinner," Divan says, pointing at the news clip, "have you seen this?"

On-screen is a talk show. Featured guests are none other than "Connor Lassiter" and Risa Ward. Divan notes the way Skinner's hands shake when he sees it. The coffee cup on the platter chatters like teeth on a cold night. The reason is obvious. Skinner knows that any business involving the Akron AWOL and Risa Ward usually sends Divan into a rage. He's probably waiting for it—but today Divan has no reason to lose his temper. "This was broadcast live earlier this morning," Divan explains. "Watch what happens next."

Just as the host is about to start the interview, shots ring out, the host's chest practically explodes, and the camera skews wildly. More shots. Risa and Connor can be seen hurried backstage by security guards, to the gasps and screams of the studio audience.

Skinner drops the coffee carafe and immediately goes down to clean it up, apologizing profusely. It is of little concern to Divan. Skinner will clean it up and get more coffee. In spite of his occasional clumsiness, he's an excellent valet.

"It appears that Risa and the imposter were unharmed," Divan says, "but I doubt they'll be doing any more interviews."

"Were you . . . were you involved?" Skinner asks.

Divan actually laughs at the suggestion. "Certainly not. I hold no grudge against Risa just because she escaped. As for the imposter, he's not worth my time—and his actions have mostly been good for business."

"Yes, sir, I suppose they have."

When "Connor Lassiter" returned to the public spotlight, it was obvious to Divan that he must be an imposter. Divan had gone down to witness the young man's unwinding, so there could be no foul-ups. His parts were sold and shipped out. And although the Swiss banker who purchased Connor's face claims he was duped and the face was someone else's, Divan knew the truth. The banker must have sold it to the American Anti-Divisional Resistance. They probably got his vocal cords too. That's all they needed to rewind themselves an imposter who looks and sounds like Connor Lassiter. As for the shark tattoo, that's easy enough to fake. The world might be fooled, but not Divan Umarov.

At their next stop—a secluded airfield in Canada—the *Lady Lucrezia* lands in a downpour. There will be guests today. Guests that Divan must reluctantly allow on his flying fortress. Once a year he meets with his sister to discuss the family business. She complains and tries to persuade him to cut costs and increase output. He refuses, citing the fact that quality is the hallmark of his product. She leaves miffed, he flies off miffed, and that's that until next year. Such is the lot when you cast your fortunes in with family.

"You will treat her with the respect with which you treat me," Divan tells his staff. "Whether she deserves it or not." Although he addresses everyone, most of the others have heard this before. It's mainly for the benefit of Argent, who has not experienced Divan's family.

Divan watches from a window in the expansive living room. Several figures approach from a large limousine, and he wonders who accompanies her today. Her spineless waif of a husband? Her lawyer? The heavy rain necessitates umbrellas and hooded raincoats. Because of this Divan doesn't get a clear picture of all his guests as they board the plane. Had he seen, he would never have opened the hatch.

3 · Argent

Argent is curious, Argent is fearful, but most of all Argent is annoyed that he will now be expected to anticipate the needs of many instead of just Divan. Divan maintains a skeleton crew. The pilots, his bodyguard, a chef, and Argent. He calls Argent a valet, but what he really is, is valet, housekeeper, and waiter rolled into one. Every task that isn't specifically assigned to someone else is left to Argent. He works long hours for little money and even less praise. And yet in spite of it, he's come to appreciate the routine and even Divan himself. It sure beats being a supermarket cashier.

Divan *relies* on him. Back home Gracie had relied on him, but that had been different. He resented having to care for his low-cortical sister. But for some reason he doesn't resent working for Divan. He has no idea where Gracie is now. Whether she's alive or Nelson killed her. Connor swore up and down she was alive last time he saw her, but Argent can't know for sure. He tries not to think about her. She's the one who abandoned him. Whatever bed she made, she made herself.

The hatch folds open into a short set of stairs to the tarmac. The *Lady Lucrezia* is so large its belly comes within four feet of the ground. Servants with umbrellas hurry a group of people from a limousine to the plane. The storm has picked up. They probably won't be able to take off until it eases. Not good for Divan's mood. He hates being grounded.

The first to enter is a woman. She wears no raincoat—instead she's covered head to toe in a massive fur coat made from an animal that is probably extinct. Her coat alone may have taken out the entire species. This clearly must be Dagmara, Divan's sister.

"Where is he?" she demands. "Why is he not here to greet us?" She exchanges a few snappish words in Chechen with Bula, Divan's bodyguard.

Next to enter is a boy of about sixteen. Divan's nephew, Malik. He's good looking in that prom-king kind of way that would make Argent want to slash his tires if he were back home. He takes one look at Argent and says, "Who the hell are you? What's wrong with your face?"

Dagmara answers. "This is Skinner—don't you remember? I told you. He sold half of his face to a parts pirate for drugs, and your softhearted uncle took him in."

Argent seethes but knows he can't show it. Her version is so far from the truth he wants to scream. "Is that what he told you?"

Dagmara shrugs. "No, but I can read between the lines."

He's about to lead them up when a final figure comes in, cloaked in a rain hood. He removes it to reveal that he's Asian, with a dark complexion. It doesn't take a genius to guess that he's Burmese.

Bula the bodyguard reaches for his weapon, but Dagmara comes between them.

"He is our guest and here by my invitation," Dagmara says.

"You bring Dah Zey scum on *Lady Lucrezia*?" Bula doesn't let go of his weapon but doesn't remove it from its holster either.

"I am unarmed," says the Burmese man. "I'm not here to cause trouble but to end it."

Bula considers this, then turns to Argent. "Close the hatch." Then he grabs the Burmese man by the arm. "You have special place to wait until Mr. Umarov decides what to make of you."

Although Argent knows it's just Bula's poor English, it's fitting. Because Divan has "made" things of the four Dah Zey assassins sent to kill him. Argent wonders if a bonsai life is in store for this man as well.

The champagne and trays of canapés that Argent serves seem a nicety that's out of place in the shouting match that ensues the moment Divan finds out there's a Dah Zey agent on board. He doesn't need to understand Chechen to know what it's about—and the storm inside seems amplified by the storm outside as the massive jet fights to climb above the turbulence.

The adults are too heated to eat or drink. It's Malik who downs the champagne and the hors d'oeuvres. "Bring more," Malik orders. Argent gets some more finger foods from the chef but decides giving the kid more champagne won't do anyone any good.

Finally the tension settles, the turbulence becomes an occasional tremor, and Divan asks Argent to bring out snacks—most of which Malik has already eaten. Whatever understanding was reached, it didn't involve ejecting the Burmese guy out of the "Sayonara Hatch," a special airlock Divan had installed for the flushing of undesirables.

I've never had occasion to use it, Divan once told Argent, *but it's a comfort to know that it's there.*

With the Burmese interloper still locked away and guarded by Bula, Divan and his family settle in to the small talk that should have started the day. Apparently Chechen is their language of anger, because now they speak English.

Argent mixes their drinks and fetches food from the galley, all the while listening, a proverbial fly on the wall. Dagmara's older son is off in college. To her embarrassment he's majoring in philosophy and has shunned the family business entirely. She and her good-for-nothing husband have separated, and he wants the family's Swiss chalet in the divorce. Malik has been expelled from yet another prep school due to bad behavior.

"It's not my fault," Malik whines. "They all suck." Usually a kid like Malik could skate by on his good looks, so Argent figures he must be a real screwup.

And then Dagmara asks, "What's behind the curtain?"

Divan smiles as if he's been waiting for the question. "Something I acquired since your last time on board," he tells her. "A work of art that also happens to be a musical instrument."

That piques everyone's curiosity.

"Skinner! Show them."

And so Argent pulls back the curtain to reveal the Orgão Orgânico. Eighty-eight faces loom above its keyboard.

Dagmara gasps. "Is that an organ?"

"Of a kind," Divan says. "A heavenly chorus awaiting a conductor."

Dagmara approaches it, not horrified as Risa was, but entranced. "May I?"

"Be my guest," Divan says.

She sits at the keyboard and begins to play.

In all the time that Argent has been on board, he's never heard the Orgão Orgânico played, except for the time Risa touched one key, and a single voice sang. Dagmara launches right into a dark and powerful piece that is familiar even to Argent, whose grasp of classical music is about the same as his grasp of particle physics.

"'Toccata and Fugue in D minor'!" says Divan. "An excellent choice."

The *Lady Lucrezia* is filled with the eerie strains of the fugue voiced by the unwound chorus, mouths opening and closing to Dagmara's touch of the keys. As it builds to a crescendo, Argent concludes that it is the most disturbing thing he has ever witnessed. Even Divan seems taken aback.

And Malik says, "Cool!"

"Play as much as you like," Divan tells his sister. "It was purchased with you in mind."

4 · Divan

Against his sister's complaints, Divan holds the Dah Zey scum in a cell for most of the day. They both need to know who's calling the shots here. This is Divan's plane, his operation—and if he deigns to speak with the man, it will be on Divan's terms, no one else's.

He chooses to release the man for dinner.

"I will feed him, and listen to what he has to say, and then put him off the plane at our next stop," he tells Dagmara.

"That is not acceptable," Dagmara says.

"I couldn't care less what you think is and is not acceptable." He wonders if all siblings are like them, or if this is unique in his family. Or perhaps it's an ailment of the wealthy: The more money a family has, the more its members despise one another. Especially when control of that money comes into play.

When Bula arrives with the Burmese man, the man does not appear disgruntled by his treatment. In fact he appears downright jovial, which Divan finds irritating.

Dagmara, the mastermind of this questionable summit, does the introductions. "Divan, I would like to present to you the honorable Mr. Sonthi, representative of the Burmese Dah Zey. Mr. Sonthi, my brother, Divan Umarov."

"A pleasure," Mr. Sonthi says.

Divan says nothing; he just offers his hand to shake, with a calculated shift of position at the last instant, making Sonthi's grip awkward. It's Divan's way of setting an adversary off balance from the onset.

There's a dining table in the plane's great room, set for five. Skinner serves with the unobtrusive formality that Divan so painstakingly taught him.

"I have a valet back at my harvest camp," Mr. Sonthi says, "but he's all thumbs." And then he laughs at a joke that only he seems to understand.

Dagmara slips right into talk of her marital woes, and Malik finds fault in everything. Divan has no patience for any of it.

Then, when Skinner serves the main course, Malik turns to Divan in practiced disgust. "Does he have to be here? Looking at him makes me lose my appetite."

"Would you prefer to serve yourself?" Divan asks.

"I would prefer you hire someone with a face."

"Malik, you must learn to be more tolerant," Dagmara chides. "This is the very type of thing that keeps getting him expelled from school. Do you want to tell your uncle why you were thrown out of Excelsior Academy?"

Malik grabs a roll and rips off a piece with his teeth. "I unwound my math teacher's Chihuahua."

Sonthi laughs.

"Well, it was a nuisance, yapping all the time," Malik says. "The guy had no business bringing a yappy dog on campus."

And then comes a voice from behind that no one is expecting to hear. "You didn't unwind it; you killed it," says Skinner, suddenly no longer unobtrusive but the center of everyone's attention.

"Excuse me?" says Dagmara seething with indignation.

"Did you really just say that to me?" says Malik.

Dagmara turns to Divan. "Is this how you train your valet? To talk back to your guests?"

Divan sighs. He needs no more drama at the table. "Apologize to my nephew, Skinner."

Skinner just stands there, refusing to look at anyone.

"I said apologize," Divan says more forcefully.

"I'm sorry," Skinner finally says.

And to keep this from escalating any further, Divan decides to remove Skinner from the situation. "You're excused. Bula will serve the rest of the meal." Bula steps out of the shadows to take over, and Skinner disappears toward his quarters at the rear of the plane.

"There should be consequences," Dagmara says. Divan agrees, but not with who those consequences should be for.

The meal continues in an uneasy silence. Malik leaves after dessert without as much as a good-bye, and once he's gone, Divan gets down to business.

"Mr. Sonthi, toward what end have you intruded on this time with my family?"

There's an uncomfortable pause. It's Dagmara who answers. "He has a proposal from the Dah Zey. I think you should hear it."

Divan takes his time, rimming his espresso with lemon rind. "I'm listening."

Sonthi leans forward. "This war between us helps no one," he begins. "It is our hope that we can pool our resources, and make a greater profit for all of us."

Divan knows exactly where this is going. "You want UNIS."

"It's no secret that your machine can perform an unwinding in only fifteen minutes. With this technology, we could downsize our harvest camps, while increasing our output. In return, we are prepared to offer you a generous percentage of our profits."

"In other words, you propose to buy me out."

"Think about it, Divan," says Dagmara. "No more attacks

from the Dah Zey, no need to fear for your life, and more money than we're pulling in now."

Divan takes a sip of his espresso. "I will not surrender my business to an organization as bloody and barbarous as the Burmese Dah Zey. Not now, not ever."

Then Dagmara finally shows her hand. "You forget, dear brother, that I control your ground operations. Without my distribution network, you can't move a single unwound part."

"Are you threatening me, Dagmara?"

"I'm merely trying to get you to see reason."

Divan turns to Sonthi, his decision made—but in truth it was made even before they began speaking. "When we land in Kamchatka, you will be put off my plane, Mr. Sonthi. I trust you'll be able to find your way home from there."

Then Divan excuses himself, not wanting to be in either of their company a moment longer.

5 · Argent

There's not much room in his tiny cabin to pace, but Argent can't keep still. Divan has entertained the likes of parts pirates and contract killers, but none have gotten under his skin the way Malik has. Perhaps because those others do what they do for money, not for pleasure. As Divan always says, it's strictly business, and no matter how illicit the business is, the joy comes more from the profit than from the act. Surely the black market is rotten with sociopaths, but Malik feels like a special case.

And Divan made Argent apologize!

There's little enough self-respect left in Argent, and that just about killed it.

There's a knock at his door. He suspects it's Divan come to

lecture him on his place in the scheme of things, but it's not. It's Malik, the beast himself, come to pay a visit.

"Nice closet," he says. "Can I come in?"

Argent knows if he denies him entry, he'll get in even more trouble. "I already apologized," Argent says. "What else do you want from me?"

"I want to give you the chance to make it up to me." Malik steps in, and Argent has no choice but to let him. "Things will be changing around here. You can either be part of the change, or be steamrolled by it."

"Nothing's changing unless Mr. Umarov says it is," Argent tells him.

Malik doesn't speak to that. Instead he says, "Show me my uncle's harvester."

Argent wasn't expecting that. "I . . . I'm not allowed."

"But you can get in, can't you? I want to see UNIS. I want to see how it works."

"I told you, I can't."

And then Malik reaches up and grips the biobandage that covers Argent's faceless half. "I could rip this off you right now."

It's a terrifying threat—because a biobandage is more than just dressing: It grows into the surrounding tissue to protect the wound. If he rips it off, the pain will be unbearable.

Argent still remembers his martial arts moves. He could have Malik in a choke hold in an instant, cutting off his oxygen and rendering him unconscious. If he holds it long enough, Malik could be left with irreversible brain damage—which might be exactly what he needs. But who is Argent kidding? He'll just get rewound brain bits to replace the damage. On the other hand, perhaps those brain bits will be better than the ones Malik came with.

Argent never gets the chance to find out, because Dagmara comes to the door. "Am I interrupting?" she asks.

Malik takes his hand from Argent's bandage. "Just having a friendly chat," Malik says, and saunters off, leaving his mother to talk business.

"I have a proposal for you, Skinner," Dagmara says. "Listen carefully, because I'm about to make you very rich. . . ."

The instant Dagmara leaves, Argent goes to Divan's quarters, making sure that no one sees him. He knocks urgently, and Divan lets him in.

"I take it that this is important, or you wouldn't be disturbing me."

"Very important, sir."

Then Argent shows him the vial that Dagmara gave him. "She said she'd give me a million dollars to pour this into your espresso at breakfast tomorrow morning."

Divan doesn't seem surprised, just disappointed. "You realize she wouldn't have given you a dime. Most likely she'd kill you."

"Most likely she'd have Malik kill me," Argent says. Divan doesn't disagree.

Divan opens the vial and sniffs it, thinks for a moment, then replaces the stopper and hands the vial back to Argent. "Do it," Divan says.

"You . . . you want me to poison you?"

"Certainly not. But I have no qualms about you putting it in someone else's espresso. Whoever you like. I trust your judgment."

The idea that Divan trusts him with anything—especially something as serious as this—is a surprise to Argent.

"You're asking me to be your assassin."

"The Eastern world calls such assassins ninjas. Many of them serve as personal aids to their masters. Is this a position you can rise to, Argent?"

It's the first time he can remember Divan calling him Argent instead of Skinner.

"Yes I can," says Argent. "And you don't need to give me a million bucks, either."

"Perhaps I will," Divan tells him. Then adds. "In time . . . in time."

6 · Malik

Malik has to admit the plane is as amazing as he thought it would be, and his own prospects are even more thrilling. His brother, the philosopher, wants no part of the family business. That leaves Malik first in line to inherit it all. His mother knows Malik is the strongest link in the family chain, which is why she's brokered this deal with the Dah Zey.

If we play our cards right, you'll be running the Dah Zey one day, she told him. Merging with them isn't a matter of surrendering, it's infiltrating, and these Burmese fools are too stupid to see it!

In the meantime, however, he'll settle for the *Lady Lucrezia* and its airborne harvest camp. But when he's in charge, things will be different. For one thing he'll have a proper staff—and his first order of business will be to jettison the half-faced freak right out the Sayonara Hatch into oblivion.

Such are Malik's musings when his uncle pays him a visit.

"Skinner tells me you have an interest in seeing UNIS in action," Uncle Divan tells him.

Malik is cautious. "He told you that?"

"Yes—he doesn't have access, so he asked if I could do it. I'd be happy to."

Malik sits up, unable to hide his excitement. "Thanks, Uncle Divan."

"Don't mention it. But before we go into the harvest drum, you'll need to put these on."

He tosses Malik a one-piece garment that looks like long underwear, only heavier. As Malik examines it, he sees that it's made of metal. A very finely woven chain mail.

"What for?"

"For your own protection, of course."

Malik quickly dons the metallic one-piece and follows his uncle to the front of the jet, where the automated harvesting unit awaits.

"Can I watch an unwinding?"

"Of course," says his uncle cheerily. "I think you'll find it an eye-opening experience."

7 · Divan

The *Lady Lucrezia* lands in Kamchatka at dawn. Several hundred stasis containers are unloaded—the result of twelve unwindings that took place in flight. There's only one small container that was not put up for auction. This box Divan takes to his personal quarters for safekeeping.

Although new AWOLs have been brought to the *Lady Lucrezia* from his Russian holding facility—enough to fill all the empty beds in the harvest drum—Divan takes none of them on board.

"Next time," he tells his confused supply crew. "Pay the parts pirates what we owe them, and next time I'll take them on board."

As for Sonthi, Divan does not put him off the plane. He tells his sister that he's had a change of heart and wants more time to consider their proposal. The *Lady Lucrezia* is refueled and airborne again in half an hour.

But shortly after reaching cruising altitude, Divan notices several things that could only be called red flags. His chef will not look him in the eye; Bula is mysteriously missing; and the portside windows bring in a spectacular sunrise—which means they're heading on a southerly course instead of due west, as is Divan's traditional flight plan. He doesn't need a compass to know that they're heading for Burma and that the pilots are now working for the Dah Zey.

All these things he keeps to himself at breakfast, playing his own hand very close to the vest. Even Skinner has a poker face this morning, although he does give Divan a surreptitious nod to indicate that they are in league.

Malik is late for breakfast. No one is concerned.

"You should send Skinner to get him," Dagmara tells Divan. "Eggs Benedict is his favorite."

"I'm sure he'll be along shortly," Divan assures her. It's as Skinner brings the morning espresso that Divan turns to Sonthi. "Now, let us discuss the terms of your proposal."

Both Dagmara and Sonthi watch with interest as Divan takes his time squeezing his lemon rind around the edge of his espresso cup.

"The terms," Sonthi says, "have already been negotiated. There is nothing left but for you to accept them."

Sonthi takes a sip of his espresso. Dagmara takes a sip of hers.

"In that case, there's nothing more to discuss, is there?" Divan says, and brings his own espresso to his lips.

8 · Argent

He pours juice. He takes away plates. He watches and listens, all the while his heart pounding so painfully in his chest, he fears it may explode. Did he confuse the cups? He doesn't trust his own memory. What a time to be uncertain.

Divan has taken a sip. All three have. How strong is the poison? How much of it must be ingested, and how long does it take to work? What sort of ninja is this clueless about his own methods?

He doesn't need to wait long for an answer. Sonthi begins to gag and froth at the mouth and falls face forward. His head smacks the table with a thud. His eyes remain open. He's dead.

Dagmara gasps, then throws an accusing glare at Argent. "You imbecile! What have you done!"

"Precisely what I expected he would do," Divan says. "Well played, Skinner."

"Do you have any idea what the Dah Zey will do when they find out he's dead?"

"That," says Divan, "is no longer your concern." Then he pulls out a gun and fires.

It's a tranq. It hits Dagmara squarely in the chest. She mumbles something in Chechen—most likely a curse—and her head rolls back instead of forward.

"I searched everywhere for Bula," Argent tells Divan once Dagmara is unconscious. "He's not on board anymore. They must have killed him when we landed."

"Or sent him out the Sayonara Hatch." Divan shakes his head. "Pool Bula, he deserved better."

"What do you want me to do now?" Argent asks.

Divan smiles. "You would do anything I asked, wouldn't you, Argent? Such loyalty is a rare commodity in this world."

Would he do anything for Divan? Argent wonders. This man who cut off the good half of his face and gave it to Nelson—then turned him into an indentured servant in order to earn back the right to have a face again? Argent finds that his answer is yes. He would do anything Divan wished of him. Argent wonders if that makes him broken, or noble.

Divan leans back, as if he has no care in the world. "Go tell the chef that we'll all be having lamb for lunch. That will keep him busy for a while. And while you're at it, please bring me another espresso."

9 · Dagmara

She awakens to find herself staring at a sea of soulless faces. For a moment she thinks it's a dream, until she realizes where she is. She is sitting before the Orgão Orgânico. Her head is still a bit hazy, but she remembers what happened.

To the left a single male face has its mouth open, intoning a deep bass *aaaaaaaaaah*. She sees a single finger depressing the lowest B-flat key and follows that finger to her brother, who sits beside her.

"Stop that," she says wearily, because the sound resonates in her aching head.

"I'm afraid that would be a mistake," Divan says, then removes his finger. Immediately Dagmara can feel the plane begin to lose altitude.

Divan puts his finger on the key once more. The voice sings again. The plane stops dropping. "You see? When I installed the organ, I made sure it was wired into the autopilot circuit, on the chance that this day might come. A mere flick of a switch has sent the control here. Now as long as the Orgão Orgânico is being played, the autopilot is engaged."

"Autopilot . . . ," mumbles Dagmara, still struggling to get her wits back as the tranq wears off."

"Yes. I'm afraid I had to kill both the pilot and his copilot. They proved themselves to be traitors. The chef as well. Pity. I doubt I'll ever find one with such talent."

Dagmara groans. What a mess things have become. Leave it to her brother to spite everyone, including himself. And then something occurs to her that brings on a wave of nausea.

"Malik . . . Where's Malik? Where's my son?"

"No longer on board. Mostly. He was put off in Kamchatka."

"You left him alone?"

"No, of course not. He's in the company of your distribution network. You'll be pleased to know that his parts fetched us more than three hundred thousand dollars."

Dagmara gapes at him. He's joking. He must be. He wouldn't unwind his own nephew. What sort of monster would do such a thing?

"While I would love to continue this chat, Dagmara, I'm afraid we're out of time," Divan says. "We've just crossed into Chinese airspace at an altitude of about 2,300 meters. We're no longer headed toward Burma, but west. Of course, at this low an altitude it will be a bumpy ride once you reach the Chinese mountain ranges, but not to worry—the autopilot will steer you clear of the higher peaks."

Dagmara struggles to grasp the things that Divan is telling her. Chinese mountains. 2,300 meters, Autopilot. And Malik. None of it seems real to her. It's all a hallucination brought on by the tranqs. Please let it be so. Please let it be so.

"I'll be leaving you now, dear sister. "Saying 'sayonara,' as it were. You see, there are two parachutes on board. One for me and one for my valet."

"Wait—you're just going to leave me here?"

"I leave you with my prize possession: the Orgão Orgânico. As long as you keep playing, the plane will fly true. At least until it runs out of gas, but her tanks are massive. You've got at least twenty hours left, maybe more."

Then Divan removes his finger from the key. The face stops wailing, closes its mouth, and the plane begins to drop.

"Better play, Dagmara."

In a panic Dagmara looks at the keyboard and quickly launches into her go-to piece as she had when she first arrived—Bach's "Toccata and Fugue in D-minor." The chorus of disembodied voices fills the space.

"Very good!" says Divan, as he strides away "Keep playing, Dagmara. Keep playing!"

"Divan!" she calls. "DIVAN!" But he's gone.

And so she plays for her life, buying herself the seconds and the minutes and the hours until there is nothing but soulless voices and fumes.

10 · Argent

Being ejected out of the Sayonara Hatch is like being launched from a cannon into an ice-cold sky. He tumbles in an uncontrolled plummet. He has no experience or skill at skydiving. He's just happy he remembers to pull the rip cord to open the chute. At last Argent lands shivering in a patch of snow on a hillside and tumbles to a stop. Divan arrives a few moments later, twenty yards away, perfectly controlled and landing on his feet. He disconnects from his parachute and comes over to help Argent release himself from his.

"Well, that was exhilarating," Divan says.

"Yeah right," says Argent, a little too riled to be respectful. "Almost dying is always fun."

Divan chuckles.

"So what now?" Argent asks.

"I have friends in China, and I've already alerted them. They'll zero in on our beacon. We won't have to wait here for long."

Argent suspects Divan has friends everywhere. Except for maybe Southeast Asia. Then Divan pulls something out of his backpack—the only object he salvaged from the plane—and hands it to Argent. It's a biological stasis cooler about the size of a lunch box.

"What's . . . inside?" Argent asks.

Divan sighs. "The only part of Malik I didn't sell. His best part, actually."

Argent doesn't dare open it. He knows what it is. "And it's . . . for me?" Argent asks, scarcely willing to believe it.

"It's an elegant solution, don't you think?" Divan says. "It fulfills my promise to you, and allows me to see my nephew's handsome face once more, without having to suffer the rest of him."

Argent holds the box closely. He feels awful, he feels grateful, he feels damned, and he feels blessed. How could something generate so many conflicting emotions? He decides to go with the positive ones, because the negative ones will surely drive him mad. "Thank you," he says.

"I do believe Malik is better off living divided," Divan says. "It's certainly better than the life path he was on."

He tells Argent that he'll arrange a private procedure to graft his new face once they arrive in Beijing.

"And then you're free, Argent. I will have you taken to wherever you want to go."

Argent looks at Divan, holding eye contact—something he never before had the courage to do. "What if I don't want to go? What if I want to keep working for you?"

"Well then, I'll pay you a wage worthy of your loyalty."

Divan looks up at *Lady Lucrezia*'s vapor trail, slowly being torn apart by crosswinds. "When the plane finally does goes down, we'll all be taken for dead. I intend to take advantage of that. Leave my business. Retire under an assumed name. Of course, I'll always need a valet."

They sit down and wait for the arrival of Divan's "friends," who will most likely come by helicopter. And as Argent ponders the electrifying prospect of his new future, a question comes to mind.

"Where will we go?" he asks. "Where do you want to retire?"

"Well," says Divan, "faking one's death does require a level of continued anonymity." He feigns to consider the question, but clearly he's thought about it before. "Did you know that with all that I possess, I've never owned a yacht? It has been a long-standing dream of mine to own one, and sail the Mediterranean—sticking only to the smaller, less traveled ports, of course."

"Sounds like a plan," says Argent, already settling in to the idea.

After all, what are the chances of running into someone they know?

Turn the page
for a sneak peek at Scythe.

We must, by law, keep a record of the innocents we kill.

And as I see it, they're all innocents. Even the guilty. Everyone is guilty of something, and everyone still harbors a memory of childhood innocence, no matter how many layers of life wrap around it. Humanity is innocent; humanity is guilty, and both states are undeniably true.

We must, by law, keep a record.

It begins on day one of apprenticeship—but we do not officially call it "killing." It's not socially or morally correct to call it such. It is, and has always been, "gleaning," named for the way the poor would trail behind farmers in ancient times, taking the stray stalks of grain left behind. It was the earliest form of charity. A scythe's work is the same. Every child is told from the day he or she is old enough to understand that the scythes provide a crucial service for society. Ours is the closest thing to a sacred mission the modern world knows.

Perhaps that is why we must, by law, keep a record. A public journal, testifying to those who will never die and those who are yet to be born, as to why we human beings do the things we do. We are instructed to write down not just our deeds but our feelings, because it must be known that we do have feelings. Remorse. Regret. Sorrow too great to bear. Because if we didn't feel those things, what monsters would we be?

—From the gleaning journal of H.S. Curie

The scythe arrived late on a cold November afternoon. Citra was at the dining room table, slaving over a particularly difficult algebra problem, shuffling variables, unable to solve for X or Y, when this new and far more pernicious variable entered her life's equation.

Guests were frequent at the Terranovas' apartment, so when the doorbell rang, there was no sense of foreboding—no dimming of the sun, no foreshadowing of the arrival of death at their door. Perhaps the universe should have deigned to provide such warnings, but scythes were no more supernatural than tax collectors in the grand scheme of things. They showed up, did their unpleasant business, and were gone.

Her mother answered the door. Citra didn't see the visitor, as he was, at first, hidden from her view by the door when it opened. What she saw was how her mother stood there, suddenly immobile, as if her veins had solidified within her. As if, were she tipped over, she would fall to the floor and shatter.

"May I enter, Mrs. Terranova?"

The visitor's tone of voice gave him away. Resonant and inevitable, like the dull toll of an iron bell, confident in the ability of its peal to reach all those who needed reaching. Citra knew before she even saw him that it was a scythe. *My god! A scythe has come to our home!*

"Yes, yes of course, come in." Citra's mother stepped aside to allow him entry—as if she were the visitor and not the other way around.

He stepped over the threshold, his soft slipper-like shoes making no sound on the parquet floor. His multilayered robe was smooth ivory linen, and although it reached so low as to dust the floor, there was not a spot of dirt on it anywhere. A scythe, Citra knew, could choose the color of his or her robe—every color except for black, for it was considered inappropriate for their job. Black was an absence of light, and scythes were the opposite. Luminous and enlightened, they were acknowledged as the very best of humanity—which is why they were chosen for the job.

Some scythe robes were bright, some more muted. They looked like the rich, flowing robes of Renaissance angels, both heavy yet lighter than air. The unique style of scythes' robes, regardless of the fabric and color, made them easy to spot in public, which made them easy to avoid—if avoidance was what a person wanted. Just as many were drawn to them.

The color of the robe often said a lot about a scythe's personality. This scythe's ivory robe was pleasant, and far enough from true white not to assault the eye with its brightness. But none of this changed the fact of who and what he was.

He pulled off his hood to reveal neatly cut gray hair, a mournful face red-cheeked from the chilly day, and dark eyes that seemed themselves almost to be weapons. Citra stood. Not out of respect, but out of fear. Shock. She tried not to hyperventilate. She tried not to let her knees buckle beneath her. They were betraying her by wobbling, so she forced fortitude to her legs, tightening her muscles. Whatever the scythe's purpose here, he would not see her crumble.

"You may close the door," he said to Citra's mother, who did so, although Citra could see how difficult it was for her. A scythe in the foyer could still turn around if the door was open. The moment that door was closed, he was truly, truly inside one's home.

He looked around, spotting Citra immediately. He offered a smile. "Hello, Citra," he said. The fact that he knew her name froze her just as solidly as his appearance had frozen her mother.

"Don't be rude," her mother said, too quickly. "Say hello to our guest."

"Good day, Your Honor."

"Hi," said her younger brother, Ben, who had just come to his bedroom door, having heard the deep peal of the scythe's voice. Ben was barely able to squeak out the one-word greeting. He looked to Citra and to their mother, thinking the same thing they were all thinking. *Who has he come for? Will it be me? Or will I be left to suffer the loss?*

"I smelled something inviting in the hallway," the scythe said, breathing in the aroma. "Now I see I was right in thinking it came from this apartment."

"Just baked ziti, Your Honor. Nothing special." Until this moment, Citra had never known her mother to be so timid.

"That's good," said the scythe, "because I require nothing special." Then he sat on the sofa and waited patiently for dinner.

Was it too much to believe that the man was here for a meal and nothing more? After all, scythes had to eat somewhere. Customarily, restaurants never charged them for food, but that didn't mean a home-cooked meal was not more desirable. There were rumors of scythes who required their victims to prepare them a meal before being gleaned. Is that what was happening here?

Whatever his intentions, he kept them to himself, and they had no choice but to give him whatever he wanted. Will he spare a life here today if the food is to his taste, Citra wondered? No surprise that people bent over backwards to please scythes in every possible way. Hope in the shadow of fear is the world's most powerful motivator.

Citra's mother brought him something to drink at his request, and now labored to make sure tonight's dinner was the finest she had ever served. Cooking was not her specialty. Usually she would return home from work just in time to throw something quick together for them. Tonight their lives might just rest on her questionable culinary skills. And their father? Would he be home in time, or would a gleaning in his family take place in his absence?

As terrified as Citra was, she did not want to leave the scythe alone with his own thoughts, so she went into the living room with him. Ben, who was clearly as fascinated as he was fearful, sat with her.

The man finally introduced himself as Honorable Scythe Faraday.

"I . . . uh . . . did a report on Faraday for school once," Ben said, his voice cracking only once. "You picked a pretty cool scientist to name yourself after."

Scythe Faraday smiled. "I like to think I chose an appropriate *Patron Historic*. Like many scientists, Michael Faraday was underappreciated in his life, yet our world would not be what it is without him."

"I think I have you in my scythe card collection," Ben went on. "I have almost all the MidMerican scythes—but you were younger in the picture."

The man seemed perhaps sixty, and although his hair had gone gray, his goatee was still salt-and-pepper. It was rare for a person to let themselves reach such an age before resetting back to a more youthful self. Citra wondered how old he truly was. How long had he been charged with ending lives?

"Do you look your true age, or are you at the far end of time by choice?" Citra asked.

"Citra!" Her mother nearly dropped the casserole she had just taken out of the oven. "What a question to ask!"

"I like direct questions," the scythe said. "They show an honesty of spirit, so I will give an honest answer. I admit to having turned the corner four times. My natural age is somewhere near one hundred eighty, although I forget the exact number. Of late I've chosen this venerable appearance because I find that those I glean take more comfort from it." Then he laughed. "They think me wise."

"Is that why you're here?" Ben blurted "To glean one of us?"

Scythe Faraday offered an unreadable smile.

"I'm here for dinner."

Citra's father arrived just as dinner was about to be served. Her mom had apparently informed him of the situation, so he was much more emotionally prepared than the rest of them had been. As soon as he entered, he went straight over to Scythe Faraday to shake his hand, and pretended to be far more jovial and inviting than he truly must have been.

The meal was awkward—mostly silence punctuated by the occasional comment by the scythe. "You have a lovely home." "What flavorful lemonade!" "This may be the best baked ziti in all of MidMerica!" Even though everything he said was complimentary, his voice registered like a seismic shock down everyone's spine.

"I haven't seen you in the neighborhood," Citra's father finally said.

"I don't suppose you would have," he answered. "I am not the public figure that some other scythes choose to be. Some scythes prefer the spotlight, but to truly do the job right, it requires a level of anonymity."

"Right?" Citra bristled at the very idea. "There's a right way to glean?"

"Well," he answered, "there are certainly wrong ways," and said nothing more about it. He just ate his ziti.

As the meal neared its close, he said, "Tell me about yourselves." It wasn't a question or a request. It could only be read as a demand. Citra wasn't sure whether this was part of his little dance of death, or if he was genuinely interested. He knew their names before he entered the apartment, so he probably already knew all the things they could tell him. Then why ask?

"I work in historical research," her father said.

"I'm a food synthesis engineer," said her mother.

The scythe raised his eyebrows. "And yet you cooked this from scratch."

She put down her fork. "All from synthesized ingredients."

"Yes, but if we can synthesize anything," he offered, "why do we still need food synthesis engineers?"

Citra could practically see the blood drain from her mother's face. It was her father who rose to defend his wife's existence. "There's always room for improvement."

"Yeah—and Dad's work is important, too!" Ben said.

"What, historical research?" The scythe waved his fork dismissing the notion. "The past never changes—and from what I can see, neither does the future."

While her parents and brother were perplexed and troubled by his comments, Citra understood the point he was making. The growth of civilization was complete. Everyone knew it. When it came to the human race, there was no more left to learn. Nothing about our own existence to decipher. Which meant that no one person was more important than any other. In fact, in the grand scheme of things, everyone was equally useless. That's what he was saying, and it infuriated Citra, because on a certain level, she knew he was right.

Citra was well known for her temper. It often arrived before reason, and left only after the damage was done. Tonight would be no exception.

"Why are you doing this? If you're here to glean one of us, just get it over with and stop torturing us!"

Her mother gasped, and her father pushed back his chair as if ready to get up and physically remove her from the room.

"Citra, what are you doing!" Now her mother's voice was quivering. "Show respect!"

"No! He's here, he's going to do it, so let him do it. It's not like he hasn't decided; I've heard that scythes always make up their mind before they enter a home, isn't that right?"

The scythe was unperturbed by her outburst. "Some do,

some don't," he said gently. "We each have our own way of doing things."

By now Ben was crying. Dad put his arm around him, but the boy was inconsolable.

"Yes, scythes must glean," Faraday said, "but we also must eat, and sleep, and have simple conversation."

Citra grabbed his empty plate away from him. "Well, the meal's done, so you can leave."

Then her father approached him. He fell to his knees. Her father was actually on his knees to this man! "Please, Your Honor, forgive her. I take full responsibility for her behavior."

The scythe stood. "An apology isn't necessary. It's refreshing to be challenged. You have no idea how tedious it gets; the pandering, the obsequious flattery, the endless parade of sycophants. A slap in the face is bracing. It reminds me that I'm human."

Then he went to the kitchen and grabbed the largest, sharpest knife he could find. He swished it back and forth, getting a feel for how it cut through the air.

Ben's wails grew, and his father's grip tightened on him. The scythe approached their mother. Citra was ready to hurl herself in front of her to block the blade, but instead of swinging the knife, the man held out his other hand.

"Kiss my ring."

No one was expecting this, least of all Citra.

Citra's mother stared at him, shaking her head, not willing to believe. "You're . . . you're granting me immunity?"

"For your kindness and the meal you served, I grant you one year immunity from gleaning. No scythe may touch you."

But she hesitated. "Grant it to my children instead."

Still the scythe held out his ring to her. It was a diamond the size of his knuckle with a dark core. It was the same ring all scythes wore.

"I am offering it to you, not them."

"But—"

"Jenny, just do it!" insisted their father.

And so she did. She knelt, kissed his ring, her DNA was read and was transmitted to the Scythedom's immunity database. In an instant the world knew that Jenny Terranova was safe from gleaning for the next twelve months. The scythe looked to his ring, which now glowed faintly red, indicating that the person before him had immunity from gleaning. He grinned, satisfied.

And finally he told them the truth.

"I'm here to glean your neighbor, Bridget Chadwell," Scythe Faraday informed them. "But she was not yet home. And I was hungry."

He gently touched Ben on the head, as if delivering some sort of benediction. It seemed to calm him. Then the scythe moved to the door, the knife still in his hand, leaving no question as to the method of their neighbor's gleaning. But before he left, he turned to Citra.

"You see through the facades of the world, Citra Terranova. You'd make a good scythe."

Citra recoiled. "I'd never want to be one."

"That," he said, "is the first requirement."

Then he left to kill their neighbor.

They didn't speak of it that night. No one spoke of gleanings— as if speaking about it might bring it upon them. There were no sounds from next door. No screams, no pleading wails—or perhaps the Terranovas' TV was turned up too loud to hear it. That was the first thing Citra's father did once the scythe left—turn on the TV and blast it to drown out the gleaning on the other side of the wall. But it was unnecessary, because however the scythe accomplished his task, it was done quietly. Citra found herself straining to hear something—anything. Both she and Ben discovered in themselves a morbid curiosity that made them both secretly ashamed.

An hour later, Honorable Scythe Faraday returned. It was Citra who opened the door. His ivory robe held not a single splatter of blood. Perhaps he had a spare one. Perhaps he had used the neighbor's washing machine after her gleaning. The knife was clean, too, and he handed it to Citra.

"We don't want it," Citra told him, feeling pretty sure she could speak for her parents on the matter. "We'll never use it again."

"But you *must* use it," he insisted, "so that it might remind you."

"Remind us of what?"

"That a scythe is merely the instrument of death, but it is *your* hand that swings me. You and your parents, and everyone else in this world are the wielders of scythes." Then he gently put the knife in her hands. "We are all accomplices. You must share the responsibility."

That may have been true, but after he was gone Citra still dropped the knife into the trash.